DUELIST FOR THE TON

Misfits of the Ton
Book Eight

by

Emily Royal

ARE YOU SIGNED UP FOR DRAGONBLADE'S BLOG?

You'll get the latest news and information on exclusive giveaways, exclusive excerpts, coming releases, sales, free books, cover reveals and more.

Check out our complete list of authors, too!

No spam, no junk. That's a promise!

Sign Up Here

www.dragonbladepublishing.com

Dearest Reader;

Thank you for your support of a small press. At Dragonblade Publishing, we strive to bring you the highest quality Historical Romance from some of the best authors in the business. Without your support, there is no 'us', so we sincerely hope you adore these stories and find some new favorite authors along the way.

Happy Reading!

CEO, Dragonblade Publishing

Additional Dragonblade books by Author Emily Royal

Misfits of the Ton
Tomboy of the Ton (Book 1)
Ruined by the Ton (Book 2)
Thief of the Ton (Book 3)
Oddity of the Ton (Book 4)
Harpy of the Ton (Book 5)
Heartbreaker of the Ton (Book 6)
Doxy for the Ton (Book 7)
Duelist for the Ton (Book 8)
The Taming of the Duke (Novella)

Headstrong Harts
What the Hart Wants (Book 1)
Queen of my Hart (Book 2)
Hidden Hart (Book 3)
The Prizefighter's Hart (Book 4)
All I Want for Christmas is My Hart (Novella)
Haunted Hart (Novella)

London Libertines
Henry's Bride (Book 1)
Hawthorne's Wife (Book 2)
Roderick's Widow (Book 3)
A Libertine's Christmas Miracle (Novella)

The Lyon's Den Series
A Lyon's Pride
Lyon of the Highlands
Lyon of the Ton
The Lyon and the Unicorn

CHAPTER ONE

Hyde Park, London

THE DAWN LIGHT stretched across the landscape, picking out the familiar shapes to be found in the park—the marble angel that bore a perpetual expression of weariness, the line of trees following the edge of the Serpentine…

And four men standing in a clearing—two combatants, and their seconds.

Through the mask, the newcomer could make out the duelists facing each other—two silhouettes against the backdrop of the water's surface that shimmered in the growing light.

Two pathetic, cowardly silhouettes who, like the rest of their sex, believe that their virility is measured by the number of women they seduce.

Or today, by how many of their fellow members of White's they shot at dawn.

To think—the world is run by such imbeciles.

The taller of the two raised his hand in greeting.

"About bloody time!" he said, his voice identifying him as the Honorable—or perhaps *not* so honorable—Ambrose Cholmondeley-Walker. "Dawn broke fifteen minutes ago."

"Hush!" his companion whispered. "Do you want every deuced runner in Town bearing witness?"

"There's nobody about, Manby-Bresswell," the first man said.

Ah—so it's Sir Baldwin Manby-Bresswell you wish me to put a hole in.

Manby-Bresswell turned.

Yes, I'd recognize that face anywhere—with its porcine features and close-set eyes reminiscent of an overfed boar.

"Something amusing?" Manby-Bresswell said, his voice tinged with a sneer.

"Most definitely," the newcomer said.

"And who are you to impose upon a private meeting at this hour?"

Sweet lord, Manby-Bresswell, you're the stupidest man to walk upon the earth.

Which was something of note, given that the entire male sex presented him with such strong competition for the title.

"I beg pardon, did you say something, Mr....?" Manby-Bresswell began.

"This gentleman is welcome to join our little party," Cholmondeley-Walker interrupted. "Tell me, man, do you delight in arriving late—or perhaps reneging on our contract?"

Man? *Oh, if only he knew.*

"Of course not, sir. My clients pay me only when I make an appearance—which guarantees my attendance."

Manby-Bresswell drew in a sharp breath.

"Fuck it, Ambrose, old chap—you've not hired *the Farthing*, have you?"

Cholmondeley-Walker let out a chuckle. "Beat you to it, did I, old chap?" He issued a bow.

"Welcome, Farthing, and your companion?"

"My manservant, Gerard."

"You're both welcome," Cholmondeley-Walker said. "I trust your aim will be true this morning."

"Naturally. It is, after all, what you pay me for. Gerard, would you see to business?"

The Farthing's companion stepped forward, palm outstretched. "Payment, if you please, sir."

Cholmondeley-Walker frowned. "It's not gentlemanly to discuss commerce."

"Neither is it gentlemanly to refuse to pay one's dues, Mr.

Cholmondeley-Walker," came the reply. "The terms are clear—you signed the contract willingly and were of sound mind."

Manby-Bresswell let out a snort that turned into a cough.

"Payment is to be made on the day of the duel," the Farthing said. "*Before* the first shot is fired. I'm a man who keeps his word. Can you say the same of yourself?"

Cholmondeley-Walker cocked his head to one side and narrowed his eyes. "You're no man," he said. "I can tell, even though you and your servant wear masks."

Sweet Lord! Am I discovered?

"You have the voice and frame of a boy," Cholmondeley-Walker continued, "a weakling boy."

"I have a bigger pair of bollocks than the man who'd rather pay another to face his opponent than risk his own skin."

Manby-Bresswell chuckled. "That's told *you*, Ambrose."

"Perhaps even a bigger pair than the two of you combined," the Farthing continued, "or else you'd have settled your differences in the drawing room rather than at the end of a pistol. Your wives are to be pitied."

"I should shoot you dead for that, Mr. Farthing," Manby-Bresswell said.

"I'm giving you that very opportunity this morning. That is, assuming you both wish to continue?"

The combatants nodded.

"In which case, pay my man, if you please, Mr. Cholmondeley-Walker, then we can conclude the matter and be on our way before London wakes."

Grumbling, Cholmondeley-Walker pulled out a sheaf of notes from his inside jacket pocket and handed them to Gerard, who counted each one, then gave a sharp nod and folded them.

"Excellent," the Farthing said. "Now we may proceed with our business."

"Dueling is not a *business*," Manby-Bresswell grumbled. "It's an act of a gentleman to settle a matter of honor."

"And what was the matter of honor that brought the two of

you here this morning?" the Farthing asked.

"This bounder seduced my wife. Under my very nose—in the library, if you please, while I was entertaining our guests."

Cholmondeley-Walker rolled his eyes. "How many times must I tell you, Sir Baldwin—your wife holds no appeal for me. I prefer sturdier women—makes for a more vigorous ride, particularly if she whinnies like a mare when I take her."

Ugh.

Men spoke with little sense when in the company of women—but among their own kind with not a woman in sight, or at least when they believed that were the case, they reverted to the words of the savage.

"What's the matter, Mr. Farthing—is our gentlemanly talk not to your taste?"

"Nothing of the sort, I assure you. I'm merely wondering whether either of you have paused to consider if the woman in question has an opinion on the matter and, if so, whether either of you place any value upon it."

"The opinion of a *woman?*" Cholmondeley-Walker laughed. "You're a bigger fool than Sir Baldwin here."

"I doubt that, if Sir Baldwin's wife is straying behind his back."

"Lady Manby-Bresswell is not straying behind her husband's back," Cholmondeley-Walker said. "She's notoriously faithful— despite ample provocation to be otherwise—as I've tried to explain to this witless fool."

"Then how would you account for my coming upon the two of you in the library that night?"

"I went in search of a book. As did Lady Manby-Bresswell. Why else would a man enter a library?"

"I can think of plenty of reasons."

"I imagine *you* would, seeing as you'd not know what to do with a book if someone shoved it up your arse," Cholmondeley-Walker said. "You're a fool if you think your wife's straying, Sir Baldwin."

"Then why have I seen you sniffing around her? I even caught the Duke of Whitcombe salivating over her at the dinner table."

Eleanor's husband? If he's strayed, I'll shoot him myself.

"You really have tripe in that head of yours, Sir Baldwin, if you think Whitcombe would stray. He's notoriously in love with the duchess. Any look he casts your wife's way is likely to be motivated by pity rather than desire."

"What would a man find in a baronet's wife to pity?" Sir Baldwin asked. "I may be a little out of sorts when another man tries to seduce her—what husband wouldn't?—but I always make it up to her. This very morning I intend to present her with the most delectable emerald necklace as a gesture of my undying devotion. After I've shot you, of course."

And well deserved the necklace is, too, Sir Baldwin, I'll warrant, given that your entire fortune is courtesy of her dowry.

"I beg pardon?" Sir Baldwin stared at the Farthing. "Did you have something to say?"

"Nothing save a proposal that you summon your second. I came here to shoot you—not listen to your justification of your treatment of your wife."

"And what will you do with *your* wife, Mr. Farthing, when you return to her bed? Tell her you've been out shooting better men than yourself?"

"Sir Baldwin, I'm not so foolish as to have entered into the marriage state," the Farthing said. "I have no wish to be ruled by another."

"Hush!" Gerard whispered.

Oh Lord! I've done it again.

But the transgression went unnoticed. Cholmondeley-Walker let out a laugh.

"A clever boy you are, Farthing!" he said. "At least *you* understand that a married man will need to leave his—how did you describe them?—his *bollocks* at the door when he enters his home, lest his wife remove them with her teeth." He turned to his opponent. "Sir Baldwin, your jealousy is no doubt costing you a fortune in trinkets for your wife—what was it after the last accusation? A diamond brooch, if I recall. But perhaps this morning the price of your jealousy may be somewhat higher—your life is at stake."

"Not if I shoot first," Sir Baldwin said. He approached the Farthing, his eyes glittering with loathing.

"I shall enjoy cutting you down. A man should not be earning a living out of the misery of others."

"I see no misery—only indignation and childish retribution styled as honor."

Cholmondeley-Walker gestured toward his second. "Bring them over, Corbett."

"Very good, sir." A tall, thin man approached, holding a wooden box. He lifted the lid to reveal two weapons nestled together on a bed of smooth velvet.

"First choice to you, Sir Baldwin," Cholmondeley-Walker said. "I'm disposed to be generous."

Sir Baldwin plucked a pistol and held it up to the light. "One firearm's the same as any other," he said.

"That's where you're wrong," the Farthing said, taking the other pistol and inspecting it. It was a Wogdon & Barton piece—in excellent condition, with a polished barrel, carrying the faint odor of gun oil. Whoever the owner was, at least they bothered to tend to them properly. "A man should never underestimate the weapon in his hand—particularly one with a set trigger."

"A *what?*" Sir Baldwin asked, waving his pistol in the air.

Oh, you fool—do you really think you'll best me when you have so little respect for the weapon in your hand?

"It matters not," the Farthing said, approaching the center of the clearing. "Are you ready?"

"Eager to earn your coin?" Sir Baldwin sneered.

"It's of no consequence, given that I have been paid," the Farthing replied. "But I am eager to maintain my reputation. If *you* wish to run off with your shirttails between your legs, it makes no difference to me."

"Why, you…"

"Sir Baldwin!" The fourth man, presumably Sir Baldwin's second, stepped forward. "It's getting light, and I'm certain I heard voices. It won't be long before the park is teeming with visitors."

With a huff, Sir Baldwin approached the Farthing.

"Back to back, gentlemen, if you please," Mr. Corbett said.

"I'd advise you to step away, Mr. Cholmondeley-Walker," the Farthing said. "You've paid me a considerable sum to preserve your skin—it would be a tragedy if you were hit by a stray bullet."

"Is that a threat?"

"Not at all," the Farthing said, with a smile. "*My* aim is true. I cannot, however, give you the same assurances regarding your opponent."

"Do you impugn my honor?" Sir Baldwin asked, his gruff tones not quite fully concealing the fear in his voice.

"Only your accuracy."

"Very good, gentlemen, that's enough of the pleasantries," Mr. Corbett said, closing the box. "Step forward on each count, then turn when I reach ten. Wait for my signal, then, when I lower my hand, you may fire at will. Are you both ready and willing for the duel to proceed?"

The Farthing nodded, curling his fingers around the grip of the pistol, relishing the smoothness of the polished wooden handle. *A little heavier than I'm used to—there will be less time to hold my aim.*

"I beg pardon, Mr. Farthing?" Mr. Corbett asked.

"I said I'm ready."

"And *I'm* more than willing," Sir Baldwin said.

"Very well. One…two…three…"

With each pace, the man's voice faded, replaced by the sound of breathing that filled the air, together with a faint heartbeat.

Breathe slowly—in, and out… Focus on your heartbeat—slow and steady.

"Nine…ten!"

A cool breeze caressed the back of the Farthing's neck. His heartbeat increased on the turn as Sir Baldwin came into view, already holding his weapon aloft.

The fool! Sir Baldwin's eagerness to gain the upper hand would be his downfall. Not even the most capable duelist could hold such a weapon steady for anything longer than a few heartbeats.

The dawn light reflected off the end of Sir Baldwin's barrel, revealing a slight tremor. His mouth was set in a grim line and his jaw bulged as if he gritted his teeth with effort.

Mr. Corbett raised his hand and held it motionless for a heartbeat. Then he lowered it.

Now…

With a slow exhalation, the Farthing raised an arm while focusing on Sir Baldwin, who now stood twenty paces away, his eyes glistening. Then, when the arm was fully raised, the barrel of the pistol came into view—smooth gray metal pointing toward Sir Baldwin, its aim steady and true. The Farthing curled a finger around the trigger and squeezed it, feeling the familiar resistance.

Mr. Corbett's hand dropped to his side.

"Fire when ready."

On the final word, the Farthing increased the pressure on the trigger. With an explosion of blue smoke, the weapon fired. Anticipating the recoil, the Farthing stepped backward, inhaling the familiar scent of gunpowder, then lowered their arm holding the now-spent pistol.

The smoke cleared to reveal Sir Baldwin. Still standing, he clutched his right ear, his weapon on the grass at his feet.

"Fuck!" he cried, aiming a kick at the discarded pistol.

"Stop that!" Mr. Corbett roared. "The weapon will discharge if you kick it—are you completely lacking in wits?"

"The bastard's shot me!" Sir Baldwin cried.

"I rather think that's the point of a duel, old chap," Cholmondeley-Walker said, a hint of amusement in his voice.

"I could be dying!" Sir Baldwin's voice took on a petulant tone—the degree of petulance indication enough of the superficiality of the injury. At least, the injury to his *body*. Doubtless the injury to his pride was of greater severity.

"It's just a flesh wound," the Farthing said. "I merely grazed your ear."

"I'm bleeding!"

Did you whine like that in the nursery when you wanted your nanny?

Gerard let out a giggle, then stifled it.

"That part of the ear bleeds profusely, Sir Baldwin," the Farthing said. "You now have a trophy befitting a duelist—a bloodied shirt, which you can show to your wife as a demonstration of how deeply you value her honor."

Sir Baldwin removed his hand from his ear, and red liquid trickled down his throat. "You could have *killed* me!"

"Give me *some* credit," the Farthing replied. "If I wanted to kill you, I'd have aimed for your heart."

"You mean you shot his ear on *purpose*?" Cholmondeley-Walker said.

"Did you want me to kill your friend?" the Farthing asked.

Cholmondeley-Walker colored and averted his gaze.

"I'm not in the habit of ending a man's life, no matter the provocation," the Farthing continued. "The terms of our contract were that I emerge victorious in a duel on your behalf. My duty, and therefore your honor, has been discharged successfully, at little cost to yourself."

"Fifty pounds isn't what I'd call a little cost," Cholmondeley-Walker huffed.

"Cheap enough, compared to a man's life."

"Sir Baldwin would never have bested me—he's a terrible shot."

"Which is a largely academic argument, given that you paid me to duel on your behalf. But I would beg to disagree. The most dangerous of opponents is a man unacquainted with the skills of marksmanship—for one never knows where his bullet will end up. A shot to the stomach is a worse fate than a shot to the heart. Both result in the same ultimate fate, but the former comes with considerably more pain."

"You seem well acquainted with the business of death," Cholmondeley-Walker said. "Do you serve in the militia?"

"I have no profession."

"A gentleman, then? Might I stand you a drink at White's this afternoon?"

"I am not a member of White's. But I give you leave to boast about your prowess at the dueling field over a brandy in the clubroom."

"Come as my guest, then. I insist on knowing to whom I'm indebted."

"There is no debt, sir. You paid me for a service, which I have rendered. Unless you wish to hire my services again, I see no reason for us to further our acquaintance."

"At least tell me your name."

"My *skill* is for hire—not my name."

"Then I'll take your mask off myself." Cholmondeley-Walker took a step forward.

"Try it, if you dare," the Farthing said. "But know this. My very existence demands anonymity—without it, the Farthing is no more. Given your penchant for eyeing up other men's wives, you may be in need of my services again. If I am, as you suspect, a mere boy, would you weather the ridicule of your friends at White's if it were known that you were both bested by an adolescent fresh from the schoolroom?"

Sir Baldwin caught Cholmondeley-Walker's wrist. "Leave the fellow be," he said. "Honor has been satisfied. You're fifty pounds lighter and I'm down the price of a necklace. You can boast of your victory and I'll have a forgiving wife waiting for me in the bedchamber. Sometimes it's best to know when to walk away."

Well, well, Sir Baldwin—there's evidence of a little wit between those ears of yours. Perhaps there's some hope for you yet.

The Farthing issued a bow. "In which case, gentlemen, I'll bid you good morning. Sir Baldwin, do give your wife my best wishes for her happiness. Sophia, her name is, if I recall?"

Sir Baldwin's mouth fell open, then he shook his head. With a chuckle, the Farthing placed the spent pistol back in the box then turned and strode along the path, Gerard following. By the time they reached the gates leading out of Hyde Park, the sun had breached the horizon and warm rays stretched across the road.

It was going to be a hot day.

CHAPTER TWO

AS THE TURNING into St. James's Street came into view, and with it White's, the front door opened. A man stumbled out and landed in a heap on the pavement. Dressed in a bright-blue jacket that bore a tear in the right shoulder and a cravat loose about his neck, he carried the air of a gamester whose luck, and cash, had just been exhausted.

He lifted his head, his red-rimmed eyes focusing on the two figures approaching, then, with a sigh of resignation, he lowered his head again and soft snores filled the air.

Raucous laughter came from within the building—profligate males seeking refuge from overbearing fathers or discontented wives. No doubt they'd been spending the night, and either their allowance or their wives' dowries, on liquor, gaming, and other, less acceptable forms of pleasure.

The Farthing and Gerard approached the fallen gentleman at the foot of the steps.

"Do you think we should help him, La—"

"Hush! You mustn't use my name while we're abroad, lest we're overheard. People are wont to poke their noses in when one least expects—*Gerard*."

"Forgive me—Mr. Farthing, sir. But the gentleman looks unwell."

"I daresay that if we were to enter the building we'd find twenty such men in the clubroom with an equally green pallor and bearing the same stench of sour brandy. And I'd question the label of *gentleman*, given his identity. Unless I'm mistaken, the man at our feet is the Duke of Dunton."

"I wonder who stood his drinks account this time?"

"Someone wishing to ingratiate himself with a duke—who's also willing to hold his nose to bear the company of *this* particular duke."

Dunton stirred and opened a single, liquor-glazed eye, before letting out a groan and closing it again.

"Bless me!" a voice said. "If I'm not mistaken, it's the infamous Farthing!"

A man stood in the doorway—handsome enough, with blond hair and startlingly pale blue eyes. But the appearance of an angel belied the blackened heart within.

"Sir Heath Moss."

The man bowed and descended the stairs toward the prone figure of the duke. "At your service, Mr. Farthing," he said. "Or perhaps I should say at *my* service, given the fortune you've made out of me. What are you up to at this hour? Or perhaps there's no cause to ask. Given that you're walking away from Hyde Park shortly after dawn, even those most lacking in wit could deduce what you're about."

"That's fortunate for *you*, Sir Heath," the Farthing said.

Sir Heath frowned and tilted his head to one side. "I don't understand your meaning."

"Exactly." The Farthing gestured toward Dunton. "I take it this…*creature* is with you?"

"His Grace and I are friends, yes."

"Friends! I'd question your idea of friendship, Sir Heath."

"It's a mutually convenient relationship with an acquaintance."

"Where your ready cash settles his gaming debts, which, in turn, makes him indebted to you."

"You also have a fondness for my ready cash, Mr. Farthing. Four hundred pounds is your tally to date, unless I'm mistaken.

Does that make us friends?"

"Payment for services rendered, Sir Heath," the Farthing said. "Where cash is exchanged, the relationship is one of business or coercion. But never friendship."

"Tut-tut, Mr. Farthing, sir. If we were all to take that attitude, it would paint a rather sorry portrait of London Society, would it not?"

"Which is rather my point."

Sir Heath narrowed his eyes. "You speak as if you're well acquainted with Society. Do you live hereabouts—on St. James's Street, perhaps?"

Sweet Lord.

"Ah!" Sir Heath continued. "I see a glint of fear behind that mask of yours."

"I fear no man, Sir Heath."

"Then you're a fool." Sir Heath cocked his head to one side. "A young buck fresh from Oxford, perhaps, desperate to show his prowess with a pistol to make up for his deficiencies in the bedroom—or perhaps a younger brother overlooked in favor of the elder and suffering from not being the heir." He gestured through the open door. "Perhaps you frequent this establishment, or aspire to if only your older brother would permit it?"

Older brother—*heavens!* Did the man possess an instinct like a pig sniffing for truffles?

"I have no desire to set foot in White's."

"Spoken with such vehemence, Mr. Farthing," Sir Heath said. "And the contempt you have for Dunton here makes me think that you're acquainted with dukes. The Duke of Foxton's residence is nearby—Number Eight St. James's Square. Perhaps you're familiar with the address?"

Sweet Lord! Sir Heath may not be the most intelligent man in Society, but he possessed a degree of acuity that came hand in hand with a vicious character.

"Are you attempting to ascertain my identity, Sir Heath?"

"Now who's lacking in wits?" Sir Heath grinned, revealing

perfectly even white teeth. "Perhaps not a *younger brother*, then."

Oh Lord—I'm done for.

"A footman, mayhap—dissatisfied with his lot and resentful enough of his master, and his master's social station, to take pleasure in shooting at his betters."

"You take equal pleasure, Sir Heath, in paying another to risk their life in a duel as a result of your dishonorable behavior. Of all my clientele, you are the one who, without exception, finds himself facing a protective husband, father, or older brother as a result of the women they love falling prey to your—*ahem*—charms."

Sir Heath stepped forward. "I ought to rip that mask off you right now."

"And where would that leave you, Sir Heath?"

"Very satisfied."

"And exposed to the risk of a bullet in your heart. You'd have to fight your own duels from now on each time you compromised an innocent. And let's be honest, sir—given that the chances of you being called out within the next month, or even the next week, are virtually guaranteed, it's a risk that a coward such as yourself is unwilling to take."

"Why, you…"

Fear flared as Sir Heath approached, hands outstretched, ready to rip off the Farthing's mask.

Then, with a cry, he pitched forward and fell onto the pavement.

"Bugger!"

He'd tripped over Dunton's prone form.

"Come on my…I mean, sir," Gerard whispered. "It's time we left. The house will be awake soon, and we don't want to be caught."

"Very good…Gerard. I'd be at a loss without you."

They resumed walking along St. James's Street, quickening the pace as Sir Heath yelled after them. "I'll have you yet, Mr. Farthing!"

"Aye—only next time I'll charge one hundred guineas."

"You bounder!"

"What will you do, Sir Heath?" the Farthing cried. "Call me out? I'll gladly accept the challenge."

Sir Heath let out another curse. At the turning into King Street, the Farthing glanced back to see him struggling to his feet, the Duke of Dunton clinging to his leg.

"You shouldn't rile Sir Heath," Gerard said.

"He's harmless enough, Gerard. He lacks the intelligence to pose any great danger."

"*All* men are dangerous. By taunting him, you risk discovery. He'll not rest until he's identified you."

"Then he'll not rest—and neither will any other man who engages in duels."

"Perhaps, but I would not have their unrest at the cost of yours."

King Street led onto St. James's Square and the familiar façade of the Foxton townhouse. A couple emerged from a side street and scurried across the road.

"I told you we shouldn't tarry, sir—half of London will be awake by now."

"That's Lady Stainton and her footman. She'll be more concerned with being discovered herself to bother with us. I daresay they didn't even notice us."

As they approached Number Eight, the front doors opened and a woman appeared, dressed in the eye-watering shade of orange that was currently adorning the ladies who frequented Madame Deliet's establishment. She issued a sharp word to the footman, flicked at her cuff as if to remove an invisible fleck of dust, then descended the steps with an air of self-confidence that metamorphosed into arrogance. The door closed behind her and, after a cursory glance in the Farthing's direction, she opened her parasol—the same shade of orange as her gown—and set off, her loose-hipped gait the only evidence that she had not been born into the lifestyle she aspired toward.

"Is that…"

"Mrs. Scarlet," Gerard whispered. "Mrs. Cerise Scarlet."

"Cherry red," the Farthing said, approaching the steps that descended to the basement of Number Eight. "Hardly the most imaginative of names."

"I doubt the master has any interest in her imagination."

"His Grace would need to be in possession of an imagination himself to appreciate that quality in others."

"Hush! Do you want him to overhear you? If Mrs. Scarlet has left, he'll be on his way to the breakfast room. He may even be there right now."

"He'll still be dressing. He takes at least an hour to get ready in the morning, whereas Mrs. Scarlet will have perfected the art of putting on her garments in a heartbeat so she can move on as quickly as possible to her next protector."

"Is not the master paying her for exclusivity?"

"If His Grace expected exclusivity from all the women he took to his bed, there would be no courtesans left over for his friends."

As they entered the scullery, a bell rang nearby.

"That'll be the master," Gerard whispered. "Be quick, now, or he'll wonder where you've got to—and you don't want the rest of the servants seeing you, especially dressed like that."

They slipped through the scullery toward the back stairs. Footsteps echoed in the distance, followed by the familiar voice of the duke's valet issuing orders to the cook.

The Farthing's stomach growled at the aroma of bacon and deviled kidneys.

"Hurry!"

They ascended the staircase, wincing at the creak of the boards underfoot, then padded along the corridor toward the familiar bedchamber, slipping inside and closing the door behind them.

"Bollocks, eh?" Gerard said. "The master would whip you raw if he heard you using language like that in the house."

"The *Farthing* uses such language. *I* do not—at least not in His Grace's presence. One of the drawbacks of indentured servitude is that my master can curtail my freedom if I displease him."

"But you are free."

"Not in any way that matters."

At that moment, a clock struck seven notes in the distance—the call to resume duties. A volley of chimes rang out in response, including the mantel clock in the bedchamber. With a sigh, the Farthing untied the mask and tossed it toward the bed. The brief bout of freedom was over.

Ten minutes later, the two of them stepped out of the bedchamber transformed, all evidence of the Farthing and Gerard safely folded away and tucked into a crate, ready to emerge when next required—which happened to be next Tuesday, on Hampstead Heath at dusk, when Sir Henshingly Crawford intended to give Mr. Simon Tewkberry a lesson in manners for having likened Lady Crawford's face to that of a pug in the process of emptying its bowels.

The duke's sharp voice could be heard from behind the breakfast room door—admonishing a footman, no doubt. The footman at the door glanced up and straightened his stance before opening the door.

Four more footmen occupied the breakfast room—two guarding the door inside, a third carrying a pot of tea, and the fourth spooning a portion of deviled kidneys onto a plate.

The sole occupant at the breakfast table glanced up, deep-set sapphire eyes gleaming with displeasure. His chiseled features, framed by thick, dark hair the color of a raven's wing, shifted in an almost imperceptible gesture that still managed to convey admonishment.

"You're late," he said, glancing at his pocket watch. "Breakfast is served at seven. You know that."

"It's barely five past."

"If a lady does not arrive on time then she is late," came the reply, carrying its familiar note of arrogance. "It matters not whether she is five minutes or five hours late—the tardiness is still a manifestation of the utter lack of propriety."

Manifestation of the utter lack of propriety? Lord save me from arrogant dukes!

His eyes flashed with anger. "I *beg* your pardon?"

"I said nothing."

He let out a huff, and nodded toward the place set opposite.

"Sit, then, sister," he said, then he gestured to one of the footmen.

"Charles, serve Lady Portia her breakfast."

CHAPTER THREE

L ADY PORTIA HAWKE slid into the seat opposite her brother. A footman approached with the plate of deviled kidneys and placed it before her.

"Thank you, Charles."

Her brother frowned and sliced through his bacon, his knife scraping against the plate.

"What now, Adam?" she asked. "Am I not permitted to thank the staff?"

"It's not your civility I take issue with, Portia," he said, taking a bite of bacon. "It's your lack of propriety…"

"And what of yours?"

"We're not discussing my behavior," he replied, his eyes darkening with anger. "My behavior does not risk bringing the Foxton title, or the Hawke family name, into disrepute. Yours, unfortunately, *does*."

Portia resisted the urge to pull a face. Her brother always carried an air of menace about him, a layer of brutality concealed beneath his perfectly tailored exterior.

Which, for some unfathomable reason, women were attracted to. Perhaps they relished the prospect of danger—the thrill to be had from throwing themselves at the mercy of a demon.

Or perhaps they believed him a wild beast whom they could tame—which she would have laughed at had her position in life been cause for jollity. But, as his sister, she was at his mercy, and there was nothing to relish from her situation in life.

Except for the occasional dawn—and dusk—when Lady Portia Hawke transformed into a different creature altogether, one who exposed the weaknesses of men, and beat them at their own game.

"Why do you smile, Portia?"

She glanced up to see his gaze focused on her. "Because I'm enjoying my breakfast," she replied. "Charles, please pass my compliments to Mrs. Winston—these kidneys are delicious."

"Thank you, Lady Portia, she will be honored."

"You'd have done the cook greater honor had you arrived at breakfast on time," Portia's brother said. "Perhaps there was some fault on the part of your maid."

"It wasn't Nerissa's fault," Portia replied. "I went for an early walk and she accompanied me. We returned just as your…*guest* was leaving."

He narrowed his eyes, and Portia caught a sheen of discomfort in his expression.

"Yes, brother," she said. "I find it somewhat ironic that you see fit to lecture me about decorum when we saw your mistress—or should I say one of your *many* mistresses—leaving our home, by the front door, if you please, for all of London to see, after presumably having spent the night in your bed."

"Do not speak of such things," he said with a growl. "It's not becoming of the sister of a duke."

"Even if that duke is free to do what he pleases, no matter how improper?"

"There's no impropriety in my behavior, Portia."

"Why, because you arrived at the breakfast table before seven?"

"No, because I'm a man."

A knot of anger tightened in Portia's stomach and she sliced her knife through a kidney, imagining it to be her brother's heart.

"So I must abide by different standards to you, Adam, because of my sex?"

"Precisely." He picked up his teacup and took a sip. "While you are unmarried, you're required to behave, in order to secure a husband. After your marriage you must also behave to avoid casting any disgrace on your husband's name. Whereas I—"

"Whereas you may do as you please?"

"Careful, sister," he said, his lip curling into a smirk. "You're sounding bitter."

"We are equals, brother. I—"

"We both have rank, Portia, but that does not make us equal. Your rank brings with it the duty to secure a respectable marriage. My rank enables me to do as I please."

"So my rank is a burden. But yours is a privilege—one that you should not abuse, even though you do."

He set his teacup aside. "You ought to be careful, sister. There's nothing so undesirable as a lady who answers back."

"Except a man who indulges in the advantages of power, without the accountability."

"You think I have no accountability?" he asked, leaning forward, his eyes gleaming with anger. "My entire life is governed by duty and responsibility—responsibility to the title and the estate—"

"A responsibility you delegate to your steward."

"—and a responsibility to the trustees," he continued, ignoring her interruption. "Each month I must present myself to them to justify the funds I spend. I'm beholden to them for our very survival."

"As I'm beholden to *you*," she said, aware of the bitterness in her voice. "I must come to you cap in hand if I want to do anything, or go anywhere. My world is restricted by the boundaries that you place around me. My life is dictated by the single objective placed before me—that of securing myself a husband, to whom you will relinquish your ownership of me at the altar. Even my fortune is nothing more than a financial inducement to tempt a man into marrying me, and it'll pass to him to spend as he pleases. Brother, I am not, and never will be, *free*."

"And you think *I* am?" he scoffed, before resuming his attention on the plate in front of him. "If so, then you're less intelligent than I give you credit for."

"I thought you placed no value on such qualities in a woman," Portia said, slicing through another kidney, and wincing as the knife scraped against the plate. "Did I not overhear you say that a woman's intellect was an impediment to her charms?"

"There's no place in *Society* for an intelligent woman."

"Mrs. Scarlet is not unintelligent," Portia said. "She's astute enough to ensure that she has several protectors rather than give men such as you exclusivity over her body, because she understands that men such as you are not to be trusted."

"Cerise does not belong in Society," he replied. "And I must remind you of the need to refrain from speaking of matters that are inappropriate for a young woman of your rank."

With a sigh, Portia resumed eating her breakfast.

There was no arguing with him. And perhaps he was right. Intelligence was an impediment to a woman in her position. Better that she could walk blindly into matrimony and accept the bit and bridle placed upon her with little understanding of the loss of liberty. Better that she were to value nothing more than a comfortable home, the ability to bear a man's heirs, and enough pin money to purchase a few pretty gowns to alleviate any despondency.

Silence stretched around the room, punctuated by the scraping of cutlery.

At length, her brother nodded to the footmen, who began clearing the plates.

"I give you more freedom than I am required, Portia," he said, his voice softening.

"Perhaps, in your own way, you believe that, Adam."

"I permit you to indulge in your little fancies," he said. "Your wounded soldiers, for instance."

"I thought tending to the sick was an acceptable occupation for a lady. Or are we supposed to merely throw a handful of coins at a hospital and let others do the work to avoid sullying our own hands?"

"Are you visiting the hospital later?"

"Don't feign an interest in my life, brother. It does not become you. But yes, I'm assisting Dr. McIver today."

"That charlatan! His overly modern ideas are, I hear, a danger to the profession."

"I suppose you heard that from Dr. Lucas?" Portia let out a mirthless laugh. "*His* idea of a cure is to cover the patient with leeches and be done with it, or to relieve a soldier of his limbs rather than use what little talent he has to treat an injury. Whereas Dr. McIver has written several papers on the treatment of fractures to ensure that young men are not maimed unnecessarily by those who profess to be experts in a field of which they understand very little."

"I take it you're championing your one-legged captain again?"

Portia bit her lip to suppress the rage swelling inside. "Captain Broom is a hero," she said. "I doubt *you* would have acquitted yourself quite so well at Waterloo, whereas he—"

"Spare me your praise of Captain Broom," Adam interrupted. "I fail to see how a man can be considered brave merely because he has one limb fewer than the rest of us. I only hope you're not setting your cap at a man like that."

"Stop it!" she cried. "He has more goodness and courage than the whole of your acquaintance put together. He has a fiancée, if you must know, and as soon as he returns to Yorkshire, they are to marry."

"Assuming she still wants him."

"Believe it or not, brother, not everyone is as shallow as you. Why wouldn't his fiancée still wish to marry him? A loyal, dependable young man who risked his life to fulfil his duty to his country. Better that than a profligate duke who spends his days gaming and cavorting with whores."

He set his teacup down with a clatter. Though she was likely to pay dearly for her taunt, it was a price worth paying for the pleasure of rattling him.

"And then there's your other fancy," he said. "Marksmanship is no occupation for a lady."

Her stomach twisted in fear. Surely he didn't know?

"Marksmanship?"

He waved a dismissive hand. "Archery, or whatever you call it."

Portia's heart rate settled and she suppressed a sigh of relief. "You have some skill with a bow, brother," she said, "or are you permitted to practice that skill because of your sex? And there are plenty of archers among our acquaintance. Lady Thorpe, for one."

He rolled his eyes. "That hoyden. Thorpe gives his wife too much freedom—"

"Which perhaps explains why she's happier than most Society wives. Her husband is not a heartless blackguard and he does not keep her in chains. It is fortunate for her, then, that she did not marry *you*."

Portia's brother rose to his feet, pushing his chair back, and she winced at the sound of wood scraping against wood.

He dropped his napkin on the table. "This conversation is over."

"Why, because I have placed a mirror before your character and you dislike what you see?"

"No, because I've better things to occupy my time with than a discontented, sour-tempered female."

"So you're off to indulge in brandy at White's to boast about your conquests and maybe compare notes on Mrs. Scarlet's particular talents with the likes of Sir Heath Moss?"

His left eye twitched.

"Of course, brother," she added, "like it or not, *you* will have to enter into the marriage state one day and temper your excesses."

He shrugged. "And?"

"Then perhaps you'll know what it's like to be imprisoned."

"A man is only imprisoned in a marriage if he has the misfortune to fall in love with his wife." He issued a bow, clicking his heels together. "I shall bid you good day."

He approached the doors, and the footmen pulled them open.

"Adam," she called after him.

He turned at the doorway and raised his eyebrows.

"One day, brother, that stone in your chest that passes for a heart will soften, and you will fall in love. And then you shall know what pain is."

"Dear sister," he said, "I, as you so frequently point out, am not in possession of a heart. At least not for women. But you are right in that the duty of matrimony comes to us all. I am generous enough to fund your third Season, but I shall expect to see you engaged to a suitable man by the end of it. Failing that, I shall, myself, find a suitable man to take you off my hands."

He turned his back and exited the breakfast room, the footmen closing the doors behind him.

Portia gripped her teacup, her knuckles whitening as she tightened her hold. What satisfaction would she get from flinging it across the room! But her brother would only laugh at her—and she'd be damned if she gave him the satisfaction, or gave the footmen more work in clearing up the mess.

I shall find a suitable man to take you off my hands.

Portia permitted herself a grin.

"Not if I've shot them all, brother."

CHAPTER FOUR

Fog smothered the battlefield, a thick gray shroud clinging to the landscape, following the contours of the land, the hillocks, the boulders…and the still shapes of what had once been living, breathing men.

Those men had sallied forth toward the enemy, their voices joining the battle cry of their general, only to be cut short with each slice of a sword, each explosion that filled the air with acrid smoke to mingle with the sour, metallic stench that choked the senses as each man's lifeblood drained into the earth.

The voices that had chanted together in a song of comradeship now filled the air with pain and despair—some calling to loved ones they would ever see again, others to the deity that had forsaken them.

"Death—death is upon us!"

A lone voice filled his mind, filled with agony, pleading for the onset of oblivion. Then the fog cleared to reveal an apparition—the remnants of a soldier, his pale face gleaming in the dying light. The soldier reached up, clawing at the air, and long, thin fingers stretched across the battlefield, reaching toward him.

"Reid…"

The voice swelled in the air, swirling around with the fog, filling his mind, thick agony hammering against his temples, and he pressed his hands against his ears to obliterate the howling of the dead—so many dead, their bodies littering the ground…

Men—better, braver men than he—who deserved to live…

"Reid!"

A hand caught his sleeve, and he jerked back. The fog dissipated to reveal a face, but it was no longer the colorless face of a dead man. Before him was a living, breathing face—rounded cheeks bearing a healthy pink glow, two warm brown eyes narrowed with concern, framed by a shock of thick, pale-blonde hair.

Captain Broom—his friend and former comrade in arms.

"I say, Reid, old chap, did we lose you for a moment? Are you well?"

"Y-yes, I'm well, Broom."

Stephen blinked and the world re-formed. The thick gray pallor dissolved into daylight to reveal not a bloodied battlefield strewn with the dead, but a vast, high-ceilinged hall with a neat formation of beds arranged in rows. Shapes moved between the beds in a slow formation, tending to the occupants before moving on to the next, like dance partners at a ball.

Most of the occupants were unlikely to attend a ball again.

"You're looking melancholy again, Reid," Broom said.

"Is it any wonder after what happened to you?"

"It no longer gives me pain, old chap," Broom said, gesturing to the lower half of his body. "And I'm better off than most, thanks to you."

"It's my fault you're in that bed."

"Aye, it is," Broom said, with a grin. "If it weren't for you, I'd be in my grave or, more likely, scattered all over that damned battlefield. I know where I'd prefer to be, and so does my Sophy."

"D-does she not mind…?"

A slight frown creased Broom's forehead and he shook his head. "You give her too little credit, my friend."

"I'm sending her fiancé back minus a limb."

"No, my friend—that particular honor goes to Dr. Lucas. *He's* the sawbones. Or, if you really wish to apportion blame, set it at the feet of the Frenchie who shot me—who, if I recall, is himself scattered across the field at Waterloo courtesy of your firearm. If you must feel pity for anyone, Reid, pity *his* sweetheart, who will be waiting forever for him to return." Broom squeezed Stephen's hand. "Or perhaps save a little compassion for yourself."

"For *me*? Why?" The familiar tide of guilt swelled within him. "I escaped unscathed where my fellow soldiers were killed or maimed. I'm the one who should have died in battle."

Broom's expression softened. "No, my friend," he said. "You didn't escape unscathed. Your wounds may not be visible, but I see them. You need to heal as much as I."

In Bedlam, perhaps? Wasn't that where they sent men whose wits had snapped? Weak souls incapable of facing the consequences of their actions—men who relived the battle every night, waking to the stench of blood in their nostrils and the screams of the dead in their ears. Men who—

"You're doing it again, old boy." Broom took his hand. "Do not let the war claim your soul, my friend. What do you think your sister would say if she knew you'd rather have died in battle than return home to her? There is no honor in death—the honor is in returning safe to your loved ones. Angela's too young to lose her brother."

"She has another brother."

"Who is too occupied with his own family to bother with a younger sister embarking on her first Season. Face it, Reid, Angela needs *you*."

"I've employed a chaperone for her."

"Angela needs a brother, not some dowdy, sour-tempered widow."

"Mrs. Stowe is not sour-tempered. She's perfectly amiable."

"Ah, Mrs. Stowe!" Broom said, grinning. "So I was mostly right, then. Her late husband was something of a profligate, or so I hear, which explains her need for employment. She's dull enough to keep Angela from straying. But your sister doesn't just need a colorless old woman to keep her from coming to harm. She needs her brother to champion her honor and protect her from rakes."

"Perhaps."

"There's no 'perhaps' about it, old chap. Your sister is the epitome of innocence. A veritable angel."

Broom's smile widened and he sat up, his eyes sparkling with delight. "Ah, speak of an angel, and the finest in the kingdom will appear."

"Beg pardon?"

Broom gestured across the ward. At the far end stood two young women. One was dressed in the garb of a servant, but the other wore a gown of bright-red silk with a matching redingote that lent a splash of color to the otherwise muted tones of her environment, as if she were a single rose blooming in a neglected garden. Illuminated by a beam of sunlight, she looked almost ethereal, as if an angel had descended to walk among mere mortals. Tall and slim, she towered over her companion. Beneath her bonnet, dark curls framed her face—the color of a raven's wing, shining in the sunlight, giving it a deep blue hue to match the color of her eyes…

Sweet heaven! Stephen had never seen eyes such as hers—the color of cornflowers under the summer sun, with a spark of sharp intelligence.

In short, he could never have believed that such loveliness could exist.

A low chuckle came from the bed.

"You like her, eh, Reid?"

"She's pretty enough."

"Ha! She's a damned sight more than that, and you know it. I'm only thankful I have my Sophy to go home to, or I'd be as smitten as you."

Indignation, tempered by shame, shimmered in the air and Stephen turned away. "Don't be a bloody fool."

The man in the bed recoiled at the savagery in Stephen's tone. "Come, come, my friend. A man would have to be blind not to want her."

"He'd doubtless have his heart torn to shreds at her feet,"

Stephen replied. "Mark my words, Broom, a woman like that has no time for men such as us—especially not *you*. You're a leg and a title short of what a woman such as *her* would deem acceptable."

"Do you insult me, or Lady Portia?" Broom said. "I assure you, she cares not for appearance—as you'll come to know."

"I've had my fill of haughty misses who care nothing for others, Broom. I have absolutely no desire to know Lady—"

"Lady Portia!" Broom cried, extending his hands. "To what do I owe the pleasure of the company of my favorite nurse?"

Damn.

The woman in question stood before them. How come ladies had the ability to glide about the floor so quietly? To catch men unawares, perhaps.

Had she heard him?

She tilted her head to one side, casting Stephen a cursory glance. Her closeness only emphasized her beauty—perfect porcelain skin, with a faint flush of rose on her cheeks. A slight grimace played on her lips, and he caught a flicker of disdain in her eyes.

Aye, a haughty miss, indeed.

Most young ladies seemed to think such haughtiness was desirable to the opposite sex, as if the prospect of being saddled with a harridan in a loveless union was a man's primary objective. No doubt she'd wed herself to a titled man, then triumph over her rivals and bask in their resentful admiration.

As to Captain Broom—no doubt she'd soon wipe the lovesick smile from his face with the put-downs so often issued by ladies such as her.

She turned to the man in the bed, and her face broke into a smile.

Sweet Lord almighty! Pretty enough she might be, but that smile rendered her breathtaking.

Stephen's heart stuttered and he fought to draw a breath. Her eyes sparkled with pleasure and compassion as she reached forward and took Broom's hands.

"Captain Broom, the pleasure is all mine," she said.

"Might I introduce you to my friend, Lady Portia?" Broom said. "Reid, this is Lady Portia Hawke. Lady Portia, this is Colonel Stephen Reid, my comrade in arms, who fought alongside me at Waterloo."

She turned her attention to Stephen once more, her expression cooling. His gut twisted at the intensity of her gaze, as if she had the ability to penetrate a man's façade and delve into his soul.

"A pleasure, I'm sure, colonel," she said, extending her hand.

He took it, and a bolt of need fizzed through his blood as he slid his fingers between hers. Her nostrils flared, and for a moment, the warmth of desire flickered in her eyes. Then she blinked and it was gone. She withdrew her hand and a sense of loss rippled through his body.

She gestured toward her companion. "My maid, Nerissa— Miss Price."

What the devil was a woman of her rank doing introducing her *maid*? Lady Portia frowned, then Stephen extended his hand to her companion.

"Miss Price, a pleasure."

Lady Portia resumed her attention on the man in the bed. "It warms my heart to see you looking so well, Captain Broom," she said, "doesn't it, Nerissa?"

"It does, Lady Portia. Will you be returning home soon, captain?"

"I leave next week, Miss Nerissa."

"I'm sure Miss Flynn will be delighted to hear that. Have you written to her?"

"I have, and I sent her the book of poems you recommended."

What was the maid doing, speaking out of turn? Her mistress was likely to admonish her forwardness, so why was Broom encouraging such behavior?

The captain let out a chuckle. "My friend is somewhat discomposed, Miss Price."

The maid colored and glanced at her mistress. A flicker of disdain shone in Lady Portia's eyes.

"Do you disapprove of my maid having a voice, Colonel Reid?" she said.

Stephen shook his head. "I merely find it astonishing that a woman of your rank—"

"Is not displaying the behavior of a haughty miss who cares nothing for others whom you have absolutely no desire to know?"

Shit. She'd heard.

An uncomfortable heat bloomed in his body at her intense gaze. Then a slight smile played on her lips, as if she found him faintly amusing, like a child trying to engage in conversation with a superior mind.

Sweet holy hell—could anything be more desirable? A fire sparked in his belly, then centered on his groin, and he shifted position to ease the tightness in his breeches.

She lowered her gaze to his lap and her eyes widened a fraction. The tip of her tongue flicked across her lips, leaving them glistening with moisture—just ripe to be tasted...

"I say, old boy! You're not being very gallant, are you?" Broom said. "A gentleman should never remain sitting in the presences of ladies standing."

Bugger. If Stephen stood now, the cockstand in his breeches would be all too apparent. What would Lady Portia think if she saw *that*?

"It's of no consequence, Captain Broom, I assure you," she said. "I am not one to lose composure over such a...*little* matter."

Her gaze flicked to his groin, and he caught a flash of amusement in her eyes as her maid stifled a giggle.

"I must apologize for my friend, Lady Portia," Broom continued. "He's not well versed in polite conversation."

"Taciturnity is to be admired, given how little sense comes from a man's lips," she replied.

Confounded female! Did she seek to insult him?

Stephen crossed his legs to ease the ache in his groin. "A hospital's no place for a woman," he said, the gruffness in his voice disguising the swelling desire. "The injuries these men have sustained are not for a woman's eyes."

"And yet it's women who tend to them daily," she replied. "Whether we ignore them or not, men are injured on the battlefield, or shot in duels, and they deserve to be tended to."

"There's no honor in a *duel*," he said. "Men who engage in such childish activities injure themselves unnecessarily and require the services of a physician at the expense of those in true need."

"But they fight for the honor of their loved ones," Broom said.

"Where's the honor in a childish spat between men who should know better?" Stephen said. "A duel arises from an act of dishonor—the seduction of an innocent, violation of another man's wife…or a silly insult at White's."

"You speak as if you've direct experience of duels, sir," Lady Portia said, directing her unsettling gaze at him.

"I'd never stoop to such antics," he replied, "but I am sensitive to the problem."

"How so?"

"His younger sister, Lady Portia," Broom said. "She will be having her come-out this season."

"Then I look forward to meeting her," Lady Portia said with a smile. "Is she excited about her debut?"

"Very—her romantic sensibilities make it so," Stephen replied.

Her smile slipped. "Romantic sensibility in a woman is a luxury she can rarely afford, for it rarely ends well for the woman."

"Do you speak from experience?" he asked.

Pain flickered in her eyes, then she averted her gaze and stooped to kiss Broom on the forehead.

"Forgive me, captain," she said. "I see I'm intruding, and I mustn't neglect my chores, or Dr. McIver will be most disappointed. I'll come and sit with you later—after your friend has gone."

She nodded toward Stephen, then approached another bed. Its occupant, who had remained still all morning, came to life, color blooming on his previously ashen face and a smile illuminating his one remaining eye.

"Lady Portia!" he cried, offering his left hand. "And the delightful Miss Price. I was beginning to worry that you'd never come today."

She touched the stump where his right arm had once been, then took his left hand, and a stab of envy needled at Stephen to see the smitten expression on the man's face.

"Captain Clarke, I promised, did I not?" she said. "Now, have you been practicing your writing?"

"Yes, but my penmanship is appalling."

"It always was, if I recall. The penmanship of a pug, my brother always said."

"Oh, is he as overbearing as usual?"

"Worse," she said, with a laugh, and they were soon engaged in conversation.

"I see she's charmed every man in the room," Stephen said.

Broom let out a snort. "Every man except one, it seems. Why have you taken against her? Is it perhaps to hide your desire?"

"I care nothing for her."

"Tell that to your cock," Broom said. "No man can be indifferent to any woman, let alone one such as her."

"She is beautiful, I'll admit…"

"Oh, you'll admit, will you?" Broom chuckled. "Lady Portia's a damned sight more than that. She's intelligent and charming. Even you would admit that a man has much to gain from the company of a beautiful woman."

"Oh *yes*," Stephen said, unable to temper the bitterness in his voice. "She'll make him the envy of his friends, and there's nothing more effective than envy in destroying friendships. Every admirer and adventurer will see her as a challenge, and eventually she'll succumb—as all women do—to temptation and flattery. In a woman's eyes, there will always be a wealthier, handsomer, or greater-titled alternative to the man she promises herself to, and thus the man who falls for her wiles will be left rejected and brokenhearted. The envy of his friends, which will have cost him many friendships, will now turn to pity and disdain."

"Reid, not all women are like—"

"Spare me, Broom," Stephen growled. "I have no intention of losing my heart, to Lady Portia or any other woman. I'll not be made a fool of again."

He squeezed his friend's hand, then rose to his feet and bowed. As he exited the hospital, he glanced over his shoulder at the elegant figure weaving in among the beds, exchanging words and smiles with the occupants.

Beautiful she might be, but Lady Portia was a woman. Even if she weren't tempted by the material benefits of a better man, what woman would want to cleave herself to a man such as he? A man who spent every night tormented by the demons of war; a man set on the path to madness.

No woman deserved *that*.

CHAPTER FIVE

"Sister, your dance card is not full."

Portia glared at her brother. "Am I not to be granted some respite, or would you have me sprain my ankle from fatigue?"

"Sir Heath Moss is eager to dance with you again."

"One dance with that rake is more than enough for any woman to stomach. I wouldn't want to be seen to encourage him by agreeing to a second dance."

Besides, at dawn tomorrow, she would be taking Sir Heath's place in a duel against Lord Maybury. It wouldn't do to spend too much time with the man in case he recognized her. The hunger in his eyes was, she assumed, merely animal lust, but it was best not to rely on it being the spark of recognition.

"A man as popular with the ladies as he does you great honor asking for a second dance."

Portia snorted. "His *popularity*, as you call it, is purely due to his looks, which he uses to his advantage."

"Granted, he's a little wild, but marriage to the right woman will settle him."

Portia's stomach tightened with nausea. *Sweet Lord*—surely her brother didn't mean to shackle her to *that* reprobate?

"I beg to disagree, Adam," she said. "His idea of the right woman is one with a title and a large enough dowry to fund his excesses. He only associates with you because of your higher rank."

"Are you saying you dislike him because he's only a baronet?"

"I dislike him because he's a rake and a bully, with a reputation for compromising innocents."

"I've not heard of any such reputation."

"You wouldn't, seeing as you're a *man*," Portia said. "He's known to have bedded half the married women in the ballroom tonight."

"I've always found him an amiable fellow."

"Of course you do, given that each time you see him, it must be like looking in a mirror."

She lifted her glass to her lips and took a sip, while his eyes darkened in anger. Most likely she'd pay for her defiance, but if she'd already earned her punishment, she might as well indulge in the crime a little further.

"I wonder, brother, if the two of you compare notes on the innocents you've ruined? Do you keep a tally in the bet book at White's? The first man to lift the skirts of twenty maidens wins half a crown?"

"Don't be so crude. It's unbecoming in a woman of your station."

"So is ruining myself with a footman," she retorted, "but I'll do just that if you persist in partnering me with Sir Heath."

"Then you'd *have* to marry him," he replied. "If you ruin yourself, I shall walk you down the aisle, in chains if need be, to the man of my choosing. There are plenty who'd be prepared to take a titled lady for a wife even if she'd been soiled by another."

"Why, you—"

She raised her hand to strike him, but he caught her wrist. His grip firm and unyielding, he lowered her hand with measured slowness.

"Sister dear, we cannot have you insulting our hosts with your behavior."

"I hate you," she spat, snatching her hand free, and he let out a sigh.

"You may hate me, Portia, but I only act out of love for you," he said. "You've no income, save that which I provide, and the trustees will only release your fortune on your marriage. Therefore, you have no means with which to support yourself without a loving brother or husband to take care of you."

"But it's not—"

"Not fair?" he said. "I know that. But it's the world in which we live. Find yourself a kind and generous husband and your position will be considerably better than mine."

"I have no need for a husband."

He let out a laugh. "You have some secret income that I know nothing of?"

A ripple of apprehension threaded through her. "Of course not," she said, averting her gaze to prevent him from seeing the falsehood in her eyes.

"Then what are you speaking of?" he asked. "Is there something on your mind?"

"My mind is my own, brother," she replied. "But I'll tell you this for free: I despise men who boast of their prowess—men who seem to think a woman will be tempted by his tales of his virility."

"Then perhaps I ought to partner you with Lord Devereaux. He'll never regale you with tales of his virility. In fact, he won't speak at all."

He gestured toward a corner where a man stood apart from the rest of the company, clutching a glass in his hand. His whole form exuded hostility. His attention, which was fixed for the most part on his drink, occasionally was diverted to the rest of the company, when his dark gaze swept across the ballroom before returning to his glass. The only acknowledgment he gave of the presence of another creature was a polite nod to their hostess.

"His disinclination to speak is an advantage," Portia said.

Almost as if he'd heard, Lord Devereaux lifted his gaze to hers, then he frowned and looked away.

"Sadly," she added, "it comes with a permanent state of sour-temperedness."

"Then the two of you have much in common." Almost as soon as her brother spoke the words, regret glimmered in his eyes. "Forgive me, sister," he said. "I only speak out of my love for you."

"So you have said, at least twice. But I judge a man by his actions, not his words."

"Then let me act and make amends for being such an overbearing brother," he said, offering his arm. "It's almost time for the entertainment. I hear Countess Thorpe has employed a fireworker."

"A *what?*"

"Come and see," he said, leading her toward the terrace. "It's all the fashion this year."

"Come, *mes amis!*" a bright voice trilled. Henrietta, Countess Thorpe, glided toward the terrace, arm in arm with her husband, and Portia suppressed a pang of envy at the tenderness in Earl Thorpe's expression as he looked at his wife. Henrietta was something of a harridan—in fact, it was she who'd introduced Portia to the delights of marksmanship—and yet she had found a husband who loved her in spite of her tomboyish ways...or perhaps because of them.

The company followed, among them the Duke of Sawbridge and his new duchess. The man once labeled as the worst reprobate of the *ton* turned to his wife and kissed her—thoroughly tamed and completely in love.

The entire company seemed to consist of people in pairs. Everyone seemed to be one half of a happy couple—or if not completely happy, then at least satisfied with their partner.

Everyone except me.

Portia spied Sir Heath Moss's blond head among the crowd. He turned to face her, and his handsome face broke into a smile. He moved toward her, and she withdrew her arm from her brother's.

"I'm in need of a little solitude, Adam," she said. "I've had more than enough of Sir Heath Moss for a lifetime, let alone an evening. I know my reluctance to marry disappoints you—everything about me disappoints you—but shackle me to him and you'll be condemning me to a life of misery."

"Don't you wish to be loved, Portia?" her brother asked, his voice softening.

"What do *you* know of love?"

"Perhaps nothing," came the reply. "But look at Sawbridge over there. Do you not wish to be loved as he loves his duchess?"

"And who among the posing peacocks here tonight do you think capable of loving me as much as Sawbridge loves his wife? Mimi is one of the more fortunate women of my acquaintance."

"But she endured much before she found happiness."

"Yes," Portia replied, unable to disguise the bitterness in her voice. "All at the hands of men. For every Mimi, I'll wager there are a thousand women who fell into ruination and despair and never found redemption."

"That fate does not await you, Portia," he said. "I'll make sure of that."

"Why must I depend on you to ensure my happiness?"

"Because I'm your brother, and I'll never forsake you."

"No matter what?"

He nodded.

At that moment, an explosion sounded outside, together with a flash of light in myriad colors. A ripple of "oohs" and "aahs" threaded through the company, followed by gloved applause.

"You're missing the show," he said.

"Then don't let me detain you," she replied. "You can occupy Sir Heath better than I."

He let out a huff, but did not attempt to stop her as she exited the ballroom. As she reached the door, she glanced back to see her brother catch Sir Heath's sleeve, thereby preventing him from following.

Perhaps her brother did love her after all—at least enough to give her respite from the company of rakes. For tonight, anyway.

But what of tomorrow?

CHAPTER SIX

As Portia made her way to the library, she passed a window and glanced outside. A burst of light filled the sky, followed by an explosion, then it shattered into a hundred stars that lingered in the air for a heartbeat. Almost like the dandelion heads she used to pick as a child. Then the lights dispersed, like dandelion seeds in a gust of wind, radiating outward then dissolving into the ink-colored background.

She entered the library and closed the door, and the cheering and laughter faded. But the explosions continued, deep in pitch, such that she could almost feel them vibrating in her bones. Two candles beside the fireplace cast a warm yellow light across the wall that flickered and danced. After each explosion outside, a flash of light filtered through the curtains, illuminating the gold embossing of the rows of books that lined the walls.

A faint scratching sound came from the opposite end of the room. Portia caught her breath and cast her gaze about, but she saw nothing save the shadows that grew deeper in the corners. Most likely a mouse had taken refuge from the Thorpes' housecat, seeking respite in the darkness.

Perhaps that's what I am, a mouse seeking refuge from predators in the shape of hungry suitors desperate to win me—or, rather, my title and dowry—with soulless flattery.

Why did every man she'd met seem to think that flattery was the way to her heart?

Every man except one—the brooding specimen she'd encountered at the hospital whose only redeeming feature was his devotion to Captain Broom, the merriest soldier in all England.

Heaven, deliver me from the male sex!

And where better to seek deliverance than a library? Particularly this one. Earl Thorpe was renowned for having an excellent library—even Portia's brother remarked on it. Among the historical and theological works and journals was a collection of literary and artistic works that had expanded over the years, courtesy of the countess. And, unlike most members of Society, the Thorpes were known to actually *read* their books.

Portia approached one wall and ran her fingertips along the spines, tracing the outlines of the titles embossed in gold leaf. She smiled to herself as she traced the name of the author.

William Shakespeare.

She continued along the row until she found the title she sought.

The hand of providence, perhaps—how else could she have found that very work in a room that must house five hundred books at least?

Clutching the book like a prized possession, she crossed the floor and settled into an armchair beside one of the candles, then she opened the book and flicked through the pages to the passage she sought.

Another explosion sounded in the distance, together with a cheer.

Then she heard it—a long, low growl.

The skin on the back of her neck tightened with apprehension.

It was no mouse. Nor was it a cat.

Holding the book in one hand, she picked up the candle, then approached the corner from where the sound had come. Her stomach clenched in fear as a shadow shifted in the darkness, moving slowly back and forth.

"Is someone there?" she said, unable to temper the tremor in her voice.

The fireworker outside let off another explosion, and a long, low moan came from the apparition in the corner. With a shriek, Portia stepped back, almost losing her grip on the candle.

You fool!

What would her brother think of her, frightened of a shadow?

She held the candle aloft, and the shadow dissolved to reveal the figure of a man.

Crouched in the corner, his arms wrapped around his knees, he rocked back and forth.

"Sir?" Portia asked.

He made no response, and she moved closer.

"Sir, are you well?"

The rocking ceased and he lifted his head. Soft brown eyes stared ahead, dark against the pallor of his face, which was surrounded by a thick mane of honey-blond hair, and a shock of recognition coursed through her.

It was the man from the hospital.

"Colonel…" Curse it, what was his name? She'd thought of him as *Colonel Crabby*, after cursing the Almighty for always blessing the handsomest men with the sourest temperaments. But perhaps he had a reason for his poor disposition—a reason that gave rise to his suffering now.

He closed his eyes and mumbled to himself.

"I beg your pardon, sir?" Portia said. "I did not hear you."

The mumbling continued, and she caught a single word…

Battle.

Then another explosion echoed outside and he flinched. His eyes opened, glazed with fear.

"They're shooting," he groaned.

"No, sir, it's merely a—"

"Death!" he interrupted. "They're dead because of me. I can see them…" His head jerked to one side. "Bodies—surrounded by bodies…everywhere."

"There's no battle here," Portia said. "You're in Earl Thorpe's library."

He shook his head with a frantic, jerking motion, and she reached for his sleeve. As soon as she touched it, he jerked away, falling back against the wall. His eyes widening, he shuffled backward until he was pressed against the wall, and lowered his head, staring at the floor.

"Colonel…" she began, and he flinched.

"Begone, demon!" he cried. "I'm destined for Hades, but you'll not take me yet."

Reid! That was it.

"Colonel Reid!" Portia cried, and he jerked his head up.

"H-have I seen you before?" he croaked.

"At the hospital," she said, "visiting the wounded soldiers, including your friend."

Recognition flickered in his eyes and he tilted his head to one side. Then his gaze began to shift out of focus.

"You're not at the mouth of Hades, Colonel Reid," she said, "and I'm no demon. I'm a mortal woman."

"N-no…"

Portia crouched beside him and set her book on the floor. "Colonel, may I take your hand?"

His lack of response she took for assent, and she slipped her hand in his. For a moment, it lay limp and unresponsive, then his fingers curled around hers, his touch solidifying as, perhaps, did his awareness of his surroundings. She caught her breath as a fizz of want bubbled in her center at the feel of his skin against hers.

Then she chided herself. Now was not the time to succumb to desire, no matter how his strong-featured face had slipped into her dreams in the nights since she'd first seen him at the hospital—his brooding demeanor in contrast to Captain Broom's more congenial disposition.

What had Dr. McIver said?

Some men suffer as much as those whom the war has maimed.

In fact, perhaps they suffered more—their injuries were not visible and therefore ignored and laughed at by an uncaring world.

What horrors had this man witnessed to cause such suffering?

"Colonel Reid, do you remember me?"

He lifted his gaze and his eyes began to focus, the wildness in their expression fading, to be replaced by a sheen of shame.

"Colonel," Portia said, lowering her voice to a gentle whisper, "tell me what you see."

He shook his head. "Don't be a fool."

At that moment, another bang sounded outside and he flinched, his forehead creasing in pain. She lifted his hand to her lips, and he drew in a sharp breath. Warm brown eyes fixed on her, then darkened to the color of mahogany as he slid his fingers across hers, interlocking their hands.

"The battlefield…"

"No, colonel," she whispered. "We're in a library. Tell me what you see."

He blinked and shifted his gaze. "A candle," he said.

"Very good. What else?"

He blinked, slowly, and his chest rose and fell in a deep breath.

"Books," he said. "Hundreds of books—lining the walls."

"Can you describe them?"

He paused, then nodded. "Row upon row, the spines glistening in the candlelight, green and gold. No—red." He looked to the book at Portia's feet. "Ah, Shakespeare. *The Merchant of Venice.*" Then his lips curved upward. "Portia," he said. "Are you Portia come to life from the page? Are you in my mind?"

"I am no character in a play," she replied. "Nor do I exist only in your imagination. I'm Lady Portia Hawke. Do you not remember me?"

"Lady Portia…"

For a moment he stared at her, then recognition filled his gaze and he colored.

"Dear Lord—what you must think of me!" he said. He tried to rise, then fell back, and she caught his hand.

"Sir, you're unwell," she said. "Perhaps you shouldn't attempt to stand until you're feeling better. May I bring you something? A brandy, perhaps?"

He shook his head.

"I understand your distress, colonel," Portia said. "Did you fight at Waterloo alongside Captain Broom?"

Shame flickered in his eyes and he looked away.

"There's nothing to be ashamed of in experiencing distress after a war," Portia said. "I cannot imagine what you must have experienced."

"I'm not injured, Lady Portia," he said, his voice hardening. "A bout of weakness is all I've endured tonight. It will not happen again. Now, permit me to stand."

He tried to move, and she placed a hand on his shoulder.

"I see no weakness," she said. "I'd sooner call it weak to deny your pain—even that which is not physical."

At a further explosion outside, he flinched, and she squeezed his hand.

"Our hosts are entertaining the guests with a fireworker," she said. "It's all the fashion this Season—or so my brother says."

"Why are you in here, then?"

"To seek respite from the crowds."

Another bang came, followed by a volley of explosions and a distant cheer.

"I think perhaps the fireworker is approaching his finale," Portia said, as the explosions increased in intensity.

He stiffened, and she sat next to him, curling her fingers around his.

"I prefer to wait somewhere quiet until the entertainment is over," she said, while he continued to shake. "A ball has three purposes, does it not? Music, dancing, and conversation. I think fireworkers are best suited to public entertainment, don't you?"

"I-I suppose so."

"Perhaps Countess Thorpe intends for her guests to enjoy a quieter mode of entertainment near the end of the evening," she continued. "I saw the Duchess of Sawbridge among the guests. She's fond of Bach, and has become quite the proficient. Perhaps she'll entertain us over supper."

"S-Sawbridge?" He raised his eyebrows in inquiry. Her attempt at Society conversation was at least diverting his attention from the noise outside.

"He's something of a reprobate, you know," she added. "I'm sure you heard the rumors. Not that I applaud the spreading of gossip—I leave that to Lady Francis. Have you had the fortune, or otherwise, of being sat next to her at the supper table? She's too apt to poke her nose in the affairs of others. Eleanor has sketched a particularly wicked likeness of her, with the nose a little too long."

His eyes flared with recognition. "E-Eleanor?"

"The Duchess of Whitcombe," Portia said. "Perhaps you know her? She's not fond of loud noises either. Or crowds."

"Y-yes, I know her."

"Then we've at least one acquaintance in common."

At that moment, footsteps approached in the corridor outside, and the colonel let out a curse. "Bugger."

"Hush!" Portia whispered. "It's likely Sir Baldwin Manby-Bresswell attempting an early visit to the buffet—though, given his portliness, I'd have expected the ground to shake under his weight."

He let out a snort, and his eyes twinkled with mirth.

"That's better," she said. "I was beginning to wonder whether you knew how to smile. Your face hasn't cracked, so you must have smiled before."

A final cheer rose in the distance, followed by applause.

"Ah," she said. "Perhaps the entertainment is done and it's time for supper. Shall we return to the ballroom?"

She rose to her feet, and he followed suit. At that moment, the library door was flung open and a dark silhouette filled the doorway.

"What the devil do you think you're *doing*?" a voice roared, and Portia's stomach twisted in apprehension as she recognized the voice.

She rose to her feet, smoothing down the skirts of her gown. "Brother, I'm—"

"Be quiet!"

Adam stepped into the library, the candlelight picking out his chiseled features and the cold fury in his eyes.

Sweet Lord.

She was ruined.

CHAPTER SEVEN

*I*T'S REALLY NOT *my day.*

Cursing his rotten luck, Stephen shrank back into the shadows.

Not only had he disgraced himself in front of a lady, whimpering like a babe at the sound of the fireworker's entertainment, he now found himself in a compromising position with her in the library—in front of her brother.

Like all men, he understood what was required of him in such situations. Even if there were no fault on either side, he'd be required to do the *honorable thing.*

Though, he had to admit, there were worse women for whom he'd be forced to do the honorable thing. The tenderness in Lady Portia's eyes belied the brittle superiority of ladies of her station, and the soft tone of voice when she'd taken his hand and brought him back from the brink of hell spoke of a far superior woman.

A woman with whom even the most hard-hearted man could easily find himself falling in love, to the point of his own destruction.

Her eyes glittered with anger as she placed her hands on her hips. "I'm not a footman you can order about, Adam," she addressed the man in the doorway, whose powerful frame filled the space. "I've"—she glanced back toward Stephen—"*we've* done nothing wrong."

"*We?*" the man said, a mocking tone in his voice. "Then what were you doing?"

"Discussing Shakespeare."

"Seriously?"

Lady Portia let out a huff. "I wouldn't expect you to understand, Adam. Didn't you once say that Shakespeare's works were books to have on one's shelf to give the appearance of gentility, but were not something one actually *read*? At least, not something *you're* capable of reading?"

"That's no way to talk to me, Portia, given the situation I find you in."

The man's voice—deep and rich—sounded familiar. Then he stepped forward and the candlelight illuminated his face.

Shit.

The Duke of Foxton.

Lady Portia's brother was the *Duke of bloody Foxton*?

In which case, no matter what Stephen said in his defense, he was done for. Foxton wasn't known for a forgiving nature—quite the opposite. Which perhaps explained his appeal to the opposite sex—too many women were drawn to a rake in the hope that they might tame him. But more often than not they were savaged, their hearts and reputations ripped to shreds.

In fact, Foxton was the very sort of man with whom Stephen wanted little to do—the sort of man he needed to protect his sister against.

"I *beg* your pardon?" the duke said, taking a step toward Stephen.

"Adam, leave him be," Lady Portia said, catching his arm. "Or would you call out everyone who expresses disappointment on your entering a room?" She let out a sharp, cold laugh. "If you did that, you'd be dueling with almost every soul in Town—except the women you've not ruined yet, of course."

Stephen flinched in anticipation, but, rather than the anger he'd expected, the duke gave a cold smile.

"Ah, so *that's* it?" he sneered. "You've decided to carry out your threat to ruin yourself in the hope that I'd demand this fellow here offer his hand?"

"Of course not," she retorted. "I've no intention of marrying him, or anyone else."

Rather than the sense of relief at being released of any obligation, Stephen felt a pang of disappointment. Her spirited defiance of her domineering brother warmed his blood, and his breeches became a little too tight.

"I apologize for my sister's behavior," Foxton said. "I trust you'll show discretion and speak nothing of what transpired here tonight? I shall of course say nothing. You have my word as a gentleman."

Lady Portia snorted, and Foxton's eyes flashed with anger.

"Will you not at least reveal yourself?" the duke said. "You'll not be in any trouble with your mistress."

Dear Lord, did the duke think Stephen a *footman*?

Stephen moved forward, and Foxton drew in a sharp breath.

"Colonel Reid!"

"You *know* him?" Lady Portia said.

"Of course." The duke's lips twisted into a smirk. "Made a fool of yourself with the younger Howard girl, didn't you? Trotting after her like a lovesick puppy, then after she rejected you, you went sniffing after her sister before *she* fled London under a cloud of gossip." He tilted his head to one side. "Perhaps my sister's not at fault here. Scandal follows you around like a cloud of flies. Are you here to sniff around the sister of a duke?"

"Adam, sometimes you can be an utter arse," Lady Portia said. "The only man who's been *sniffing around* me, as you so elegantly put it, is that horrid Moss creature. And, to be frank, any man you feel the need to deter me from is, by definition, more favorable in my eyes than a man you'd recommend."

"You don't trust my judgment?"

"I trust your judgment as much as I trust your literary intelligence." She picked up the book from the floor. "Do you even know the story—who the lead character is in *The Merchant of*

Venice? It was our mother's favorite play."

The duke shrugged. "I care not. But if you think I'll let you make a fool of yourself because of your romantic sensibilities…"

She threw back her head and laughed, and Stephen's heart tightened at the expression in her eyes. Ye gods, she was a beautiful creature when angry, but when she laughed, her beauty rendered her otherworldly.

Then she sobered and met Stephen's gaze. "Forgive me, colonel," she said. "Were you very much in love with Juliette Howard, or Lady Staines, as she is now?"

Stephen's cheeks warmed with shame at the memory of how he'd trotted after Juliette, mesmerized by her beauty, with no consideration of her character—and then how he'd fancied himself in love with Juliette's sister merely because she reminded him of her.

But in the months since he'd shown himself to be an utter fool, his eyes had been opened to the superficiality of Society and its obsession with beauty—at least beauty on the surface. The ugliness of war, the broken bodies and stench of death, had taken root in his soul, bleeding into his very essence and changing him forever.

Men like Broom, with their cheerful optimism, could weather the horrors of war.

But not me. I'm weak, unworthy of the uniform I wear.

"There's no shame in it, colonel," Lady Portia said.

Dear God—had he spoken aloud?

"In *what*, sister?" the duke said, frowning.

"In falling in love. The rules of our Society prevent men and women from discovering enough about each other to make an informed decision as to whether they will be happy partnered for life. And men, as the weaker sex"—she shot a look at her brother—"will always value a woman based on her appearance. Juliette Howard is an exceptionally beautiful creature, but she is happy with Lord Staines. The two of them are a perfect match, therefore she could never have made you truly happy, colonel."

"What nonsense you utter," the duke said.

"So speaks a man who cares little for a woman's happiness."

"A woman's happiness!" he scoffed. "Your needs are simple—a secure home, a strong husband, and a position in Society. I daresay Lady Staines is happy, given that she's been elevated from a commoner's daughter to an earl's wife." He glanced at the door. "Perhaps we should return to the ballroom before we're missed—to preserve my sister's reputation."

Stephen nodded. "Of course."

The duke offered his arm to Lady Portia. She hesitated and his expression hardened, then she sighed and linked her arm with his and they exited the library.

"Colonel, I trust you'll say nothing of what transpired in here tonight," Foxton said.

"Of course," Stephen replied. "Nothing untoward happened. Besides, I have more to lose than she."

Lady Portia glanced at him, and Stephen's heart ached at the compassion in her eyes.

The duke chuckled. "Hardly," he said. "You're a man and should have nothing to fear from a little scandal, at least not compared to a woman. With that attitude, how the devil did you survive Waterloo?"

"Adam!" Lady Portia snapped. "It's not the done thing for a man who languishes in the comfort of his townhouse to question the character of those who risk their lives for their country."

"But—" he began, but she interrupted.

"Colonel, I sympathize on your having endured the rejection of someone you loved—or at least believed yourself to be in love with."

"Rejection!" the duke scoffed. "I wouldn't stand for such treatment."

"That's because you're a rake, brother."

"I'll take that as a compliment—shouldn't I, colonel?"

Lady Portia saved Stephen the need to respond. "Yes, *you* would, Adam," she said. "But rakes only amuse in fiction. I prefer to live in reality. Residing in fiction will only result in ruination and despair."

"Aye," Stephen said. "I loathe any form of deceit. Anyone who is not who they seem is deceiving the rest of the world."

"A little subterfuge can be forgiven if the objective is honorable," Lady Portia said. "Don't you recall the Phoenix?"

"The Phoenix?" Stephen asked.

"An infamous thief," the duke said. "How he escaped the gallows, I'll never know."

"Rumor has it that he was a *she*," Lady Portia said.

"I trust you're mistaken," Stephen said. "No woman in possession of her wits would undertake such a dangerous venture."

Her eyes flared with indignation, then she looked away.

"Well, whoever he—or she—was," the duke said, "they stole a number of precious heirlooms a year or so ago, and evaded justice."

"Only it wasn't theft," Lady Portia said. "It was redemption. Those heirlooms belonged to another, and the Phoenix returned them to their rightful owner."

Surely she wasn't defending the perpetrator of a crime? Or perhaps she knew more about the identity of the Phoenix than she cared to admit. After all, no man knew precisely what women talked about when they indulged in their tea parties and afternoons of gossip promenading in the park.

"Very well, then," the duke said. "What about this masked duelist—the Farthing, or whatever he calls himself. Surely you cannot leap to *his* defense."

Lady Portia stiffened, a flicker of apprehension in her eyes.

"The Farthing?" Stephen asked.

"A man who serves cowards," the duke said, his voice laced with contempt. "A duelist who profits from dishonor, acting as a proxy—for a fee, of course—for men who are too weak to face up to the consequences of their actions."

Stephen shook his head. "A man who takes payment for killing others?"

"Is that not the same as a soldier, colonel?" Lady Portia said.

Ye gods! Perhaps there was some truth in the maxim that a woman's place was in the home, if she harbored such notions.

"It most certainly is not, Lady Portia," he said, unable to temper the vehemence in his tone.

She flinched. "I meant no offense."

"Forgive me, Lady Portia, neither did I—but soldiering is a necessity to maintain the peace. No soldier takes enjoyment from shooting another man, even if that man is the enemy. A soldier who takes pleasure in killing does not deserve his uniform, and anyone seeking to shoot another at dawn in the name of honor does not deserve to be called a man, let alone a gentleman."

"Perhaps the Farthing's intention is to *prevent* death," she said.

"I doubt that," Stephen said. "He sounds like the very worst of reprobates, profiting from such activity."

"Pay no attention to my sister, colonel," the duke said. "Women know little of such things. But I must disagree with you on the matter of fear. A man who fears is a coward, and the militia is not in need of cowards."

"There's no cowardice in admitting one's fear," Lady Portia said. "Quite the opposite."

"How so?" Stephen asked.

She turned her sapphire gaze onto him, and a spark of need ignited in his heart.

"Courage—true courage—is admitting to your fears and still sallying forth into battle. I daresay each and every soldier at Waterloo experienced fear at some point."

They neared the entrance to the ballroom, where the guests milled about the floor.

"Ah!" Foxton said. "The dancing's about to resume. I trust you'll not disappoint me again tonight, sister."

Lady Portia frowned, but Stephen caught a flicker of despair in her eyes.

"Perhaps, Lady Portia, if you're not engaged, you might partner me for the next dance," he said.

"Partner *you?*" Foxton raised his eyebrows.

"I submit myself to the prospect of your rejection, Lady Portia," Stephen said, offering his hand.

"Sir Ambrose Cholmondeley-Walker wishes to dance with you, sister," Foxton said. "That's why I came to find you. He made such a point of asking me."

"Then he ought to have asked *me* first, given that you're not the one who'd have to dance with him," she retorted. "You may be my gaoler, Adam, but you're not my owner. Besides, I cannot think of anything worse than dancing with a man with whom it would be impossible to enjoy a conversation."

"How so?" Stephen asked.

She met his gaze and grinned, and his heart was lost. "With a name like *Cholmondeley-Walker*, each time I address him, I'll have run out of breath before I can make my point, and the dance will be over."

"Portia," the duke warned. He fixed his gaze on Stephen, disapproval in his eyes.

Stephen backed away. The pain and humiliation of Juliette Howard's rejection still ached, and, as any professional soldier understood, some battles were lost even before the first shot was fired. A weak soldier still suffering from the nightmares of war was no match for the Duke of Foxton with his reputation for ferocity and strength of will, and nor was he a match for the sister of such a man.

But, before he could withdraw completely, Lady Portia took his hand, and he caught his breath at the fizz of need as her warm fingers slid against his.

"Colonel, it would be my pleasure to dance with you."

CHAPTER EIGHT

T HE COLONEL'S EYES widened in surprise as Portia took his hand. She shot her brother a look of warning, then led her partner into the center of the ballroom, giving Sir Ambrose Cholmondeley-Walker a cursory nod.

She could have weathered Sir Ambrose's insipid company for a dance, but it was more prudent not to dance with the man with whom she'd undertaken a business transaction only a few nights before. He lacked the wit to recognize her—and, like all men who believed themselves the superior sex, he'd never consider the notion that the Farthing was a *woman*. But all astute business-men—or *businesswomen*—avoided unnecessary risks.

Let him dance with Lady Manby-Bresswell.

But the lady in question was already partnered with Sir Heath Moss, under the watchful eye of the lady's husband.

Good. It might present another business opportunity for the Farthing if Sir Baldwin saw fit to call Sir Heath out. Beneath the veneer of arrogance, Sir Heath was a coward and a notoriously poor shot—which made him the perfect client.

The couples lined up, and Portia's heart soared to see dear Mimi at the head of the line with her husband, the Duke of Sawbridge. Nobody in the room, not even the snobbish Miss Peacock, would daresay anything untoward about Mimi's reputation. It was the benefit of being a duchess, and no matter how much Portia despised Society's obsession with rank, that very same obsession saved her dear friend from ridicule and censure.

Colonel Reid stiffened, tightening his grip on Portia's hand. She glanced up to see him staring at a couple placed further down the line—Earl Staines and his wife, formerly Juliette Howard.

She gave his hand a reassuring squeeze. "There's naught to be ashamed of, colonel," she said. "You're a man, and like all men, rejection and refusal is the price you pay for having the power of choice."

"The power of choice?" he asked as the dance began.

She took his hand and stepped forward in time to the music. "When it comes to anything—dancing or matrimony—my sex is required to wait to be asked," she said. "Your sex has the freedom of choice to ask, or more often *demand*, whatever you wish—a commission in the army, a dance partner, a wife, or a business opportunity. You may make your wishes and desires known at any time and Society will applaud you for it, whereas we are required to keep silent until the final moment, where we are only given two responses to choose from—yes or no."

"Do not underestimate the freedom to say 'no,' Lady Portia."

The despondency in his voice pricked at her heart, and she caught sight of Lady Staines dancing, of the adoration in her eyes as she gazed at her husband.

"Did you love her very much, colonel?" Portia couldn't help asking.

Colonel Reid frowned.

"Forgive me," she said. "My brother's always admonishing me for speaking out of turn."

He caught her hand, and they moved in a figure-of-eight motion to the music. "You're an accomplished dancer, Lady Portia," he said.

"You needn't divert my question with flattery, colonel," she replied. "You have my permission to refuse to answer my question. As you put it so eloquently, do not underestimate the power of refusal."

"It's not flattery when I speak the truth, Lady Portia. Did I not say that I despise deception and those who perpetuate it?"

She flinched inwardly at the undercurrent of loathing in his voice when her brother had mentioned the Farthing. Trust Adam to say the wrong thing at the wrong moment! Though, of course, Adam had no knowledge of her clandestine business activities…or so she hoped.

No—if her brother knew, he'd keep her under lock and key at all hours of the day, only permitting her out on a leash to be paraded around the Marriage Mart.

"Lady Portia? You seem distracted," her partner said. "In answer to your question: yes, I believed myself very much in love with Miss Howard—Lady Staines, as she is now. But I was merely blinded by her beauty. I am resolved never to trust a beautiful woman again. With beauty comes a lack of compassion."

"And is that how you classify the women of your acquaintance, colonel, in terms of whether they are beautiful or not? And, by extension, you conclude that beauty and compassion are mutually exclusive?"

"Forgive me, Lady Portia. I did not mean *you.*"

Anger flared in the pit of her stomach. Though his suffering on account of his experiences at Waterloo should elicit compassion, his view of her sex was not to be borne.

"I thought you said you did not stoop to flattery," she said, not bothering to disguise her irritation. "Perhaps my friend broke off your engagement because of your insincerity."

Regret needled at her as hurt glimmered in his eyes. Not half an hour earlier he had been gripped by the nightmares of war, and here she was now, criticizing his gallantry toward her.

Perhaps Adam was right when he said she was too prickly a creature to reside in a man's heart.

Not that her brother knew anything of hearts.

The dance concluded, and Colonel Reid offered his arm to escort Portia to the edge of the ballroom, steering them toward their host and hostess.

"Countess Thorpe," Portia said. "Dear Henrietta—a most delightful evening."

"Lady Portia," the countess said, dipping her head in greeting, "I was most upset to see you not dancing earlier when there were so many gentlemen unpartnered, but I applaud your choice of partner this time. Colonel Reid's talents on the dance floor are renowned, are they not, colonel?"

Portia's partner dipped his head in acknowledgment. "You are most kind, countess."

Their hostess offered her hand. "I find myself disappointed that dear Angela was not with you tonight. I trust she is well."

A spike of jealousy stabbed at Portia's heart. Was he courting another?

The colonel took the countess's hand and lifted it to his lips. "My sister is not ready for a public occasion just yet."

His *sister*…

Portia drew in a sharp breath, then felt her cheeks warming as Earl Thorpe fixed his gaze on her, a flicker of knowing in his eyes.

How was it that some men were able to penetrate a woman's defenses with a single glance? Portia would have called the earl the most formidable man in the room—were it not for the presence of her brother, who always seemed to be in the periphery of her vision, watching her with his disapproving sapphire gaze.

"I trust you're not hiding Angela from the world, colonel," Henrietta said. "A wide-eyed young woman's behavior must be tempered, of course, for her own safety, but she will chafe under too much restraint. You are at least permitting her to venture outside?"

"I've taken her to Hyde Park," he said, his expression softening with brotherly love. "She was particularly fond of the swans, and I plan to take her again."

"Excellent! I cannot abide the notion of an older brother behaving as if he were his sister's gaoler," Henrietta said, glancing in Portia's direction. "You could have brought her here tonight, for my balls are hardly *public* occasions. Though, I admit, there are one or two guests among the party whom I invited merely for the sake of appearance than out of friendship." She exchanged a glance with Portia then fixed her gaze on the figure of Sir Heath Moss, who was escorting Lady Cholmondeley-Walker toward the terrace.

"Henrietta…" the earl warned, and she let out a snort.

"Pshaw, Giles!" she said. "I'll be polite to the face of those I dislike to maintain propriety, but you cannot expect me to speak dishonestly when among friends." She gave a warm smile. "Colonel, you must take supper with us some time and bring your sister. I'll not countenance any response other than your acceptance."

"Then it will be my pleasure to give it, on behalf of us both."

"Excellent!" she cried. "Now, please excuse us."

Their hosts continued circulating around the ballroom, and the colonel let out a sigh.

"Henrietta's a formidable woman," Portia said. "I pity anyone who dares say no to her."

"She's been very kind toward my sister."

Portia sighed. "I'd have liked to have a sister. But I have been cursed with an overbearing older brother."

"He loves you, I am sure, Lady Portia," he replied. "An older brother will always wish to protect his sister, even if he must assert himself when that sister is spirited and headstrong."

"Is your sister a troublesome charge?"

He shook his head, and a gentle smile curved his lips. His eyes softened to the color of warm chocolate, and a little pulse of yearning fluttered in her center at the love in them.

"Perhaps a little headstrong," he said. "She has yet to lose the youthful enthusiasm for everything. I fear that I should caution her more."

"You fear for her?"

"London's no place for an innocent."

"But she has a loving brother to keep her safe," Portia said. "I envy her in that."

"You have a brother."

"But he's not *you*, colonel."

A spark of desire flickered in the depths of his eyes.

"You do not act in the manner expected of a woman of your rank, Lady Portia," he said, a hoarseness in his voice.

"In that I am not a… What did you call it?" She cocked her head to one side and lifted her forefinger to her chin, frowning in mock confusion. "Oh yes, that was it—a *haughty miss who cares nothing for others.*"

To his credit, he blushed. "You weren't meant to overhear that."

"You *do* surprise me," she said, smiling. "I trust you'll make sure your sister does not overhear when you're criticizing our sex. You wouldn't want her to be influenced by such sentiment."

"Which is why I have engaged a chaperone to care for her—that, and for her safety."

"Has she no female relatives to chaperone her?"

"None, other than my brother's wife, but she's much occupied at the family seat in the country. Angela has no mother or sister to care for her." He let out a sigh. "The appointment's out of necessity more than choice. I dislike the notion of a woman compelled to earn a living."

Pompous fool!

"What nonsense!" Portia said. "A woman should be permitted to make her own way in life as much as a man, and not all women are compelled to earn a living—some of us do by choice."

"Surely *you're* not engaged in commerce, Lady Portia?"

Her stomach twisted in apprehension. "N-no, of course not."

"Commerce is a *man's* world," he said.

"There are plenty of women earning a living in the City."

"Not women of your station. I wouldn't want my sister to earn her living. In that, I'm in agreement with your brother."

Portia caught sight of her brother at the far end of the ballroom, striding across the floor with all the insufferable arrogance of the superior male, turning the head of every unattached female—and most of the attached. It was as if he cast a spell that caused women to lose all reason and rationality.

Were he not so overbearing, Portia might have pitied him. But, as with all men, the unwanted attention of the opposite sex did not pose any danger to his person or his reputation.

"There she is," Colonel Reid said.

He gestured toward a lone woman sitting in the corner, her gown a shade of blue that could only be describe as *somber*. She wore no jewelry save a brooch in the center of her neckline. Her hair, a rich, dark chestnut with streaks of gray, was scraped back into an unflattering matriarchal style. She sat, back stiff, a folded shawl on her lap, gazing out toward the center of the ballroom, but as Portia's brother passed, the woman startled and her wide, expressive eyes focused on him. Portia caught a flicker of yearning, but unlike the hunger seen in the other female guests, her expression carried an undertone of despair.

Despite the crowd in the ballroom, Portia had never seen anyone who looked so utterly *alone*.

"That's Mrs. Stowe," the colonel said, "whom I've engaged to chaperone my sister."

"She doesn't seem to be enjoying herself."

"That's the price a woman pays for her independence."

"It's a price that Society imposes on her, colonel," Portia said. "Why is nobody talking to her? It's as if she doesn't exist. The world is not going to descend into anarchy if a woman earning a living is accepted into Society."

He steered Portia toward the woman, and she lifted her head in recognition, then rose to her feet and dipped into a curtsey.

"Colonel Reid," she said, her voice a rich alto. "Is your sister here tonight? Forgive me, I thought her first social engagement was next week."

"It is, Mrs. Stowe," he replied. "I am alone tonight."

She settled her gaze on Portia.

"May I introduce you to Lady Portia Hawke?" Colonel Reid

said. "Lady Portia, this is Mrs. Stowe."

Portia offered her hand, and Mrs. Stowe curtseyed once more. "Delighted," she said. "Have we met before? You look familiar."

"I don't think I've had that pleasure, ma'am," Portia said. "But perhaps you know my brother? He's the Duke of Foxton."

Mrs. Stowe's eyes widened. "Oh…yes, of course. *Hawke*. I-I'm aware of His Grace, but we've not been introduced."

"Then let me—" Portia began.

"Please don't trouble yourself, Lady Portia. I…" Mrs. Stowe colored. "Forgive me for speaking out of turn."

"Very well," Portia said. "It's no great loss to you. My brother disapproves of the notion of an independent woman."

"As do all men."

"But not your husband, Mrs. Stowe?" Portia said.

"I'm a widow, Lady Portia."

"I'm sorry. Do forgive me."

A slight smile curved Mrs. Stowe's lips. "My late husband would not have approved of my earning a living. Widowhood brings with it the kind of freedom that may be socially acceptable, but it elicits an excess of pity."

"And there's nothing worse than being *pitied*," Portia said.

"Quite so, Lady Portia. I—" Mrs. Stowe broke off and lowered her gaze. At that moment, Portia's brother appeared, together with Lord Maybury—the very man whom Heath Moss had engaged the Farthing to shoot at, as soon as dawn broke tomorrow.

"*There* you are, sister." Adam gave a cursory glance at Mrs. Stowe, then resumed his attention on Portia. "Do you have a partner for the next dance?"

"No."

"Then you should circulate," he said. "You'll never find a partner if you loiter about at the edge of the ballroom."

"Particularly if it's the *dowdy* edge," Lord Maybury said, eyeing Mrs. Stowe.

Portia's brother let out a laugh and clapped Maybury on the back.

"Please excuse me," Mrs. Stowe said, her voice tight. "I must attend to Miss Turton. It's rather cold and she needs her shawl." She approached a young woman at the center of the ballroom.

"I say, Maybury, there's no call for that," Colonel Reid said.

"Oh, don't be so stuffy!" Maybury chuckled. "A man attends a ball to look at pretty girls, not down-at-heel maiden aunts." He gestured to Mrs. Stowe's retreating back. "Women like *that* make the place look deuced untidy."

"Women like Mrs. Stowe protect young ladies from rakes, Maybury," Colonel Reid said. "She's no maiden aunt, she's a hired chaperone, and has as much right to be here tonight as you or I."

"A paid subordinate?" Maybury said. "I trust she'll be eating her supper downstairs tonight."

Portia glanced toward Mrs. Stowe, who was draping the shawl over a young woman's shoulders, her eyes bright with moisture.

A gong sounded, and Henrietta clapped her hands. "Time for supper, *mes amis!*"

Colonel Reid offered his arm, and Portia took it. Out of the corner of her eye she spotted Henrietta and her husband approach Mrs. Stowe and her charge. Earl Thorpe offered Mrs. Stowe his arm and escorted her to the dinner table, Lord Maybury watching with a scowl.

"Bravo, Thorpe," Colonel Reid said.

Bravo indeed. Few men possessed enough kindness to defy social convention.

Perhaps Colonel Reid was one such man. As her brother and Lord Maybury were not.

But tomorrow, at dawn, the Farthing would take much pleasure from aiming his pistol at Maybury's head.

CHAPTER NINE

"E IGHT…NINE…"

As Portia raised her arm, a shot rang out, and a puff of smoke exploded in the air. She heard a faint whistling, then caught sight of something moving fast toward her. She flinched, anticipating the hit.

Her opponent had shot wide.

"No!" Nerissa cried.

The acrid stench of gunpowder in her nostrils, Portia continued to raise her arm until the muzzle of her pistol was aimed directly at Lord Maybury.

"The devil fired before the count!"

The ringing in her ears could not completely muffle Sir Heath Moss's indignant voice.

"How dare you insult me so, Maybury, you bounder!" Sir Heath continued. "Do you have no honor?"

Portia gritted her teeth. How typical of a man! To be more concerned with propriety than the fact that Maybury had cheated and could have taken her life.

Her heartbeat hammering in her ears, she willed her fingers not to grip the pistol too tight. For, as Mr. Greaves had taught her, the tighter the grip, the poorer the aim.

Slow and steady, your ladyship… A true shot is earned by a stable hand.

She drew in a breath then exhaled slowly until her aim was

focused on her opponent, who now stood cowering at the far end of the lawn.

Oh, Mr. Greaves, if only you could see me now!

Withdrawing from the world around her, she focused on her breathing and the target. The muzzle of her pistol moved, faintly, in time to her heartbeat.

The right shoulder, I think.

Enough to incapacitate Maybury for a day or two, and ruin his jacket.

I'd like to see you explain that *to your valet—or to Lady Maybury.*

On the next heartbeat, she squeezed the trigger.

Slow and steady…

The weapon fired, and she let her arm relax, absorbing the recoil. To flinch in anticipation of the recoil was the marksman's downfall.

Nerissa rushed to her side. "Oh, La—"

"Hush, Gerard!" Portia whispered.

"I mean…sir, are you all right?"

"A little shaken, Gerard, that's all," Portia said, willing her body to stop trembling.

When the smoke cleared, she caught sight of her opponent, bent over, clutching his shoulder.

"You cad!" he cried. "You shot me."

"Isn't that rather the point, Lord Maybury?" Nerissa said, her voice laced with loathing.

"Jephson, get your arse over here. *Fuck*, that hurts."

Maybury's second rushed over and inspected Maybury's shoulder.

"I'm mortally wounded, I know it," Maybury said, flinging his uninjured arm out in a dramatic gesture. "Tell my wife that I lo—"

"It's just a flesh wound, Maybury old chap," his second said. "No need to make such a fuss. Not when you shot before Bodkins finished the count."

"I did *not!*"

"You did," the adjudicator said. "I had not yet reached ten."

He turned to Portia. "Sir, you're lucky to be alive."

"So is he," Portia said, gesturing toward Maybury. "You're fortunate my aim is true, sir."

"You mean you *meant* to shoot me in the shoulder?" Maybury's voice took on a nasal whine reminiscent of a petulant child who'd been refused a second bowl of custard.

"Did *you* deliberately aim wide?" Portia asked. "That bullet went right over my head."

"Ha!" Sir Heath laughed. "Maybury's a poor shot—he'd have had a better chance hitting you if he'd aimed at that tree over there. Perhaps, Maybury old chap, you should consider hiring the Farthing yourself the next time you accuse someone of compromising your wife—though if others are as dishonorable as you and shoot out of turn, the Farthing may not be with us much longer."

Nausea rose in Portia's throat as the realization sank in. Today was the first occasion her life had been truly at risk. All it took was one man not obeying the rules of the duel, the unspoken oath of trust. And when had any man shown himself to be worthy of trust?

"You're quite right, Sir Heath," Maybury said. No longer clutching his shoulder—evidence enough that the injury was not as fatal as he'd previously declared—he approached Portia and fished several notes from his pocket. "I think five should suffice."

"Or ten?" Portia said.

"You drive a hard bargain, sir. I may want to use your services in the future."

"Then consider the extra five as a down payment for future services."

She held out her hand, and he counted an additional five notes and placed them in her upturned palm.

"You have small hands, sir," Maybury said, "and a rather light voice. You're no man."

Oh no...

"Perhaps if I removed that mask of yours, I'd find a mere

boy."

Portia forced a smile at the contempt in Maybury's voice. "Imagine what your friends at White's would think if they knew you'd been bested by a *mere boy*."

I shall have to laugh with Nerissa in secret about the fact that you were bested by a woman.

"If your father knew you were here, he'd give you a bloody good hiding," Maybury said.

"The head of my family *would* give me a hiding, sir, were he to know. But you should consider yourself fortunate that I was not aiming for your heart, Maybury. Perhaps next time I'll aim elsewhere."

"Next time?" Maybury asked.

Sir Heath barked with laughter. "Come, come, old chap. I'll wager you'll find yourself here again within a week—after your wife has parted her thighs for the next man."

"So you *did* lift her skirts, Sir Heath?"

"I did nothing that she didn't beg for. Come to think of it, she spent most of the night on her knees. Which is where every woman should be."

Dear Lord! Was this how *all* men spoke of the female sex?

"Perhaps," Maybury said, "but it's not the done thing to rut another man's wife."

"I consider myself to be performing a service," Sir Heath said. "Lady Maybury likes to be ridden daily—twice daily, so De Blanchard tells me. If she gives your friends a little distraction once in a while, where's the harm? You already have your heir and spare, so there's no risk of any of my by-blows taking your title—unless she was sharing her favors during your honeymoon."

"Why, you—"

"Oh, stow it, Maybury!" Sir Heath said, offering his hand. "Let's shake on it and speak no further on the matter. Honor has been satisfied and we're free to go about our lives."

"Fair enough."

"What about your wife, Lord Maybury?" Portia asked, unable to restrain the anger simmering inside.

"What of her? She's content enough, having performed her duty."

"Which is?"

"To furnish me with a dowry, and an heir." Maybury let out a sigh. "If only a man could dispense with his wife once she's carried out her duty. It would save his ears from the nagging. But you'll soon learn that yourself, young fellow."

Despicable man—they're all *despicable!*

Anger flared, and Portia curled her hand into a fist. She may have only grazed Maybury's shoulder, but there was nothing to stop her knocking out a tooth or two.

A calm hand touched her sleeve.

"No, your ladyship," Nerissa whispered. "It would serve no good."

"What's that you say, young man?" Maybury barked.

"My manservant was reminding me of the necessity for haste," Portia said. "Gerard, you're right, of course. It's almost light. And Lord Maybury needs to get his wound seen to." She gestured to his shoulder.

"Waste of a damned good jacket," Maybury said. "My valet has no skill at removing bloodstains."

"Then next time I'll aim for your head to preserve your jacket."

"And there'll be a next time," Sir Heath said. "Lady Maybury's shared her favors with almost everyone: De Blanchard, of course, Cholmondeley-Walker, naturally…even Foxton's been between those thighs, and he's usually more discerning. He's always said his cock refuses to perform if the woman has a face like a horse."

"He *what?*" Portia cried before she could stop herself.

Sir Heath chuckled. "I didn't take you for a greenhorn, Mr. Farthing. Have you not been broken in yet?"

Portia opened her mouth to reply, but Nerissa placed a warning hand on her arm.

"It matters not," Sir Heath continued. I'm sure once you've been broken in, you'll shag with the best of us. And, of course, no man would dare call you out—unless he's a cheat, like Maybury here."

"I swear I heard Mr. Bodkins finish the count," Maybury said.

"And that's what you'll tell the company at White's, but take care, my friend, not to make your point within my earshot," Sir Heath said. "Or this fellow's," he added, gesturing to Portia, "which may prove a challenge, given his anonymity." He stepped toward Portia, his gaze searching.

There came a time, after every duel, when the client grew a little too eager to discover the Farthing's identity.

She bowed, bade them good morning, and retreated, Nerissa at her side.

"Heavens, Nerissa! That was the closest one yet."

"Perhaps you should stop, your ladyship. It's getting too dangerous."

"I doubt Sir Heath would reveal my identity when he's in constant need of my services."

Nerissa let out a sharp sigh. "I meant the danger to your *life*. Lord Maybury fired before you were ready."

"You saw what a poor marksman he is," Portia said. "Gentlemen are such idle creatures—they lack the tenacity to perfect the skill at anything other than gaming and debauchery."

"Not every man in London displays such idleness."

"It's fortunate then, Nerissa, that duels are mostly the province of the idle rich."

"You were lucky today," Nerissa said, "and luck always runs out. I sometimes wonder if you're truly aware of the danger you're placing yourself in."

"It's no more dangerous than surrendering my person in matrimony. At least as the Farthing I am *living*, not merely existing."

"And it's precisely my wish for you to continue living that

compels me to caution you."

"I cannot surrender my responsibilities, Nerissa. Dr. McIver depends on me—or, at least, the money I provide him."

"Your brother would, I'm sure—"

"No," Portia said, bitterly. "He *wouldn't*. He would see any expenditure a frivolity unless it were to make myself more attractive to a potential suitor."

"Then perhaps you should take his counsel and find yourself a generous husband."

"Good Lord, Nerissa, what nonsense!"

"You cannot be the Farthing forever," Nerissa said. "Sooner or later, your secret will be out. I pray that the revelation happens as a drawing room anecdote and not when someone pulls the mask off your lifeless body in Hyde Park at dusk."

They continued in silence, and as they approached the entrance to the townhouse, Nerissa took Portia's hand.

"Forgive me for speaking out of turn, Lady Portia. I speak only out of concern for you. I'd be distraught if anything were to happen to you. So would your brother."

"He'd merely be angry that I was disobeying his orders."

"His Grace is a harsh man, but it's out of necessity in a harsh world. But he does possess a heart, even if he hides it well."

Portia squeezed her maid's hand. "What would I do without you, my lovely Nerissa?"

"You'd be late for breakfast," Nerissa said with a smile. "Make haste. Go directly to your chamber and I'll fetch your clothes."

Portia made her way up the back stairs, pausing as she heard the bustle of activity in the kitchen. From the aroma, Mrs. Winston was preparing kedgeree, and Portia's stomach growled with hunger.

As she slipped into her chamber to await Nerissa, the maid's words hung in the air.

Luck always runs out.

CHAPTER TEN

"LOOK AT THE swans!"

Stephen's heart lifted to hear the delight in Angela's voice. How might she react to her first ball?

"Do hurry, brother," she continued. "They're getting away. Oh, they're so *beautiful!*" She let out a squeal of excitement and tugged on his sleeve. "Come *on!*"

"Angela," he said, "do you think Mrs. Stowe would approve of your outburst of enthusiasm?"

"She never said anything about not enjoying myself."

"But I'm sure she's warned you about the folly of expressing emotions so freely. Like it or not, Society prefers those who restrain themselves."

"Like you, you mean?" She pursed her lips in a pout. "You never laugh—at least not since you returned from the war. I'd have thought you'd be glad to be back in England."

"I am."

"Then why don't you show it?"

"Angela, just because I don't smile every waking moment, doesn't mean I'm happy to be here, with my beloved sister."

"I suppose I must be content with that."

"Are *you* happy here?" he asked.

"Oh, yes!" she said brightly. "And Mrs. Stowe isn't nearly so staid as you said."

"Is she kind?"

"You saw her at tea yesterday."

"But what about when I'm not there? The true test of her character is how she behaves when she's alone with you."

Stephen shuddered at the memory of his nursemaid, who used to pinch him before presenting him to his mother and father before bedtime, then make a show of comforting him when he cried. At all costs, Angela wouldn't suffer as he had.

"She's perfectly amiable."

"Are you sure?" he asked. "I'll not hesitate to dismiss her at the slightest cross word."

"Dear brother!" Angela laughed. "You've nothing to fear. I like Mrs. Stowe. She's like an older sister, or…"

She hesitated, then looked away, her cheeks flushed a delicate shade of rose.

Or a mother.

Poor Angela. She'd grown up not only lacking a mother's love, but being subject to Father's condemnation for her entry into the world having facilitated their mother's exit from it.

Was it any wonder that the urge to destroy anyone who gave Angela even the merest slight often rendered him unable to draw breath?

But he had to temper his fear, or he'd keep his sister at home under lock and key, safe from predators—the very predators who paraded about Hyde Park in their finery, using their sophistication to corrupt an innocent.

"Mrs. Stowe said something very odd yesterday," Angela said.

"Which was?"

"She said that to love was to be enslaved. What could she mean by that?"

Doubtless Mrs. Stowe meant that she'd suffered heartbreak. The late Mr. Stowe had, by all accounts, been a respectable man of means, but if his widow had been reduced to earning a living escorting young women about while she sat in a dark corner subject to the taunts of the likes of Foxton, then she had not benefited from the marriage.

But Angela need not have her eyes opened to the miseries of the world. No, she needed protection from them. And until she'd found a husband to care for her as she deserved, Stephen would devote his life to providing that protection.

"I suspect Mrs. Stowe meant that you must not give your heart too easily," he said. "And I agree. You must not lose your heart to the first handsome man who pays you a compliment."

"Oh, no," she replied. "I intend to have a whole flock of suitors and then take my pick of the best."

"Then take care not to break their hearts," he said, giving her hand an affectionate squeeze.

"Have *you* had your heart broken, brother?"

At that moment, as if Fate played a trick, he spotted Lady Staines arm in arm with her husband, and a small pulse of pain flickered in his heart at the memory of her rejection. But Lady Staines was not the woman she had once been. The socially ambitious Juliette Howard was now the serene and blissfully happy countess, having married for love.

"Colonel Reid!" she said, steering her husband toward them. "What a pleasure. And who's this delightful young lady? Though perhaps I needn't ask. You're so alike that she must be your sister."

Angela gave a shy smile and moved a little closer to Stephen. He placed a protective hand on her shoulder and bowed. "Angela, may I introduce you to Lord and Lady Staines? Lady Staines, this is my sister Angela."

"The pleasure's all mine, my dear," Lady Staines said. "Eleanor! Do come and meet Lady Angela Reid."

Stephen's stomach clenched with discomfort. It was awkward enough facing one Howard sister, let alone both of them.

"Duchess," he said, as the duke and duchess of Whitcombe appeared.

Angela's grip on his hand tightened. "D-Duchess…" she whispered.

But she had no cause for fear. The duchess's peculiarly intense emerald gaze flicked over Stephen before settling on his sister.

"Lady Angela," she said, nodding. "Is this your first Season? Are you out yet? I trust you have a chaperone other than your brother."

Angela's eyes widened. The duchess was not known for engaging in social pleasantries. She preferred to speak more directly, often saying what was on everyone else's mind, but they were too polite to voice.

"I-I am out, Your Grace."

"Excellent," the duchess said. "Then I can invite you to our house party at Rosecombe Park. I trust you'll come."

"Eleanor, my love," the duke said in a low voice, and the duchess colored.

"Oh, forgive me—I'll send you an invitation, of course." She turned to Angela. "I hope you'll come. There will be pall-mall and archery for the ladies and shooting and fishing for the gentlemen—though if you prefer to fish or shoot, you may do so. Portia likes to shoot, though she's promised to teach the other ladies archery. She's rather good, you know."

"Lady Portia Hawke?" Stephen said.

"That's right. We had shooting at our house party last winter, and Portia bested all the gentlemen, didn't she, my love?" She exchanged a smile with the duke. "What was the name of the fellow you engaged to teach us?"

"Greaves."

"That was it, Mr. Greaves. Poor Foxton was so incensed at Portia besting him that he threatened to throw Mr. Greaves into the lake."

Angela, who'd been watching the duchess with wide-eyed admiration, tugged at Stephen's sleeve. "Oh, *can* we go, brother? It sounds wonderful—my first house party!"

"I'm not sure if Mrs. Stowe will be available to chaperone you," he said.

"*I* can chaperone your sister, colonel," the duchess said.

Two pairs of eyes focused on him—one green and enigmatic, the other a warm brown to match his own, filled with eagerness.

How could he refuse Angela, the innocent soul he loved more than anyone in the world?

"Very well," he said, and smiled inwardly at Angela's squeal of pleasure. "We'll be delighted to accept, Duchess. But on one condition. My sister is *not* to partake in the shooting."

"Not even the archery?" Angela asked.

"I've no objection to your wielding a bow and arrow," he replied, "but I disapprove of firing a gun for pleasure, and find it particularly unbecoming for a woman."

"The pheasants on your brother's estate must be very grateful to hear that," Lord Staines said.

Stephen shook his head. "My brother does not share my sensibilities."

"Neither does most of Society," Whitcombe said. "But I agree with you, colonel, that women and weapons do not mix, and that includes Lady Portia Hawke."

"My, my, Your Grace, are you indulging in gossip?" a female voice said from behind.

Stephen caught his breath as he turned to see the subject of their conversation standing in the pathway, arm in arm with her brother.

"Portia," the duchess said, "my husband was just telling the colonel here what an excellent shot you are."

Lady Portia's eyes widened. For a moment, Stephen caught a flicker of fear in her expression before she blinked and glanced at her brother, but Foxton was staring at Lady Staines.

"Don't tell my brother that," she said, "or he'll throw you in the Serpentine. He cannot bear the notion of a woman—even his sister—besting him at anything requiring any level of skill."

"Do *you* intend to shoot at Rosecombe?" Stephen asked.

"I intend to concentrate my efforts toward the archery competition, colonel. I have my eye on the prize."

"Which is?"

She gestured toward the duchess. "A portrait of the winner, at Eleanor's hand. She's something of an artist, you know."

"Of course!" Stephen said. "You exhibited at the Royal Academy last year, didn't you, Duchess? I'll wager the competition for that particular prize will be fierce, for it's that rare thing—a prize that money cannot buy."

"Such as love," Angela said, glancing from Stephen to Lady Portia and back, a smile playing on her lips.

"There's a prize for the best shot also," Whitcombe said. "The man—or woman—who bags the most birds stands to win a case of Trelawney's finest brandy."

"Then I'll stick to archery," Lady Portia said. "I cannot stand brandy, and I've no intention of furnishing my bother with yet more means to reduce himself to a state of inebriation each night."

Foxton's expression hardened, and he opened his mouth to speak, but the duchess intervened.

"Your Grace, Lady Portia, have you met Colonel Reid's sister, Lady Angela Reid?"

Lady Portia turned to Angela, her eyes gleaming with interest.

"Angela," Stephen said, "this is the Duke of Foxton and his sister, Lady Portia Hawke."

"Y-Your Grace." Angela dipped into a curtsey, her voice tightening with apprehension and shyness.

Lady Portia wrenched herself free from her brother's grip and clasped both of Angela's hands. "It's such a pleasure to meet you," she said. "I'd know you anywhere. You look so like your brother."

"Nonsense," Foxton said. "She's nothing like him."

"That's because you only *look* at people, Adam," she retorted. "You don't bother to *see* them. The likeness is obvious—the shape and color of their eyes is identical, and the mouth—"

She broke off, and a flare of desire ignited in Stephen's blood at the delicate bloom on her cheeks.

"Do you enjoy firing a weapon, Lady Portia?" he asked.

Her smile disappeared, and a hunted look flickered in her eyes. "I don't see why I should be denied the pursuits that men enjoy merely because of my sex," she said.

"Sister," Foxton admonished her, and she shot him a look of defiance.

Whitcombe let out a laugh. "I daresay, Foxton, your sister will be insisting on membership of White's if you give her too much freedom."

"Then I shall have to curb her freedom."

Lady Portia let out a laugh. "You think I want to spend every waking afternoon drinking brandy and congratulating myself on how many fellows I've bested at the card table or how many maidens I've seduced?"

A collective intake of breath rippled through the company, and Foxton snapped at her. "Portia, I've warned you before—"

"Have I said anything untrue?" she said. "You may admonish me for speaking out of turn if you like, but do not attempt to chastise me for speaking the truth. I would rather hear the truth, even if it gives me discomfort, than be placated with a lie merely to keep me quiet."

"Portia, I've a good mind—" Foxton began, but Duchess Whitcombe interrupted.

"Quite so, Lady Portia. I often find myself voicing an uncomfortable truth, though it drives my poor husband to despair—does it not, my love?" She turned to Whitcombe, who lifted her hand to his heart.

Sweet Lord—what must it be like to be so in love? But the love Whitcombe held for his wife was not a slavish devotion where he ignored her flaws and exposed himself to heartbreak and rejection. It was a love borne of knowing—*really* knowing—his wife's soul and recognizing her as his true mate.

Stephen's gaze shifted to Lady Portia, who watched the couple with understanding and envy in her eyes. Then she met his gaze and held it for a moment, before she colored and looked away, while Angela watched the exchange.

At that moment, the sound of splashing and honking carried across the air, and Angela turned her attention to the waters of the Serpentine, which glistened through the trees, reflecting the sunlight like a thousand tiny stars dancing across the surface.

"Lady Angela, shall we go and see the swans?" Lady Portia said. "I fear my brother is about to chastise me in public, and I'd rather he wait to dish out his admonishments at home."

Foxton frowned, and Lord Staines let out a laugh. "You've a headstrong young lady there in your sister, Foxton. I trust you appreciate the benefits of having such a spirited young woman in your home. Consider it good practice for your marriage, for I'll wager that only the most strong-willed of women will suit you."

"On the contrary, Staines," Foxton said, giving Lady Portia a hard look. "I find that a lifetime of my sister has made me appreciate the benefits of a silent, biddable partner in marriage all the more."

Angela stared at Foxton.

"Does *your* brother admonish you as much, Lady Angela?" Portia said.

Foxton let out a snort. "And does *your* sister run wild as much, colonel?"

Lady Portia linked her arm with Angela's. "I think the swans may be more congenial company for us. Certainly they'll be more adept at intelligent conversation."

"Y-yes please…" Angela stammered. "I mean, I'd be delighted, Lady Portia."

"Call me Portia," came the reply, and the two women approached the water's edge.

"Don't stray too far, Angela," Stephen said.

"Leave her be, colonel," Lady Staines said, approaching him. "Portia's sensible enough, for all her brother says. She'll make sure your sister comes to no harm."

He offered his arm, and she took it, her cheeks blooming. Did she recall the last time they promenaded together in the park—

when he'd offered his hand, believing himself in love?

She glanced toward the rest of the party, but her husband was in conversation with Foxton while Whitcombe and his duchess had eyes for none but each other.

"You must forgive me, colonel," she said.

"Whatever for?"

Her color deepened and she let out a sigh.

"There's naught to forgive, Lady Staines," he said. "In fact, I ought to thank you for breaking our…" He hesitated as she drew in a sharp breath. "I mean…you had the foresight to understand that continuing on the path we'd set ourselves would have led to contentment at best, but ultimately unhappiness. You did us both a service—and you suffered more than I. But in the end, you were rewarded for your bravery."

She blinked, and her eyes glistened with moisture. "You are too good, colonel," she said. "I could never have hoped to deserve a man such as you."

"We all deserve someone to make us happy, Lady Staines."

"Then," she said, glancing toward the two women by the water, "my greatest wish is that you'll find the happiness that I have found for myself—the happiness that you deserve."

"Mama, Mama!" a voice cried, and a child of five or six years approached them at a run, followed by a young woman in a pale-blue gown.

"Master Gabriel, a little slower, please, or you'll tumble over!"

"Ah, *my* happiness," Lady Staines said.

The child tripped forward and fell onto the grass. But, unlike most children who wailed with petulance, he leaped up and continued forward, laughing as he barreled into Lady Staines and wrapped his arms around her skirts.

The young woman reached them, panting. "Master Gabriel, careful of your mama's gown."

Lady Staines glanced at her skirts and the smudge of mud on the fabric. "Not again!" she said, and the boy's smile disappeared.

"Never mind. I'm sure it'll wash out, Flora. Gabriel can help—won't you, my darling?"

The boy nodded, then turned his expressive blue gaze toward Stephen.

"And who might you be, young sir?" Stephen said.

Lady Staines's eyes took on a look of wariness. The gossips had done their work—almost everyone in Society knew that Gabriel was a natural child.

Foxton, who'd been deep in conversation with Staines, cast his gaze over the boy, a slight sneer on his lips.

"This is my son," Juliette said. "Gabriel Staines. Gabriel, my love, this is Colonel Reid."

"I'm very pleased to meet you, Mr. Staines," Stephen said, offering his hand. The boy stared at it, then looked back up at him.

"Are you a *soldier*?"

"Aye."

"You must be terribly brave."

"I don't know about that."

"Oh yes you *are*," Gabriel said, his eyes shining with admiration. "Mama says that soldiers are the bravest men in the world. They do what they do so that everybody in England is safe. That's what you said, Mama, was it not?"

"Yes, my darling," Lady Staines said, stroking the boy's head.

"What do soldiers do?" the boy asked.

"This soldier, not very much at present," Stephen said. "I'm in town for the foreseeable future, taking care of my sister."

"Oh, like Flora? She takes care of me and my brother."

"Is your brother with you today?"

"He's too young to walk in the park. Mrs. Smith's taking care of him at home in the country. He's a viscount, you know."

A look of discomfort darkened Lady Staines's expression, but the boy had yet to understand the implications of his younger brother having the title that he did not.

"Is this your first visit to London?" Stephen asked.

Gabriel nodded. "I didn't like it at first—so many people, and they all stared at me. But Mama says it's rude to stare, so I didn't stare back."

"And now?"

"I like coming to the park. They have swans here. We don't have swans in the country, but there are moorhens on the lake. Do you know what a moorhen is?"

"A hen that lives on the moors?" Stephen said.

"No, silly! Hens don't live on the moors."

"Gabriel, hush," Lady Staines said. "Remember what I said about needing to be polite when we're out, and why?"

The boy colored. "You said not everyone would be kind to me."

Stephen's heart ached at the stricken expression on Gabriel's face, and the fear in his mother's eyes. At that moment, Angela returned from the water's edge with Lady Portia. Lady Staines glanced from Stephen to Lady Portia, then extended her hand to Angela.

"Lady Angela, would you walk with me?"

Angela took the proffered arm, and Stephen approached Lady Portia. She linked her arm through his as if it belonged there, and his heart warmed with hope as a spark of desire flickered in his blood.

"Who might you be, young sir?" Lady Portia said, glancing at the boy with a smile.

"I'm Gabriel Staines."

Her smile slipped and she glanced toward Lady Staines, then back at the child.

"Of course," she said. "I'm very pleased to meet you, Mr. Staines. I've heard much about you."

Stephen stared at her. *Yes, I'll wager you have—you and all the gossips.*

"This man's a soldier, you know," Gabriel said, tuning his admiring gaze to Stephen once more. "He saves everybody."

"Everybody?" she said, curling her lips into a smile. "A remarkable feat. Do you think we're in danger here in the park?"

"Mama told me London can be dangerous."

"And she's right," Lady Portia said. "I trust you listen to your mama. I confess, I don't always listen to my brother, but you ought to be a better person than I and do as your mama says, at least until you're old enough to make your own way in the world."

"Are *you* old enough to make your way in the world, Lady Portia?" the boy asked.

She let out a laugh. "I'm afraid I'll never be given the freedom to do so, Master Gabriel. That is the curse of being a woman, and of having a title. Whereas you…"

She faltered, her cheeks reddening.

"It matters not," she said. "If Society's rules cannot be broken, they can at least be molded to our satisfaction." She bent down and lowered her voice to a conspiratorial whisper. "And what my brother doesn't know about my antics cannot hurt him."

"What doesn't your brother know, Lady Portia?" Stephen couldn't help asking.

A hunted expression flickered in her eyes, then she straightened up, taking Gabriel's hand.

"Permit a lady to preserve *some* secrets, colonel. Come, Gabriel, shall we take a look at those flowers?" She led the boy toward a raised flower bed, filled with blooms in a vibrant mix of pinks and oranges. "Do you like flowers?" she asked.

"Mama likes them, so I'd like to pick some for her to take home."

"I think the gardeners here would object. Besides, you wouldn't want everyone else to be deprived of enjoying them. It would be like taking one of the swans home."

"I couldn't do that," the boy said. "The moorhens on the lake wouldn't like it. Do you know what a moorhen is?"

"It's a bird that lives on the water," came the reply. "A pretty little thing that stays hidden due to his dark plumage, but you can always spot his bright beak, a flash of red and yellow. And he has a very distinctive call that echoes across the water. I prefer them to swans, which are graceful enough, but are known to attack you if you get too close."

"I prefer them too," the boy said. "The colonel didn't know what they were."

She glanced over her shoulder to Stephen and grinned. "Let me guess, he thought they were hens that lived on moors?"

The boy let out a squeal of laughter, lost his balance, and fell back. Lady Portia caught him and tumbled onto the grass, and Stephen braced himself for a fit of temper. But she merely brushed the dust from her gown, righted herself, and swept the boy into her arms.

"Gabriel!" Lady Staines said, an undertone of warning in her voice, and the boy's laughter died. Stephen glanced toward her, but she was not looking at her son. Her attention was fixed on the gentleman approaching the party on the path.

Foxton was the first to greet him. "Ah, Sir Heath. Pleasant morning for a promenade."

"Provided the company is to one's taste," Sir Heath said, staring at Gabriel. Then he turned his cold blue gaze toward Lady Staines and inclined his head. "Lady Staines, a pleasure."

"How *kind* of you, Sir Heath," she said. "I commend your effort at gallantry."

He turned his attention to Angela. "And who's this delightful creature?" he said, his mouth curling into the sort of smile that ladies found alluring.

"I'm Lady Angela Reid."

Sir Heath glanced at Stephen, and his smile broadened, revealing white, even teeth that gleamed in the sunlight, giving him a predatory air.

"Is that so?" he said. "I went shooting with your late father, don't you know?" He took her hand and made a great show of bowing over it. "Sir Heath Moss, at your service, Lady Angela."

"Pleased to meet you, Sir Heath."

"I'm *very* glad to hear that." He lifted her hand to his lips, and

Stephen's gut twisted at the lascivious expression in his eyes. "Are you embarking on your first Season, Lady Angela?"

"Yes, I'm here with my brother."

"Of course." Sir Heath inclined his head in Stephen's direction. "I believe that of all the gems in London this Season, you will be the brightest. I trust the time will come when I have the opportunity to partner you for a dance."

"I say, is that not a little forward?" Stephen said.

"There's no harm in declaring my intentions, colonel," Sir Heath replied. "Your sister's a beautiful creature, and there will be many young bucks vying for her hand."

"I have often observed, Sir Heath, that you do not always declare your full intentions—at least not as openly as the recipient of your gallantry might wish."

"Come, come, nobody could accuse me of not giving a woman what she *wishes*."

Sir Heath kissed Angela's hand once more, then released it. For a moment, she stared at the back of her hand, then she colored and lowered her arm.

"Ah, Lady Portia!" Sir Heath said. "A somewhat unusual activity for you, what?"

"I don't understand your meaning, Sir Heath."

He gestured toward Gabriel. "One could almost mistake you for an urchin, grubbing about in the dirt with all manner of individuals."

She placed a protective arm around the boy's shoulders. "One encounters such a variety of people in a public park," she said. "It enables us to widen our acquaintance. But with such variety comes the risk of having to encounter those with whom we'd rather not associate ourselves."

"Quite so," Sir Heath said, staring at the boy.

"Gabriel, my love, come here!" Lady Staines said. Lady Portia released the boy, who ran to his mother, then Sir Heath tipped his hat and continued along the path.

Lady Portia approached Stephen, and he held out his arm,

which she took. "It's such a pity," she said, her gaze on Lady Staines and the boy.

"Does it bother you that Gabriel is some other man's natural son?"

She wrenched her arm free, and her sapphire eyes flashed with anger.

"Not in the way that men such as you think. What bothers me is that Gabriel will forever be tainted by the sins of another."

"You think Lady Staines a sinner?"

"Colonel, how dare—"

She broke off and drew in a sharp breath as Stephen grasped her hand, her eyes widening. A fizz of need ignited in his blood, and he shifted position as his breeches became too tight. Desire flared in her eyes before the anger returned.

"Unhand me, sir."

Out of the corner of his eye, he caught sight of Lord Staines staring at them. "I apologize if I misunderstood you, Lady Portia."

"Do you also apologize to Gabriel?"

At the mention of her son's name, Lady Staines turned her attention toward them, holding Gabriel close.

"You accuse me of having contempt for an innocent child and his mother, who were wronged by others?" Lady Portia said.

"Society thinks—"

"Society can rot, colonel," she retorted. "Gabriel is a sweet boy and his mother is one of the kindest women I know. As for his father…"

"You know the identity of his father?"

"I mean Lord Staines," she said, "the father who matters. He's to be commended for recognizing and loving Gabriel as his own. Most men would have insisted that Gabriel be sent away. But that is the very worst sin a man can commit."

"Perhaps not the *only* sin," Stephen said, glancing at Sir Heath's retreating figure.

"It's our misfortune that men rule the world and therefore

behave as they wish with no consideration of the consequences to others. Few, if any, men in our Society would have acted as Lord Staines did. But he's enlightened enough to understand."

"Understand what?"

"That no loving mother should be parted from her child. Not for propriety—not for *anything*. Please excuse me."

She pulled her hand free and approached Lady Staines. Then she reached for Gabriel and lifted him in her arms.

"Sweet boy!" she cried. "Lady Staines, you must come to tea and bring Gabriel with you. Our cook is particularly fond of children, and she makes the most delicious sweet buns. Would you like that, Gabriel?"

"Sweet buns?" Gabriel said, his eyes gleaming with excitement. "Mama, can we?"

"Of course, my love," Lady Staines said, kissing the top of her son's head. "You're very kind, Lady Portia."

"It's out of self-interest, I assure you. I find myself in want of congenial male company at home."

"That's put *you* in your place, Foxton," Lord Staines said with a chuckle.

The party continued along the path, and Stephen fell into step with Lord Staines.

"Your son's a delightful boy," he said, "though I suspect he's a handful."

"Most children are at that age. He's old enough to move about of his own accord—poor Flora is kept on her toes trying to keep up with him, but still young enough that his enthusiasm for everything and everyone about him has not yet waned. That enthusiasm will soon be tempered by a better understanding of the world, but for now, it is something to be celebrated."

At that moment a shot rang out, and Stephen froze in fear. He closed his eyes as the distant screams of his fallen comrades filled the air, together with the stench of smoke, dirt, and pain. The image thrust into his mind—the landscape stretching toward the horizon, the colors fading in the dying light, the blurred shapes of men littering the ground, mortal enemies united at last in death…

"Witless fools!"

A sharp voice cut through the fog, and Stephen opened his eyes to see Lord Staines standing by the edge of the Serpentine gesturing to two young men across the water.

"What the devil do you think you're *doing*?" he cried. "Ignorant pups, firing a pistol in the middle of a park filled with people? Save that sort of behavior for dawn or dusk, when, with luck, you'll rid the world of each other."

"But sir, we—"

"I don't want to hear it," Staines said. "Now go, or I'll tell your papa."

The young man who'd spoken paled and sheathed his pistol. "Come on, Dudders, best get going."

They turned and fled, and Staines returned.

"That Gillingham fellow will find himself on the wrong end of a pistol one day, mark my words," he said.

"The one who spoke?" Stephen asked.

"Earl Gillingham's eldest. His father's notoriously strict, but it seems to have made the boy more determined. Duddington, the boy with him, is, I suspect, being led stray. But if Gillingham finds out, they'll both have sore hides. Gillingham's not above using the strap for the slightest infraction."

"Are you an advocate of corporal punishment?"

"I'd never take a hand to either of my boys," Staines said. "There are other ways to teach them to understand the consequences of their actions. For example, when Gabriel let the chickens out at Radham Hall, he was tasked with helping our under-gardener retrieve them, then cleaning out the chicken run afterward."

"And did he?"

Staines smiled. "He needed a little help, but he did it uncomplainingly when I explained to him that the under-gardener had had to spend his afternoon off retrieving the chickens, and it was therefore only fair that Gabriel undertake some of his duties the following day."

He tilted his head to one side and fixed his gaze on Stephen. "Are you ailing, my friend?"

Stephen glanced across the Serpentine where the two young men had now disappeared. "It's nothing. I'm merely beset by the occasional memory of the battlefield, that's all."

"Waterloo?"

Stephen nodded.

Staines placed his hand on his arm. "Though it would be fatuous of me to say that I understand, because I don't, I know how some events can impact a man's soul. But it wasn't that to which I was referring."

He nodded toward Lady Portia, who still had Gabriel in her arms.

"I recognize the signs," he said. "A man may not be able to acknowledge such an ailment when he suffers it himself, but once he's experienced it, he can recognize it in others. Though, of course, I'd hesitate to use the term 'suffering,' lest my Juliette admonish me."

"I'm afraid I don't follow you," Stephen said.

Staines gestured toward Lady Portia, then lowered his voice. "There's nothing that captures one's heart more than the sight of a woman showing love to a child, especially when that child is not her own, and when that child is..." He made a random gesture, then smiled. "Lady Portia seems fond of Gabriel, though I'm not certain her brother approves."

"Foxton's a stickler for propriety," Stephen said. "He's not the sort of fellow to embrace anyone who does not fit into his idea of the perfect Society gentleman—or lady. Personally, I think perfection is overrated. Society, in its desire for perfection, can often be unbelievably cruel." He nodded toward the boy. "Is Gabriel aware that he's"—he hesitated as Staines frowned—"not like his younger brother?"

"He's beginning to suspect," came the reply. "A look here, a casually dropped word there…" Staines let out a sigh. "It's not necessarily what anyone says, but *how* they say it. But, for the moment, we can shield him from the worst."

"Then he's fortunate to have you as his father."

"As am I, to have him as my son," Staines said, his eyes glistening with love. "My Juliette taught me that we can build a little society of our own—of our *true* friends. Society will always be filled with men, and women, who stand by a desire to observe their superiority of rank by exhibiting cruelty to those they consider beneath them. But I measure a person's worth by their behavior, particularly their behavior toward Gabriel."

He turned his attention to the boy once more. Lady Portia had set him on his feet, and he clung to her legs while she held his hand, seemingly oblivious of the mud stain on her skirts.

"It's perhaps fortunate that Lady Portia is not like her brother," Staines said. "There's a spirit hiding behind her eyes that is unlikely to be tamed. The man who captures her heart will be fortunate indeed."

"Ought you to speak of such things?"

"As Earl Staines, perhaps not. But I was never intended to take the title—my vocation was the church."

"Do you miss your occupation?"

"About as much as you miss yours, I suspect, colonel," Staines said. "I miss the sense of purpose it gave me, but the reality of the position was never the same as the dream I once had when I took up the cloth, all youthful eagerness, unaware of the obstacles I'd have to face. My occupation is much respected and often envied by those who have an idyllic, overly romantic view of what it entails. I daresay it's the same for you."

Sweet heaven—it was almost as if Staines had delved into Stephen's mind to unlock his soul.

"Will you sell your commission and retire from the army?" he asked. "I daresay the world will attempt to persuade you otherwise."

"Are you bothering the colonel, Lord Staines?"

Stephen turned to see Lady Portia standing before him, holding Gabriel's hand.

"Are you in the habit of listening to private conversations, Lady Portia?" Staines said.

"No, but Gabriel wanted to be with his father, and who am I to deny the sweet boy anything he wants?"

"Come here, young sir, Staines said, taking the boy into his arms. "It's time we took you home for your supper." He called out to his wife, "My love, ought we take Gabriel home?"

"Ah yes," she said. "We're at Vauxhall Gardens tonight. Are you going, colonel? Eleanor and Monty are, as I believe are Foxton and Lady Portia."

"What's happening at Vauxhall Gardens?" Angela asked, turning her expressive gaze onto Stephen. "Can we go?"

"I hadn't intended us to."

"It will all be very jolly," Lady Staines said. "Jugglers, acrobats, musicians—and Lady Rivers told me there's to be a fire-eater."

"A what?" Angela asked, her eyes widening.

"A man who eats fire. It's a most extraordinary sight."

"That sounds wonderful!" Angela cried. "Can we go, brother? Please say we can?"

She turned her gaze on him, and his heart was lost. There was nothing in the world he wouldn't do to make her happy.

"Very well," he said with a sigh.

"Excellent! Might I beg a place with you tonight, Lady Portia?"

Lady Portia glanced at Stephen. "If you wish it."

Oh, I do wish it, Lady Portia.

She curved her mouth into a smile, and his heart gave a little sigh.

Perhaps Staines was right—he was sickening for something.

Love.

CHAPTER ELEVEN

"Y OU COULD HAVE at least changed your gown."

Portia glared at her brother as they approached the entrance to Vauxhall Gardens. "Why?" she said. "You haven't changed your jacket."

"I'm a *man*. I have no need. Your position as a lady requires you to maintain the appearance of elegance at all times. And that means not wearing the same gown on consecutive social occasions."

"I didn't think you were so interested in fashion, Adam," she replied. "Though perhaps, given the vast number of gowns you purchase for your hundreds of mistresses, it should come as no surprise."

"Hundreds!" he scoffed. "Don't be a fool."

"Oh, forgive me, I forgot a man's inability to understand proportion when it comes to numbers."

He rolled his eyes. "What are you talking about?"

"Well, when a man counts his mistresses, something akin to twenty is deemed not very many at all—but when a woman takes a single lover, she's vilified as being too generous with her favors."

"We're not talking about lovers, Portia. We're talking about your gown."

"No, *you're* talking about my gown—which nobody will be looking at, given that it'll be dark in the gardens."

"Will you at least promise to behave with decorum?" he said.

"Don't I always?"

He linked her arm with his. "I'm only thinking of you, Portia. I wish I didn't have to be so strict with you at times, but you often drive me to distraction."

Did she imagine it, or was there a flicker of compassion in his voice? Surely her cold-hearted brother wasn't in possession of a soul?

He steered her toward the crowd in the center of the gardens. The air seemed to vibrate with anticipation and the buzz of animated voices. In a corner, a small group of musicians played a merry air, and around the perimeter of the gardens, liveried footmen held aloft torches, which flickered in the cool evening air, casting a vibrant orange glow over the crowd.

Portia glanced across the gardens, and her gaze settled on a woman dressed in a shade of red that could only be described as scandalous. Her hair was piled atop her head in an elaborate fashion, dotted with diamonds and rubies, the value of which must be enough to rival most dowries.

Doubtless my brother has contributed in no small part toward their cost.

Portia gestured toward the woman. "I see Mrs. Scarlet's here tonight. May I suggest a wager?"

"Ladies don't enter into wagers."

"I thought we could place bets on which gentleman's arm she'll be adorning tonight."

His eyes narrowed, and she caught a flicker of guilt in them.

"Ah, brother, I see now why you're reluctant to enter into a wager," Portia said. "Very well, I release you from your obligation toward me. I'm sure she'll enjoy your company tonight more than I, and when you take her for an intimate walk among the rosebushes, she'll express her enjoyment most vocally."

His jaw bulged as he gritted his teeth, but before he could admonish her, she caught sight of Whitcombe, flanked by his wife and sister.

"Ah!" she said, with exaggerated brightness, "it's Eleanor, and she's brought Olivia."

Her brother let out a snort. "Another *natural child*. London is littered with them this Season."

She slapped his arm. "They'll hear you."

"And what if they do? Whitcombe has no right to parade his father's by-blow about as if she were a lady."

"Why must you be so cruel?" Portia said. "Olivia's a delightful creature, charming and kind."

"I'm not disputing that, but there's no denying the misfortune of her birth. No matter how much Whitcombe parades her about in Society in an attempt to marry her off, he cannot overcome such an obstacle. No respectable man of Society will want to wed a bas—"

"Hush!" she whispered. "Do you want Whitcombe to call you out? He's a better shot than you."

She approached the Whitcombes, hands outstretched.

"Dear Eleanor! What a delight to see you!"

The duchess took her hands. "You act as if you didn't expect to see us, Portia."

"I know you dislike crowds." Portia turned to the sweet-faced young woman standing beside the duke. "Olivia, I'm delighted to see you tonight. We missed you in Hyde Park this afternoon, but I daresay you have many engagements now you've had your come-out."

Olivia colored, and Whitcombe placed a protective hand on her shoulder. "My sister was a little…*indisposed* this afternoon," he said, an undertone of anger in his voice.

"I see," Portia said. "Well, Olivia's among friends now—isn't that right, Adam?"

Her brother, who'd been staring across the garden, resumed his attention on them and nodded.

"Of course," he said. "A pleasure to see you—Miss FitzRoy, is that right?"

"It's Miss *Whitcombe*," Portia said, "as you well know. Why don't you go and speak to your mistress instead, Adam? *She'll* at least enjoy your company."

He shot her a look, then nodded to Whitcombe. "I trust your sister does not display the same lack of decorum as mine."

"Certainly not, Foxton."

Olivia blushed and turned to meet her brother's gaze, and Portia caught a glimpse of a redness about her eyes.

"Miss Whitcombe is much better behaved than I could ever be," she said, "aren't you, Olivia?"

"Y-yes, Lady—"

"I've already told you to call me Portia. We're friends, are we not?"

Olivia nodded, and Portia took her arm.

"Take no notice of my brother," she whispered. "I don't think I've heard him speak a civil word to anyone, save a few male friends."

Olivia managed a watery smile.

"Are you enjoying the Season?" Portia asked. "I found my first rather trying—far too many parties and balls—so I spent most mornings prostrate in my bedchamber with a headache."

"That, at least, is a problem I've not had to face," Olivia said.

"And the ceaseless chatter!" Portia added. "Some ladies must consider their desirability to be in direct proportion to the number of fatuous remarks they make about the weather, the cut of each others' gowns, or whether it is altogether too *nouveau riche* to issue invitations to a ball on paper edged in gold."

"I-I confess, I've not been subjected to many such fatuous remarks," Olivia said. "At least not to my face."

Her eyes glistened with moisture, and Portia's heart ached to see her expression. No wonder Olivia had been absent that afternoon. No doubt she'd been subject to the cruelty of the ladies who circled the waters of the *ton* like predators on the lookout for lesser beings to rip apart with their put-downs.

"Well, nobody cares what *they* think," Portia said. "At least nobody of any merit. If the witless ladies of Society see fit to exclude you from their conversations, it's their loss."

"Perhaps, but I fear I'm letting my brother down. He wanted my first Season to be a triumph, but not even the sister of a duke is acceptable in Society if she's a bas—"

"I'm sure your brother cares only for your happiness," Portia said, casting an envious glance at Whitcombe, who was gazing at his wife with devotion. "You're fortunate in *that*, at least."

"Oh, he's the best brother in all the world!" Olivia said, turning her adoring gaze on Whitcombe. "And I love Eleanor as a sister. But not everyone in London is as kind. I know I'm less than them, but I wish it were not so."

Portia's heart ached for the resignation in Olivia's tone. Why must the world be so cruel as to blame a person—usually a woman—for the circumstances of their birth? And why did Olivia feel she had to accept her status as being *less*?

Then her heart gave a little flutter as the familiar, tall figure emerged from the crowd, arm in arm with the delicately featured debutante she'd met in the park that afternoon.

"Colonel Reid"—Whitcombe inclined his head in a bow— "and Lady Angela. A pleasure."

"A pleasure indeed," Eleanor echoed. "Lady Angela, I was beginning to fear your brother had changed his mind and you weren't coming. May I introduce my husband's sister, Miss Whitcombe? Olivia, this is the young woman I told you about, Lady Angela Reid."

Olivia dipped into a curtsey, and Lady Angela tilted her head to one side, then glanced at the duke. "You're His Grace's sister?" she said. "A pleasure to meet you, Lady Olivia."

"It's *Miss Whitcombe*," Olivia said, blushing.

"But I thought a duke's sister was—"

"Miss Whitcombe," Colonel Reid said, extending his hand and issuing a broad smile, "a pleasure to see you again."

"I-I don't..." Olivia stammered, but he continued.

"Don't you recall we were introduced at the Royal Academy exhibition, where your sister-in-law's portrait of you graced the walls and was, in my opinion, the finest exhibit in the room?"

Olivia glanced at her brother, her eyes widening, and Eleanor came to her rescue.

"Colonel, you flatter my talents," she said. "I'm not so conceited as to consider my little pencil sketch to rank among the work of some of the finest artists in the country." She glanced at Olivia. "Perhaps it was the subject, not the artist, whom you were praising."

He bowed to the duchess, then took Olivia's hand and lifted it to his lips. Portia tempered the little spike of jealousy as he brushed his lips against Olivia's fingers. He was a handsome enough man in his usual brooding attitude, but when he smiled he was rendered godlike.

And she found that she didn't at all like seeing that smile turned toward another woman.

"You underestimate your talent, Duchess," he said to Eleanor, "but you are correct in your recognition of your sister-in-law's beauty."

He resumed his attention on Olivia. "I trust you'll favor me with a dance when next we meet at a ball, Miss Whitcombe."

She glanced at her brother. "I—I do not know when I'll next be attending a ball."

"Well, mind you reserve a space for me on your dance card before it fills." He smiled again, then released her hand. "Perhaps you might visit us for tea some time? My sister would appreciate widening her acquaintance, and you're just the sort of young lady I'd like her to get to know better."

Angela leaned close to her brother. "Stephen, why isn't she Lady Olivia?"

Though she had lowered her voice to a whisper, the rest of the party had caught her words. Whitcombe's expression hardened and Olivia colored.

"Olivia is a lady," Portia said, stepping forward. "At least in every quality that matters. Dear Olivia, I hope to see more of you at your sister's house party next month."

"In the meantime, perhaps you'd like to get to know Miss Whitcombe a little better, Angela," Colonel Reid said, steering her toward Olivia, and smiling as the two young women linked arms. He exchanged a glance with Portia, and her heart gave another little flutter.

"You see, Adam?" she said, turning to her brother. "There are some men who understand the true meaning of gallantry."

His eyes darkened, but he before he could admonish her, a familiar nasal voice uttered an overly bright greeting.

"Foxton! How delightful to see you. And Whitcombe, of course."

Sir Heath Moss approached, arm in arm with Lady Francis. He inclined his head to Adam, then bowed toward Portia and Eleanor.

"Lady Portia, Your Grace," he said. "Charmed, I'm sure." He turned his gaze toward Olivia and curled his lip in a sneer. "I see you've brought the *whole* family with you tonight, Whitcombe. Very charitable."

"In what way is my husband *charitable*?" Eleanor said.

"In his more modern sensibilities, Duchess," Sir Heath said, "which have extended to many of the choices he's made in life."

"Such as?" Whitcombe said, his voice growing quiet as he took his wife's hand and drew her close.

Sir Heath stared at Whitcombe's hand, then smiled, his pale gaze shifting to Eleanor. "I have always spoken of my admiration of *you*, Duchess, and of the unexpected elevation in Society that your family has enjoyed—which is, I'm sure, down to the"—he lowered his gaze to her neckline—"the *talents* both you and your sister possess."

"Do you intend to insult me?" Eleanor asked.

His eyes widened in mock horror. "On the contrary, Duchess, I have nothing but praise for you. Tell me, when shall we expect to see your sister-in-law gracing the dance floor at a ball? I noticed you and the duke at Countess Thorpe's party last week, though *Miss Whitcombe* was absent. Was she not invited? Earl Thorpe is *such* a stickler for propriety."

"My sister was not inclined to attend, Sir Heath," Whitcombe said.

"Which was a great loss to the rest of us," Portia said, extending her hand to Olivia. "I trust you'll be inclined to attend the next ball. There will be many young men eager to dance with you, and with whom it would not be a sufferance to stand up for more than a minute or two." She met Sir Heath's gaze and smiled coldly. "With a few notable exceptions."

"Portia…" her brother growled, and she let out a laugh.

"Of course *you're* not one of those exceptions, brother," she said. "I've heard there are some women who can endure your company for a whole evening—even a whole night."

He shot her a look that foretold of future admonishments. "Please excuse my sister, Sir Heath."

"There's nothing to forgive, Foxton," came the reply. "I'm fond of a spirited woman, am I not, Lady Francis?"

The lady blushed and curled her fingers around Sir Heath's arm in a possessive grip.

Portia suppressed a laugh. Lady Francis was welcome to him. In fact, by keeping Sir Heath occupied in her bed, she was doing the innocents of Society a great service by removing the predator from their midst.

As was Lady Maybury, and the other bored wives whose husbands Portia had found herself facing at dawn while she earned a pretty penny—or rather, fifty pretty pounds—from Sir Heath's cowardice.

"A-are you attending the house party at Rosecombe next month, Sir Heath?" Angela asked.

Whitcombe frowned, and Eleanor's eyes widened in apprehension.

"Angela…" Colonel Reid whispered in warning, and his sister cast her gaze down.

"F-forgive me. It was improper of me to ask."

"Your impropriety comes from kindness, Lady Angela," Sir

Heath said, "and for that, you can only be commended. You truly do live up to your name—as an angel." He extended his hand, and she took it, coloring as he lifted her hand to his lips while Lady Francis scowled, turning her overly made-up face quite ugly for a moment.

Jealousy never became a woman well.

Including my own.

But the colonel's gallantry toward Olivia was not borne out of desire—it was out of the kindness that was clearly a characteristic of the family. In that aspect, if nothing else, Portia could agree with Sir Heath. Lady Angela was an angel.

"I find myself quite overcome with so much beauty before me," Sir Heath continued.

Lady Angela smiled. "You're very gallant, Sir Heath."

"*Your* admiration is something I believe I shall come to value greatly."

Surely women didn't fall for such a speech, uttered, as it was, with such obsequiousness?

"You value much, Sir Heath," Portia said. "I'm convinced I heard that selfsame phrase used on Miss Bonneville. Do you perhaps keep a note of the phrases you deploy when attempting to flatter unsuspecting young women?"

"You think Sir Heath misguided in his gallantry toward me, Lady Portia?" Lady Angela said, a hint of frost in her voice.

"My dear Lady Angela," Sir Heath said, giving her an indulgent smile, his teeth glittering in the torchlight, "we must forgive Lady Portia, for she is on her... How many Seasons is it, Lady Portia? Is this your fourth?"

"Her third," Adam said, a hard edge to his voice.

"An unnecessary expense for you, Foxton," Sir Heath said. "You have my sympathies."

"Not every young woman can expect to find love in her first Season," Colonel Reid said, and Portia's heart soared at the warmth in his voice.

"You're mistaken," Adam said. "The purpose of a Season is to find a *husband*, not love."

"The two ought to go hand in hand, surely?"

"Colonel, with that attitude, your family may find itself in for a very expensive few years," Adam said. "Young women don't fall in love. They succumb to the occasional childish infatuation, but they soon grow out of it."

"Since when have I suffered a *childish infatuation*, brother?" Portia said. "Or were you perhaps referring to the unfortunate debutantes who've fallen at your feet? I wouldn't call *that* a childish infatuation—I'd call it a sickness of the mind."

"Then perhaps you're destined never to fall in love, Lady Portia," Lady Angela said. "But *I* hope to fall in love." She directed a shy smile at Sir Heath, who bowed once more.

"Bravo, Lady Angela!" he said. "An admirable attitude, one that will yield you much success this Season."

Lady Francis's scowl deepened. "Ought we to take our leave, Heath?" she said, her tone petulant. She dug her fingernails into his arm. "You promised to buy me ice cream. It will all have melted if you persist in speaking to everyone we pass by."

"I doubt that," Eleanor said. "They keep it cool with blocks of ice."

Lady Francis shot her a look of spite.

"Duty calls," Sir Heath said. "But I hope to enjoy the pleasure of your company another time"—he glanced toward Portia—"perhaps when we're not in the company of those who would be jealous of a young lady whose beauty surpasses theirs."

Lady Angela blushed and inclined her head while he kissed her hand once more, then took his leave. Shortly after, Lady Francis could be heard expressing discontent with everything— the gardens, the cold…and the company.

"I wonder what he finds attractive in her," Portia said.

"For heavens' sake!" her brother snapped. "Why do you *persist* in speaking out of turn?"

"It's not anything you don't discuss at White's," Portia said. "But perhaps she's very…*talented*. Isn't that how you men describe a woman?"

"Are you jealous of her, Lady Portia?" Lady Angela said.

"Angela, that's enough," Colonel Reid said. "You'd do better to find friendship with Lady Portia than Lady Francis—or Sir Heath Moss, come to that."

"I think—" Angela began, but Olivia interrupted.

"Lady Angela, shall we take a look at the jugglers? I've never been able to fathom how they can keep all those batons in the air without dropping them."

"May I, brother?" Angela said.

The colonel nodded. "Of course, but at first you must apol—"

"I'd recommend the fire-breathers, also," Portia interrupted. "I saw them near the pavilion. You know the way, don't you, Olivia?"

Olivia nodded, and the two young women made their way toward the building across the lawn.

"I commend you on having such a sensible sister, Whitcombe," Colonel Reid said. "She'll be a steadying influence on Angela, who I'm afraid is a little impulsive."

"I'm sure she'll grow out of it," Eleanor said. "How old is she, eighteen?"

"She's not yet sixteen, Duchess."

"Then you must guard her closely."

"I intend to," he replied. "There's nothing so precious as a woman's virtue. Except, perhaps, her honesty and civility. Angela ought to have apologized for her incivility toward you, Lady Portia."

"An apology obtained by request is no true apology," Portia replied. "Besides, there's no need for her to apologize. I often speak out of turn."

"That's the most sensible thing you've said all day," her brother said.

"Which is *your* opinion, Adam," she retorted.

"And the opinion of everyone here, no doubt."

"My opinion, Foxton, is that your sister speaks perfect sense,"

Colonel Reid said. Though it was dark, she could sense his nearness as he shifted closer, and her breath hitched at the faint aroma of masculinity. She moved toward him until she brushed up against his jacket, and the aroma intensified—deep, woody spices and an earthy scent of the outdoors, like a fresh spring meadow.

Then a hand touched hers. She caught her breath at the sensation of the callouses on his fingers brushing over her skin. Had those hands wielded a weapon, defending his life and the lives of others on the battlefield? Had they touched other women to elicit the same sensations that now swirled deep in her belly?

"I commend you for championing Miss Whitcombe earlier," she whispered. "Duke Whitcombe's desire to further his sister's acceptance into Society is one of his most admirable features— that and his love for dear Eleanor, of course."

"It's a pity that, in our world, Miss Whitcombe and others like her, such as young Gabriel Staines, are in need of a champion due to their birth. You are also to be admired, Lady Portia, for coming to their defense." He lowered his voice, and the gravelly tone resonated in her bones. "In fact, I find much to admire in you."

She let out a low whimper, and he curled his fingers around hers then brushed the palm of her hand with his thumb. How could such a simple touch cause a fizz of need to ignite in her veins?

She leaned toward him, inhaling his rich scent, then tilted her head back. In the darkness, she could not tell whether he was smiling.

Please let him be smiling.

She closed her eyes, imagining the expression in his eyes were he to smile at her—how the warm chocolate color would deepen to rich mahogany, perhaps punctuated with glimmers of golden light.

Then a cheer filled the air as the crowd surged forward. A bright light soared into the air, before igniting into rainbow-colored stars. An explosion filled the air, resonating through her body, as if the earth vibrated beneath her feet. Then the fireworker set off another explosion to "oohs" and "aahs" from the crowd.

Portia turned to the man beside her, but when the shower of light illuminated his face, there was no softness, no smile, but an increasing horror—a fear so primal that her heart froze to see it. His face glowed whitely in the diffused light, and his eyes were a black as night, as if they had absorbed all light, and all hope. And reflected in his eyes, she saw…

Her gut twisted with fear.

In his eyes, she saw the shadow of death.

CHAPTER TWELVE

*S*WEET *L*ORD, *NO!*

Explosions filled the air, resonating through Stephen's body until he was, once more, on the battlefield, the stench of death and smoke in his nostrils while his fallen comrades—brave men he'd failed to save—lay dying, crying for the deity that had abandoned them.

He closed his eyes to block out the world, but the nightmare followed, burying itself to fester like a canker, blackening his soul from the inside. The canker swelled with each pulse of his heartbeat, glistening black and red, until it formed a shape—the tall, thin form of a hooded creature wielding a scythe. It rose, towering over him until he fell into its shadow, the coldness seeping into his veins. Then the figure spoke, a whisper as cold as the slow hiss of a blade unsheathing, ready to slice through his throat.

Coward! That's what you are, Reid, a coward!

No…

Squealing like a babe—and for what? You escaped unscathed while your friends fell at your command, yet you're the one sniveling, crying the tears of a wretched animal while your wits snap…

A high-pitched laugh sliced through his mind, followed by another, and another, until a whole host of voices tittered and taunted, a coven of cackling phantoms…

He shook his head to dispel the image of broken bodies, but they swelled and pulsed, their expressions accusatory, condemning him for surviving, mouths open, ready to utter the incantation to send him into hell…

"Colonel."

A voice spoke in the recesses of his mind, sliding between the taunts—a voice unlike those that haunted his dreams. Then gentle fingers curled around his own, pulling him back from the mouth of hell. The demons receded, then another explosion filled the air and he let out a whimper as they surged forward again.

"Colonel Reid!"

The voice came again, pulling him from the nightmare of pain and death, flowing into his mind like cool liquid to soothe the burning agony. Then it lowered to a whispered caress.

"Stephen…"

A hand touched his face.

"Stephen, look at me."

He opened his eyes.

The dark gray of the battlefield was gone, replaced by a clear blue—as if an ocean were staring right into his soul.

"Breathe…" The voice said, and he complied, drawing in a lungful of air. Then soft fingertips caressed his chin. The ocean focused into two sapphires, wide, expressive eyes in a porcelain-skinned face framed by glossy black curls. He lowered his gaze to her mouth—full, plump lips with the promise of the sweetness of a kiss.

"That's better," she breathed.

He looked into her eyes once more and caught his breath at the flare of desire in them.

A desire to match his own.

"Breathe…" she whispered, her lips curving into a gentle smile.

He inhaled again, then exhaled, slowly.

"That's better, colonel. Tell me what you see."

He blinked, and the world around him swam into focus—blurred nighttime shapes illuminated by flickering torches.

"I see flames."

"What can you see in the light of the flames?"

"A garden," he said. "A path leading toward a building with arched windows that reflect the torchlight."

Her eyes sparkled with pleasure. "Good," she whispered. "Very good. What else?"

He shifted his focus to the woman before him. "I see beauty."

Her smile slipped and a flicker of annoyance glimmered in her eyes.

"Can you not speak the truth?" she said, an edge to her voice.

"I lack the strength to lie," he replied. "I see a pair of eyes of the deepest blue, the color of midnight, with silver stars glimmering in their depths that speak of the soul hidden within. In those eyes I see kindness, and compassion."

He lowered his gaze to her mouth.

"I see lips, full and red, set in a determined expression that speaks of a strength that I lack. Yet I also see softness—a softness that I long to surrender my soul to. Tell me, Lady Portia, what kind of man, save a fool, could see anything other than beauty in that?"

He lifted his hand to her face and caressed her chin with his fingertip, a nugget of need threading through him at the feel of the silken softness of her skin.

Closing her eyes, she leaned into his touch.

"Lady Portia…" be breathed.

"Stephen…" Her soft whisper as she spoke his name swelled his heart. Then she parted her lips and let out a soft sigh. He had only to lower his head a fraction to claim that sweet mouth…

Fool! You're a weak fool!

He pushed her back.

"No." He shook his head. "Forgive me. You must think me a fool—a weakling and a fool."

"Why would you say that?" she asked, her eyes glistening with moisture.

Ye gods, did she harbor *pity* for him?

He stepped back, but she caught his wrist. "No, colonel—do

not run away from me a second time."

"A second time?"

The compassion in her eyes returned. "You left my world just then. Do not do so again, not when you have only just returned."

"I-I do not understand you."

"Yes, you do," she said, touching his cheek once more. "Your body might not have left, but your mind…"

"You think I'm prone to insanity, Lady Portia?" he said, shame filling his heart as he caught her meaning. "Is that why you asked me what I could see, to test that I was not so out of wits that I couldn't recognize my surroundings?"

She flinched. "No. You were merely besieged by a memory so vivid that it threatened to break into your consciousness. A memory is like a dream. When we dream we believe it is real, do we not? The more vivid the memory, the more real it seems."

"Only a madman would say such things."

"Would you call Dr. McIver a madman?"

Stephen shook his head. "McIver's a clever man, unlike that charlatan Dr. Lucas and his cursed leeches."

Her mouth curved into a smile. "Then you must accept what I say, for I merely repeat Dr. McIver's words. He has written a paper on the impact of great suffering on the mind, though men such as Dr. Lucas have ridiculed him for it. But I have seen it for myself—soldiers wounded in the hospital, their bodies broken, minds suffering while they relive the horrors of war."

"My body is not broken, Lady Portia," he said. "I'm one of the lucky ones."

"Perhaps not," she said. "Tell me, do you believe you deserved to return from Waterloo with no physical injury while men such as Captain Broom lost their limbs?"

"Of course not," he said, before he could stop himself.

She took his hand, and the urge to withdraw and hide his shame warred with the desire to pull her close.

"There is no law that dictates whether a man deserves to be wounded in battle," she said. "Every man who returns from war is a different man to the one who rode out to it. You all sustained wounds."

"I escaped with barely a scratch, Lady Portia," he said. "How is that fair? How can I look into the eyes of those who call me a hero of Waterloo when I survived while better men did not?"

"In what way were they better?" she said. "Because they were injured or killed, and you were not?" She caressed his cheek. "You *were* injured, colonel, and you suffer those injuries still. Just because your injuries are invisible to most, that doesn't render them any less deserving of compassion, or any less in need of healing."

"Insanity cannot be healed."

"An immaterial argument, given that you're not insane."

"I'm weak, then," he said. "My poor sister does not need a weakling for a brother."

"Your sister is fortunate to have you as a brother. Perhaps she's the most fortunate sister in the world."

"At least *your* brother is no weakling."

"It depends on your definition of weakness," she replied. "Any man can behave like a rake when he has a title and a fortune, together with the kind of looks that make women swoon in droves."

At that moment, a harsh voice called out from the darkness, and Lady Portia's smile disappeared, the softness yielding to a hunted expression.

"Sister, where are you?"

Stephen glanced at his surroundings. "Where's the rest of our party?"

"I steered you away."

"So that they might not witness my weakness?"

"No, to give you privacy, so those who do not understand are given no opportunity to gossip. Not that I don't trust dear Eleanor, but I cannot trust my brother—or that reprobate Sir Heath—to be discreet." She offered her arm. "Shall we return before we're missed? I think the fireworker has finished."

He nodded and took her arm, and she steered him along the path toward Duke and Duchess Whitcombe. Angela was nowhere to be seen.

"Where's my sister?"

"With Miss Whitcombe. They've gone to look at the fire-eaters. She's in safe hands with Olivia, you know."

He nodded. "I still fear for her. An unmarried young girl in London is in far greater danger than a soldier on the battlefield."

"Perhaps you should equip her with a pistol."

He shuddered. "I abhor the use of weapons for sport, Lady Portia."

Fear flared in her eyes, but before he could ask what frightened her, Foxton approached with the woman in the scarlet dress he'd noticed earlier. As she saw Stephen, a look of hunger flickered in her eyes. She lowered her gaze to his feet, then raised it slowly, settling on his groin for a heartbeat—then she licked her lips and resumed her attention on her companion.

Most men would call her beautiful, but her beauty was the kind that women used to shatter men's hearts and empty their purses. Foxton was welcome to her.

"*There* you are, sister," the duke said, patting the woman's arm with a gesture of possessiveness. "I was beginning to wonder where you'd got to."

"Well, I'm here now," Lady Portia said, an edge to her voice.

"You shouldn't wander off. As a lady, you must be mindful of your reputation at all times."

"I'd have thought the reputation of a *lady* would be the last thing on your mind at the present moment." She cast her gaze over Foxton's companion. "Miss Scarlet, is it not?"

"Mrs.," came the reply, accompanied by a sneer.

"Where did you go, Portia?" Foxton asked, his gaze wandering over Stephen, as if he were searching for evidence of transgression.

Stephen's gut twisted with shame. Would Lady Portia reveal his weakness, that he'd been on the brink of madness and she'd spirited him away from the party to conceal it? What would the party think of being in the presence of a witless fool?

"We went searching for ices for everyone," she said. "We were all getting a little hot. I asked the colonel to help me carry them."

Her voice carried not even the slightest flicker of guilt at her deception. How was it that some individuals could utter a such a bald falsehood without the slightest impact on their conscience?

Foxton lowered his gaze to her hand on Stephen's arm. "I see," he said.

"Isn't that right, colonel?" she said, turning her attention to Stephen.

Was it not enough that she could lie to her brother so convincingly that she wanted Stephen as an accomplice? No matter how she'd come to his aid earlier, nobody had the right to compel him into deception.

Foxton's expression hardened, and Lady Portia fixed her gaze on Stephen, awaiting his response. He remained silent, and she withdrew her hand, her brow furrowed.

"Did you not say you wanted ices, Eleanor?" she asked, and Stephen caught the plea in her eyes.

The duchess tilted her head to one side as if in concentration, then she nodded. "Monty saw ices being sold earlier. Didn't you, my love?"

"I beg pardon?" Whitcombe said, turning his attention from a group of jugglers across the path.

"Ices," the duchess said. "Wasn't there a man selling them near the main entrance?"

"Not that I know of, my love," came the reply, "but I believe the proprietor of Gunter's is here tonight. I saw a sign beside the pavilion—near the fire-breathers, I think. Perhaps they're selling ices there. But surely you don't want an ice, Eleanor—you're still recovering from that cold you took when we went sea bathing. Dr. McIver said you were to take care."

"If I recall, Dr. McIver said I should take plenty of fresh air, Monty."

"Fresh air, perhaps, but not *ices*. Who the devil eats ices out of doors in the evening?"

"Our entire party, apparently," Foxton said, fixing his cold stare on his sister.

"Well, *I* want one, at least," Lady Portia said.

"As do I," the duchess added. "Their brown bread ices are delicious."

"Brown bread?" Foxton said with a sneer. "Who the devil would want to eat an ice that tastes like *bread*?"

"Perhaps someone with a discerning palate, Foxton," Stephen said, catching the distress in Eleanor's eyes. "I've tasted the brown bread ice cream myself and recommend it."

"Do you like ices, Mrs. Scarlet?" the duchess asked.

The brightly attired peacock on Foxton's arm turned her sharp-nosed gaze on the duchess, looked her up and down, then shook her head.

"I must beg to be excused from a discussion of ices, Your Grace," she said. "The consumption of an abundance of desserts is not a recommended practice for a woman who wishes to retain her figure. And I always find that an overly"—she lowered her gaze to the duchess's neckline—"*healthy* figure is considered unattractive in some circles, for it is evidence of a lack of self-discipline and self-restraint, not to mention the expense of always having to have ones clothes altered."

"Is it not better to enjoy life rather than deprive oneself of pleasure?" the duchess said.

"Of course, Your Grace," the courtesan replied, her smile broadening to reveal gleaming white teeth. "There are few among my acquaintance who understand the nature of pleasure as I do. But some things can be enjoyed a little too much. And, after all, as women, we have a responsibility to maintain our appearance to give pleasure to others. Is that not right, Foxton, darling?"

The duke nodded. "Quite right, Mrs. Scarlet. As insightful as ever."

"Very well," Stephen said, "with the exception of Mrs. Scarlet, who chooses not to have one, shall Lady Portia and I bring ices for everyone who deserves one?"

"None for my brother, then," Lady Portia said. "You wouldn't want to disappoint Mrs. Scarlet, would you? Or is it only members of the female sex who must deprive themselves of treats in order to keep a man's attentions?"

"Do forgive my sister, Mrs. Scarlet," Foxton said. "Perhaps we ought to take a turn about the garden."

The courtesan nodded in the manner of a queen acknowledging a humble subject, then he steered her away.

"One ice each for my wife and me," Whitcombe said, taking the duchess's hand and lifting it to his lips. "I, for one, find much to admire in a woman who takes pleasure in devouring brown bread ice cream, especially when it's smeared over—"

"Monty!" The duchess let out a squeal, her face turning bright pink as Whitcombe pulled her into his arms.

Stephen's heart fluttered with envy. Was there ever a couple so much in love? Plenty of husbands and wives gave the appearance of happiness—or at least satisfaction—yet took no genuine pleasure in each other's company. Foxton and his mistress, for example, seemed very pleased with themselves, but there was little to no joy in the duke's eyes.

Perhaps Lady Portia could be forgiven for wanting to deceive her brother. To have one's entire life dictated by such a man was not a state to be envied.

As they approached the pavilion, Stephen spotted a sign erected at the far end of the façade depicting a pineapple placed atop a vase, bearing the legend *J Gunter, ices.*

"There they are," he said. "Whitcombe spoke the truth."

"Good for Whitcombe," Lady Portia said.

She began to withdraw her arm, and Stephen caught her hand.

"Forgive me," he said. "I-I ought to have helped you back then with your brother, but I cannot bear any form of deception."

"Then you won't survive long in London Society. In any case, I was only trying—"

"To help me, I know. And for that I'm grateful, believe me. But I abhor any form of dishonesty, and I cannot bear the notion of your having a trait I dislike when I admire you so much."

"If you think to ingratiate yourself by flattery, colonel, I—"

She let out a gasp as he pulled her close.

"Can't you see it's not mere flattery, Lady Portia?" he said. "I'm a soldier. I have no time for deception or the petty niceties of drawing room conversation. I see little merit in speaking anything but the truth, and if I cannot speak the truth, then I have no wish to speak at all. I do not flatter you because you're beautiful. I admire you because, more than anyone of my acquaintance, you *see* me. I-I cannot fathom how you understood what I needed when I…" He paused, the memory of the battlefield threatening to rise once more.

Then slim fingers curled around his hand and a thrill rippled across his skin.

"Stephen, look at me."

He met her gaze, letting the cool blue of her eyes fill his senses and soothe his soul, until the image of the battlefield faded. The anger in her expression had gone, replaced by compassion and understanding and a tiny spark that swelled his hope.

A spark of desire to match his own.

He drew in a sharp breath to temper the surge in his manhood.

"I must apologize also for my sister, Lady Portia."

"Angela? For what?"

"She was most uncivil toward you earlier. I fear her naiveté makes her prone to flattery."

"The kind that men such as Heath Moss employ to entrap the innocent?" She smiled. "It matters not. She has a big brother to keep her safe from harm. She's young and spirited, that's all—as we all were at that age. I love the freeness in her soul, her enthusiasm for life."

"But she must learn to be more guarded."

"She will," Portia said. "There comes a time when our eyes are opened more fully to the world about us, when the unbridled enthusiasm we have as children is tempered by the need to survive in a world of those who would judge us, or seek to take advantage of us for their own purposes."

"Such as those who would deceive us," Stephen said. "Men such as Sir Heath, for example—fair in face, gallant in demeanor, yet his gallantry does not come from his character, but from a desire to persuade others that he is to be trusted. He behaves very differently when in the company of men compared to when among your sex."

"As do all men, colonel."

"Then I apologize on behalf of all of my sex."

"I fear the majority of your sex is past redemption—though there may exist one or two notable exceptions."

A smile played on her lips, and his heart gave a little jolt.

"You are blessed to have a sister," she said. "I should have liked to have a sister."

Perhaps, one day, you will.

He closed his eyes, letting the dream take shape in his mind—Lady Portia in his home, and his life, gently steering his beloved little angel, teaching her the meaning of true beauty…

When he opened them, she was staring at him, her lips parted in surprise.

Sweet Lord, he'd spoken aloud!

He drew her close, and the spark of desire in her eyes swelled. Her lips parted further. Sweet and plump—would they taste as sweet as he'd imagined in his dreams? Would she sigh with pleasure as he claimed them for his own?

"Stephen…"

Her soft, whispered words shattered his resolve, and he pulled her close then placed his hand on her cheek. A whimper escaped her lips as he caressed her cheek with his thumb, relishing the softness of her skin. He traced the outline of her mouth and she sighed, her warm breath fluttering over his skin, sending a bolt of heat through his veins. He shifted his thighs as his breeches tightened, and her eyes widened as his manhood stiffened against her body.

"Lady Portia…"

"Stephen…"

He dipped his head and claimed her mouth.

Heavens! She tasted sweeter than he could ever have imagined—rich honey with a deeper, warmer taste of cinnamon and spice. And yet, unlike the camp followers who had given him and his fellow soldiers a little comfort in the field for a coin or two, she carried a taste of innocence.

It was the taste of a woman who had yet to be awakened to the pleasures of her body.

His own body surged with the anticipation of claiming her, to be the first to awaken her to the unimaginable pleasure of the intimacy of…

Bedsport, his fellow soldiers called it, as they'd cheered each other on, celebrating their prowess. But what might such an act be when there was love involved, a meeting of minds and souls as well as bodies?

No—she was an innocent, and a lady, not some cheap doxy wanting to earn a crust for gratifying a camp full of soldiers. She did not deserve to be treated as such.

But before he could withdraw, she parted her lips further and pressed her body against his, and he almost spent in his breeches at the feel of two stiff little peaks pushing against his chest.

He slipped his tongue between her lips. She gave a low mewl of satisfaction, curling her tongue around his in a slow dance of seduction. She reached up and buried her fingers in his hair, pulling him closer as he deepened the kiss. A low growl swelled in his throat as she shifted her thighs against his manhood, and he fought to maintain his resolve against the urge to bury himself inside her.

But she was not some wench to be rutted in the bushes, no

matter how pleasurable it would be to take her swiftly. No, the first time he took her, he wanted to relish every moment, every heartbeat, as he awakened her to the pleasures of her body and slide inside her…

What the devil am I doing?

He jerked back, shame warring with his desire. For a moment she stood before him, eyes closed, lips parted, bruised and swollen from his kiss, her hair in disarray. The flush on her cheeks spoke of raw pleasure, but when she opened her eyes, the pleasure faded.

"Forgive me, Lady Portia. I-I shouldn't have done that."

Disappointment flickered across her face. "Colonel, you did nothing that I did not desire."

"Then—"

He was interrupted by a shout.

"Well, old chap, you've been caught with your breeches down, haven't you?"

The voice was Foxton's.

Lady Portia's eyes widened in fear, and she smoothed back her hair, glancing about her. Stephen drew her close to preserve her from her brother's fury.

Then he saw him.

Foxton was standing with his mistress—but he was not looking toward them. His attention was on another couple.

Sir Heath Moss and Lady Francis stood beside the building, not completely concealed in the shadows. By the state of the lady's dishabille, and the expression of triumph on the gentleman's face—if Sir Heath could be called a gentleman—there was no doubt what they had been doing.

And beside them stood Lord Francis.

"Heavens!" Lady Portia said. "Have Sir Heath and Lady Francis been—"

"Hush!" Stephen whispered as Foxton glanced in their direction. He pulled her deeper into the shadows. "Or do you want him to catch us?"

"I thought you disliked deception."

"I dislike the notion of your brother running me through even more."

She stifled a giggle.

Several onlookers approached, whispering to each other, some holding ices.

"I see the crowd is in search of some entertainment while they enjoy their dessert," Lady Portia whispered.

At that moment, the crowd let out a cry in unison as Lord Francis stepped toward Sir Heath, pulled off his glove, and hit him smartly across the cheek.

"You blackguard!" he cried. "I'll see you at dawn tomorrow."

Lady Portia stiffened and took a step toward them.

"Make it dusk," Sir Heath replied. "I must make the proper arrangements."

"If you need to find a second, I'm sure Dunton will oblige," Lord Francis said. "I saw him wandering about tonight with that sour-faced wife of his. You've been standing him drinks at White's all month, so it's the least he can do."

"A duel," Stephen scoffed. "Why must they engage in such a thing, as if it's a trivial matter to take a life?"

"I doubt that'll be the outcome," Lady Portia said. "Sir Heath's a coward, and Lord Francis a poor shot."

"How the devil do you know that?"

She stiffened, and he caught a flash of fear in her eyes. Then she shook her head. "Everyone knows Sir Heath's a coward—after all, isn't that the one trait shared by all bullies? As for Lord Francis, I competed against him in archery at a house party once. Isn't archery the same as marksmanship?"

"No, it's a different sport entirely. But Sir Heath—"

"Do *you* enjoy archery, colonel?"

"I confess that I do."

"I'm very much looking forward to the archery at Eleanor's house party. The competition reminds me of what it must have been like hundreds of years ago, hunting for rabbit—though, of course, the targets will be fixed, which makes it a little less challenging."

"Fixed?"

"Yes, they're placed all over the grounds, and the competitors have to find them."

"Isn't that dangerous?"

"The gamekeepers will ensure we keep to the path, and they keep score to make sure nobody cheats. Though that's unlikely, given that Eleanor has better taste in friends than most. Sir Heath, for example, will not be at the party."

Stephen glanced over to the man in question, who was bowing to Lord Francis, a sneer on his lips.

"Much as I despise that man, I have no wish to see him, or Lord Francis, come to harm," he said. "I hear Sir Heath employs that Farthing fellow to fight for him."

"Oh?" she replied, her voice tight.

Stephen shook his head. "If Sir Heath is despicable, that's nothing compared to the black soul of that particular creature. To make a profit from such an act… I hope one day he hangs."

She shrank back, the fear in her eyes intensifying. Then he took her hand.

"Forgive me. We're not here to speak of men who are too rotten to deserve our attention. We're here to fetch ices, are we not? We mustn't keep the duchess waiting. She is perhaps one of the few women in Society for whom I have any admiration—save yourself, of course."

She nodded, but her smile did not resume, and he steered her toward the queue for ices.

What had given rise to such fear in her eyes? And why did it pierce his soul to see her so afraid?

Perhaps if he discovered the cause of her fear, he could shatter it. For he wanted nothing more than to see her safe and happy.

Sweet Lord—he was falling in love.

CHAPTER THIRTEEN

THE SUN HAD long since slid below the line of trees in the park, casting shadows that stretched across the ground until they merged into the darkness.

Three figures stood, silhouetted against the moonlight reflected in the Serpentine—Sir Heath Moss, his second, and the referee. Sir Heath had managed to persuade the Duke of Dunton to act as his second. Portia would have recognized Dunton's portly frame anywhere, not to mention the stench of sour brandy and unwashed garments that followed him like a thick fog wherever he went. Why Sir Heath saw fit to pay Dunton's expenses made little sense, apart from Dunton's title, which rendered him attractive to men such as Sir Heath who sought to collect titled friends.

And other men's wives.

Nerissa at her side, Portia adjusted her mask then drew her cloak about her. Despite the warmth of the day, a chill had descended since the sunset. Each time she exhaled, her breath formed a mist. It was fortunate that Sir Heath had insisted on the duel taking place at dusk. By dawn, the ground would be covered in frost. And with a frost came footprints, the pattern of which would declare to the whole world that a duel had taken place.

"Will you not come closer while we wait, Mr. Farthing?" Sir Heath said.

"My master's not here to engage in conversation," Nerissa

said.

"You're not going to bolt, are you? You've my fifty pounds in your pocket."

"My master's fifty pounds," Nerissa said. "According to the terms of the contract—"

"Yes, yes," Sir Heath said, irritation in his voice. "According to the contract, the client pays whether his opponent shows or not. That damned contract exists for *your* benefit, not mine."

"Only if you place little value on your life."

"Well, it seems as if *your* life is not at risk tonight," Sir Heath said. "I always said Francis was a coward—in addition to being unable to satisfy his wife."

"No man is enough for that woman," Dunton said, his voice slurred. "*I've* had her."

"That's nothing to boast about," Sir Heath said. "I doubt there's a man in London who's not had her. Lord Francis had to dismiss his entire body of male staff after catching her *in flagrante delicto* with three footmen last Christmas. I even hear he's jealous of the stallions in his stables."

"Which proves my point that all women are whores," Dunton said. "Give a woman an ounce of freedom and she'll spread her legs for anything that moves." He let out a coarse laugh. "And several things that don't," he added. "I suspect she's a patron of Madame DilDoul's establishment. Not that I object, of course. Madame has the most delectable items for her more discerning customers—carved out of ivory, don't you know! I myself have used—"

The referee cleared his throat, and Dunton let out a laugh.

"Squeamish, are you, Johnson?"

Before the man could respond, footsteps crunched on the gravel and Portia turned to see two men approaching, Lord Francis and…

"Sweet Lord—Adam!"

"Hush!" Nerissa whispered.

Lord Francis approached Sir Heath and extended his hand.

"Well met. Dunton, I didn't expect to see you outside at this hour. That must be a great loss to the bawdy houses of London."

"I might say the same for your friend there," Dunton said. "I'd have thought you'd be buried inside that slut of yours at this hour, Foxton."

Portia's brother approached Dunton, then he paused and turned toward her, his eyes glittering with distaste. For a heartbeat, brother and sister stared at each other, and she bit her lip to stem the cry of fear.

"Have a care," Nerissa whispered, taking her hand.

Then he resumed his attention on Dunton.

Portia exhaled, but the knots in her stomach failed to loosen. She curled her hands into fists to stem the shaking, but she couldn't temper the tremors.

"He's not recognized you," Nerissa whispered. "And he won't if you stay silent. I'll do the talking."

"He might recognize *you*."

"I doubt that. Your brother wouldn't recognize any of his servants out of uniform. He can't tell one from the other."

"What's that you're saying, Mr. Farthing?" Sir Heath said.

"Nothing to concern you, Sir Heath," Nerissa said. "My master is merely eager to proceed."

Lord Francis turned toward Portia. "Oh, *fuck*."

"Precisely," Sir Heath said, triumph in his tone. He gestured toward Portia. "My friend's reputation precedes him."

I am not *your friend.*

"I don't suppose you fancy calling it a night?" Lord Francis said. "I'll stand you a brandy at White's for your trouble."

"Ahem," Dunton said.

"And Dunton too, of course. I appreciate the effort it must have taken to tear yourself away from Mrs. Green's bawdy house to come here tonight."

"Good God!" Adam said. "Is Mrs. Green still alive? She must be sixty at least."

"With age comes experience and a wealth of talent," Sir

Heath said. "That thing she does with her tongue—I've never had the like. Not even Lady Fra…" He trailed off and cocked his head to one side, staring at Lord Francis.

"So it's *you* she learned that from," Lord Francis said. "I ought to be grateful."

Sweet Lord! Portia swallowed her nausea. No matter what Lady Francis's faults might be, she was Lord Francis's wife and his duty was to defend her honor.

"Perhaps you ought to charge for your wife's services, Francis," Adam said. "It would help settle your debts."

"That's not a bad idea, Foxton," Lord Francis said, with a chuckle. "What say you, a guinea a time? She's been lusting after *you* since her first Season."

"I doubt that," Adam said. "I was still in the cradle back then. Perhaps you mean my grandfather? By all accounts, members of the weaker sex couldn't resist his talents in the bedchamber."

"Bloody hell, Foxton, I ought to call you out for that." Lord Francis glanced in Portia's direction. "Though doubtless you'd hire this fellow to do the deed for you."

"Hire him yourself," Adam said, wrinkling his nose in a sneer, and she shivered at the loathing in his voice. "I wouldn't stoop to dealing with such an underhand creature. Worse than a whore you are, Mr. Farthing—or whatever your name is."

He stepped toward her, and Nerissa squeezed her hand.

"Have a care," she whispered. "Say nothing, lest you reveal yourself."

"Steady on, Foxton, old chap," Sir Heath said. "The Farthing may be a whore, but he's a damned useful one. His aim is as useful as Lady Francis's cunny, which we've all enjoyed to the full. I'd rather he were left unscathed."

"But perhaps not anonymous," Adam said. "We should reveal his identity."

Portia's gut tightened with knots of fear, and she stepped back.

"I say, old chap," Lord Francis said, "there's no call for that sort of talk. A gentleman would never act so dishonorably."

Despicable creatures, all of them! They thought nothing of making bawdy remarks about Lady Francis and sharing her among themselves as if she were a cut of beef—but the notion of unmasking a duelist was considered *dishonorable?*

It would serve them right if she revealed herself, let them know they'd been bested at their own game by a member of the so-called weaker sex.

Adam paused, his gaze fixed on her. He narrowed his eyes and tilted his head to one side.

"Do I know you?" he said.

Portia dug her nails into her palms to stop the tremors in her body. Then her brother let out a snort of derision.

"Most likely you're some footman eager to earn a few extra coins. Does your master know where you are?"

Portia shook her head. Her brother grinned, revealing sharp white teeth. She'd always known him to be a rake, but how had she not noticed until now how much of an air of menace he carried about him?

Heaven help the women who fell for his charms.

As to the woman who became his duchess, whoever that unfortunate soul would be… Not even the Almighty and all His angels would be able to help *her*.

Was this how all men behaved? Whitcombe, Staines…

Surely not Stephen?

No…

Adam gave a slow, lazy smile, his savagely handsome face giving a predatory air that women found irresistible, though it was a manifestation of the blackened soul within.

"Do I discompose you, Mr. Farthing?" he sneered. "Perhaps my friends and I ought to rouse our households on our return tonight to see who's missing?"

Using her fury to conquer her fear, Portia stared her brother straight in the eye.

His eyes were the same shape and shade of blue as hers,

enough to cause a jolt of recognition, as if she were looking into a mirror. But the similarity ended there. In them she saw a predatory air and degree of confidence that only a man of his rank could possess—the confidence that came from knowing that the world would bow to him in everything, that he had the power to destroy the livelihoods, reputations, and souls of others at the merest word or casual flick of the wrist.

A thread of ice rippled through her veins as he continued to glare at her, his eyes glittering with dominance.

Sweet Lord! Many times had she been on the receiving end of his anger, his disappointment, but never before had she faced such ice-cold fury, delivered with such control.

The corner of his lips twitched into the ghost of a smile, as if, like a predator, he relished the terror in his prey at the moment before he tore her apart. But, as Stephen had once told her, the best generals only stepped into battle when they were assured of victory—sometimes the battle was won before a single shot had been fired. By staring down his opponent, Adam was attempting to triumph even before he made the first move. Doubtless he expected her to turn tail and flee.

Her fingers itched with the urge to challenge him, and she curled her hand, imagining what it might be like to aim a pistol at her brother's head. Would he blubber like a toddler, as Viscount de Blanchard did when he faced the end of the Farthing's pistol, or soil his breeches like Dunton?

"Challenge me, Your Grace, if you dare," she whispered. "But you don't have the balls."

His gaze faltered, then he looked away and laughed.

"Waste of bloody time coming here tonight, Francis," he said, clapping his friend on the back. "You don't have the balls to face this fellow in a duel."

He glanced back toward Portia, and she grinned.

Yes, brother. Sometimes the battle is won before a shot is fired.

But while confidence might be the combatant's ultimate weapon, complacency was his, or *her*, greatest danger. And the danger of her identity being revealed still lingered in the air.

She issued a bow toward Sir Heath. "A pleasure," she said.

"Easiest fifty pounds you've ever earned," came the reply.

"Stop grumbling, Moss," Lord Francis said. "If you'd not been caught shagging my wife, there'd have been no need for this."

"Every man and his dog knows Sir Heath is shagging your wife," Dunton said. "Ha! Most likely every man and his dog *is* shagging her."

"Perhaps," Lord Francis said, "but it's not the done thing to make such a public show of it." He gestured toward Portia. "Be off with you, young fellow, before I change my mind," he said. "Be thankful I decided to save your skin. I'd have shot you dead, you know."

Resisting the temptation to point out his lack of prowess, Portia merely placed her hand over her heart and bowed. Then, taking Nerissa's arm, she retreated to the park entrance. When the men were out of sight, they broke into a run.

By the time they reached the townhouse, night had fallen. Under cover of shadows, they slipped through the back entrance, their footsteps clattering on the stairs.

As Portia caught sight of the door to her bedchamber—and safety—she let out a sigh of relief.

Then a deep voice called out from behind.

"Who goes there?"

Her skin tightened in fear, but Nerissa placed a gentle hand on her arm.

"Hush, your ladyship," she whispered. Then she called out, "Mr. Reeve? It's just me, Nerissa."

The butler let out a huff. "Don't try to fool me, girl. I heard more than one set of footsteps. If you've been lying to me, I'll have you horsewhipped—if you're entertaining a man, I'll have you horsewhipped then thrown out on the street. His Grace won't suffer sluts in his house." Heavy footsteps approached.

"It's all right, Reeve," Portia called out. "Nerissa was accompanying me on a visit."

"At this hour?" came the reply. "Most inappropriate."

"You forget your place," Portia said. "I'm not answerable to you."

"Does the master know you've wandering the streets at this hour?"

"Hardly *wandering the streets*, Reeve, and I'll thank you not to take that tone with your mistress. Please have some hot chocolate brought to my chamber. I shall speak to my brother about you when he returns."

For a moment, silence filled the air, then the butler let out a huff and retreated, grumbling to himself, his heavy footsteps receding on the stairs.

"Pompous arse," Portia said. "I cannot think why my brother employs him."

"He served your family for many years," Nerissa said. "Your father and grandfather."

"And his grandfather as well, I'll wager. Perhaps it's time he was put to pasture. Doubtless he believes we've been visiting the docks, giving favors to sailors."

They slipped into Portia's bedchamber and Nerissa placed the fifty pounds on the dressing table, then helped her out of her clothes and into a fresh gown. She folded up the Farthing's garments and placed them at the bottom of a trunk before slipping the trunk under the bed. Then she returned to the dressing table and picked up a hairbrush.

"Come sit here, and let me fix your hair."

"There's no time," Portia said. "You'd best get yourself changed first. If anyone spots you, send them to me and I'll deal with them."

"Even Mr. Reeve?"

"Especially Reeve," Portia said, steering Nerissa toward her dressing room. "Quick, now!"

The maid slipped into the dressing room, closing the door behind her.

Just in time. Heavy, determined footsteps approached and

stopped outside the bedchamber door, then someone knocked smartly, three times.

Portia opened her mouth to call out, then spotted the pound notes on the dressing table. Just as she reached for them, the door opened.

"Reeve, have I not told you before it's most improper to open the door without—"

"I'm sure you have, sister."

She turned, her heart fluttering with apprehension. Her brother stood in the doorway, a cup in his hand, from which wisps of steam rose.

"For you, I believe," he said, holding it up.

She rose, shifting position to conceal the notes, and reached behind her back to pick them up. He arched an eyebrow and lowered his gaze to her hand.

"What's that you have there?"

"Nothing of any concern, Adam."

He stepped inside the chamber. "I know that look," he said.

"What look?"

"That determined look in your eyes. You've been up to mischief."

"Everything I do counts as mischief in your eyes."

He let out a sigh. "Where have you been?"

"Nowhere."

"Reeve caught you on the back stairs with that maid of yours."

"I-I wanted a cup of hot chocolate, so we were on our way to the kitchen."

He tilted his head to one side. "Reeve caught you going *up* the stairs, not down. And he saw you both coming in via the back entrance."

Oh, Lord…

"So," he said, stepping closer, his huge, powerful frame seeming to fill the room, "I'll ask again—where have you been?"

"Have you employed that cockroach of a butler to spy on

me?" she said. But while the actions of the Farthing might intimidate her brother, the actions of a sister over whom he knew he held ultimate power did little to even dent his dominance.

"Do I have reason to?" he said. Then he glanced at the dressing table, and understanding flickered in his cold expression. "Ah, my sister has been creeping about outside like a thief, carrying a pile of money with her. A woman's place—especially a woman of your rank—is in the home."

"What, behind, or perhaps beneath, the man who owns me?"

"Don't be crude," he said. "It doesn't take a fool to work out where you've been."

"Giving favors to sailors at the docks?" she sneered, unable to disguise the tremor in her voice. "Is that what Reeve told you when he gave an account of my whereabouts? There's good money in it. In fact—"

She broke off as he caught her arm and pulled her hard against him. He tightened his grip, and she groaned in pain.

"Don't be a fool," he snarled. "I know exactly what you've been doing. Did you really think you could fool *me?*"

Sweet heaven! He'd recognized her in the park.

"Let me go!" she cried.

"Not until I have satisfaction," he said. "I see I've been too lenient with you, letting you run wild. I knew it would come to this—but you, with your whining and cajoling, sought to persuade me to give you every concession. Do you want to drag our good name into the gutter?"

She shook her head.

"Look at Sawbridge!" he said, his voice heightening in pitch. "He almost destroyed his good name by gallivanting about the park, half drunk—and he's a man! It's a hundred times worse if a *woman* is caught behaving in such a manner. Do you want to ruin yourself?"

"Brother, I—"

The adjoining door burst open and Nerissa rushed in.

"Your Grace, sir!" she cried. "Please don't hurt Lady Portia!"

"Ah, the accomplice," he said coldly. "I ought to have you dismissed."

"Leave her alone!" Portia said. "Nerissa was only acting on my orders. You can't dismiss her for being loyal."

"Her loyalty should be toward *me*, as head of this family. Do you have any idea the danger you're putting yourself in? Dear God Almighty, Portia, even if you care little for your own safety, are you so negligent of your maid's?"

"Brother, I—"

"No!" he interrupted. "I'll not hear another word from your lips. Speak again and I'll have you thrashed and your maid dismissed, and I'll ask Reeve to make sure that she never finds employment anywhere within fifty miles of London."

Portia opened her mouth to respond, then glanced at her maid's face, pale with terror, and closed it again.

"You're not to visit that damned hospital again, do you hear me?" he said.

"The *what*?"

"The hospital. I take it that's where you've been, wandering the streets at the dead of night."

Hardly the dead of night, given that it was barely nine o'clock, but Portia bit her lip and refrained from answering him back.

"It's in a dangerous part of town," he continued. "Anything could happen to you, two women on their own."

"I can take care of myself."

"Dear God, why must you be so belligerent!" he cried. "Of course you can't! No woman can. London's a den of thieves and brigands at the best of times."

"Are you speaking of yourself, brother? Are men like you a danger to women?"

He narrowed his eyes, and she caught a flicker of guilt. "We're not speaking of me, we're speaking of you. I can take care of myself."

"And I can't?" she retorted. "Do you even know what I'm

capable of, whether I can defend myself?"

"You shouldn't have to!" he said. "Don't you see? My responsibility as head of this family is not simply to order you about and tell you what to do—it's to… I…" He paused, his voice breaking, then shook his head. "Portia, do you know what was the one thing that our father made me promise on his deathbed?"

"To maintain the family honor, no doubt."

He blinked, and a sheen of moisture gleamed in his eyes. "No, sister," he said. "He made me promise, above all else, to keep you safe—and happy."

"And do you think I'm happy, Adam?"

He flinched at her use of his name, then he sighed.

"But you're *safe*," he said, taking her hand. "At least, that's what I would have you be."

"I suppose you think I'm dishonoring the family name by enjoying a bit of freedom, that I'm failing you somehow."

"No," he said quietly. "I'm failing *you*." He gestured to the cup. "Drink your chocolate. I take it the money you're attempting to conceal is for that McIver fellow? You know Dr. Lucas thinks him a charlatan."

"It's Dr. Lucas who's the charlatan," Portia said. "Even his daughter thinks so."

"Dear Lord, you're not associating yourself with a doctor's daughter?"

"Miss Lucas volunteers at the hospital. She and I have assisted Dr. McIver on many procedures—not least Captain Broom's wound when it got infected after Dr. Lucas failed to treat it properly."

"Spare me the details of wounded soldiers, Portia. It's bad enough to have to associate oneself with them at all, let alone go out of one's way to visit them in the sickbed."

"Do you vilify the militia because you see in them the courageous man you wish to be thought of?"

He let out a sigh. "I'm not in the mood to spar with you tonight. I've had a trying evening."

"Did Mrs. Scarlet not give satisfaction?"

"If you must know, I was ingratiating that fool Francis, who was ill-minded enough to challenge Sir Heath Moss to a duel, knowing full well that blackguard would turn up."

"What blackguard?"

"That Farthing fellow. So perhaps you understand now why I've no wish to see you wandering about the streets. What if the Farthing accosted you?"

"I'm sure he doesn't go about shooting everyone he meets."

"How would you know? Are you acquainted with him?"

He tilted his head to one side and focused his pale blue gaze on her.

Heavens, why can I not keep my mouth shut?

At length, he shook his head. "I'd suggest the Farthing was Colonel Reid, but he seems too fearful of weapons—unless that's a ruse, of course."

"No," she said. "He *dislikes* guns. His view is that weapons should be used only when necessary, and restricted to the militia. The notion of shooting at another man abhors him."

"A little lily-livered for a soldier. I take it he's not averse to shooting game?"

"He dislikes any form of shooting."

He let out a snort. "It's a wonder he survived Waterloo—unless, of course, he's stretching the truth about his escapades on the battlefield. Perhaps he hid on the sidelines, shivering like a coward while his friends risked their lives."

She drew her arm back and struck his cheek. Stinging pain exploded in her palm with the force of the blow, and he staggered back, knocking into the dressing table. The cup rattled in its saucer before tipping over and falling onto the floor, shattering into shards, splashing hot brown liquid over the carpet.

He rubbed his cheek, a smile curving his lips.

"You're a wildcat when defending your lover, are you not? Ought I to call him out?"

"He's not my…"

She paused as the memory of Stephen's kiss filled her senses—the scent of masculine spices, the soft sweep of his tongue, and the delicious warmth that had spread into her bones, settling in her center, that wicked, secret place she dared not touch.

"I'm only defending a man whose courage you seek to impugn."

"You should take as much care with your honor, Portia." Adam gestured to Nerissa. "You, fetch something to clear up the mess." Portia frowned, and he sighed. "Clear up the mess, *please.*"

Nerissa glanced at Portia.

"It's all right," Portia said. "My brother won't dismiss you—will you, Adam?"

He shook his head, and Nerissa exited the bedchamber. Then he stopped to pick up the shards.

"I suppose I'm partially to blame," he said, setting the pieces on the table.

"Careful, Adam, that came dangerously close to an apology."

"Perhaps there's hope for me yet."

"I wouldn't go *that* far."

He let out a laugh and patted her cheek. She flinched, and a flicker of pain shone in his eyes.

"You think I'd strike you back?" he said. "No matter how badly you behave, I'd never hurt you, Portia. I only act out of wanting what's best for you." He smiled. "I almost envy the man who wins you—he may be beset with many trials, but boredom won't be one of them. If this soldier fellow is the one you've set your cap at, then I'll not object. Ought I to speak to him?"

Portia shook her head. "The last thing I want is you interfering."

"He'll feel the end of my sword if he does anything to dishonor you."

"He's done nothing to dishonor me, Adam. I don't even know if he likes me, at least enough to—"

She broke off, her cheeks warming at the direction of her thoughts.

"I suppose there's worse men to be had," Adam said. "He keeps himself to himself. I can't recall ever seeing him at White's."

"That's something to recommend him, is it not?"

"I find it hard to trust a man incapable of holding his liquor."

"But you don't go to White's merely to drink brandy, do you?" she said. "You go to escape the tyranny of female company and boast about your conquests to your fellow men."

He let out a laugh. "Surely you wouldn't deny me sanctuary from the rest of the world?"

"I would deny you nothing, brother, as long as you do not bring others, or yourself, to harm."

"Then we are of one mind, sister, for that is what I desire for you."

She turned to the dressing mirror and began brushing her hair.

"Perhaps I should give you some respite from your overbearing old brother," he said, an undercurrent of sadness in his voice. "Please assure your maid—"

"Nerissa."

"Yes, Nerissa. Please assure her that her position is safe." He glanced at the notes in her hand. "Would you like me to pass that to Dr. McIver?"

"Really?"

He nodded. "Yes, really. If you wish to help the hospital, then I've no wish to stop you."

She opened her mouth to respond, and he held up his hand.

"I shan't waver in my resolve to forbid you from visiting the hospital at night, but I'll not object to your visiting in the day, provided you take a footman with you. I'm sure James would oblige."

"You mean Charles?"

"James, Charles—it's all the same to me."

"I daresay it is."

"Very well," he said. "Will you be joining me for supper later, or retiring?"

"Are you not visiting Mrs. Scarlet tonight?"

"I prefer the company of my sister."

"Is that because you can bully me, whereas Mrs. Scarlet is free to leave if she tires of you?"

"No, Portia," he said. "Mrs. Scarlet, and her like, will always return when I open my purse. But as for my beloved sister, when you leave, you will never return. Which is as it should be. A wife has a duty to her husband as a sister has to her brother. But it is the brother who must yield in the end, and I therefore wish to enjoy the time we have left before you are no longer in my life. As you must defer to your husband, so must I."

He placed a kiss on her forehead, then opened the door, almost colliding with Nerissa in the doorway.

"Take good care of your mistress," he said. Nerissa bobbed a curtsey, then entered the chamber.

"That was close, your ladyship," she said, placing a cloth on the stain.

"Yes, you almost collided, but he's assured me you'll not be dismissed. And besides, I'd never let him."

"No, I mean in the park," Nerissa said. "I thought His Grace had recognized you. There will come a time when your luck will expire—and then, I fear, so will you. Perhaps it's time to hang up the Farthing's cloak for good."

"How can I help Dr. McIver if I were to do that?"

"Dr. McIver has many benefactors. He'll not think any less of you if you cannot contribute as much as you did before. And I'm sure His Grace would increase your allowance if you asked him. He's a kinder man than most, despite how he appears. He just likes to hide it behind all that sternness."

"Perhaps."

"And besides…" Nerissa paused and looked away.

"Besides what?"

"You may not be able to help Dr. McIver as much if the Farthing ceases to exist. But it's better than the alternative."

"Which is?"

"You'll not be able to help him at all if your dueling gets you killed."

Portia shivered at the memory of the previous duel, when the bullet whistled past her ear. An inch or two to the right and…

No. Do not think about it.

"Perhaps you're right." Portia sighed, staring at her reflection. "Once I come into my fortune, I'll have no need to earn it."

"Provided you have an obliging husband."

"Then I must ensure I marry an obliging man." Portia placed her fingertips on her lips, where Stephen had kissed them. "Very well," she said. "I promise that on my marriage, the Farthing will cease to exist."

"And if you don't find a husband?"

"I promise that once the Season is over, the Farthing will be no more. Lady Portia will restrict her activities to archery."

Nerissa placed a gentle hand on her shoulder. "You swear?"

Portia placed her hand over her maid's and squeezed it. "To please *you*, I swear."

The maid nodded and smiled. Then she picked up the hairbrush. "Shall I fix your hair for supper, Lady Portia?"

"I'm not hungry."

"I'm sure your brother would appreciate your company tonight. He loves you as much as I—more so, even, for he's prepared to treat you harshly to express his love, whereas I—"

"Whereas you cannot, for fear of dismissal?" Portia smiled at her maid. "Nerissa, promise never to leave me. I fear I shan't survive without you taking care of me."

Nerissa's smile disappeared. For a moment, a spark of fear glowed in her dark eyes, then she blinked and nodded. "You must also promise not to leave *me*, Lady Portia."

For a moment, they stared at each other in the mirror, then Nerissa's smile resumed.

"How about some pearls?" she said brightly. "They'll set off the color of your dress delightfully."

Portia nodded, and they settled into a companionable silence while she watched Nerissa's nimble fingers fashion her hair into curls then pin them into place.

I wish to enjoy the time we have left before you are no longer in my life.

As her brother's voice echoed in her mind, a cold hand slid across her heart. What if his words were not a reference to the possibility of her marriage…

…but a death knell?

CHAPTER FOURTEEN

THERE WASN'T A house in England to match the beauty of Rosecombe Park. Not because of the size of the grounds, though they were extensive, but the air of understated elegance and lack of artifice. The road inclined upward toward the main building, which dominated the landscape, stretching from left to right, the red-bricked façade three stories high. What must be at least a hundred windows stared out across the land, all-seeing and ever watching.

It ought to have shrouded the surrounding countryside in an aura of oppression—and, perhaps, like most grand houses, it was most likely designed and constructed with that objective in mind. But this particular building, though grander than any other structure for several miles, instead carried a nurturing air, like a benevolent parent standing guard over the world, harboring pride over everything in its vicinity, ready to nurture and inspire.

Not all grand houses carried such a welcoming air.

But then, not all grand houses had a mistress like the Duchess of Whitcombe, who, like the house that had been her home for two years, stood silently, serenely, in understated attire, waiting to greet her guests.

The carriage drew to a halt beside the main building, and a liveried footman approached and opened the door, placing a block on the ground. He bowed, then stepped back.

"Thank you, Charles," the duchess said, approaching the

carriage. "Colonel Reid, I'm so glad you're come. I was beginning to fear you'd decided to remain in London."

Stephen climbed out of the carriage and bowed. "Forgive me, Duchess, for I was delayed on the road."

"And…your sister?" She peered into the carriage.

"Angela's still in Town."

"She's well, I trust?"

He nodded. "Perfectly so, I thank you. But I decided that she should remain in London."

"What a pity. I was looking forward to seeing her again."

"I fear she's not quite ready for Society. She…she acted a little inappropriately at Vauxhall Gardens."

"And you took it upon yourself to punish her by leaving her behind? I think…" She paused then shook her head. "Forgive me, I spoke out of turn and do not have my husband here to temper my frankness."

"I find much to admire in your frankness, Duchess," he said, smiling. "You say that which others yearn to say, but lack the courage."

She let out a laugh. "That's exactly what Portia said to me this morning when I told Foxton that he was acting as if he were her father, not her brother."

"Is Lady Portia here?" he said, aware of the tightness in his voice.

"Let me take you to her," came the reply. "She was most distracted earlier, and I feared for her success in the archery competition. Then, as soon as we heard the carriage, she confided in me that—" She broke off and shook her head. "I'm doing it again, colonel. My poor husband despairs that I will never become presentable in Society. I never say the right thing."

"That rather depends on one's definition of the *right thing*," Stephen said, fighting the urge to ask her to continue. What had Lady Portia confided to the duchess about? "I prefer honesty over propriety."

"A quality common among your profession, I think. Soldiering requires a degree of honesty that most gentleman lack." She turned to the footman. "Charles, would you see to the colonel's belongings and show him to his room? We'll delay the archery until he joins us."

"Don't wait on my account," Stephen said.

Her lips curved in a smile. "Colonel, my guests—at least *one* guest—would never forgive me if we started without you, unless you wish to join my husband and the rest of the gentlemen? Charles can escort you to the shooting party. My husband has set aside a shotgun for you, a Westley Richards, which, he says, is one of the finest."

At that moment, a crack echoed through the air, and Stephen flinched, fighting the image of the battlefield that rose in his mind.

Then a soft hand touched his arm.

"Or perhaps you might prefer to come to the aid of Earl Hardwick. He's the only gentleman partaking in the archery, and I'm sure he'd appreciate a little male company."

The garden came into view, a vast stretch of green, dotted with trees and shrubs, in a seemingly random formation, yet it gave an air of harmony. Birdsong filled the air, together with the rush of the wind through the trees. Then Stephen caught the sound of voices, punctuated by laughter.

As they turned a corner, Stephen caught sight of the party beside a vast lawn, at the far end of which, three targets had been set up, concentric circles of bright colors that shimmered in the sunlight. Earl Hardwick and his countess sat apart from the others, who stood in various attitudes—some holding teacups, deep in conversation, such as Countess Thorpe and Countess Weston, and others inspecting an array of bows set out on a long table. Stephen caught sight of Lady Trelawney picking up a bow, helped by Miss Whitcombe, before she set it down again.

Where was…*she?*

Then he spotted her. Standing at the end of the table, holding a bow, was Lady Portia. Her hair, swept back in a simple, elegant style, shone in the sunlight, the color of a raven's wing that glimmered with an almost blue sheen. Her eyes, the color of sapphires, were creased into a frown of concentration as she stroked the carved wood of the bow. Her dress, a simple gown of pale blue, was a more muted tone than the silks of the other ladies, but it emphasized the color of her eyes, rendering her the loveliest creature in the garden—nay, the loveliest thing he had ever seen.

He caught his breath and stared at her, drinking in the sight like a man dying in a desert. If only she would remain in that attitude so that he might feast on the sight all day.

Then a male voice called out, "Ah! Come to help me entertain the ladies, Reid?"

Lady Portia stiffened and looked up, and the frown disintegrated, morphing into a smile as her eyes sparkled with delight.

Earl Hardwick, who'd spoken, rose from his seat.

"I thought you might enjoy a little male company, Lord Hardwick," their hostess said. "Ladies, we've another gentleman to entertain us."

After taking Hardwick's hand, Stephen greeted the ladies in turn, until he reached the lone figure at the end of the table.

"Lady Portia."

She took his hand, and he lifted it to his lips.

"You greet me last," she said, an edge to her voice, "even though you had to pass me by to speak to Olivia."

He tempered the little devil in the back of his mind that let out a cheer. Most men would consider jealousy in a woman to be a mark of his virility. But she had no need to be jealous—how could she, when every other woman was nothing to him, compared to her?

"Consider how one eats a fine meal, Lady Portia," he said. "I myself prefer the savory course near the end. Once I have undertaken the duty of tasting the earlier courses—the roasted meats, soup, and some such—I can permit myself to linger on the final course in the knowledge that I am not obliged to move on to the next."

She tilted her head to one side, and her eyes darkened. "Are you likening me to a *cheese straw?*"

"Lady Portia, I meant no offense. I—"

The corner of her mouth twitched into a smile. "I'm rather partial to a cheese straw." She glanced about the garden. "I cannot see your sister."

"Angela is still in London," he said.

"I should have liked to see her again."

"Even after her incivility toward you at Vauxhall Gardens?"

She smiled. "I'm not one to take offense at a little incivility from a young girl—and I'd never forgive myself if I were the reason for your not bringing her with you today."

He took her hand. "Rest assured, you are blameless. I acted out of Angela's benefit. I fear her impetuousness may lead her to harm. She's not ready to attend a house party."

"Then you must permit me to invite her to family supper once we've returned to Town," she said. "And Olivia also, of course. I should like to see Olivia gain a wider acquaintance with those who would not judge her for her birth. Her Season proved something of a disaster, and while Whitcombe seems convinced that she'll make a successful match, I know it pains dear Eleanor to see Olivia being subjected to the spite of others." She nodded toward Miss Whitcombe, who was laughing with Lady Trelawney. "Of course, there's no such danger today—she's in good company."

"The best company," Stephen said, bowing over her hand.

"I feel a little sorry for poor Earl Hardwick," she said.

"How so?"

"For the duration of the morning, he's been the only gentleman among a company of women. A large group of ladies in a social gathering can be a fearsome prospect for a gentleman."

"It depends on the ladies, surely?" he said. "Though I confess surprise at Hardwick's deciding to forgo the shooting. He's an excellent shot, or so I hear."

"He's also an overprotective husband. Lady Hardwick's expecting their fourth child." She lowered her voice to a whisper. "Given the history regarding Hardwick's first wife, he is to be forgiven for wanting to remain by Beatrice's side at all times. He remained in her bedchamber through each confinement—can you credit that?"

"Is that not the definition of love, for a man to act out of character?"

"I doubt Hardwick is acting out of character, but he is acting contrary to what's expected by Society of a man of his rank."

"Is that not the same thing, Lady Portia?"

"For most men in Society, perhaps, yes. But Hardwick possesses something that most men lack."

"Which is?"

"The right sort of character. Whitcombe's the same—the evidence of which is plain to see."

"Evidence?"

She gestured toward their hostess, who was laughing at something Miss Whitcombe was saying, her emerald eyes sparkling in the sunlight.

"I don't believe there's a happier creature on the earth than dear Eleanor."

"Perhaps marriage to a duke makes her happy."

He winced as she slapped him on the arm. "I trust you're jesting, colonel. A woman can make her own happiness rather than rely on a man to give it to her. Though I must admit that a man such as Whitcombe is impossible to ignore."

Stephen tempered the flare of jealousy. "Because he's a duke?"

"Partly," she said. "With the title comes a degree of entitlement and arrogance that renders him impossible to disregard."

"You speak as if you admire him."

"I admire him for loving Eleanor—as I admire Hardwick for loving Beatrice." She let out a sigh. "Your sex often forgets that sometimes, a woman simply wants to be *loved*."

The undercurrent of pain in her voice pierced his heart, and he reached for her hand. A jolt of need rushed through him as their fingers came into contact. Then she colored and withdrew her hand.

"Forgive me, I spoke out of turn again. My brother's always admonishing me for it."

"He's another man who cannot be ignored," Stephen said.

"And there the similarity with Whitcombe and Hardwick ends. I doubt my brother capable of loving *anyone*, let alone the woman he eventually marries." She gestured toward Lord Hardwick, who was staring at his wife with unabashed devotion.

"For an overprotective husband, I confess surprise that Hardwick gave her permission to come here," Stephen said.

Lady Portia laughed. "I'm sure he *thinks* he gave permission. Lady Beatrice is the sort of wife whose duty to her husband can be summed up in a simple fashion."

"Which is?"

"To make him believe that any and all decisions made are his."

Stephen glanced at the sweet-faced countess with the elfin features and delicate porcelain skin. "She doesn't look like a harridan."

"Beatrice is an angel," Lady Portia said. "But just because a woman is mild in looks, that doesn't mean she lacks an iron will."

"I'm beginning to wonder if all women have a will of iron," he said.

"Perhaps we do." She turned the bow over in her hands. "But we must conceal it in order to survive, at least when among those we cannot completely trust."

"And what might it take for a man to earn *your* trust, Lady Portia?"

A faint bloom colored her cheeks. "Perhaps you already have."

He reached for her hand again, anticipating the surge of desire as she curled her fingers around his. "Have I done aught to merit such a reward?"

"A woman can never wholly trust a man until he has given her *his* trust," she said. "We live in a man's world, where the men have all the power—they rule over others, and we women are defined and dictated by the men who own us. Men, therefore, have no need to trust, for in trusting another, they stand to lose more than a woman who has little ownership of her fate."

He lifted her hand to his lips, and her eyes flared with desire.

"Most men believe that women only desire gifts," she continued. "But the truth is that we *all* desire gifts. The mistake men make is that we want material gifts—jewelry, trinkets, pin money. Those are the gifts that are given with the expectation of something in return, such as our obedience, forgiveness, or bodies. The only gift given with no expectation of return, and therefore the only gift that truly comes from the soul, is trust."

Her lips curved into a smile, and he fought the urge to claim them.

"I knew," she whispered, "from that moment in the library that night, that I could trust you."

"The moment in—"

He broke off as he recalled the ball—the night he'd taken sanctuary in Lord Thorpe's library, besieged by the memories of the stench of battle…when an angel had come to him, taken his hand, and delivered him from the brink.

"Portia…"

Her eyes darkened at his use of her name, and she parted her lips. Might he taste them again, capture an illicit kiss while the party were occupied elsewhere?

He raised his eyebrows in a plea, and she again smiled.

"Ladies!" the duchess called out, and he jerked free, his cheeks warming with shame, as if he were a lovestruck adolescent caught ogling an angel. "And gentlemen, of course," the duchess added. "Would you take your places? The first round of the competition is about to begin. Then afterward we'll break for luncheon with the rest of the gentlemen."

Stephen turned to see the competitors lining up, facing the

targets at the far end of the lawn. Lady Portia plucked a bow and quiver from the table and handed them to him. "Shall we?"

"If it pleases you," he replied, with a smile.

They lined up with the rest of the party, ten competitors in total, with their hostess and Lady Hardwick watching.

"Are you not going to join us, Duchess?" Stephen asked.

"I lack the talent for it, colonel," she replied.

"So do I, Your Grace," Hardwick said. "You can take my place if you wish."

"I'm afraid, Lord Hardwick, that my talent at archery is such that those standing behind me are in greater danger of being hit than the target. Besides, do you not want to claim victory for your wife?"

"Here, Augustus," Lady Hardwick said, pulling out a hand-kerchief from her reticule. "Take my favor."

He took it, pressed it to his lips, then slid it into his jacket pocket over his heart.

Such gallantry in most gentlemen was considered merely a gesture, but sincerity shone in Hardwick's eyes. He adored his wife unreservedly.

What must it be like to adore such a woman—and be adored in return?

"Five arrows each," their hostess said. "The four highest scores will compete in the afternoon. In the event of a tie for fourth place, you must each shoot one more arrow, until we have four clear winners."

As it transpired, there was no tie. Lady Portia's bow seemed to be a part of her, and her first four arrows hit the center of the target. When, just before she let her fifth arrow fly, Lady Hardwick sneezed and dropped her teacup, which shattered on the terrace, Lady Portia flinched and shot wide. Laughing at her folly, she offered her shawl to Lady Hardwick then admonished Lord Hardwick for not taking proper care of his wife while she sat outside in the cold. When he apologized, she laughed again, her body shaking with mirth. Then she turned her clear blue gaze on

Stephen and his heart was lost.

"Lady Portia, I distracted you—you must take your final shot again," Lady Hardwick said.

"Absolutely not, Beatrice. The proficient archer should be able to focus entirely on her quarry and conquer any distractions from around her."

"It matters not, anyway," the duchess said. "Lady Portia still scored higher than everyone save Colonel Reid."

Miss Whitcombe approached and linked her arm with her sister-in-law's. "How did you become so proficient with a bow, colonel?"

"My father taught me when I was a boy," Stephen replied, smiling at the memory. "He used to tell me that a true marksman must master two skills."

"Which are?"

"A steady hand and the ability to breathe."

"I'd have thought a true aim would be the most important skill," Miss Whitcombe said. "Is not the ability to see also important? We can all breathe, surely?"

"But you use your whole body to shoot, Olivia," Lady Portia said. "Of course, we need to see to aim in the right direction, but consider *how* we aim—we use our bodies to stand and hold the weapon. Most of us strive to hold the weapon still, but we will never manage such a feat. Our bodies are never completely still. We breathe in and out, and our hearts are always beating. We must therefore steady our breathing—adopt an attitude of calm, lift the bow into position, and let the arrow fly once the position is reached. Only then do we use our sight, and contrary to what most believe, the ability to see clearly can work against us."

"I see!" Miss Whitcombe said, smiling. "Because while we strive to see more clearly, we hesitate, hold our breath, and our bodies grow tense, at which point the game is lost. Which explains why I missed the target each time."

"As did Mrs. McIver," the duchess said. "Archery is more difficult than it looks. Portia, you do us a disservice by making it look easy."

Lady Portia smiled and nodded. "You're very kind, Eleanor. It's not easy, but I've a keen interest in marksmanship. Whilst the technique may be a little different, the skills required to fire a weapon are similar to those required to shoot an arrow. Men call it a sport, but that's because they consider the number of birds they can shoot out of the sky, or the number of gentlemen they can shoot at dawn or dusk, to be a mark of their virility. But it's more of an art form. I have yet to encounter an opponent who…"

Her voice tailed off, and she colored.

"An opponent on the archery field, I trust, Portia," the duchess said. "I trust you don't make a habit of firing a pistol at others."

Lady Portia glanced toward Stephen, a flicker of apprehension in her eyes, then she gestured toward the other ladies. "Who are my competitors to be this afternoon?"

"The colonel, of course," the duchess said, then she gestured to Lady Trelawney and Countess Weston. "And Alice and Lavinia."

"Not Lady Thorpe?" Stephen said, nodding toward a tall woman dressed in dark blue, cascades of rich brown hair tumbling about her shoulders. He'd half expected her to be wearing breeches, given her reputation for engaging in the pursuits of men and despising any activity attributed to ladies.

"Henrietta is a better with a sword than she is at marksmanship," Lady Weston said.

"Whereas you're better, Lav, at climbing up walls when nobody's looking," Lady Thorpe said. She slapped Lady Weston on the back. "Take care, Ellie, lest your guests find themselves a diamond necklace or two lighter come the end of the week. But then, you've been known to act as her accomplice, have you not?"

The duchess colored, and Lady Weston drew an arm about her shoulders. "Be mindful, Hen," she said, "or I'll tell your husband you were climbing trees in the orchard again. Didn't he say he'd discipline you in the sternest manner were he to catch you acting in an unladylike manner this week?"

Lady Thorpe grinned and flicked her tongue out to moisten her lips. "Who's to say I don't relish the particular style of discipline that my Giles doles out?"

Lady Hardwick burst into laughter. "Ah yes, my cousin has a firm hand."

"Delectably so," Lady Thorpe said.

"What do you mean, discipline?" Miss Whitcombe said, her eyes widening. "Does your husband *punish* you?"

The duchess blushed, and Lady Weston took her hand.

"Forgive me, Ellie, I'm speaking out of turn." She turned to Miss Whitcombe. "Olivia, take no notice—I was only jesting. Henrietta and her husband are very much in love, aren't you, Hen?"

Lady Thorpe gave a smile, mischief and satisfaction gleaming in her eyes. Then she met Stephen's gaze and giggled. "Oh dear, I fear I may have shocked your guest, Eleanor. Do forgive us, colonel. I'm afraid our conversation is not for the ears of gentlemen."

"Much as gentlemen's conversation is not for the ears of ladies," Lady Portia said.

"I thought ladies discussed the weather," Stephen said. "Or their accomplishments."

"Oh, we do," Lady Thorpe said. "But our idea of...*accomplishment* may differ from most ladies in Society who confine their conversation to embroidery, music, the cut of their gowns, and their superiority over their rivals."

"I'm afraid you find yourself among misfits here," Lady Portia said. "Dear Eleanor is most particular about whom she invites to her house parties."

"Meaning I'm a misfit?" Stephen said.

"Meaning you possess qualities that set you apart from the rest of Society. Today, colonel, you're an honorary misfit."

"Is it some sort of club for which membership is by invitation?"

"Perhaps!" Lady Weston laughed. "And, in your choice of activity today, we might also declare you to be an honorary lady."

"What's all this?" a deep male voice said, and Stephen looked up to see Portia's brother approaching, followed by the rest of the gentlemen. "Is the colonel turning into the weaker sex?"

"Are you asking if he's turning into a man, brother?" Lady Portia said, an edge to her voice.

"Of course not, sister, but his reluctance to shoot is a trait he shares in common with women."

"Not all women."

"Quite so, Lady Portia," Whitcombe said. He approached his wife, took her hand, and lifted it to his lips. "I've missed you, my love," he whispered. The other gentlemen smiled, save Foxton, who rolled his eyes.

"Lord Hardwick chose to remain with us here," Duchess Whitcombe said, leaning into her husband's touch. "A preference for archery is not exclusive to my sex."

"Ah, but everyone knows Hardwick is in thrall to his wife," Foxton said.

"I say, there's no need for that, old chap," Whitcombe said. "A man who loves his wife is more of a man than one who doesn't, is that not so, gentlemen?"

A murmur of agreement rippled through the men, who dispersed among the ladies, pairing up with their wives to form happy couples.

"Your sister performed remarkably well, Your Grace," their hostess said to Foxton.

"I trust she didn't behave out of turn," he said.

"Lady Portia is perfect in every way. I would not have her any different."

She glanced toward Stephen with that curiously unsettling gaze of hers—dark with intensity, as if she were looking into his soul.

"My sister has much to learn," Foxton said. "But perhaps, given that she was born into nobility, she must uphold higher standards of decorum than those who were not."

"That's enough, Foxton," Whitcombe said, holding his wife close. "I'm afraid you must forgive our friend here. He bagged the fewest of the whole party—even McIver here bested him, and McIver's not fired a gun before." He turned to Lady Portia. "Ma'am, we'd have fared better had you accompanied us in Foxton's stead. Mr. Greaves continues to tell me how much more proficient you are at marksmanship than your brother, though he takes care to say it when your brother's out of earshot for fear of being tossed into a lake again. Men don't like the notion of being bested by a woman—well, some men, at least. Men who believe they have something to prove."

"My love, you mustn't tease our guest," the duchess said. "I'm sure Foxton meant no offense."

To his credit, Foxton colored, and he bowed to her. "Forgive me, Duchess. I fear I'm not at my best today."

The duchess nodded to him, then to the footman in attendance. "Charles, would you have luncheon brought out?" She turned to the party. "It's such a pleasant day, I thought we could have our luncheon outside ahead of the afternoon's competing, unless anyone objects. Beatrice, would you mind?"

"I'd love that," Lady Hardwick said. "And my doctor is at hand should I be in need of him."

Dr. McIver nodded. "Aye, yer ladyship, the air will do ye good." He approached Stephen and offered his hand. "Colonel, a delight to see ye. I take it ye're well? No concerns about"—he glanced about, then lowered his voice—"about the war?"

"Nothing I cannot deal with, Dr. McIver."

"There's no shame in admitting yer fears, lad. Yer injuries from Waterloo are as potent as those suffered by the likes of young Captain Broom, even if they cannot be seen by the untrained eye. There's those among us who know and appreciate that, and will value ye no less for yer struggles."

Stephen glanced across the guests to Lady Portia, who watched them both, a smile on her lips. "Those who display such understanding also deserve to be valued, colonel, do you not think so?"

"Yes," he said, returning her smile. "They deserve to be valued above all others."

The doctor glanced toward Lady Portia, then let out a soft chuckle.

"H-have you seen Captain Broom lately, doctor?" Stephen asked.

"He's returned to Yorkshire," came the reply. "I believe he's to be married in September."

"Then his fiancée didn't abandon him."

"Why would she? What woman in charge of her wits would forsake such a fine lad? He's a hero from Waterloo, and the sort of level-headed young man who'd only fall in love with the right sort of lass. As are ye, colonel."

Stephen shook his head. "I made a fool of myself trotting after Miss Howard—Lady Staines—as is."

"But I'll wager ye've learned from yer mistakes and would now only lose yer heart to the right lass. Or perhaps ye already have. She's as fine a lass as I'd hope for ye."

"Dr. McIver, I've no idea who—"

"Yes, yes," the doctor said, with a chuckle. "It's not the done thing for a man to reveal his heart too often, lest he risk it coming to harm. But ye're a courageous enough lad to know that some risks are worth taking if the reward is yer heart's desire."

Most gentlemen would ridicule such words, for they often spoke them with a desire to flatter and cajole. But Dr. McIver had one quality that set him apart from most of Stephen's acquaintance—he was no gentleman. He had no time in his occupation for the insincerity of thoughtless praise or pretty stories to elicit false hope.

Stephen glanced again toward Lady Portia, who was chatting with Earl and Countess Thorpe. As soon as his gaze fell on her, she stiffened, as if they were connected by an invisible thread, and glanced over her shoulder.

Yes—some risks were worth taking, especially if his heart's desire was before him.

CHAPTER FIFTEEN

LUNCHEON CONCLUDED, AND their hostess made preparations for the afternoon's archery final, issuing instructions to the servants to distribute the targets about the grounds. As Portia took up her bow and quiver, Dr. McIver and his wife approached.

"Talented lass ye are, I'll say," he said, nodding to the bow in her hand. "I was just saying to Mrs. McIver, wasn't I, my love?"

"Aye, ye did, my darling."

"How can you speak of the talent of others when you possess qualities that we can only dream of?" Portia said.

He let out a laugh. "I was privileged enough to have the opportunity to study under the most excellent tutors, Lady Portia, by fortune of my birth and sex."

"I'll grant that a fine education is almost the exclusive province of men whose families can afford it," she said, "but consider what you've done with your education, Dr. McIver—used your education for the good of the world." She gestured about the party. "Compare yourself to the rest of the gentlemen. My brother, for example, who had the benefit of an Oxford education, yet I saw no improvement in the quality of his mind after he returned compared to before. He's supposed to have read mathematics, yet our steward manages the estate's ledgers."

"As do most stewards of great estates, Lady Portia. Yer brother is a gentlemen, after all—and not just any gentleman. He has one of the most exalted titles in the kingdom. Some men are not suited to a life of academia, or a life of business."

"But the value he brings to the world is nothing compared to you, Dr. McIver. Consider the benefits that have arisen from your research on injuries—not only to the body, but the effect that traumatic events can have on the mind. In fact—"

She broke off as she caught sight of Colonel Reid approaching.

"It's an area of research that has long been neglected," Dr. McIver continued, "though Dr. Lucas would disagree with me."

"Dr. Lucas is a charlatan," Portia said. "Even Miss Lucas knows it, though she dares not criticize her father openly. Have you seen her lately?"

"She was at the hospital last week and assisted me in a rather tricky procedure—a young maid whose foot got trapped in the coal cellar. The poor lass, I'll wager her screams could be heard all the way to Aberdeen. Her master dismissed her on the spot, and Dr. Lucas refused to treat her."

"Because, presumably, there was no fee in it," Colonel Reid said, shaking his head. "I wonder at the injustices in the world. What happened to the girl?"

"I treated her myself, of course. I had to remove her foot, poor child. I thank the Almighty that Miss Lucas was there to assist. I'm afraid my nurse fainted when she caught sight of the injury."

"Captain Broom always speaks highly of Miss Lucas," Colonel Reid said. "That is, when he's not extolling Lady Portia's virtues."

"But Euphramia Lucas has a talent for medicine that I lack," Portia said.

"A pity, then, that she's been denied the education her father enjoyed. She'd make a capable doctor."

"Aye, she would," Dr. McIver said. "I teach her what I can, but, of course, I'd need her father's permission to take her as my apprentice. But I have embarked on a small venture that I believe not even Dr. Lucas would prevent her from assisting with."

"Which is?"

"A convalescent institution, where patients can recover until they are well enough to return home."

"Can they not remain in hospital?" Colonel Reid asked.

"There are too many acute cases needing treatment, and the hospital lacks capacity."

"Then they should be sent home."

"Not all patients are as fortunate as Captain Broom, with a loving sweetheart ready to care for him. Take young Tilly, the maid I treated. She must learn to walk again before she can seek employment elsewhere. Her master won't take her back, and she has no family."

"Poor girl," Portia said. "Perhaps I could take her in."

"And what of the hundreds of others I treat, Lady Portia? Ye cannot save everyone."

"Och, let the lass help the wee girl if she's so inclined," Mrs. McIver said. "Ye've still to raise the funds for yer venture, and she'll have nowhere to go until then."

"I've another donation for you, Dr. McIver," Portia said, lowering her voice and glancing toward her brother—but he was engrossed in conversation with their host. "I can send it over as soon as I return to London."

"I'm afraid ye must wait until next month, lass," Dr. McIver said, taking his wife's hand. "My wife and I are taking a vacation in the Highlands. It's almost twenty years to the day that she made me the happiest man alive."

Portia's heart swelled at the love in their eyes as they exchanged a glance. Would she ever experience such a love—a love that lasted for decades?

"Then, with your permission, I'll bring it to you myself on your return and you can tell me all about your vacation," Portia said. "It's fifty pounds. Perhaps it will be sufficient for your venture. And I might have more to give you next month."

"That's too generous of ye, lass. What must yer brother think?"

She linked her arm with his and glanced toward her brother.

"What Adam doesn't know brings him to no harm."

"I wouldn't want ye to deceive yer brother, Lady Portia. He's a fine man. What say ye, colonel?"

Stephen narrowed his eyes. "That it's wrong to conceal the truth."

"Even for a good cause?" Portia asked.

His expression hardened. "No matter the nobility of the objective, I cannot condone any form of deception. To show such a lack of integrity is most reprehensible."

At that moment, Eleanor's voice rang out. "Colonel! We're about to begin. Come choose your bow."

"At your service, Duchess," he said, his smile returning, and approached her.

"I'm afraid ye must excuse me for a moment," Dr. McIver said. "I fear I've taken a little too much of our hostess's fine lemonade." He trotted off toward the building, and Portia linked her arm through Mrs. McIver's.

"Does your husband need to raise a substantial sum to fund his venture?"

"One hundred and fifty pounds will secure the building. We can fund very little of it ourselves. Alastair will insist on treating those who cannot afford to pay, though I love him all the more for it." She turned her adoring gaze on her husband's retreating back and sighed.

"Dr. McIver is fortunate in his choice of wife," Portia said.

"I'm the fortunate one, Lady Portia. Alastair loves me enough to indulge my wish to assist him in his work rather than insist I remain in the home. Marriage is a step into the unknown—we know so little of our prospective partners that uniting ourselves to them for life carries such a risk."

"And that risk is greater for a wife, because she's the one surrendering her body and her freedom to her husband."

"Precisely. We women must ascertain that our prospective partner for life is in possession of a good soul. Of course, I knew Alastair was a man of honor, but nevertheless, he's granted me freedoms that I could never dream of having had I married a gentleman. Though, of course, there are some fine gentlemen here today."

"Eleanor is to be applauded for her choice of guests," Portia said.

"One in particular, perhaps?" Mrs. McIver gave a shy smile. "I trust I've not spoken out of turn."

"Of course not."

"Excellent. In which case, permit me to say that I trust when your time comes, you will choose as wisely for yourself as I did for myself."

"Portia, darling, do join us!" Eleanor called out. "We're ready to begin." She gestured to the man standing beside her in a tweed jacket. "Our gamekeeper James has concealed ten targets in the woodland between here and the line of fir trees in front of the lake. Thank you, James."

"My pleasure, ma'am."

Eleanor continued. "Our footmen are manning each target to keep a tally of your scores. You each have ten arrows, one for each target. If you fire more than one arrow at a target, you forfeit your score for that target. If you deviate from the path, you forfeit the game." She smiled. "After all, deviation from the path risks your being hit by a stray arrow, and I would not send you home injured, even if we are in the company of the finest doctor in the country."

"Who is currently languishing on the privy," Portia's brother said, chuckling. "Oh no—here he comes." He waved to Dr. McIver, who was returning from the building. "Glad you could join us."

"We're fortunate to have Dr. McIver here today," Stephen said, "unless you know how to bandage a wound, Foxton?"

Portia suppressed a laugh. "My brother is hardly capable of dressing himself unaided."

"That's what a valet is for, Portia," Adam said. "I wouldn't sully my hands with—"

"Foxton, that's enough," Whitcombe said, taking Eleanor's hand. "Would you take advantage of my wife's hospitality by teasing the other guests?"

"Certainly not, old boy."

Stephen nodded, then his gaze settled on Portia, and her heart lifted at the warmth in his eyes.

Adam turned to Eleanor. "Forgive me, Duchess. I meant no offense."

"None taken," she said, a smile dancing in her dark-emerald eyes. "It's only possible to take offense if you value the opinion of the alleged offender. You are therefore at liberty to speak freely."

Adam nodded and smiled. Stephen let out a snort, and when Portia met his gaze again, he'd covered his mouth with his hand, and mirth flickered in his eyes.

"When the hour is up," Eleanor continued, "James here will fire a single shot in the air, after which the winner will be declared. Are you all ready? Then begin. And remember, don't stray from the path!"

ELEANOR'S GAMEKEEPER WAS to be commended for his creativity. Out of the first eight targets Portia located, five were as expected—at eye level and approximately fifty yards from the path—but the other three were partially concealed among the rhododendrons.

As for the ninth…

Someone had set it halfway up a tree.

She retrieved an arrow from her quiver and nocked it, then heard a voice from behind.

"That'll require an entirely different technique, given the angle."

She turned to face the owner of the voice. "Colonel Reid, are you following me?"

"Can you not call me Stephen?" he said with a lopsided grin.

"Can you not answer a question with another question?"

He let out a laugh, then gestured to the target. "You'll have to aim higher than you'd expect."

"How much higher?"

"Come, come, Lady Portia, you wouldn't expect any favors from your rival, would you?" He glanced over his shoulder. "You'd best get on with it. I saw Lady Trelawney coming this way."

She gestured to the target. "Then be my guest."

"A gentleman always follows the rule of *ladies first*."

"You know enough of me by now to appreciate that I'm not fond of the rules that gentlemen adopt. Why should you treat me differently because of my sex?"

"Gallantry, of course."

"Which is the man's excuse for restricting a woman's freedom."

Understanding flickered in his eyes, and he nodded, then spoke more softly. "Is your brother overly strict with you?" He gestured in the direction of the main lawn. "Far be it for me to speak out of turn, but I noticed today—"

"You're very kind, colonel."

"*Stephen*, please," he said, moving closer, until she could almost feel the warmth of his body on her skin.

"Stephen," she said, suppressing the little pulse of longing as her tongue curled around his name. "My brother is a little…" She made a random gesture, trying to find the words.

"Overprotective?"

"He has a good heart."

He tilted his head to one side and raised his eyebrows.

"Perhaps not one that is entirely visible to the rest of the world," she continued, "but in his own way, he loves me. He's not the type to tell me openly, of course, for in his eyes that would show weakness. I may not always approve of his methods, but I believe his desire to maintain the unfathomable rules of

Society comes from a wish that I come to no harm."

"Then in that, if in little else, I find myself in agreement with him."

His eyes darkened and he leaned closer. She had only to tilt her face upward, offer her lips for a kiss…

Laughter filtered through the air, followed by animated voices, and she jerked back.

"That's Lady Trelawney," she said. "With Lavinia, by the sound of it. It seems they've teamed up and become a pair."

"Then perhaps you and I should become a pair."

The voices drew near, and Portia tempered the flare of desire at his words, spoken with a low growl.

"If we're of one team, then I suggest we deal with this target as quickly as possible then find the rest," she said, "and you must go first."

"Very well." He smiled, then nocked his arrow, drew back the bow, aimed upward, and let it fly. The arrow hit the inner ring, just shy of the center.

"Not too incompetent," she said, nocking her own arrow. "How many targets have you found so far?" She tilted her body upward until the target came into view.

"Nine, including this one," he said as she let her arrow fly. The arrow sailed upward in an arc, then landed in the center of the target.

A footman stepped out from behind a tree. "Excellent shot, colonel, and Lady Portia. That's two points for you, colonel, and three for the lady."

"How much time is there left?" Portia asked.

"A few minutes, if that," Stephen said, pulling out his pocket watch. "Good man, can you tell us where the last target is?"

"How would he know which target you mean?" Portia said. "They're dotted all over the place."

"I've not been toward the lake yet, so perhaps it's there. Am I right, good man?"

The footman opened his mouth to reply.

"Say nothing that will give him an advantage, I beg you," Portia said. "The colonel is a paragon of honesty, and I would hate for you to be the object of his derision."

Stephen frowned, then let out a sigh. "Very well. I'm going toward the lake."

"Keep to the path, mind," the footman said. Stephen nodded, then offered his arm unsmilingly, and Portia took it.

After they had followed the path far enough for the footman, with luck, to be out of earshot, Portia spoke.

"Forgive me…Stephen, I did not mean to criticize you, and certainly not in front of Eleanor's footman. I meant no offense."

"I cannot say I took no offense."

Her heart sank.

Heavens—did she care so much for his opinion of her? "Then I must apol—"

"The reason I cannot admit to not having taken offense is because such a statement would imply, as our hostess says, that I care nothing for your opinion."

He turned toward her, a gleam of mischief in his eyes, and her heart lifted a little.

"You understood what Eleanor said earlier?"

"The duchess has a rather odd turn of phrase, but rather than fill her sentences with bland niceties that most ladies are fond of, she speaks the absolute truth—even if that truth is not deemed acceptable."

"Eleanor speaks literally, and takes what's said to her in return literally also. She has no time for social niceties. She's the most honest soul I know."

"Oh, I don't know," he said, smiling. "I'll wager there's another lady here today who displays a similar penchant for honesty. You're not afraid to speak up, even if your brother disapproves—or even if *I* disapprove. I take it you find my desire for honesty officious?"

"A little. Is it not better to aspire to goodness?"

"Ah, but I consider honesty and goodness to walk hand in hand."

"But is there not merit in considering the principle—the *spirit*, if you will—of goodness? Honesty and goodness are not mutually exclusive, but where the two come into conflict, then I can see justification for concealing the truth, even molding it a little, while not actively telling a falsehood."

"But do you not understand that even the slightest deception opens the door to falsehood, which may never be closed again? Consider the wounded man who takes a little laudanum, and then a little more because he enjoys the feeling it elicits—and then, after indulging in it over a long period, he finds himself unable to live without it."

She let out a huff. "I know enough about laudanum addiction, colonel, to understand the risks of overdependence."

"Perhaps enough about what Dr. McIver has told you, but I doubt you've seen the effects for yourself."

"What do you think I do when I visit the hospital? Rearrange the flowers?"

At that moment, they entered a clearing and a target came into view, nestled among a holly bush, its concentric rings shining in the sunlight.

"Ah, Eleanor has made the final target easy for her guests," Portia said. "I had wondered if she'd have the last one concealed in the lake."

She reached for her final arrow, and he caught her hand, his long, lean fingers curled about her wrist. Her skin tightened at the sensation of the callouses on his fingers, so unlike the smooth skin of men such as her brother, who'd never known a day's toil. She met his gaze, and her stomach fluttered at the intensity of in his eyes—the faint undertones of pain that still lingered and, no doubt, the guilt that plagued him for having survived the war while his comrades fell about him.

He gestured to the target. "Do you wish to go first?"

She shook her head. "You can."

He took his final arrow, drew back the bow, and let it fly. The arrow sailed in a perfect arc, landing in the center.

"Excellent shot," Portia said, and he flinched. She drew out her final arrow.

"Forgive me for my words earlier," he said. "I'm not trying to impugn your skills or knowledge. I'm only trying to explain the danger of treading the wrong path, even though one might set upon that path with good intentions. If a man attempts to justify his dishonesty, then he clearly wishes to move further along that path."

"Not necessarily," she said, nocking the arrow.

"I disagree. I don't believe anyone to be truly evil, but men do evil things. And the only way to prevent evil is to consider what caused the seed of evil to grow in the man. Even the most reprehensible of men will have, at some point, made a decision that they believed to be justified that set them on the path. Some may even be redeemable."

"So you believe men such as Sir Heath Moss had the capacity for goodness at some point and can be redeemed?"

"Yes, even men such as him. Of course, some men are beyond redemption, whatever Lord Staines may say."

"Lord Staines is a vicar—or at least he was before he inherited the title. It is a vicar's duty to believe every lost soul is capable of redemption."

"I'm sure most are, but some men are beyond it."

"Such as?"

"That Farthing fellow."

Her gut twisted with apprehension at the loathing in his tone, and she gritted her teeth to stem the tremors in her body.

"He's not killed anyone," she said.

He snapped his head around and stared at her, his eyes darkening.

"At least…that's what I've heard. My brother speaks of him."

"He shouldn't discuss such matters with you, Lady Portia."

"Why not? Is it not deception to conceal information?"

"But why should you want to know about such a despicable creature?"

"Perhaps he's just earning a living," she said. "He might use the money he earns for good, to support a family or to help others."

"By risking lives?"

"He might be proficient enough to leave his opponent injured just enough to satisfy everyone's honor, but not so much as to cause permanent damage," she said. "You might argue that he's *saving* lives, not putting them at risk."

"And you think that justifies taking up a weapon and shooting at an innocent man?" he said, his voice rising. "Not only is dueling illegal, it's morally reprehensible. Men who take part in duels do so to satisfy their inflated opinions of themselves, and nothing more. This Farthing fellow is profiteering off that and placing their lives at risk."

"But—"

"No, Lady Portia," he said, his eyes bright with emotion. "He does not deserve our understanding. He deserves our censure, and…"

He hesitated, and the emotion in his eyes turned to hatred.

"He deserves to be hanged."

"Surely such a punishment should be reserved for the very worst crimes imaginable."

"I cannot imagine anything worse than what the Farthing does," he said, his voice almost a snarl. "I would gladly place the noose around his neck myself and see his body dance in agony while he draws his last breath!"

The breath left Portia's body as nausea swelled inside her stomach and she let her arrow fly. It sailed over the top of the target. Her eyes misted with moisture and she blinked. As her vision cleared, Stephen's concerned face swam into view.

"Forgive me. I didn't mean to upset you. Perhaps the footman in attendance will permit you to take the shot again." He tilted his head upward. "Hello there!"

A footman emerged from behind a tree. "Yes, sir?"

"Would you be so kind as to let Lady Portia—"

"There's no need," she said. "The damage has been done."

At that moment, a shot rang out in the distance. Stephen winced and glanced about, fear glazing his eyes.

"No need for alarm, sir," the footman said. "That's the signal for the end of the game." He pulled a notebook out of his pocket and wrote in it, before slipping it back in his pocket. "Shall I escort you back to the lawn for tea? There's strawberries and cream."

"No need," Portia said. "I know the way." She hooked her bow over her shoulder and set off on the path, not bothering to see if Stephen followed.

Before she reached the edge of the woods, she caught sight of Alice and Lavinia. They turned as she approached.

"Portia, darling!" Lavinia said. "Did you find all ten targets? We only found nine."

"Did you see the one hidden among the holly near the lake?"

Alice nodded. "Oh yes, I almost hit the center of that one. And we found the ones hidden in the rhododendrons."

"What about the one up a tree?"

"Up a tree?" Lavinia raised her eyebrows. "Are you jesting?"

"No, it was up that large oak tree in the center of the woods."

"Oh, we walked right past that," Alice said. "I'd have thought you'd have spotted it, Lavinia, given your penchant for climbing." She let out a giggle. "Though, of course, you prefer to climb into people's bedrooms and steal their treasures."

"Only when they deserve to be stolen," Lavinia said. "There's nothing wrong with a little mischief if it's in a good cause, don't you think, Lady Portia?"

Portia glanced over her shoulder in the direction from which she'd come. "Yes," she said. "I certainly do."

"Was Colonel Reid not with you?" Alice asked. "Lavinia and I paired up. We would have asked you to join us, but we thought you'd prefer to make a pair with the colonel."

"No," Portia said quietly, tempering the pinch of sorrow in her heart. "The colonel and I are not a pair."

Nor are we ever likely to be.

CHAPTER SIXTEEN

*H*EAVEN HELP ME, *I've done it again.*

Why did he have to preach at Lady Portia and force his own opinions into the conversation? Most would have interpreted the distress in her eyes when her arrow had shot wide as frustration, her pride being hurt at not being able to best him. But she lacked the pride that most ladies had in abundance. No, her distress was at him trying to emerge victorious in their debate by use of emotion and anger.

And, as any soldier understood, anger and emotion did not win a battle, let alone a war.

But she had not granted him the opportunity to explain himself. When he'd emerged from the woods and rejoined the party, hailed already as the victor by Whitcombe, Lady Portia was nowhere to be seen. Foxton had said something about her being a poor loser, but Duchess Whitcombe had admonished Foxton, expressing concern that Lady Portia has taken too much sun. And, despite the duchess's kind attentions, Stephen couldn't bring himself to enjoy the tea. The strawberries left a sour taste in his mouth that not even being hailed the victor of the day could sweeten.

At dinner, Lady Portia was seated between Whitcombe and Sir Ross Trelawney. Her spirits seemed to have improved, but though she gifted her dining companions with her smiles, she didn't even glance in Stephen's direction.

By the time the gentlemen finished their cigars and brandy and moved to rejoin the ladies, the urge to be close to her and to ease her pain—though he had been the cause of it—had gripped his heart, and as soon as they entered the drawing room, he moved toward her. But she was sitting among a group of ladies and he had no opportunity to be close to her. And though she did not look at him, the fact that she steadfastly focused her attention away from him said that she was as aware of him as he was of her.

Their hostess approached him. "Colonel, I must congratulate you once more on your prowess this afternoon. An almost perfect score, save one target."

"The one in the tree."

"Dear Portia made a perfect shot on that one. Such a pity she missed the final target. But, I suppose, that's the true test of proficiency—one must be consistent in one's accuracy."

"You are a fortunate man indeed, Reid," Whitcombe said, joining them. He took the duchess's hand and lifted it to his lips. "My wife does not bestow her portraiture skills on just anyone. You must make arrangements for your sitting. We can either accommodate you here, or when we return to London."

"Actually, I'd rather not have my portrait painted," Stephen said. The duchess's smile slipped and he caught a flare of hurt in her eyes. "If you'd not mind very much, Duchess, I'd like to gift the prize to my sister. I believe it would benefit her more than I. Angela deserves the best, and perhaps it would atone for my not bringing her with me—if you have no objection?"

She smiled. "None at all."

"And you would benefit from the exchange, for you'd have a far prettier subject for your brush."

"Beauty is not defined by appearance, colonel," she said. "But I applaud your generosity toward your sister. I would be delighted to paint her, and I'm sure Olivia would appreciate seeing her again. Perhaps we could invite her to stay with us for a few days? Just the family, of course—I understand your sensibilities about inviting her to larger parties, though I hear you've hired a chaperone for her."

"There's no need. Angela has a chaperone. A Mrs. Stowe."

"Ha!" a voice cried, and they turned to see Foxton holding a glass that, according to Stephen's count, contained his fifth brandy. "The dowdy widow."

"Foxton, may I offer you coffee?" the duchess said. "I believe we've some strong enough to meet your needs." She deftly plucked the brandy glass from Foxton's hand and smiled, her emerald eyes gleaming with insight. "I find coffee particularly beneficial when the necessity arises to offset the symptoms of overindulgence." She lowered her gaze to the brandy glass, then smiled again. "But—"

"Come, Foxton," Whitcombe interrupted, "our coffee is excellent. Not content with procuring the finest brandy in the land, Trelawney here has expanded his business into coffee."

"I can't abide the stuff," Foxton said. "Give me a brandy any day. Besides, we've yet to toast Reid's success this afternoon." He turned his blue gaze—so like his sister's, save for the lack of warmth—to Stephen and raised an imaginary glass. "I commend you on your victory."

He glanced across the room, toward Lady Portia, who was now looking in their direction.

"You've demonstrated our superiority over the weaker sex and proven what I have believed all along, that women should not engage in pursuits that the Almighty never intended them to partake in. Is that not right, sister?"

Lady Portia colored, then she met Stephen's gaze and her eyes narrowed. But she made no attempt to respond.

Where had that determination—which he so admired in her—gone?

Perhaps you should ask yourself that.

Silencing the little voice whispering in his mind, Stephen turned to Foxton.

"If you must know, Lady Portia outshot me," he said. "That

target up the tree that our hostess mentioned earlier? Your sister hit it dead center, despite the awkward angle. The mark of a true proficient is the ability to succeed in every circumstance—even the most unusual."

"And yet you emerged victorious overall," Foxton said. "The weaker sex will always be defeated in the end."

"It's my fault that I won," Stephen said. "I distracted her on the final target and she shot wide."

Foxton nodded. "Women are easily distracted."

"Yes, brother," a voice said, coldly.

Lady Portia had joined them.

"We're exposed to the tricks of men who distract us into believing that they can be trusted. And when we succumb, you take advantage of us for your own ends." Then she turned to their hostess. "Eleanor, let me assure you that Colonel Reid won the competition fairly. Perhaps it's time for a little music, to distract us from conversations we'd rather not engage in."

"An excellent idea," Countess Weston said, rising. "Alice, if I sing, would you accompany me on the pianoforte?"

"Gladly," Lady Trelawney said. "Anything to spare us a debate on the superiority of the male sex. We ladies are willing to let you gentlemen indulge in your little fantasies, but you've already had a full half-hour in the library to congratulate yourselves on your prowess over brandy and cigars. It's now time to return to the world of reality."

"Lord save me from a woman who speaks for herself," Foxton muttered.

Stephen suppressed a laugh. Foxton might consider himself superior to most, but among the company of intelligent, independently minded women supported by their equally intelligent, appreciative husbands, he lacked the courage to voice his opinions too loudly. Lady Trelawney, despite her outwardly gentle appearance, had a will of iron. She had endured much suffering before her marriage to Trelawney—rumor had it she'd spent some time in an asylum—yet she had emerged stronger because of it, with a devoted partner who understood the demons that plagued her dreams and loved her in spite of, or perhaps even because of, them.

Perhaps there's some hope for me, *after all.*

Stephen's gaze drifted toward Lady Portia, like a boat in a storm seeking safe harbor, the only creature in the world to come close to understanding the demons that plagued him. As if she sensed his gaze, she turned toward him, her eyes gleaming in the candlelight—the color of a deep ocean he longed to plunge into.

Then she turned away.

The music began, and the party focused their attention on the musicians, Lady Trelawney at the pianoforte and Countess Weston singing in Italian. Though the words meant nothing to Stephen, the richness of her voice transcended the language, while Earl Weston looked on with such devotion in his eyes that Stephen's heart ached to see it.

Would he ever experience even a fraction of the love that the husbands and wives here tonight shared?

He spotted Lady Portia approaching the doors. The footman in attendance raised his eyebrows, then quietly opened the doors to let her slip outside. At the threshold she glanced back, her eyes glistening, then she disappeared.

Before the footman could close the door behind her, Stephen followed. Their hostess caught sight of him, but she made no move to stop him. She merely nodded, then resumed her attention on the music.

When Stephen stepped into the corridor, there was no sign of Lady Portia. Perhaps he ought to leave her be, but he couldn't bear the notion of her pain, not when she had gone to such lengths to ease his own pain when he'd been beset by memories of the battlefield. In fact, he'd rather suffer pain himself if it could ease hers…

Sweet heaven—was that not the very definition of love? His admiration she'd long since earned, but on seeing the love shared at Rosecombe, between the duke and duchess and their married guests…

Love in a marriage was a rarity—he'd been brought up from a young age to understand that among his class, the best he could hope for was a companionable regard and mutual respect. But, if nothing else, his visit to Rosecombe had shown him that love in a marriage was not such a rarity that a man should neither hope nor expect it. The happiness in the air tonight showed him that love was there for the taking—it was just a matter of finding the right partner to share that love.

Where are you, Portia…?

He made his way along the corridor, the music fading into the distance, and rounded the corner at the end. Another passageway stretched into the distance, presumably spanning the width of the whole house, lined with thick-framed paintings depicting generations of Whitcombes. About halfway along, he saw her approaching a half-open door.

"Lady Portia."

She froze, then turned to watch him approach, her eyes bright with moisture. "Colonel Reid."

He reached for her hand. For a moment, she began to withdraw, then she relented and let her hand go limp while he drew it to his breast.

"Will you not call me by my name?"

She blinked, and a single tear spilled onto her cheek. He brushed it away with his thumb, and as his skin touched hers, a fizz of need ignited in his blood. Her lips parted and she drew in a sharp breath.

"Stephen," she whispered, "I…" She hesitated as voices came from along the passageway. "I've no wish for anyone to see me like this."

The voices drew nearer, and she slipped through the doorway. Succumbing to impulse, he followed, closing the door behind them.

"Portia, I wanted to apologize for this afternoon," he said. "The last thing I wanted to do was distress you. I—"

"Hush!" she whispered. "Someone's coming."

Footsteps approached, and she leaned toward him, trembling.

"Ask Sarah to have another bedchamber made up, Simon," a voice said in the passageway outside.

"Are you sure, Mr. Jenkins, sir? He's unlikely to wish to stay the night."

"Has his horse been stabled?" the first voice said.

"Sam's said to leave him be for the moment. Lady Star's in season."

"Ah, quite so. The duchess won't appreciate anything happening to her horse. Well, I'm sure Sam knows what's…"

The voices faded, along with the footsteps, and Lady Portia exhaled. Then she stiffened, withdrew from his embrace, and moved toward the center of the room.

Stephen's eyes had adjusted to the darkness, but most of the room was still in shadow, despite the light from the candle on a large mahogany desk at the far end of the room. The flame cast a soft light that, though it failed to reach the corners of the room, illuminated a book on the desk, picking out the gold embossing on the spine. Shadows seemed to shift about in the corner beside the curtains—a trick of the candlelight, perhaps.

"I ought to return," she said. "Eleanor will be wondering where I am."

"The duchess saw me leave the drawing room," Stephen said. "Something in her eyes told me that she knew."

"Knew what?"

"That you were distressed—and I'm the cause."

She shook her head. "I was merely a little out of sorts. Too much sun, perhaps. Dr. McIver's always warning me about the dangers of it."

"What about the dangers of being in the company of a judgmental, sanctimonious arse?"

Her eyes widened, two sapphires glowing in the candlelight, and he took her hand and drew her to him once more.

"Permit me to beg forgiveness for what I said. The very last thing I want is to cause you pain."

"Is that why you followed me here, to apologize?" She let out a bitter laugh. "There's no need. After all, according to your moral compass, I'm the one in the wrong—*you're* the paragon of honesty and integrity."

"Honesty, perhaps, but as to integrity, you are my superior."

"Ah, you're here to flatter," she said. "Have I not said that flattery is akin to an insult, for it's based on the assumption that I'm empty-headed enough to succumb to a few meaningless words?"

"Will you not let me explain myself?" he said. "Don't you now know why I followed you?"

"Pray tell me, colonel," she said, her voice cracking with emotion, "why not bestow some of that honesty you value so much upon me? Why did you risk my reputation by following me here?"

"Heavens, woman, must you be so infuriating?" he said. "I followed you here because I love you!"

Her hand flew to her chest and she drew in a sharp breath.

"You…" She shook her head. "B-but what you said earlier…"

"You think I'm only capable of loving a woman who agrees with everything I say?" He reached toward her and cupped her face. She let out a low groan and closed her eyes, and another tear rolled down her cheek.

"On, Portia, my dear one, I love you not in spite of our differences of opinion, but *because* of them—because you trust me enough to give me your opinion, freely and openly. And dare I begin to hope that your ability to speak freely to me is due to some regard you have for me also?"

Another tear spilled onto her cheek, and he wiped it away with his thumb.

"Stephen, I must tell you—"

"Hush, my love," he whispered, lowering his mouth to hers. "The time for speaking is done."

With a low whimper, she tilted her head up, offering her lips, and he claimed them, tasting, at first, the salt of her tears, before he slipped his tongue between her lips to relish the sweetness within.

A low growl resonated in his chest as his body surged with desire. She shifted against him, and he caught his breath as his manhood strained against his breeches. He shook with the urge to be buried inside her, and closed his eyes, drawing forth the image of her reclining on that mahogany desk, legs parted, skirts around her waist while she welcomed him into her warm, wet—

The door opened with a crash.

"I knew it!" a voice roared. "I bloody *knew* it!"

Stephen broke the kiss and whirled around.

Two men stood in the doorway. The first, Whitcombe, folded his arms and tilted his head to one side. The second stepped into the room, his face twisted with fury.

"Reid, you blackguard! You've ruined my sister! I insist on satisfaction. You will marry her."

"Brother, I—" Portia began.

"Silence!" Foxton roared. "You've done enough. Let another take responsibility for your behavior, for I've failed at every turn to bring you to heel."

"I'm not some dog you can train, Adam."

"Nevertheless, sister, it's time you were put on a leash."

"I've…*we've* done nothing!" Portia said. "I merely came here because I craved solitude, and the colonel followed me. I—Oh!"

She let out a shriek and leaped back as the shadow in the corner moved.

"What the devil…" Stephen trailed off as the shadow morphed into the shape of a man. "You there! What are you doing? Come forward."

The man stepped into the light, revealing a sharply handsome face framed by a thick head of shoulder-length hair. A shiver threaded through Stephen at the soulless expression in the man's deep-set, dark eyes.

"Ah, Devereaux, *there* you are," Whitcombe said. "My butler said you were in the library. Charles must have brought you here instead."

The man inclined his head.

"What the devil were you doing hiding in the shadows?" Stephen said. "Why did you not speak or reveal yourself when Lady Portia and I entered?"

Foxton let out a laugh. "Is that a serious question?" He gestured toward the silent man. "Devereaux hasn't said a word in all the years I've known him."

"Had we not agreed to meet *tomorrow* evening, Devereaux?" Whitcombe said.

The man inclined his head almost imperceptibly.

"Well, you're here now. Why don't you stay the night? I can introduce you to my wife and the rest of our guests. You know Foxton, of course."

Devereaux flinched, then shook his head.

"Ah, Devereaux, old chap," Foxton said, "the women of our acquaintance could learn a thing or two from you—I'm a great advocate for the rule that women should be seen and not heard."

"So you value Mrs. Scarlet for her taciturnity, do you, brother?" Portia said. "I thought you placed great worth on what she can do with her tongue."

Foxton turned to Stephen. "I wish you luck," he said. "You'll not want for fortune, of course—she comes with forty thousand, which should be compensation enough."

"I'm not some commodity you can sell," Portia said. She turned to Devereaux. "Sir, if you possess any honor, I beg you tell my brother what you saw. The colonel and I were not behaving improperly, and I'll not have Eleanor upset by any rumors of scandal in her home."

Devereaux's dark gaze shifted toward her, but he remained silent.

"There'll be no scandal, sister," Foxton said, "because you'll marry this man. I've no qualms about putting you on a carriage to Scotland—bound and gagged, if need be. As for this fellow here…"

He turned to Stephen. "I insist on being satisfied, Reid. Do as I bid, or"—he stepped up close, his eyes cold with fury—"face me at dawn."

CHAPTER SEVENTEEN

*S*WEET HEAVEN—NOT A *duel!*

Portia's stomach cramped with horror. The last thing she wanted was the two men she loved the most in the world risking their lives over her.

Then she caught her breath.

The two men I love the most.

Infuriating as he was, Adam was driven by the need to accomplish what he believed was in her best interests, and she loved him for it.

As for Stephen…

Since when had he secured a place in her heart? Perhaps that was why his intransigence on his views about honesty and integrity gave rise to so much pain—because it meant that he could never accept her in her entirety.

Because it meant that she—or at least that part of her that satisfied her craving for freedom and autonomy over her life— would never be good enough for him.

"Adam, please," she said. "There's no need for—"

"There's every need," her brother said, his eyes gleaming in the candlelight. "And I fail to see why you're so distressed. You set your cap at him—now you can have him."

"Brother!"

"Why deny it? You can trust everyone here. Reid, I'm sure, will concede defeat, and Whitcombe won't engage in gossip for fear of distressing his perfect wife. As for this fellow here"—he gestured to the silent, darkly brooding figure that had materialized from the shadows like a phantom—"Devereaux won't speak a word either way. Bravo, sister—an excellent evening's work."

Stephen turned toward her. "Did you plan this?"

"How dare you make such an accusation!" she said. "Just because our opinions differ on honesty, you think me capable of something so underhand?"

"You defended that Farthing ruffian."

"Ah, the Farthing," Adam said. "Perhaps I'll hire him if you refuse to marry my sister."

"Don't you dare!" Portia cried.

"Then what would you have me do?" her brother said. "Await your ruination?"

"I'd rather be ruined than have a good man forced into marriage with me. Would you condemn us both to a life of misery?"

"And would you condemn yourself to a life of solitude, never to have a home of your own? For heaven's sake, Portia, I—"

"Foxton, perhaps we should let this be," Whitcombe said.

"Would you let it be if it were *your* sister placed in such a compromising situation?"

"No, but Lady Portia is not my sister."

"Quite so, Whitcombe. My sister has a title and respectability of birth that is at risk of being besmirched, whereas yours—"

"If you wish to remain under my roof, Foxton, I'd advise you to stop there," Whitcombe said, a low growl in his voice. "Perhaps we should continue our discussion elsewhere."

"Or we should cease talking altogether, like that fellow there," Portia said, gesturing toward Devereaux. "I'll not be discussed by you, or anyone else. Your Grace, please convey my apologies to Eleanor. It's time I retired."

"Portia, I—"

"You've said enough, colonel," she said, her brother raising his eyebrows at the familiarity of Stephen's address. "In fact, every man of my acquaintance has said more than enough for me to bear tonight."

Before Stephen could respond, she exited the room, closing the door behind her, almost colliding with the butler in the corridor.

"Are you well, Lady Portia?" he said.

"Perfectly so, Mr. Jenkins—at least, I will be now I'm not in the company of men who are no better than beasts."

His face remained impassive, save a slight twitch to the corner of his mouth. "Will you be rejoining the ladies in the drawing room?"

"No, I shall retire."

"Very good. I'll send for your maid."

"Please don't disturb her."

He bowed, then approached the study door, while Portia slipped away. She waited until she reached her chamber before she could succumb to her fury. Angry tears spilled down her cheeks as she removed her gown then fumbled at the laces of her corset. The final lace refused to come undone, and she tugged at it, cursing under her breath as it tore in her hands.

Finally undressed, she flung the corset across the chamber.

Damn him!

She slipped on her night rail, then approached the fireplace. The fire had already been laid, ready for a servant to light it. Doubtless her brother—and Stephen, most likely—thought her incapable of lighting it herself.

I'll show them.

Her gaze fell on a jar at the end of the mantelshelf containing long, thin tapers. She took one and held the tip against the flame of the candle on one of the wall sconces until it ignited. Then, shielding the flame with her hands, she crossed the floor and held the tip at the base of the fire, until the kindling began to glow. Leaning over, she blew gently on the kindling until a small flame sprang into life. Smoke curled upward into the hearth, then disappeared up the chimney.

At least the chimneys at Rosecombe were better swept than

those at Forthridge Park.

When I am mistress of my own home, I'll make sure my housekeeper engages a better sweep.

What had her brother said? *Never to have a home of your own…*

Was that the fate of every woman who stuck to her principles? To live a life without love?

What *was* love? Was it the meeting of like minds and souls, always to be in agreement, of one mind, and blissfully happy? Or was love the recognition and acceptance of those who were different, in both mind and temperament, in challenging one's partner for life and responding to the challenge in return, in order to grow and flourish?

Perhaps that was why the couples gathered together tonight at Rosecombe were so suited to each other, why they were so in love, even after marriage—because they were so different. Eleanor, whom Society had viewed as an oddity—silent, awkward, oddly intense—and Whitcombe were as different as two souls could be, yet no one who knew them could dispute the love they shared. As for Henrietta, the sword-wielding, tomboyish hoyden, and Earl Thorpe, the stickler for propriety, the two seemed such an odd match, yet they, as the other couples here tonight, were different from most of Society in that they genuinely loved each other.

Drawing her shawl about her, Portia settled into the chair beside the fireplace, watching the flames dance and flicker. The soft crackling of the wood and the occasional hiss of coal filled the air like a gentle lullaby, and she leaned back, relishing the warmth on her skin, and closed her eyes. She drew in a deep breath, letting the air fill her lungs, then exhaled, slowly, picturing in the mind her cares drifting away, dissipating in the air.

No matter what trials awaited her in the world, at least here, in her bedchamber, she could relish a moment's respite, drawing strength in the solitude to face the world again.

Footsteps approached—most likely one of the other guests. Beatrice's chamber was next door, and in her delicate state of health, she was likely to retire early, on her husband's insistence if nothing else.

Portia let out a sigh.

So many couples in love…

The footsteps drew near, then stopped outside her chamber door. She opened her eyes and caught sight of a shadow at the foot of the door.

Curse that butler! Doubtless he'd ignored her instructions and, out of a wish to maintain propriety, had disturbed her maid from her supper. Perhaps he believed, as most men did, that she was incapable of dressing and undressing herself.

She rose and approached the door.

"Nerissa, there was no need…" she said, opening the door, then she froze, her voice trailing away.

It wasn't Nerissa.

The man in the doorway stared at her, his eyes darkening, and she caught her breath as her skin tightened with want. A pool of heat swelled in her center, and she curled her hands into fists, digging her fingernails into her palms to stem the tremors in her body.

"Wh-what do you want, *colonel?*"

Stephen's eyes narrowed and a flicker of pain gleaned in their dark depths. "You were distressed."

"And that bothers you how?"

"No, Portia, I…I mean…" He shook his head. "I've made a mess of this, have I not?"

"I thought you stated your position clearly and firmly."

"Yes, but…" He stiffened and glanced over his shoulder, and her stomach fluttered as she heard footsteps. "I'm here to declare myself."

"Have you not already done that?"

"I-I've spoken to your brother."

"I'm very pleased for you both. Could you not wait until morning to speak to me?"

"No, it cannot wait until morning. You see, I…" He colored,

glanced over his shoulder, then lowered his voice. "I-I've agreed to marry you."

A little thrill coursed through her body, settling in her center. Ignoring it, she folded her arms.

"Oh, you have, have you? On pain of a shooting, no doubt."

A smile played on his lips. "Your brother's an insistent man. I shan't say I'd relish having him as a brother-in-law, but I'd rather that than have him as my enemy."

Hurt swelled in her soul, and as he reached for her hand, she drew back.

"And is this how you declare yourself? Not content with accusing me of scheming to entrap you into matrimony, you now tell me that you will succumb to the state on account of not wanting my brother as an enemy?" She let out a snort. "If that's the case, I suggest you marry *him*. He's incapable of making any woman happy, so you'd be doing womankind a favor."

"Don't be—"

"Don't be *what*?" she said, her voice rising. "Ungrateful that you'll slide the parson's noose over your neck to preserve your skin?"

"Of course not," he said. "I thought it's what you wanted. It's what *I* want, Portia. Can't you see that? I've wanted to marry you for a long time. And tonight made me realize as much."

"Well, as my brother says, there's a sizeable dowry in it."

"I'm not marrying you for your dowry, woman!" he said, taking her shoulders. "I'm marrying you because I *love* you!"

"Don't—" she began, but he silenced her with a kiss, claiming her lips with his own. A whimper escaped her as she surrendered, parting her lips as he thrust his tongue inside like a condemned man ready to devour his last meal.

"Oh, Portia, Portia…" he whispered, peppering her face with tiny, open-mouthed kisses that sent a firebolt of desire straight to her center. "I cannot bear the notion of you in pain, and I curse myself for being the one to cause it." He paused and cupped her face in his hands. "I've hurt you today—so many times…"

His voice cracked and he closed his eyes. When he opened them again, they were bright with moisture.

"Your pain is my pain, my love," he whispered. "But I shall spend the rest of my days easing your pain, worshipping you and loving you."

"You cannot love me," she said. "You love your idea of what you wish me to be—and I cannot be that, Stephen."

"Do you think I don't know that?" he said. "Do you think love happens when a man comes face to face with his idea of perfection?" He shook his head. "No, it is what differentiates us that I love—that you and I are willing to challenge each other, to express our differences and to celebrate them. It is that which makes us perfect for each other."

He tilted her chin up and lowered his mouth to hers once more, but before their lips met, a voice called out.

"Quick!" Portia said, pulling him into the chamber and closing the door. "That's Beatrice, and she's with her maid. We can't be seen."

"You don't want Lady Hardwick to see how much I love you?"

She slapped his arm, and he gave an expression of mock hurt.

"You wound me, my darling."

"Hush! I don't want the shock of seeing us in a compromising position bringing on Beatrice's confinement," she said. "Not that she's particularly timid. Henrietta told me that she used to keep a pistol under her pillow." She lowered her voice to a whisper. "She shot her husband once, thinking him an intruder."

"Heavens!" he said. "Am I surrounded by hoydens?"

"Would you prefer timidity in a woman?"

"Certainly not." He approached the door and turned the handle.

"No!" she whispered. "If Beatrice is retiring, her maid will soon follow. You don't want to get caught."

"But I shouldn't stay here, much as I'd like to."

She turned toward him, her cheeks warming at her impending boldness. "Why would you like to stay here?"

He gave a lopsided grin. "There's a warm fire—and I admit the prospect of being harangued by a harridan in the passageway is not my idea of an enjoyable evening."

"As opposed to the harridan in this room?"

He lifted her hand to his lips. "I would never consider you a harridan, Portia."

His tongue flicked out and caressed the back of her hand. A shiver of need rippled through her, and she squeezed her legs together to ease the ache in her center.

How could such a simple touch elicit such wicked sensations?"

He licked his lips, and her stomach fluttered at the raw hunger in his gaze.

"I confess I'm disappointed in you, colonel," she said. A flicker of rejection gleamed in his eyes, and he tried to release her hand but she curled her fingers around his wrist. His pulse beat faintly against the tip of her thumb—his lifeblood, coming from a heart he'd professed as belonging to her.

"H-have I failed you?" he whispered, an undercurrent of vulnerability in his tone.

"I thought you valued absolute honesty above all else," she said, tilting her head sideways in the manner of a coquette. "Do you expect me to believe you when you say you wish to remain here merely because of the warm fire?"

He drew her close, and a thrill coursed through her veins as his hot breath caressed her neck. Then he lowered his head and his hair brushed against her ear.

"Not merely the warm fire, my lady," he said, his voice a low growl, "but the warm body I have in my arms—the body I intend to spend the rest of my life worshipping."

She lowered her gaze to conquer the shame of her wantonness—and the fear of his rejection. "And…tonight?"

"Ohh…" His voice carried undertones of agony as he trembled against her. "Sweet Lord, what have I done to merit such temptation?"

She lifted her gaze. His eyes were closed and his jaw bulged as if he gritted his teeth with restraint.

"Stephen…" she whispered.

"Oh heavens, what you do to me!" he groaned. "What you have always done to me when I hear my name on your lips. If only you knew how I long to hear you cry my name!"

She lifted a hand to his cheek, and he drew in a sharp breath. He placed his hand over hers and exhaled.

"Portia…"

He traced a line along her arm, sending ripples of desire with each touch, the heat of his body seeming to burn through the thin fabric of her nightgown.

A whimper escaped her lips as her body began to pulse faintly, and she shifted closer to him, chasing the delicious sensation.

Heavens, was this what happened when a man seduced a woman? Was this why so many innocents fell to ruin—all for the sake of a single taste of…this?

He traced a line with his fingertips along her throat, then the ripples in her body increased as he followed the neckline of her nightgown. How could a touch be so soft, yet elicit such potent sensations deep inside her body?

Then he slipped his hand inside her nightgown, letting his fingers slide over her breasts. She tilted her head back, drawing in a lungful of air, as her whole body tightened with an unfathomable sensation, wicked in its deliciousness. He cupped one breast, and tears stung her eyes at the tender reverence of his touch, as if he treasured her.

His lips curved into a smile, then he flicked his thumb over her nipple. It hardened to a painful point against his palm, and she let out a low cry. Her breasts grew heavy and warm, and she arched her back, offering them to him, succumbing to her body's instinct to chase the pleasure.

"Stephen!"

At her cry, he withdrew his hand, his cheeks coloring. "Forgive me. I-I cannot do this."

Blushing with shame at her wantonness, Portia folded her arms over her chest. "Go, then," she said, stepping back. "You're under no obligation. I can speak to my brother tomorrow."

"Oh, heavens!" he said. "Do you still believe I don't desire you more than anything—that I don't want to be with you, to make love to you for the rest of my days? I—" He broke off. "I-I cannot take your innocence like this—a stolen moment in another man's house. It's not…"

"Not what?" she said. "Not proper? Perhaps not by Society's standards, but is not admitting our feelings and desires an expression of honesty?"

He blinked, and a sheen of moisture glistened in his eyes. Then he leaned forward and pressed his forehead against hers. His chest rose and fell in a sigh.

"Yes, my love," he said, brushing the tip of his nose against hers, "it's the ultimate expression of honesty."

"Then stay," she said. "If you love me, stay."

He glanced toward the bed, and a thrill of anticipation coursed through her at the flare of need in his eyes.

"Are you certain?"

She nodded. "Yes, Stephen. I have never been more certain."

He lifted his hand to her breast and grazed it with his knuckle, and she let out a low cry as the nipple again hardened, poking hungrily at the fabric.

"Shh…" he whispered. "You must be quiet."

"But—"

He pressed a finger against her lips. "I will stay if you promise not to make a sound—however much you wish to."

She met his gaze, and her soul surrendered at the tenderness in his eyes.

"Yes, my love," she whispered. "I promise."

He brushed his lips against hers, then lifted her into his arms and carried her over to the bed.

"Stephen," she protested, "I can walk."

"Perhaps, but I want to carry you," he whispered. "Always."

He placed her on the bed, then lifted the hem of her nightgown.

"May I?" he whispered.

She nodded, then lifted her arms while he peeled off her nightgown. Her skin tightened in the air, and she shifted her arms in an instinctive move to cover her breasts, but he caught her hand.

"No," he whispered. "You have nothing to fear, nothing to be ashamed of. Let me look at you—at your beautiful body."

"More flattery?"

"No, devotion. Now hush—be still while I show you. Lie back."

He placed a hand on her shoulder and gently pushed her back. For a heartbeat she resisted, then she yielded to his touch and sank onto the bed.

"That's it," he breathed. "Now, let me look at you."

He took her hand and pressed his lips against the center of her palm. His tongue flicked out against her skin, and she drew in a sharp breath.

"Hush," he whispered again. "Not a sound, remember?"

He peppered her hand with featherlight kisses, pressing his lips against each fingertip. Then he took her forefinger into his mouth, caressing its length with his tongue. He curled his tongue around her fingertip, and she suppressed a groan at the little pulse of desire in her center.

"That's it..."

He climbed onto the bed, which shifted under his weight, then placed a hand on her belly, his fingers warm as he caressed her skin, almost with reverence. He traced a path toward her breasts. She held her breath in anticipation of his touch, and her nipples tightened with a delicious ache. The urge to cry out—to beg him to ease the ache—was almost too much to bear, and she arched her back, her breath catching as he lowered his head and she felt his warm breath on her skin.

Then he lowered his head and took her breast in his mouth.

"Mmm!"

Her body jerked upward, and she clamped her lips together to stem her cry at the burst of pleasure that tore through her.

He lifted his head and smiled, his eyes wide and dark with desire. "Good girl."

Sweet heaven! Her body pulsed again at his gentle praise, and she shifted her thighs to ease the growing ache between her legs.

"H-how did you know that—" She broke off, her cheeks warming with shame.

He had done this before—with other women.

"Hush, my love," he said, kissing her breast, his warm breath caressing her skin. "You are the only woman I want—and tonight I give myself to you, wholly and utterly."

He kissed her other breast, drawing it into his mouth, then he flicked out his tongue and traced a path along her body, toward the juncture of her thighs. When he reached the nest of curls at her center, he drew in a long, slow breath.

"Ahh—have you any idea how I've longed to breathe in your scent?" he whispered. "The most delectable scent in the world, and it's for me." He pressed his lips against her curls. "All for me…"

A surge of moisture swelled in her center, but she conquered her shame as his nostrils flared.

"*Only* for me."

The fierceness in his voice held a note of possession, and though her mind warred against it, her body pulsed with longing, aching to be claimed.

Then he parted her thighs, his fingers gentle but insistent, and a rush of shame engulfed her.

Surely he didn't want to look at her…*there*?

She looked up to see him staring at her, his eyes the color of midnight with silver stars pulsing in their depths, as if he were revealing his soul, while she bared her…

"Shh," he whispered. "Do you trust me?"

For a heartbeat she hesitated. Then she nodded, fisting her hands in the bedsheets while he nudged her thighs apart. Then he grew still and lowered his gaze to her thighs. His eyes flared and a slow smile curled on his lips, as if he could devour her with a single look.

"May I?" he breathed.

She nodded, and he flicked his tongue out, running the tip along his lips until they glistened with moisture. Then he parted her thighs further and dipped his head.

She let out a whimper at the tickling sensation as he placed kisses on her skin, his hair brushing against the inside of her thighs. Then he dipped his tongue into her curls. A low groan escaped her, and he stopped, looking up.

"Does it pain you?"

"N-no," she whispered. "I feel only pleasure."

"Ahh—pleasure…" His whispered word brushed over her skin again. Then he dipped his tongue in and caressed her flesh. She bit her lip to stem a cry as pleasure swelled deep inside her, and the wicked moisture between her thighs surged once more.

"No…" she panted. "I-I'm… I mean…down *there*… It's…"

He lifted his head again and fixed his gaze on her.

"Forgive me," she said, her cheeks warming with shame at the slickness between her thighs. "I-I didn't mean to…"

He smiled, then licked his lips.

"Oh, Portia," he breathed. "You have nothing to fear, and nothing to be ashamed of. Your body is only giving me a sign of your pleasure."

"I-it's a sign of *pleasure*?"

He nodded. "Our bodies show nothing but honesty. There's no need for words."

"Stephen, I—"

"No, my love," he said. "Say nothing—listen to your body. It speaks so prettily."

He lowered his head once more then caressed her with his tongue, gently at first, then more insistently, until the tip reached that part of her where the first fizz of pleasure had ignited. As if he knew her body's desires, he circled his tongue around it until a shock of pleasure ignited in her center, sending soft ripples through her body. She gritted her teeth, but could not temper the low groan in her throat.

He kissed her thigh once more, then lifted his head and sat up, a soft smile on his lips.

"Are you ready for me?" he whispered.

"Have we not just…"

"Oh no, my love," he said, shaking his head. "That was the appetizer. Are you ready for the main course?"

"Yes," she whispered. "I'm ready."

He fumbled at the buttons on his breeches, then his manhood sprang free. A pulse of fear threaded through her.

It's so…so big.

He smiled, took his length in his hand, and stroked it—almost as if in pride.

Sweet Lord. Had she just spoken aloud?

He slid his body against hers, and her stomach fluttered in delicious apprehension as she felt him, hard and hot, moving slickly against her flesh. His scent filled her senses—spicy and woody—and she drew in a sharp breath as its potency almost overwhelmed her.

"Yes, my love," he whispered. "Can you not hear my body also, saying that he is ready for you?"

"He?"

His eyes glittered with desire. "He is here to serve you, worship you, if you'll welcome him."

"I…" She caught her breath, and the world shifted out of focus. "Wha… What's happening?"

He grew still. "I have no desire for you do to anything unwillingly, Portia," he said. "I can wait—a lifetime if I must—until you're ready. For I fear it will hurt you."

"H-hurt me?"

"The first time," he said. "Only the first."

"Did your first time hurt?"

He shook his head. "Only the woman feels pain the first time—but afterward, there will be no pain."

She fought to dispel the images from her mind of his lying with other women. But had she really expected him to be different from other men?

He placed his hand on her cheek and brushed his lips against hers. "The only woman I want to lie with is you," he said, "but I'll not take you if you're not certain."

She hesitated, as two paths stretched before her. Then she stepped onto the path leading to happiness.

"I am certain, Stephen," she whispered, nodding. "I *love* you."

His nostrils flared at her words, and a sheen of moisture glistened in his eyes.

"Sweet Lord," he whispered, "what have I done to deserve you?"

He shifted his body, then thrust forward, and she suppressed a whimper at the sharp sting.

He leaned against her, trembling, his breath coming in short, shallow pants.

"D-did I give you pain?"

"Only a little."

"My sweet, brave girl." He kissed the tip of her nose, then remained still while her body stretched around him and the pain began to ease to a delicious ache that held the promise of pleasure.

Then he moved, slowly at first, and her body pulsed with pleasure at the delicious sensations that ignited the flame flickering in her center.

"Oh!"

"Hush, my love," he whispered, his breath hot against her cheek. "Not a sound, remember?"

She clamped her lips together, battling the urge to cry out. With each movement, the flame swelled, and a low groan reverberated in her chest as he quickened the pace.

Then the flame ignited and her body disintegrated as waves of pleasure tore through her. She threw back her head, drawing in a lungful of air. Unable to suppress the cry, she parted her lips, his name filling her mind until nothing else existed in the world—only him.

"Ste—"

He plunged into her once more and silenced her cry with his mouth, thrusting his tongue in, mirroring the actions of his body to mark her as his. Her cries were joined by a deep groan coming from the man inside her. He shuddered while she writhed beneath him, chasing the pleasure. Setting aside all shame at her wantonness, she parted her legs further, then wrapped them around his body, drawing him in deeper.

A primal growl escaped his lips, and he nipped her earlobe, a beast laying claim to his mate. Such baseness—such wicked wantonness—and yet she could never have imagined such pleasure could exist.

Holding her close, he shifted onto his side, still inside her, their bodies entwined as if they were a single creature. She curled into his embrace, nestling her head against his chest until she could hear his heartbeat, thick and strong.

A heart that belonged to her.

He caressed her hair, entwining his fingers through her tresses while she relished the warmth of his body and the tiny pulses of pleasure in her center.

If only they could lie together in that attitude forever! The world outside mattered not compared to the man who cradled her in his arms as if she were the most precious thing on earth.

"Portia," he whispered.

"Mmm?" she murmured, unwilling to open her eyes.

"There's something I ought to have asked you."

She smiled. "Isn't it a little late for that? You're already in my bed."

"No, something else."

She opened her eyes, and her heart fluttered at the expression in his eyes, the rawness, as if he were baring his soul.

"Lady Portia, will you do me the honor of becoming my wife? I…" His voice faltered and he inhaled and continued. "Forgive me for not asking as you deserved to be asked. But I ask now—will you marry me?"

"Well…" She tilted her head to one side and frowned.

His forehead creased, and his eyes filled with apprehension. Then she smiled.

"Given that you're still inside me," she said, feeling her cheeks warm at such unseemly language, "it really would be rude to refuse, would it not?"

He laughed, softly, then kissed her. "Not the most conventional of responses, but then, you're not the most conventional of women. Perhaps that's why I love you. Would my fiancée permit me to hold her for a moment and bask in my good fortune?"

She closed her eyes once more, lulled by his heartbeat, until she drifted into a doze.

When she woke, he was sitting on the edge of the bed pulling his breeches on.

"Colonel, am I to be insulted that you leave my bed so soon?"

He turned and smiled. "Much as I wish to remain in bed with you all night, I must at least give the appearance of propriety to prevent your brother from horsewhipping me in the courtyard."

"Is there any likelihood of that?"

He straightened his stance and pursed his lips. Then he lowered his voice to a deep growl, made an exaggerated gesture, and spoke.

"Make the slightest attempt to dishonor my sister and I'll feed you to Whitcombe's dogs, then have you stripped naked, carried into the center of the village and horsewhipped for the entertainment of all."

"Is that supposed to be my brother?" she said, suppressing a giggle.

He nodded. "Foxton is many things, but one aspect of him that I admire is his determination to do right by you."

She let out a snort. "Pity, then, that his and my idea of what's *right* seldom coincide."

"Ought I be insulted?"

"Perhaps this once instance is the exception to the rule," she said.

"Which is why I must ensure that we're not caught in the morning." He leaned toward her to place a swift kiss on her lips. "But tomorrow at breakfast, I shall announce to the party that we are to wed—if my future wife consents, of course."

She nodded, and he kissed her again. Then he exited the chamber, pausing at the door to blow a kiss in her direction before slipping outside, closing it softly behind him.

She lay back, squeezing her thighs together to relive the delicious sensations he'd elicited. Then she drew the bedcovers over herself and turned onto her side, watching the flames of the fire while they danced and crackled.

My future wife…

To think! She finally understood what made her friends—Eleanor, Henrietta, and many others—so blissfully happy.

And tomorrow she would witness their joy on knowing that such happiness awaited her.

CHAPTER EIGHTEEN

Portia woke to the familiar sound of her maid bustling about the bedchamber—the rustle of clothes being set out ready to dress her with, and the delicate chink of bottles being moved on the dressing table.

Nerissa had the innate ability to know precisely when Portia woke and how to rouse her from her sleep with the minimum amount of violence. While Portia lay on the bed, the sounds grew a little louder—footsteps crossing the floor, then the swish of the curtains being pulled back.

She opened her eyes, then drew in a long, languorous breath, stretched her arms, and rolled over, letting out a sigh as she found a cool spot on the pillow. The delicious dream from last night caressed her mind—when her lover had brought her to pleasure, whispering sweet words of love.

Then she caught her breath.

It hadn't been a dream…

She sat up, exhaling sharply. The young woman silhouetted against the window turned.

"Lady Portia! Forgive me—did I wake you?"

Portia shook her head. "No, Nerissa."

"Are you certain? You sound a little pained."

Only the woman feels pain the first time—but afterward, there will be no pain…

She squeezed her legs together, and her cheeks warmed with

shame at the soreness between them—the memory of last night…

…the image of his head between her thighs while he delivered the most exquisite pleasure…

Oh!

"Lady Portia?" Nerissa's concerned face swam into view. "Perhaps you'd prefer to sleep a little longer before I dress you? It's early yet, and I'm sure the duchess will take no offense if you arrive for breakfast a little late."

Tomorrow at breakfast, I shall announce to the party that we are to wed…

Her heart soaring with joy, Portia pulled back the covers.

"No, Nerissa, I mustn't be late for breakfast."

"The duchess won't mind," Nerissa said, retrieving a pair of stockings from Portia's trunk. "She's ever so kind. Did you know that she insisted on the guests' maids and valets having a special dinner last night? And she came to visit us while we were eating. She said that there was no reason not to treat us as her guests. She's not at all what I expected of her. But then, perhaps you know that yourself if you're her friend."

Nerissa rattled on, extolling Eleanor's virtues while Portia approached the dressing table. Then she stopped and let out a cry.

"Oh, Lady Portia! Forgive me. I didn't bring any cloths for you."

"Why should you?" Portia said. "It's not my…" Her voice trailed away as she lowered her gaze to her nightgown—and the patch of red staining the fabric.

"Have you injured yourself?" Nerissa asked, reaching for Portia's nightgown. "Perhaps yesterday, or last night, or…"

She hesitated, then lifted her gaze, and Portia felt her cheeks warm with shame as a flicker of understanding shone in her maid's eyes.

"L-Lady Portia?"

"Colonel Reid and I are engaged," Portia said, flinching as she braced herself for her maid's censure.

"A-and you…"

Portia bit her lip.

"Did he…?" Nerissa colored and gestured toward Portia's nightgown.

"He visited me last night."

The maid frowned. "It's not my place to say such things, but I'm disappointed in him—compromising you while you're guests of the duchess."

"I was willing," Portia said. "H-he only came to ask me to marry him…b-but I asked him to stay. He's going to announce our engagement today. So you see, I've done nothing wrong."

"Of course not—*you* could never do wrong. But you wouldn't want everyone here to…" Nerissa tilted her head to one side. "I'll see to your nightgown, so nobody need know."

"Y-you won't tell my brother?"

"Not if the colonel does right by you, Lady Portia," Nerissa replied with a grin. "But if he does not, I'll see to him myself. After all, the Farthing isn't the only marksman capable of teaching a dishonorable man a lesson. Gerard can wield a pistol almost as well."

"The colonel is a man of honor," Portia said.

"Then let him prove his worth at breakfast."

Portia stood obediently while her maid removed the nightgown, folded it, and tucked it into the bottom of the trunk, only feeling a moment's shame when Nerissa helped her to wash, removing the smear on her mistress's legs with her usual soothing touch, remarking in a soft voice that a woman only bled the first time.

By the time Portia stepped out of the bedchamber in a fresh gown, her hair fashioned into a neat chignon and dotted with daisies, her apprehension had faded.

Perhaps Eleanor's house was the best place to have given herself to Stephen—and to announce their engagement. For they were among friends, and half a day's ride from London Society and all its judgment of those who placed love over propriety.

When Stephen announced their engagement, their friends would express genuine pleasure and celebrate their love.

Her head held high, she strode toward the breakfast room, and the murmur of chatter interspersed with the laughter of her friends. As she entered, the chatter stopped and Eleanor rose to greet her. Portia cast her gaze about the breakfast table—to the empty space between Henrietta and Beatrice.

Where was he?

A knot of apprehension twisted in her stomach and she glanced across the table toward her brother.

"Is the colonel not joining us for breakfast?" she said, flinching inwardly at the tightness in her voice.

"The poor colonel was called away urgently last night," Eleanor said. "Is that not right, my love?"

Whitcombe nodded. "A messenger from London arrived shortly after dawn," he said. "He's downstairs now, taking tea while my man's tending to his horse."

"And…the colonel?" Portia said, aware of her brother's dark gaze on her.

"He left shortly after receiving the message," Whitcombe replied. "My valet attended him and he asked him to convey his regrets and to say that he hoped to see us all again in London."

"Did he say—"

"He said he'd pay us a visit," Adam interrupted, and when she met his gaze, he nodded, his expression softening, as if conveying his reassurance.

Have no fear, sister.

"It's all rather mysterious," Lord Hardwick said, reaching for his teacup. "Dashing off in the middle of the night. What is he running to?" He let out a chuckle. "Or from? Soldiers retreat as well as advance, do they not?"

"I fear the weather will not be kind for the journey back to London," Eleanor said. "Lord Hardwick, are you returning to London or will you be taking Beatrice directly back to Hardwick Hall?"

Hardwick tilted his head and raised his eyebrows in question. "Duchess?"

"You wouldn't want dear Beatrice to endure more carriage rides than necessary," Eleanor continued. Then she turned to Whitcombe and smiled. "Do you not recall, Monty, how our carriage went into a rut and you feared it would bring about my confinement there and then?" She turned her attention to the rest of the guests. "My poor husband not only feared that he'd be present at the birth, but that he'd be forced to deliver the child himself!"

A ripple of laughter threaded through the guests, and the conversation turned to the hazards of riding a carriage on poorly maintained roads. Eleanor met Portia's gaze, and Portia dipped her head in a nod.

Thank you, she mouthed.

How Eleanor had understood Portia's distress was a mystery—as were so many aspects of Eleanor's insight. There was little point in attempting to understand her ability to look deep inside a person's soul, but every reason to be thankful for it.

As the party gathered at the front of the building to say their goodbyes, Eleanor approached Portia and linked her arm through hers.

"He really was called away," she said, lowering her voice. "Monty's valet said he was most agitated, and he particularly wanted to convey his regrets to you and say that he'll call on you as soon as he settles his business in London."

"How did you…?"

"Know that he's in love with you?" Eleanor said with a smile. "By the way he looks at you, and"—she glanced toward Adam, who was issuing orders to the footmen placing their trunks on the back of their carriage—"by the way your brother looks at him. Mark my words, when you return to London, you'll find a message awaiting you—either that, or you'll find the colonel waiting on your doorstep, begging forgiveness."

I hope so…

"I *know* so," Eleanor said, with a smile, as if she'd read Portia's mind. "Have no fear, it's only three hours to London—less than that if your brother hurries your driver, and I suspect he will. I'm sure you can wait that long. After all, you've waited your entire life to find the one man capable of deserving you."

"Are you coming, sister?" Adam said, approaching. He took Eleanor's hand and kissed it. "Duchess, a pleasure, as always, but I trust you'll understand my eagerness to return to London."

"I understand it perfectly, Foxton," Eleanor said.

He offered his hand. "Sister, shall we?"

Portia took it and let him lead her into the carriage. After it had set off and Rosecombe was no longer in sight, he spoke.

"Reid's agreed to marry you."

"I know."

He arched an eyebrow and tilted his head to one side. "How…?" Then he shook his head. "Best not to say, lest I find I'm obliged to face him at dawn."

Portia leaned toward the window, letting the air cool her cheeks. Then she startled as her brother took her hand.

"I only want what's best for you, Portia," he said, his voice wavering. "I know I can be harsh—but it's because I want to see you happy. I want you to enjoy happiness in marriage without the burden of duty." He hesitated, then averted his gaze. "It's something I shall never have, but I'll be content knowing that you will."

He squeezed her hand, then patted it and released it, leaning back.

"Let us hope the duchess is proven wrong and that we have fine weather on the way home. We can stop off at the Crown for luncheon if you wish, or we can return home directly. Mrs. Winston promised to have luncheon waiting on our return. I wouldn't want her to have made such an effort in vain."

"Who is this man I see before me?" Portia said. "He looks like my brother, and sounds like my brother, but does not utter the words of Adam Hawke, Duke of Foxton."

"Or perhaps he does, even if it's for the first time."

His expression softened for a moment, as if he'd opened a shutter to gift her with a glimpse of his soul. Then he blinked and the shutters closed—once more, the cold duke sat before her.

"I'm a little tired," he said. "Wake me when we reach Dorking, if you wish to stop." Then he leaned back and closed his eyes.

The hard edge to his voice had returned, but the glimpse of a tender heart beneath gave her hope that whatever might befall her, her brother loved her, even if he could hardly bear to admit it to himself. And if that tiny glimpse of love was all he could find in his heart to gift her with, then she'd cherish it.

CHAPTER NINETEEN

PORTIA JOLTED AWAKE as the carriage drew to a halt. Her brother exited the carriage then helped her out, steadying her as she caught her foot on the step.

She cast her gaze over the white-fronted façade of Number Eight St. James's Square, then she approached the open door, where the butler stood waiting.

"Welcome home, Your Grace, Lady Portia," he said. Then he barked orders to the footmen as they helped Nerissa down from her seat. "Do you require luncheon, Your Grace?"

Adam pulled out his pocket watch and opened it. "Have it ready in half an hour, would you, Reeve?"

"Very good, sir."

"Are there any messages for me, Reeve?" Portia asked.

The butler turned his pale gaze on her, then shook his head.

"None at all?"

"There's a message for your maid."

"For me, Mr. Reeve?" Nerissa asked as she approached the steps leading to the basement.

"Your brother delivered it not half an hour ago," he said. "Knocked on the kitchen with much insistence. Most unbecoming."

"Surely there's no harm in Nerissa receiving a message from her brother?" Portia said, eyeing the butler with dislike. "I can understand how his knocking on the *front* door might send you into a fit of apoplexy, but—"

"Portia, perhaps you might freshen up for luncheon," her brother interrupted. "It was rather hot in the carriage, and the road's always so dusty." He gestured to the butler. "I'll take a brandy in my study, Reeve, and Lady Portia will have some tea."

"Very good, sir." The butler bowed, then stepped aside while Adam escorted her through the doorway.

"I can't think why you continue to employ him, brother," Portia said. "He's insufferably rude."

"His family has served ours for five generations. Would you reward his loyalty by insisting I dismiss him?"

"I'm not questioning his loyalty," Portia said. "But has nobody told him that it's possible to be both loyal and kind?"

"He merely wishes to observe propriety, which is his duty as butler."

Recognizing the belligerence that rendered any argument futile, Portia nodded and climbed the stairs, making her way to her bedchamber. By the time she reached it, her maid was already there, unpacking her trunk.

"I swear, Nerissa, you must be capable of flying."

Nerissa smiled, then slipped across the chamber, closed the door, and pulled out a slip of paper from her pocket.

Portia's heart lifted with hope. "The message," she said. "Is it from Stephen?"

Nerissa raised her eyebrows at the familiarity of Portia's address, then shook her head. "It's truly from my brother," she whispered. "Mr. Grimes has given him another instruction for the Farthing."

Portia reached for the note, then hesitated. Hadn't she resolved never to deceive again?

"I can tell him that the Farthing has decided to hang up his cloak and mask," Nerissa said. "Sir Heath will just have to find another proxy—or fight his own battles." She grinned. "Perhaps that'll make him think twice before compromising another man's wife. And, of course, you cannot keep up the masquerade after you're married."

"Are you about to tell me that I must, from now on, remain quietly in the home awaiting my husband's orders?" Portia said.

Nerissa shook her head. "I wouldn't dream of it. But the colonel loves you—it's plain to see—and you love him, do you not? He wouldn't want to see you placing yourself in danger unnecessarily. And you know he'll give you as much freedom as you want, not only with your fortune, but with your person and your life. He'll not stifle you in a cage."

Nerissa was right—her wisdom belied her years, though perhaps her status below stairs meant that she witnessed more of life than Portia ever could.

But there was no denying the little rush of satisfaction from knowing that someone, a man who considered himself a ruler of the world, sought Portia's skills enough to pay for them.

And one more outing as the Farthing couldn't hurt.

Could it?

"Very well," Portia said. "But this is to be the last time. Tell your brother to instruct Mr. Grimes as usual, but from then on, he'll have to find another marksman to fight Sir Heath's duels for him." She grinned. "If this is to be my final outing, then I must make it worth the effort. Tell him to instruct Sir Heath that the Farthing's fee is one hundred pounds."

"He'll likely refuse."

"Then he must face the consequences—or, at least, the end of his opponent's pistol," Portia said. "Tell him one hundred pounds, and nothing less. I can spend the rest of the summer resting easy that Dr. McIver has sufficient funds for his venture. Then, when I'm married, I can resume my donations and nobody will be the wiser. When is the duel to take place?"

"Dawn, tomorrow," Nerissa said. "Hyde Park, the usual spot."

"And Sir Heath's opponent?"

"He didn't say."

"Very well," Portia said. "Now go, and let me know if Sir

Heath accepts the Farthing's terms."

"But Mr. Reeve…"

"I'll see to Reeve," Portia said. "Heavens! At least when I'm married, neither of us will have to deal with that pompous arse."

Nerissa let out a giggle, then slipped out of the bedchamber, while Portia finished fixing her hair. Her brother would just have to cope with her not having changed her gown for luncheon. Not that he'd notice—no doubt now he'd returned to London, his attention would have turned to the sparkling Mrs. Scarlet and how she'd keep him occupied tonight.

All the better to enable me to slip out unnoticed.

She approached the trunk tucked away in the corner and lifted the lid. Then she plucked the item from the top and held it up, running her fingertips along the ribbons and across the black silk. The gong sounded for luncheon, and she dropped the mask back into the trunk and closed it.

One more time…

As Portia anticipated, her brother didn't notice her apparel at luncheon, though he made a cursory remark about her not having arrived on time. And, as predicted, as the light faded and the day slipped into evening, he informed her that he was dining at his club and would see her at breakfast tomorrow. She hadn't the heart to needle him over his obvious falsehood—he was wearing a necktie that Mrs. Scarlet had gifted him, most likely to flatter her into ensuring he had a pleasurable evening.

A little pulse throbbed in her center at the notion of pleasure, and she met her brother's gaze, basking in the warmth of the memory.

To think, brother, I've done what you have—experienced pleasure. I am no longer a child, or your younger sister, I'm—

"Portia, is anything the matter?"

She shook her head. "No, brother. Have a pleasant evening."

Rather than continue to interview her, he nodded, then placed his hand against her cheek.

"All will be well, I assure you," he said. "If Reid hasn't called on us by tomorrow, I shall break down his door myself. Or…" He hesitated. "Would you prefer it if I didn't go out tonight?"

She shook her head. "No, brother, I would not deny you the pleasure."

He patted her cheek. "I confess I shall miss you when you're married. I trust you'll not forget your bad-tempered older brother."

"How could anyone forget *you*, Adam?"

He let out a laugh. "I'd wish you luck, but I rather think it's Reid who'll be in need of it."

"Anyone marrying into our family will need luck on their side, brother."

He smiled, then took his leave. His orders echoed through the house until the front door opened and closed behind him.

Rather then disturb the staff, Portia chose to take supper in her bedchamber while Nerissa set out the Farthing's and Gerard's attire. That way she could refrain from taking any wine without Reeve noticing. Doubtless the butler viewed a woman who spoke her mind as akin to a harpy—one who deserved to be bound and gagged until she learned her place.

By the time she slid into bed, her body seemed to thrum with excitement. Not the usual sense of anticipation that beset her on the eve of a duel, but something more—a sense of having reached a pinnacle, the completion of her quest, in knowing that this duel was to be her last.

As she rose an hour before dawn, Nerissa already moving about her chamber, a sense of completion filled her soul. Rather than regret not being able to continue as the Farthing, she felt a sense of relief.

I'm ready to bid you goodbye.

"Beg pardon, Lady Portia?"

"I realize that I don't mind giving all this up as much as I expected," Portia said, holding up the mask.

"It's only natural," Nerissa said. "You're different now you've..." She blushed and averted her gaze. "I-I mean...everyone changes. Our wants and needs change. You're about to embark on a new life—one that will give you new freedoms and challenges. And you are doing the right thing by stepping toward that life with the determination to succeed."

Portia laughed softly. "Since when did you become so wise, Nerissa? Or is it that I've only noticed it today?"

Nerissa blushed, plucked the Farthing's tricorn hat out of the trunk, and brushed it.

"Perhaps it is I who has changed," Portia said. "I'm more willing to heed the counsel of others rather than assume I know the best course of action."

She crossed the floor and glanced out of the window. Through the thin mist, she could discern a diffused light—fingers of pale blue stretching across the sky. Birdsong filled the air, the first rush that came as the birds, having woken, began their day by asserting ownership of their territories and calling to prospective mates.

"It's going to be a hot day," Nerissa said.

"Yes, and by the time the sun has risen, the Farthing will be no more."

The mist had almost completely dissipated by the time Portia entered the park, Nerissa at her side. The crunch of their boots on the gravel echoed across the park. But there wouldn't be anybody about to hear, save Sir Heath, his opponent, and their seconds. Anyone else wandering about at this hour was unlikely to wish to be seen—ruffians meeting to trade items obtained through nefarious means, illicit lovers conducting clandestine liaisons among the rhododendrons...

Portia smiled to herself. To think, at last, she understood not only what activities those illicit lovers engaged in, but why. Such wonderful, wicked pleasures were hers for the taking.

Now he's changed me forever—from a girl into a woman.

Then the little voice of doubt slithered into her mind.

Why has he not called?

"There you are!"

A sharp voice cut through the haze in her mind, and Sir Heath Moss appeared before her. Beside him stood his second, and Portia recognized Lord Maybury.

A lone man stood a little way back, beneath a tree, his features in shadow.

Sir Heath's opponent—but where was his second?

"It's about bloody time," Sir Heath said.

"We're here at the appointed hour, Sir Heath," Nerissa said, lowering the pitch of her voice.

"Insolent creature, your manservant is, Mr. Farthing," Sir Heath sneered. "I'd have thought, given how much you're extorting from me this time, you'd at least behave like a gentleman and arrive on time."

A snort came from the lone figure, and Sir Heath let out a laugh.

"Despise me all you like, old sport, but you're the one who challenged me. If you lacked the foresight to employ the Farthing's services, then you must suffer the consequences."

The figure turned and approached in long, slow strides.

A blackened knot of horror twisted in Portia's gut as her gaze wandered over the form, taking in his gait, the precision with which he took each step…the lean, powerful build, the broad shoulders, and the thick head of hair, softened by the haze of the first rays of dawn light.

And his eyes…eyes that she knew were capable of a warmth that soothed the heart and caressed the soul—eyes that were now almost black, lacking that spark of desire and affection that had captured her heart; eyes that now glistened with pure hatred and the soldier's resolve to kill his enemy as he glared at her, his mouth set in a firm line.

No. It cannot be…

She blinked, willing the nightmare to recede—but instead, the image of him filled her senses, until nothing else in the world existed except him, the man who would, in less than a few heartbeats, aim a pistol at her with the intent to kill.

Sir Heath chuckled, and bile rose in Portia's stomach as she fought to temper the nausea.

"I don't believe the two of you are acquainted," he said, "though, of course, you may have come across one another at White's." He turned to his opponent. "That is, if you stopped hiding yourself away in your lodgings playing at nursemaid and bothered to attend White's like a gentleman."

Then he let out a laugh. "It matters not." He gestured toward Portia. "Mr. Farthing, let me introduce you to your opponent—Colonel Reid."

Portia bit her lip to focus on the pain to prevent the world from shifting out of focus around her, as Sir Heath confirmed what she'd feared, and what her eyes were telling her, though she tried to deny it.

Stephen curled his hands into fists.

"At the very least, you can shake my friend's hand like a gentleman, Reid," Sir Heath said. "*Most* unseemly."

"I've no intention of shaking that blackguard's hand," Stephen said, his voice quiet and cold. Portia flinched as pure hatred dripped from his words. "There's little point in acquainting myself with a creature whom I intend to stamp out." Then he stepped closer, his body seeming to vibrate with pure, unadulterated hatred.

"Make peace with your maker, Mr. Farthing," he said, his lips curled back in a snarl, "for I intend to ensure that you'll not live to see another dawn."

CHAPTER TWENTY

S TEPHEN STARED AT the creature before him.
His hands itched to rip the mask off the blackguard's face, to wrap his fingers around the man's throat and crush the life out of him. Sir Heath was a rake, and a profligate. But the creature who stood before him now, lacking the common decency, let alone the courage, to face him like a man, instead choosing to hide behind a mask...

The Farthing was an apt name for a creature that cared only for coin. What kind of a man would stoop so low as to earn a profit from the suffering of others—the ruination of innocents?

"Have you nothing to say, sir?" Stephen said.

The Farthing flinched, and a pair of bright-blue eyes glittered behind a black silk mask. For a heartbeat Stephen's resolve faltered at the shock of familiarity. The image of another pair of blue eyes filled his memory...

Portia, the woman he'd left behind at Rosecombe to race back to London to defend his sister's honor. His Portia, whom he'd cast from his mind in his desperation to save Angela from a life of misery and ruination.

Sweet swiving heaven, when the messenger had turned up at some ungodly hour at Rosecombe, he'd feared the worst! But he had arrived home to find Angela penitent, ashamed—and terrified of whatever punishment he might mete out. No amount of reassurance on Mrs. Stowe's part would placate his anger, and though he believed her when she'd assured him Angela was still a maiden, he'd still tossed the woman out of the house, promising to expose her as the chaperone who facilitated the ruination of young girls.

And only now, on the brink of defending Angela's honor and destroying the man who'd forced him to take arms once more, did his mind wander to where his heart lay.

To her. His beloved Portia.

Did she think he'd abandoned her? Most likely not, or her brother would have been at his doorstep yesterday calling him out.

Curse you, you bastard, for profiteering from my sister's ruination, and keeping me from the woman I love.

The Farthing flinched again, and Stephen forced his lips into a cold smile. If he'd learned any lesson from Waterloo, it was that most battles were won or lost before the first blow was dealt—that an enemy who showed fear of their opponent, or doubt over their honor, or motives, was an enemy who, no matter the strength of his arms, could always be defeated by the exploitation of his weakness.

And the Farthing—even if his reputation as a superior marksman preceded him—was afraid.

Very afraid.

"Come, come, old chap," Sir Heath called. "I thought you a gentleman. At least behave like one."

Stephen turned on the man. "You have the audacity to call out *my* behavior after what you did to my sister?"

The Farthing let out a whimper. Surely the rogue wasn't in possession of a conscience?

"That little chit!" Sir Heath scoffed. "Hardly more than a morsel for a man like me. She came to me willing—couldn't get away from her big brother quickly enough. Mounted your garden wall to escape that dowdy widow of a chaperone, so that I could mount—"

"Stop right there!" Stephen roared. "Do not speak of my sister or, so help me God, I'll shoot you dead, Farthing or no Farthing!"

"Oh, *please!*" Sir Heath said. "Do you really think I'd waste my efforts on a child fresh from the schoolroom, pretty enough though she may be? My tastes run to *real* women."

"Yet you still saw fit to ruin her reputation."

Sir Heath grinned. "A harmless little jape from an infatuated child. Your sister's not the first—and she'll not be the last. But you can trust me, old chap. I'll not breathe a word of your sister's…weakness for me. After all, it's not a characteristic that sets her apart from other women."

"Don't flatter yourself, Moss. No woman of any sense would deign to touch you—for one thing, she doesn't know where you've been."

"Inside Lady Francis, for one."

Stephen wrinkled his nose.

"Had her as well, did you?" Sir Heath chuckled. "Still, she parts her thighs with little fuss at almost no expense. Think on that, a whore willing to offer her services for free."

"You disgust me."

"You're hardly a monk, Reid. Word has it you were a favorite among the camp followers in the militia—fucked more females than Wellington's prize stallion."

Maybury approached, a polished wooden case in his hands. "Gentlemen, perhaps we should proceed before it gets too light. There will be time enough to trade insults at White's over a brandy. What say I stand you both a round when we're done?"

"You think I'd drink with a man such as you?" Stephen said.

Sir Heath smiled. "Not if my man sends you to your maker." He gestured to the Farthing. "Choose your weapon."

Maybury opened the box to reveal a pair of pistols nestled together on a velvet cushion, like lovers. The Farthing approached it and reached for one, then he hesitated and stepped back, gesturing toward Stephen.

"Most gallant, I'm sure," Sir Heath said. "Very well—Reid, you have first choice."

Stephen approached the box, met the Farthing's gaze for a heartbeat, then reached for a pistol. The Farthing plucked the other one and held it in his hands, lifting it up and down as if to test the weight. Then he nodded.

"Excellent," Maybury said. "Now, I think you both know what to do—or shall I explain it to you, Reid?"

"Just get on with it," Stephen growled, suppressing the knot of fear swelling inside him at the prospect of his mind returning to the battlefield. But at least this morning, the enemy was a man he'd gladly rid the world of.

The Farthing approached, and they stood back to back. Then Maybury began to count—one, two, three…

Stephen's palm grew slick as he gripped the pistol. The memory of the battle threatened to surface as he stepped forward, one pace for each count. The shadows stretching across the grass from the trees surrounding the park seemed to morph into the shapes of his fallen comrades, and the metallic stench of blood clung to the air.

"…ten!"

He turned, the sounds of battle ringing in his ears, and cocked his weapon. His opponent stood, arm down, weapon in hand, body shaking.

Was this really the infamous Farthing, whose deadly accuracy was born of a cold detachment, a man rumored to have no soul? Or was the shivering creature before him an imposter?

Out of the corner of his eye, he caught sight of a white hand-kerchief fluttering to the ground, and slowly, he raised his arm, leveling his aim at the man before him.

But still, the Farthing made no move.

"For fuck's sake, man!" Sir Heath cried. "Get on with it! I'm paying you enough, aren't I? Bloody hell, I should have shagged her—then I'd at least have got my money's worth."

"How dare you!" Stephen cried. "She's worth twenty of you."

"She's a child," Sir Heath scoffed. "Take my advice, Reid—put her on leading strings until she turns into a woman."

"You wouldn't know a real woman if she bit you on the arse," Stephen snarled.

"Ha! That's where you're wrong. Take the delectable Lady Portia. She's—"

Rage boiled in Stephen's gut. "Do *not* speak her name!" he roared.

"Aha! So you've been sniffing round Foxton's sister?" Sir Heath taunted him. "I wouldn't bother if I were you—her brother chases off all the dogs, even if she's like a bitch in heat."

Stephen's knuckles whitened as he gripped the pistol. "Do not speak of Portia—"

"*Portia* is it?" Sir Heath said. "Such familiarity. Don't say you managed to slink past her gaoler of a brother and mount her? How does it feel to know that I got there first?"

A squeal came from across the lawn, and the Farthing's man-servant moved toward his master. Foolish fellow—didn't he know he was stepping right into the line of fire?

"Hush!" Stephen yelled.

But the Farthing let out another whimper, his trembling becoming more violent.

"Moss, you lie," Stephen said. "Perhaps I ought to expose you at White's for peddling falsehoods about respectable women."

"You can't know that for sure," Sir Heath said. "Unless…" He threw back his head. "Of course!" he cried. "*You've* fucked her, haven't you?"

"Damn you, Moss!" Stephen's arm shook as he tried to temper the rage swelling in his gut, rising like a boiling, raging wave.

"Oh ho—that's better than anything I might say in relation to your sister," Sir Heath said. "To think, the strait-laced Lady Portia, who I always thought had a frost between her legs, has been stoking a fire for the gallant colonel! Bloody hell, I'll lose ten guineas in my wager with De Blanchard, but it's worth it to know that Foxton's sister is a much of a whore as any other—"

The wave broke, and Stephen pulled the trigger, the instinct to destroy his enemy burning in his soul.

The sharp crack filled the air, followed by a puff of acrid blue smoke. Stephen's arm jerked upward with the recoil, and he bit his lip to stem the image of battered, broken bodies in the ground.

Damn you, Moss, for making me do this.

And damn the Farthing.

He closed his eyes, willing the image to recede, welcoming the blackness. His heart thudded against his chest, and he focused on the solid ground beneath his feet.

What had she once told him?

Focus on the world around you, Stephen—the real world. Then you can retreat from the battle in your mind and return to me.

He drew in a deep breath, counting to three, then exhaled slowly, picturing the battlefield melting into nothingness as he emptied his lungs.

"Oh, shit," a voice said.

The battlefield had almost receded, and as Stephen opened his eyes, only one lifeless form remained, on the grass, twenty paces in front of him. He closed his eyes, willing the shape to disappear, but when he opened them again, there were now two forms—a second shape, bending over the other.

"Bloody hell, you've killed him!" Maybury cried.

"Bugger," Sir Heath said. "Mind you, the fellow had declared that this was to be his last duel. Perhaps he expected this, eh?"

"Is that all you can say?" Maybury said. "The least you can do is fetch a doctor."

"That's what his manservant is for—Gerard, is it?"

The second shape looked up. "My mis—my master's alive. He's…"

A deep groan came from the prone form.

"There!" Sir Heath said. "He lives to fight again." He strode over to the two forms and fished a wad of notes out of his pocket. "Payment for services rendered."

"Aren't you going to help the fellow?" Maybury said.

"I've discharged my obligation by paying him. One hundred

pounds, I'll have you know. If he was determined to get greedy and double his price, then he can afford a doctor."

"Perhaps I ought—"

"Maybury, you should return to that wife of yours. You never know who might have slid into her bed the moment you left it."

Maybury let out a laugh, and the two of them sauntered off. No doubt they'd be toasting each other at White's that morning. As for the creature who'd been in their employ…

Stephen approached the Farthing's prone form.

"You fool," he said.

The Farthing stirred, and Stephen let out a sigh of relief. At least he'd not killed the fellow—even if he loathed him.

The manservant glanced up at him and spoke in a light, boyish voice. "Sir, please help us."

"Help yourself," Stephen replied. "That's what you've been doing, is it not? And do not cross my path again. You survived today, but next time you see me, you'll not be so lucky."

He reached for the Farthing's mask, and the man let out a groan. Then he hesitated.

"No," he said. "Best that I never discover who you are. If I do, I'll end your life with my bare hands when next I see you. But I pray, with my whole soul, that you rot in hell."

Suppressing a flicker of remorse, he turned his back on his fallen opponent and strode out of the park.

CHAPTER TWENTY-ONE

PAIN FLOODED PORTIA's senses, as if she were being ripped apart. Gritting her teeth to stem the scream, she tried to lift her head and caught a glimpse of Stephen's booted feet disappearing as he strode away from her without even a backward glance.

"Don't try to move," Nerissa whispered. "You've been shot."

"Ner—"

"Hush!"

Portia reached up, and a spike of agony tore through her arm.

"Keep still, *please*! I must stop the bleeding before I move you." Nerissa lifted her head and called to the retreating figure. "Colonel Reid! *Please* help us!"

But his footsteps continued to crunch on the gravel path as he walked away.

"No!" Portia cried, her voice tight. "He m-mustn't know…"

"Would you rather die than have him discover your identity?"

"Nerissa, do what I ask."

"I care not what you want, Lady Portia," Nerissa said, her voice sharpening. Then she tilted her head up and cried out, "Colonel Reid!"

The footsteps did not slow, but he called out, his voice cutting through the air, "Devil take you!"

Stephen…

Portia lifted her head again, and a low cry escaped her lips.

"Devil take *him!*" Nerissa said. She tore at her neckerchief until it came loose. "Stay still while I bind your wound, but I fear it will hurt you."

I fear it will hurt you…

Tears filled Portia's eyes as she recalled Stephen's words—spoken with such tenderness when he took her for the first time.

Then she cried out again as the pain ripped through her arm. When it dulled, she opened her eyes, blinking to remove the fog of moisture until her maid's face solidified in front of her.

"Nerissa…"

Dear, faithful, loyal Nerissa, who served her unquestioningly—not merely because it was her duty, but because she wanted to, out of loyalty and friendship.

Portia reached up, and Nerissa took her hand. She curled her fingers around her maid's, drawing strength from Nerissa's solidity and calm, tender care.

"Is that better, my lady?"

Portia nodded.

"The bleeding's stopped. Let me help you up—we need to leave. The park will be full of people soon."

Fueled by the urgency in her maid's voice, Portia tightened her grip on Nerissa's hand and, gritting her teeth, struggled to her feet. She glanced at her arm and suppressed a cry. The thin neckerchief was already stained, dark red and glistening.

"Come, quick!" Nerissa said, and they set off.

Each footstep caused another pulse of pain in Portia's arm, but they increased the pace as the sound of voices filled the air—tradesmen going about their business, lovers indulging in an illicit liaison—but they couldn't obliterate the one voice that swirled in her mind, the voice of the man she loved.

I pray, with my whole soul, that you rot in hell.

Perhaps, today, his prayers would be answered.

By the time they slipped through the servants' entrance on St. James's Square, Portia's arm was engulfed in an inferno of agony, as if it had been thrust into a furnace. Sweat dripped from her brow, stinging her eyes, and she stumbled as Nerissa steered her toward the back stairs.

"Quick, my lady, we must get you safe before Mr. Reeve sees us!"

"I-I can handle Reeve," Portia said.

"Do you want His Grace to discover you?"

Portia shook her head and let her maid steer her to the third floor, pain stabbing at her with each step, until they reached a tiny room, less than half the size of Portia's dressing room, with a bed nestled in a corner beneath the sloping ceiling and a four-paned window overlooking the London skyline.

"Is this your room, Nerissa?"

"It's the safest place for you. Nobody comes here."

Not even I've been here—and I'm her mistress.

Nerissa led her to the bed, and Portia lay back, inhaling deeply to dispel the nausea swelling in her gut.

"Stay there, Lady Portia. I'll be as quick as I can."

"Don't leave me, Nerissa!"

"You need a doctor. The ball is still in your arm."

"N-no—I'll be all right."

Nerissa shook her head. "You know better than I what will happen if your wound isn't treated. Remember Mr. Draper?"

Portia sank back on the bed. Her maid was right. Mr. Draper, a young man under Dr. Lucas's care, had sustained a wound to his leg in a duel that had festered when Dr. Lucas failed to remove the ball. Despite Dr. McIver's attempts to save his life by removing the leg, the poor young man had died, screaming in agony.

It was one of the reasons why the Farthing had come into existence—to prevent other foolish men from suffering a similar fate as a result of their pride.

"Very well, bring Dr. McIver. I just hope he forgives me for—" She broke off with a cry. "No! Dr. McIver's not in Town—he's taken his wife to Scotland."

"Dear God!" Nerissa cried, and Portia's stomach heaved with

nausea as her maid's demeanor of calm concern turned into one of horror. Then she nodded. "Never fear. I know what to do. Be as quiet as you can, Lady Portia, and I'll return directly."

Portia opened her mouth to ask where she was going, but a ripple of nausea gripped her insides and she closed it again. The thick, dark cloud that had risen in the back of her mind now came to the fore, and before her maid had closed the door behind her as she exited the chamber, it claimed her and she drifted into oblivion.

Soft, feminine voices shimmered in the distance, fading in and out, until a single voice sharpened into focus, issuing instructions with crisp efficiency.

"Pass me the candle."

Candle? Am I dreaming?

"Hold her arm still… No, not like that. Let me show you…"

"What about the laudanum?" another voice said, its timbre comforting in its familiarity.

"There's no time for it to take effect. We must act now."

"Forgive me, Lady Portia…"

A hand gripped her elbow, while another took her hand, interlacing her fingers, then pulled it taut, and the her arm began to throb.

"Yes, that's it. Don't forget to hold steady, no matter how much she struggles."

"But she's unconscious."

"Not for long. If she moves, it may do more harm than good. Ready?"

The question was met with silence, and Portia let her mind drift back into nothingness. Then a shard of agony tore into her arm. Her body jerked with the force of the pain, and she fought to tear her arm away, but her torturers only tightened their grips as the pain continued to swell, slice after slice, cutting deeper into her body, until she became nothing but a creature of pure sensation—an animal baring its teeth while being ripped apart by dogs. She bit down, and a sharp metallic taste filled her mouth.

Then she threw back her head, opened her mouth, and drew in a lungful of air. The scream swelled in her throat, but before she could set it free, something hard and unyielding was thrust into her mouth.

"Bite down!" a voice cried. She complied while the pain rose higher until, at last, it receded, washing back until it faded to a glistening ache.

She opened her eyes to see two faces—her maid, flushed scarlet and contorted with distress, beads of moisture on her forehead, and another, displaying the calm, reassuring detachment of a surgeon.

But it was no surgeon. The face had delicate features and pale-gray eyes with a shimmer of green, framed by soft chestnut curls.

Euphramia Lucas.

Which means that Dr. Lucas…

Panic rose, and Portia struggled to sit up, but a light hand touched her shoulder.

"Euphramia?"

"Stay still, Lady Portia. Let the pain subside. Here, drink this."

A spoon was held in front of her, and she pushed it aside. "Not laudanum, please. I don't want to sleep. Not if your father—"

"Dr. Lucas is at home in his bed, Lady Portia," Nerissa said. "Surely you didn't think I'd bring *him* when his daughter has more aptitude for medicine in her right hand than he…" Her voice trailed off, and she sighed. "Forgive me, Miss Lucas. I've been worried about my mistress, and spoke out of turn. I meant no insult to your father."

"It matters not," Euphramia said. "I'm loyal to Papa, but not to the point of foolhardiness." She arched an eyebrow and pressed the spoon against Portia's mouth. "I trust *you're* not stubborn to the point of foolhardiness, Lady Portia. Now, would you be so kind?"

Her gentle persuasion breached Portia's defenses, and she parted her lips, bracing herself for the bitter taste.

"It's for your benefit," Euphramia said, her tone almost apologetic.

"Perhaps, but why must everything for our benefit be so unpleasant?"

Euphramia gave a soft laugh. "It's a question my patients at the hospital are always asking. Before he left for Yorkshire, Captain Broom asked the same question when I removed the stitches from his wound."

"We can't all be as courageous as Captain Broom," Portia said, smiling at the memory of the soldier's infectious optimism.

"Or the man who saved his life," Euphramia replied with a sigh. "Colonel Reid is a most—"

"Shall I apply another bandage, Miss Lucas?" Nerissa interrupted.

Euphramia frowned. "You ought to know by now, Nerissa, that too tight a bandage for this type of wound can hamper recovery."

"Of course. Forgive me, Miss Lucas."

"The tincture should prevent putrefaction, but I'll need to check it again in a day or so—that is, if you've no objection to my visiting again."

"Why should I object?" Portia said. "You've likely saved my life."

"There's been an outbreak of smallpox in the hospital. I am, of course, taking every precaution, but I wouldn't want to risk exposing you to danger."

"I've done enough of that myself," Portia said, nodding to her arm, which was bandaged below the elbow.

"But you'll not be placing yourself in such danger again, will you?" Nerissa said, her tone that of a nanny chiding a wayward child.

"Is the pain lessening at all?" Euphramia asked.

"A little," Portia replied.

"Good, the laudanum's taking effect."

"I don't want to sleep."

"In which case, I'd recommend you sit up…and perhaps return to your own chamber if you don't want anyone finding out how you were injured."

Portia glanced at Nerissa. "You didn't tell Euphramia what happened, did you?"

"I've just removed a bullet from your arm, Lady Portia," Euphramia said. "And given that your injury was sustained before dawn, I can make an educated guess as to the circumstances leading to your sustaining that wound. But I care not what those circumstances were—my only concern is your recovery."

Euphramia's words were such that Portia could almost have imagined that Dr. McIver spoke them. What a misfortune, the circumstance of her birth! Had Euphramia been born a man—and born to Dr. and Mrs. McIver—she would have thrived as a surgeon, with her crisp efficiency and dexterity. But no, her sex prevented her from getting the recognition her expertise merited, and her father, with his medieval attitude to medicine, would hamper her dreams at every turn.

Whereas I, born into privilege and wealth, ignored the advantages of my birth, sought the self-indulgent gratification of a spoiled child— and nearly brought about my own destruction.

And even if she had escaped physical destruction, she'd destroyed the one thing she craved more than her own freedom.

The unbridled love of a good man.

Portia blinked, and a tear splashed onto her cheek.

"Do you need something else for the pain?" Euphramia asked.

Portia shook her head. No amount of laudanum would lessen the pain in her heart.

"Let me escort you to your chamber," Nerissa said. "Miss Lucas, I can take care of Lady Portia now. You need to return home before you're missed."

Euphramia nodded, then gave Portia's hand an affectionate squeeze. "I'll visit you on Thursday," she said. "Papa is taking tea with Reverend Gache, so I can slip away unnoticed."

"Let me show you out," Nerissa said.

"There's no need," came the reply. "You take care of Lady Portia."

"Very well. Use the stairs we came up," Nerissa said. "If Mr. Reeve spots you, just say you were tending to Lady Portia's monthly bleed. If he doesn't faint, he'll run away faster than a deerhound."

Euphramia smiled. "Men! They consider themselves the superior sex, yet most of them faint at the mere thought of a woman's courses. Papa is just the same. He—" She broke off, blushing, then took her leave and slipped out of the chamber, her footsteps fading into the distance.

Nerissa placed her arm around Portia's shoulders and escorted her to the door. After checking that the passageway was quiet outside, she led Portia toward her chamber on the floor below. Once inside, she helped her out of the Farthing's clothes and dropped them in a trunk.

"I'll burn these after I've brought you breakfast, then the Farthing and Gerard will be no more."

"I-I can't have breakfast in bed," Portia said. "What will I tell my brother?"

"That you're having your courses," Nerissa said. "His Grace may not swoon like Mr. Reeve at the thought of the workings of the female body, but he'll not inquire further if I tell him you're in a delicate state of health this morning." She held up the blood-stained neckerchief. "One glimpse of this will convince him to refrain from further discussion."

"And afterward?" Portia said, gesturing to her bandaged arm.

"A long sleeve will conceal that until you're fully healed," came the reply. "We're fortunate that long sleeves are fashionable this Season."

"Very well," Portia said, and Nerissa helped her into the bed and drew the sheet over her.

"There! All we need now is a warm fire—I hope you'll have no objection if I send Poppy up to light it. She's a sensible girl and won't gossip."

Portia reached toward Nerissa, who took her hand. "Thank you," she said. "I don't know what I would do if I didn't have you in my life. You're my friend, my confidante, and…" She shook her head as the world shifted out of focus. "I-I'm sorry that your room's so small and dull, tucked away upstairs. I-I didn't—"

"It's better than most maids' rooms."

"But it's not as good as you deserve. When I have a home of my own, I'll…"

Portia's voice trailed off as the reality of her situation gripped her heart, and a tear slid down her cheek.

"The colonel doesn't know it's you," Nerissa said. "He was only protecting his sister."

"I know," Portia replied, "and he'd already made his dislike of the Farthing plain when we discussed the matter. But to witness such hatred, directed toward me…"

"He hates what's happened to his sister, that's all. But he loves *you*—I know it, and so do you. If there's one person in this world he's capable of forgiving, it's you. And there's nothing to forgive. I'm sure he'll come to understand that."

But what if he doesn't?

Nerissa bustled about the room, tidying away all evidence of the Farthing, then took her leave, promising to return with a tray as soon as she'd changed into her uniform. Portia leaned back onto the pillows, wincing at the soreness in her arm, and let the languor induced by the laudanum wash over her, soothing her senses with a gentle detachment from the world around her.

At length, footsteps approached, and she rubbed the sleep out of her eyes as the door opened to reveal a blurred shape.

"I hadn't expected you to be so quick, Nerissa. Did you tell my brother—"

"Tell me what?" a deep voice said.

The world snapped into focus and Portia's stomach tightened as Adam stepped into the chamber, closing the door behind him.

"Wh-where's Nerissa?"

"Your maid's tending to your breakfast. You're taking it in

bed, I see." He approached the bed and drew up a chair. "May I?" he asked.

"Of course."

He sat, then leaned toward her. "I hear you're indisposed."

She nodded. "My health is—"

"Delicate, yes. May I see it?"

She squeezed her thighs together, her cheeks warming with embarrassment.

"You can't blame me for being curious."

Heavens! What was he about? She gestured toward her body. "Brother, I hardly think it's appropriate to—"

"Be fair, sister," he said, his tone casual. "I've never seen one before, you see."

"A…what?"

"A bullet wound."

Her stomach fluttered, and she opened her mouth to deny it. He fixed his gaze on her, then shook his head.

"I have no wish to be angry with you, Portia, but I'd advise you not to disappoint me. I do not like to be disappointed."

"Please…" she said, then swallowed.

"Please what?" His voice remained calm, his body still, but the slight tightening in his tone warned of a simmering rage beneath his calm exterior.

"Please don't dismiss Nerissa. She was acting on my instructions. If that cockroach of a butler—"

"Reeve has nothing to do with this. I spoke to your maid myself."

"H-how did you—"

"Do you think me incapable of looking out of a window? I saw two men entering the house just after dawn." He folded his arms and fixed his gaze on her, "Well, what I *thought* were two men."

"Are you spying on me?" she asked. "Or perhaps you were on the lookout for Mrs. Scarlet while she paid you a visit?"

"*I've* had no visitors, Portia, but I understand that doctor's daughter arrived here, unchaperoned, and presumably without her father's permission."

"She had every right to be here."

"In which case you'll have no objection to my discussing the matter with Dr. Lucas."

"Leave Miss Lucas alone. I'll not have you causing trouble for her."

"I'm causing trouble for no one, sister," he said. "Perhaps you should consider your own actions and the consequences that they reap. Not only the consequences for yourself"—he gestured toward her bandaged arm—"but the consequences for others who are not protected by the same degree of privilege that you seem to take for granted."

He lifted his hand to his brow and wiped it. When he lowered it again, sadness flickered in his eyes.

"Perhaps the only way to teach you a lesson in propriety would be to punish those closest to you. You seem to have no regard for your own suffering, but mayhap the suffering of others would have some effect. After all, you are not entirely without feeling."

"Unlike *you*, brother. You are devoid of all feeling."

"Do you really think you're in a position to answer me back thus? Your maid—"

"Leave Nerissa alone!" Portia cried. "She was only acting on my instruction."

"In that, if I nothing else, I agree with you."

"But you still intend to torture me by punishing her for something I've done?"

"Portia, can't you see, I…"

He trailed off, and the emotion in his eyes threatened to shatter her defiance. She had earned his irritation from the moment she'd arrived in the world—an arrival that had resulted in their mother's exit from it. She was the little sister who trotted behind him, clinging to his shirttails, seeking the comfort from a brother that only a mother could have given. As they'd grown into adulthood and Adam had been thrust into the responsibility as head of the family after their father's passing, that irritation had turned into frustration and anger—anger at her refusal to conform to the constraints of Society, and frustration from having to shoulder the responsibility of a dukedom. Even his disappointment she could weather, given that it was never directly solely at her. He seemed permanently disappointed with the rest of the world.

But his sorrow… That was something she had witnessed only in others. Even the most stoic of rakes expressed a hint of sorrow, their shuttered expressions never quite concealing their inner pain. But as for Adam, his clear blue gaze had always spoken of rationality and determination. Even as a boy when she'd broken his toy boat, he'd calmly explained the folly of her actions—as if a child of two summers would learn from her mistakes. But Portia had never believed him capable of sadness.

Until now.

"I don't blame your maid," he said, his voice heavy with weariness. "Nor do I blame you. I blame myself."

"You…?"

"Permit me to speak while I have the inclination," he said. "I have failed you. It was my duty to care for you when Mother died, but instead, I blamed you for taking her from me, for giving me the responsibility of a child who was not the younger brother I'd hoped for." He let out a sigh and shook his head. "Then, when Pater died, I found myself not only responsible for the sister I never…"

He hesitated and closed his eyes. Portia's heart ached, and she placed her hand over his. "The sister you never wanted?"

"I was young at the time," he said. "Barely sixteen—old enough to be a man in the eyes of the law, but…"

"But not so old as to suppress your true feelings and portray the wishes and desires that were socially acceptable?" She smiled. "Fathers want sons, and sons want brothers. I cannot blame you for that—or, at least, if I must blame you, then I must blame every other man in Society, and most of the women, who perpetuate that belief."

"If it's any consolation, I have, for many years, regretted my wishes, and I'm grateful to have you as my sister, even if…"

"Even if I disobey you at every turn?"

"Even if you secretly indulge in the business of dueling."

Her stomach clenched with fear.

"Who told you?"

He paused, then tilted his head to one side. "You just did."

"Brother, I—"

He raised his hand. "I suspected it when I saw you entering the house this morning. But it made sense. You always were a bloody good shot—better than I could ever be."

He *knew*? Why, then, did he not rage at her—threaten to confine her in her chamber, under lock and key, until she learned to behave?

"You're not angry?"

He sighed. "I've expended too much effort in being angry at you, sister, to no avail. I've no wish to be angry with you merely to punish you. My anger was only ever a result of my wish to do right by you—and to have you do right by yourself."

Then he blinked, and the shimmer of sorrow disappeared, replaced by the resolution of a man who held her life and freedom—and that of countless others—in his hands.

"I take it the Farthing is no more," he said.

She nodded.

"Good. Your maid told me as much."

"*Please* don't punish her," Portia said.

"Her punishment will be to tend to you for as long as you see fit, knowing that by her complicity, she placed your life at risk— something she values almost as much as I. Each day she watches you in the mirror, or dresses you, or styles your hair… Each day she tends to you at night, comforts you in moments of distress or acts as your confidante, she will be reminded of the mistress she cares for—the mistress who could so easily have departed this earth today."

He squeezed her hand. "I've lost a mother and a father—we both have. I have no wish to lose my beloved sister as well." Then he smiled. "But, at least, the burden of ensuring that you do not place yourself in further danger will be shared. I have some good news for you. Colonel Reid's card came this morning. He sent a message expressing his eagerness to call on me, though I'll wager it's not *me* he wishes to see. I took the liberty of issuing an invitation for tea."

Her heart soared with relief.

"So, like you, he doesn't mind what I've done? Or…who I was?"

He frowned. "Surely you don't think I'd be so foolish as to tell *him* of your antics? Good Lord, no—but it's in the past, so is best forgotten. What he doesn't know won't harm him."

"B-but…"

"But what?" he said, his voice sharpening.

"I-I thought…"

"Best not to think, Portia," he said. "And we must keep this between ourselves. Nerissa can be trusted. As to the man who shot you, though I wish very much to know who he is, it's best if you don't tell me."

She nodded. "Because you already know who he is."

"No, sister," he said, his voice cold and steady. "It's because if I ever discover who he is, I'll deal with him myself. Permanently."

Ice-cold fingers clung to her heart at the grim determination in his eyes.

Then he patted her hand and rose. "I'll leave you to your breakfast," he said. "You might wear long sleeves today. We wouldn't want the colonel to see your arm."

In that, her brother was right—for if Stephen's role in her injury became known, he was a dead man.

CHAPTER TWENTY-TWO

S OFT FOOTSTEPS APPROACHED Stephen's study in a tentative, timid gait. Then they stopped.

He looked up from his desk. "Come in, Angela."

The door opened to reveal his sister, her eyes almost black in her pale face. "Brother, I—"

"Speak no more," he said. "The matter is settled."

"Did Sir Hea—"

"I'd advise you not to mention that man in my presence."

Her cheeks stained pink and her lip wobbled. "I-is he…?"

"He's alive, if that's what you're asking. Do you care for his welfare?"

"No, I care for *yours*."

"You're best off tending to your own wellbeing," he said. "Not to mention your reputation."

She winced. "Am I ruined?"

"Perhaps."

The hope in her eyes died.

"If you're seeking reassurance, Angela, you're best avoiding questions that require me to speak the truth."

A tear splashed onto her cheek.

Stephen gestured to the chair across the desk, and she slid into the seat and placed both hands on her lap.

"I'm not angry with you," he said.

She curled her hands into fists, gathering the material of her skirts.

"You'll ruin your dress," he said quietly.

"A-a dress can be mended."

Another tear splashed onto her hand, and she trembled, her chest heaving with each shuddering breath.

He rose and moved toward her. She flinched as he touched her shoulder, then he drew her to him.

"You know how precious you are to me, don't you?"

Her body vibrated as she sniffed. He pulled out a handkerchief from his pocket and held it in front of her.

"It's clean."

She gave a watery smile, took it, and dabbed her eyes.

"Your reputation is intact for now," he said. *"He* won't say a word."

"Why not?"

"Like most arrogant souls, he's a coward. He hired someone to duel on his behalf."

She looked up, her eyes widening. "You mean…the infamous Farthing?"

"Aye. A man worse than Sir Heath, making a living by such nefarious means. But he'll not be seen again."

"Sweet Lord!" she cried. "D-did you kill him?"

"I shot him, but he was alive when I left. He ought to consider himself fortunate that I spared his life."

"So you intended only to injure him?"

"No," he said. "In my anger, I shot to kill."

"Brother, no! How could you have done such a thing?"

His conscience, which had been hammering that same question into his soul since the moment he'd pulled the trigger, swelled in his mind, whispering of his own sins.

"I can never forgive myself for taking up arms again," he said. "But I did it to defend your honor. Better that than have you face certain ruination. Perhaps now you understand the gravity of your folly."

She lowered her gaze.

"But if I cannot forgive myself for having shot a man," Stephen said, "neither can I forgive him for placing me in that position, where I had no choice."

"There's always a choice," she whispered.

"None that were acceptable to a loving brother."

"D-do you for—" she began, then her body shook with sobs. He placed his hand under her chin and tilted her head up with his fingertips until she met his gaze.

"Yes," he said, caressing her cheek. "I'll forgive my little sister anything."

"Th-then…" Her color deepened.

"Yes?"

"Can you not forgive Mrs. Stowe?"

He withdrew his hand.

"Please!" she said. "She had no knowledge of what I was doing. I-I climbed over the garden wall while she was taking her rest. You see, she'd had a letter from her son and was suffering one of her headaches, and her hand was giving her pain. She looked so distressed that I suggested she take her rest. Then I…"

"You took advantage of her weakness?"

She nodded, as more tears rolled down her cheeks.

"So you came to see me this morning not to plead on your behalf, but hers."

She nodded. "Punish me all you like. I shall remain within these walls until you declare me fit to venture outside. I-I'll mend the sheets—even do the laundry—anything you name, if you'll only tell Mrs. Stowe she can remain."

"And why's that, so you can take advantage of her again?"

"I promise I won't," Angela said. "I-I didn't like seeing her in pain, but Heath said…" She flinched, and he drew her close once more.

"Very well," he said. "Speak his name no more and I'll reinstate Mrs. Stowe. I'll admit that until yesterday I was very satisfied with her services. She's even encouraged you to practice your music—something *I* never managed to achieve."

"She's very proficient at the pianoforte, at least when her

hand doesn't pain her."

"Her hand?"

"I saw it once," Angela said, "when she took off her gloves—the fingers were misshapen. But when she caught me looking, she put her gloves back on and looked so angry, I didn't like to ask her."

"Quite right," Stephen said, recalling how the quiet, demure chaperone always seemed to favor her left hand. When she'd signed their contract with her left hand she'd hesitated, a flicker of fear in her eyes. But he'd refrained from asking. After all, which hand a person favored did not affect their ability to undertake their duties, no matter what Society thought.

Society be damned.

He smiled as Portia's voice whispered in his mind. His beautiful, intelligent, courageous fiancée, who doubtless would think nothing of scaling a garden wall to meet her lover. Why punish Angela for having the same impulse when her only sin had been to believe that Heath Moss loved her? Countless women of greater experience and sophistication had succumbed to that rake's charms. Angela was an innocent—and did not deserve to be censured for behaving as many others would have done.

What mattered was that she'd learned her lesson.

Stephen took his sister's hands and guided her to her feet. "I'm pleased that you came here to plead the case for another," he said. "For that alone, I shall ask Mrs. Stowe to continue to chaperone you until the end of the Season."

"And can you forgive…him?"

"Surely you don't mean…"

"Not *him*," she said, wrinkling her nose. "I meant the Farthing. After all, you shot him."

"I fear I must ask you not to make a request that I cannot honor," he said. "You must pray, for my sake and for his, that I do not encounter any injured young men over the next few days, for I don't know if I'll be able to restrain myself."

She took his hand and squeezed it. "Then for that, I am truly sorry. I cannot bear the thought of the brother I admire harboring such hatred for another."

He placed a kiss in her hair. "Then do not think of it, dearest sister," he said. "It's my burden to bear—and I shall bear it alone."

CHAPTER TWENTY-THREE

"H E'S HERE."

Portia glanced up from her embroidery. Her brother stood, silhouetted against the drawing room window.

"He has the largest bouquet of roses I've ever seen."

"Larger than the bouquets you're continually sending to Mrs. Scarlet?"

"Careful, puss," he teased. "You sound envious."

"I wouldn't envy any woman who'd fallen in love with *you*."

He laughed. "And quite right. But I have it on good authority that Mrs. Scarlet is incapable of love."

"Which explains why the two of you are such good friends. I believe that's what they call it—*friends*?"

He grinned. "Do you speak like this to the colonel?"

"Not yet."

"Very wise," he said. "Best to keep him in the dark with regards to your faults until you've slipped the parson's noose around his neck. A man's best not knowing everything about the woman he's to wed."

In that, at least, she agreed with him.

Adam moved to sit beside her while footsteps approached. Then the door opened. Portia's heart gave a little flutter as Stephen stood in the doorway, resplendent in his uniform, bearing a bouquet of roses in various shades of pink and red.

He met Portia's gaze, and a little jolt impacted her heart at the expression in his eyes—one of remorse, and love. But as she continued to gaze at him, her breath caught at the memory of the pure hatred in those dark eyes when he'd promised to end the Farthing's life…to end *her* life.

I cannot tell him—I simply can't.

Nor could she tell her brother what Stephen had done. Adam stared at him, his face grim, ready to punish him for disappearing from the house party without so much as a message. Were he to know that Stephen was the man who'd shot her…

"Reid," her brother said, rising, his voice laced with ice.

"Foxton, I-I must apologize," Stephen said, not moving from the doorway. The footman beside him shuffled from one foot to the other, and Adam let out a sharp sigh.

"You may go, Simon. I'm not about to toss our guest out on the street."

The footman disappeared, and Adam tilted his head to one side.

"Not yet," he added.

Stephen bowed his head and stepped inside the room. He glanced over his shoulder. "Shall I…?"

"Close the door, yes," Adam said. "I take it you've something to say to my sister."

Stephen's cheeks reddened, and he approached Portia, holding out the bouquet. She reached toward it then withdrew, wincing at the flare of pain in her arm.

Heaven! That hurt. She'd refused to take laudanum with her breakfast, despite Euphramia's instructions. Today, she needed her wits about her.

On no account must he know who I am—or who I was.

He narrowed his eyes. "Portia? Are you well?"

"Quite well, thank you," she said.

"Right," Adam said, crisply. "That's the pleasantries concluded. Now's the time for explanations."

"Adam," Portia warned, but Stephen nodded.

"Your brother's right, Portia. I must explain my uncivil behavior toward you—at the very least, I ought to have sent you a note when I left Rosecombe. You see, it was a rather delicate matter. I…" He glanced toward Portia's brother.

"You can have nothing to say to my sister that you cannot also say to *me*, Reid."

Stephen nodded. "Of course. I presume I can trust you to be discreet."

Adam frowned. "Discretion is a quality I value most highly—as do all men of a similar rank to mine."

Portia shot her brother a warning look while Stephen shifted from one foot to the other, mirroring the footman's earlier nervousness.

"Very well," he said, lowering his voice. "I received a note that my sister had been compromised."

"Good heavens!" Adam said. "And had she?"

"I believe her when she says the man in question did not ruin her—but, of course, I was compelled to act to preserve her honor."

"You mean you challenged him to a…"

Adam trailed off and turned toward her. His eyes darkened with understanding as he continued to stare at her. Then he lowered his gaze to her arm and it began to itch, as if it burned under his scrutiny.

"I see."

Though his voice was almost a whisper, it seemed to resonate through the room, thickening the atmosphere with menace.

"Adam, perhaps we should serve tea," Portia said, rising. "I'll send for someone to tend to the flowers. Thank you, Stephen, for such a beautiful bouquet."

"Back to pleasantries again, I see," her brother said, as he continued to stare at Stephen.

Portia reached for the bellpull, then let out a soft moan as the pain in her arm deepened. Placing a protective hand over her arm, she returned to her seat, aware of her brother's eyes on her.

"I-I trust Angela is not too distressed by what happened?" she said.

"She's almost fully recovered," Stephen said, "though she's aware of the folly of her actions and the danger she placed herself in. But I trust you understand why I had to rush to her side—and take up my responsibilities as an older brother."

He glanced at Adam, who seemed to be shimmering with barely controlled anger. "I am well aware of the responsibilities of an older brother, colonel," he said, his voice cold and hard. "He would do anything to defend his sister's honor—even kill those who brought her to harm."

Stephen flinched and took a step back. "Have I said anything amiss?"

"Not *said*," Adam replied. "Am I right, sister?"

Please don't, Portia mouthed to her brother, but he curled his hands into fists.

"Adam!" she cried. "We should serve tea before it gets cold. If Mrs. Winston has gone to the trouble of baking shortbread, we should at least offer a slice to our guest."

He turned toward her. "*Shortbread?* Is that all you can speak of?"

"Forgive me," Stephen said. "I'm afraid I don't understand—"

"Then I'll *make* you understand, given that you consider yourself the expert in an older brother's responsibilities."

"Adam!" Portia said. "Please, I-I'm sure Stephen has no intention to harm Sir Heath, and I—"

"Sir Heath?" Stephen's head snapped round as he shifted his gaze to her. "How the devil do you know it was Sir Heath who compromised Angela?"

"You really are a simpleton, aren't you, Reid?" Adam sneered.

"Stop it!" she said. "I-I merely assumed, given Sir Heath's reputation."

"Sir Heath isn't the only rake in Town," Stephen said, and she flinched at the hardness in his voice—the tone that had made her blood freeze with terror only that morning. "Is he, *Foxton?*" he continued, his voice almost a snarl. "You've not exactly been a paragon of gentlemanly behavior."

"We're not calling *my* behavior into question, Reid," Adam said. "Besides—"

"What the devil is that?" Stephen said, gesturing toward Portia's arm. She lowered her gaze and suppressed a cry of horror.

A dark red stain had appeared on her sleeve. Glistening and wet, it seemed to grow with each heartbeat.

"How did you sustain that, Lady Portia?"

"I-I dropped my cologne bottle, and—" she began, at the same time her brother spoke.

"She fell off a horse and cut—"

She met her brother's gaze.

"Which is it?" Stephen said. "Cologne bottle, or horse? Or…"

He approached Portia, his body seeming to fill the room, his eyes so dark that they were almost black.

"Or gunshot wound?"

Fear flared in her as the first seeds of hatred began to shimmer in his eyes—cold sparks of ice.

"I—"

He raised his hand. "Speak no further, madam, if you wish to deceive me. Or should I say, if you wish to *continue* to deceive me. If you possess a shred of decency, pay me the courtesy of telling me the truth. Answer the question you know that I must ask."

"How dare you?" Adam said, raising his hand. "I hardly think you've the right to—"

Portia caught her brother's wrist. Then she turned to face the man she loved—the man who loved her—and uttered the confession that would destroy that love irrevocably.

"I am the Farthing."

He cradled the bouquet, his chest rising and falling with each breath. The ticking of the clock on the mantelshelf filled the air, a steady beat marking time from the moment of the dissolution of her hopes. With each beat, the love seemed to drain from his eyes until, at last, there was no trace of emotion. No love, no anger, no hate.

As if she no longer mattered to him.

"Stephen," she said, and he narrowed his eyes, "won't you hear what I have to say—or tell me how you feel?"

"I feel nothing," he said, his tone flat. "I therefore have nothing to say."

"Are you not at least angry?"

He shook his head. "Only disappointed. But not with you—with myself, for having been deceived by you."

Adam let out a cold laugh. "You express disappointment when *you're* the one who shot my sister?"

"I didn't shoot Lady Portia," Stephen said. "I shot the vile creature who took pleasure in profiteering from the misery of others."

"I didn't do it for profit," Portia said. "I-I give the money to Dr. McIver."

"Good God!" he cried. "You mean to say you've persuaded that good man to enter into your deception?" Then he shook his head. "I suppose you believe you were in the right."

"It's not a question of right or wrong," Portia said.

"I'm afraid it's exactly that," he replied. "A man—or in this case, a woman—is either honest or deceitful, right or wrong, good or…" He made a dismissive gesture. "It matters not."

"Good or evil?" Adam said. "Is that what you were going to say?" He stepped toward Stephen, his expression grim with determination. "Let me tell you what the good, honest thing to do is. You are to make amends for what you have done to my sister. Our acquaintances expect you to marry her, and therefore, although I would rather her shackle herself to any man but you, I insist on your doing the honorable thing, seeing as you set such store by honor."

"No!" Portia cried, taking her brother's hand. "Do not make me. I couldn't bear to marry a man who hates me."

Stephen blinked, and for a moment she caught a sheen of regret in his eyes. He lowered the gaze to the bouquet in his hands, then sighed.

"I do not hate you, Portia," he said. "I may think what you've done is beyond despicable, but I can never hate you."

A small flame of hope swelled in her heart—which his next words doused.

"I have no feelings toward you at all." He cast another glance at the bouquet, then dropped it onto a chair. "Do with those what you will."

"P-perhaps Angela might care for them?" Portia suggested. "She's in need of comfort."

"What my sister is in need of is no concern of yours," he said. "And I would thank you to refer to her as *Lady Angela*."

"Damn you, Reid," Adam said, "I ought to—"

"No," Portia said quietly, forcing her sorrow into the back of her mind. "Let us not stoop to the sort of display of feeling that befits those of lower rank."

Stephen frowned, but she tilted her head up, ignoring the gleam in his eyes.

"Brother, please ring the bell for Charles, so he can escort your visitor out."

"If you're so desirous of my absence, I can see myself out."

"Then please oblige us before I fetch my pistol," Adam said. "We wouldn't want you collapsing in a fit of apoplexy at the sound of a gunshot, would we? Or perhaps you're less of a blubbering coward when you're shooting a woman."

"Adam, leave him be!" Portia said.

The resoluteness in Stephen's expression almost faltered, then he turned his disapproving gaze on her.

"Please refrain from attempting to speak on my behalf, madam," he said. "I reserve that privilege for those whom I care about." He gave a stiff bow. "Good day, Your Grace."

Adam opened his mouth to respond, but she squeezed his hand. Then Stephen turned to her, and her heart shuddered at the soullessness in his eyes—as if he were no longer alive…

Or as if she were dead to him.

"Lady Portia," he said with a nod. Before she could respond, he turned and exited the drawing room. His footsteps faded, followed by a murmur of voices as Reeve intercepted him at the front door. Then the door opened and closed in the distance, followed by silence.

Adam picked up the bouquet. "I'll dispose of this."

"Please don't," she said. "Although I've no wish to have them, they're pretty enough and would brighten someone's day. I could take them to the hospital—the soldiers always appreciate a little color in that dreary ward."

He let out a sharp sigh. "Portia, don't you think your devotion to that place has landed you in enough trouble?"

She wiped her eyes. "You didn't have to be quite so harsh on Ste"—she checked herself—"on the colonel about his fear of gunshots."

He snorted. "I was generous—*more* than generous. He left our home with his balls and head intact. By rights, I should have shot him on the spot. It would have restored the honor attached to our name and given me much gratification."

"Then why didn't you?"

He turned toward her, and his expression softened. "Because it wouldn't have made you happy. Perhaps had I considered your happiness a little more over our family's honor"—he gestured to her arm—"none of this would have happened."

He picked up the bouquet and strode to the window.

"We should leave Town."

"Are you ashamed of me?"

"I cannot deny I'm disappointed at the turn of events, but I doubt you'll relish the prospect of remaining here for the rest of the Season. After all, there's always the next. And you can recover at Forthridge Park in peace."

"Tucked away in your country seat in obscurity so I don't disgrace you?"

"No," he said, shaking his head. "Kept safe away from prying eyes and the gossipmongers' tongues. And..." He grinned, though his eyes were glazed with moisture. "You can spend your days shooting game rather than rakes."

She shook her head. "I intend never to pick up a pistol again. I'll stick with a bow and arrow."

"Then I can rest easy that you're no longer placing yourself in danger and that you'll never suffer hurt again."

Hurt to her person, perhaps. But as for her heart, it was too late.

It was broken beyond repair.

"Very well," she said. "Let us retire to the country. I only ask one thing."

"Which is?"

"I wish to be gone from London within the hour."

CHAPTER TWENTY-FOUR

*B*LOODY, FUCKING HELL!

Stephen gritted his teeth as he strode away from the Foxton residence.

How could he have been so blind? The signs had been there, only he'd been too weak-minded to notice them—her insistence on justifying dishonesty, her defense of that creature the Farthing.

No…*she* was that creature.

Fuck! Fuck, fuck, fuck!

"I *beg* your pardon, young man?"

He looked up and startled as he almost collided with a couple strolling arm in arm along the pavement.

Bloody hell, that was all he needed—Earl sodding Thorpe and his mother.

The dowager countess tilted her head to one side and glared at him, her eyes the color of ice. Then slowly she arched a perfectly formed brow and waited.

"Lady Thorpe, I must apologize," Stephen said. "That was most unseemly of me." He bowed, offering his hand. But she made no move to take it.

"What are you about, Reid?" Thorpe said. Then he glanced toward the white-fronted building from which Stephen had emerged. "Ah! Foxton gave you a hard time about bolting from his sister?"

"Giles, please refrain from being so coarse," the dowager said, her gaze still fixed on Stephen. "No matter the provocation."

Stephen opened his mouth to tell Thorpe exactly what he thought of Foxton's sister, then he closed it again.

"Lady Thorpe, I've had a somewhat trying afternoon—but that is no reason to act so dishonorably in your distinguished presence. Please accept my unreserved apology."

The eyebrow lowered, but the frown remained. Then she turned to Thorpe.

"Giles, darling, is Society so unchanged that young men still seek to flatter a woman with vacuous words? I'd rather subject myself to brutish honesty than flattery any day."

"But you're more intelligent than most, Mother," Thorpe said. "Perhaps the colonel has encountered few women who are truly immune to flattery."

Stephen ignored the little voice in his head telling him of the one woman he knew who cared nothing for flattery.

"We cannot waste our day standing around on the street," Lady Thorpe said. "Henrietta will be waiting for us."

For a heartbeat, Thorpe's expression softened and Stephen tempered the spike of jealousy when faced with a man who loved his wife, and whose wife loved him.

He tipped his hat, then resumed his journey home.

Inside, he heard soft music. Angela was singing in the morning room, accompanied by Mrs. Stowe on the pianoforte. As he entered, Angela rushed toward him, arms outstretched.

"Brother!" She buried her head in his chest while he embraced her, and his heart filled with love. He'd feared that her sweet innocence and joy for life had been irrevocably crushed.

Over the top of his sister's golden head, he saw Mrs. Stowe watching them, a mixture of wariness and sorrow in her soft gray eyes.

"Angela has been coming along very well with her music, colonel," she said. "We were about to take tea—but perhaps you'd like to spend some time alone with your sister. I've several errands to run and have no wish to be in your way."

"You could never be in my way, Mrs. Stowe," he said. "I'm only glad that you agreed to resume your duties, given how unfairly I treated you."

She colored, then moved to the pianoforte to gather the music. "Your desire to protect your sister is to be admired," she said. "You have taken on the responsibility of a parent, and a parent always places their child above all other considerations."

"We've been learning a love song," Angela said. "In Italian, would you believe! I found the language difficult at first, but I can speak a few phrases. I thought it might be useful if ever you took me to Rome. Lady Hardwick told me that Rome is the most beautiful city in the whole world, and..."

She rattled on excitedly. At the far end of the room, Mrs. Stowe bustled about, tidying up the various papers. She reached for a book, then cringed. It slipped out of her grasp and fell to the floor with a clatter. She bowed her head, eyes closed, and massaged the fingers of her right hand. At length, she opened her eyes, which were bright with moisture. She met Stephen's gaze and lowered her arms, moving her right hand to conceal it behind her back. Her lips curled into a smile that did not reach her eyes.

"I'll leave the two of you in peace," she said. "I can ask Mrs. Green to make tea."

She exited the room, and Stephen retrieved the book she'd dropped.

"Latin?" he asked, opening the first page.

"It belongs to Mrs. Stowe. She's been teaching me a few phrases."

"I trust you're not taking advantage of her, Angela. She's your chaperone, not your governess. Though perhaps I should be grateful that she's managed to encourage you to further your education. Poor Miss Treacher quite despaired of you."

"I don't see Mrs. Stowe as a governess," Angela said. "Nor do I view her as a chaperone—she's a friend. Which was why we were going to take tea together after—" She broke off, frowning. "Were you not supposed to be taking tea with Lady Portia?"

He nodded, and she fixed her clear gaze on him.

"What's wrong, brother?"

"Nothing."

"I can see you're distressed. Something's happened." Then her frown deepened. "Oh no—I've ruined your life as well as risking my own, haven't I?"

"What the devil do you mean?" he asked.

"She can't forgive you, can she?"

No. And I daresay she never will.

Stephen ignored the taunts of his conscience.

"You left Duchess Whitcombe's house party because of me." She withdrew from his embrace and approached the door.

"Where are you going, Angela?"

"To explain to Lady Portia that it's my fault you left early."

"It won't make any difference."

"I can try, brother. She might listen to me."

"The fewer people know about your little escapade, the better," he said. "We're trying to prevent gossip from spreading."

"Lady Portia isn't a gossipmonger. You've said yourself, she's the most honorable person of your acquaintance. And if she's to become my sister—"

"There's no chance of that, now."

Her face creased with distress. "No…" she whispered, her eyes glistening with sorrow. "Oh, brother, I'm so sorry!"

"I thought you disliked her," he said. "After all, it was your incivility toward her that resulted in your not going to Rosecombe."

She blushed. "I was angry because she seemed to dislike Sir Heath, and thought she was jealous. But I know now that I was wrong." Then her smile returned. "Perhaps if I apologized, it would set things right? If she knows that I'd like nothing more than have her as a sister, she might—"

"No!" he said, and she flinched at the harshness in his voice. "Lady Portia and I will not be marrying—and that's an end to the matter."

"But you said she was the only—"

"She was," he said. "But she no longer is."

"Why?"

"It's not your place to ask why."

"It is if it's made you so unhappy!"

"I'm not unhappy."

"Don't lie!" she said. "Aren't you supposed to be a paragon of honesty? Don't you always lecture me about how it's important not to utter falsehoods, and not to harbor secrets?"

"Some secrets are best kept hidden."

She let out a snort. "I recall others saying that very same thing, and your criticizing them for doing so."

Others such as Lady Portia—but what a secret *she'd* kept hidden!

"I'll not rest until you tell me."

"Lord save me from belligerent, stubborn females!" he said. But perhaps it *was* best if Angela knew the awful truth—then she might reconsider any foolish escapades.

He took her hand, steered her toward a chair, and sat her down.

"Brother?" Her voice wavered with apprehension. "Have *I* done something wrong?"

"No, sweet sister," he said. "It's only that…" He drew in a deep breath and braced himself. "Lady Portia Hawke is the Farthing."

For a moment, she stared at him, open-mouthed. Then she threw back her head and laughed.

"Oh, brother!" she cried. "You almost completely fooled me! I ought to strike you down, for you had me so worried. But you can be forgiven, considering the worry I've caused you."

"No, Angela, I—"

"You can't be *too* distressed over Lady Portia if you're capable of making such a jape of it," she continued. "Though I'm not sure she'd find such a tale amusing. So I take it you've not broken faith with her and that she *is* to be my sister?" Her eyes narrowed. "In which case, why have you returned so early when you were supposed to be taking tea with…" She hesitated. "I mean, you wouldn't…"

The color drained from her face, and her mouth formed an "O."

He took her hands, and she lowered her gaze, then looked back up at him.

"L-Lady Portia?" she whispered. "B-but…" She shook her head. "I always thought she was different to other… Oh!" She let out a cry. "Does that mean you…you *shot* her?"

"Angela, I didn't know she was—"

She withdrew her hands. "You shot her," she said quietly.

"I shot the *Farthing*."

"Is she badly injured?"

"Just her arm."

"*Just*," she said, with a snort.

"Angela, if she hadn't chosen to play a man's game, she wouldn't have suffered a man's punishment."

"Do you really believe that, brother? Or is that your argument to justify what you've done?"

"Surely you're not condoning what *she's* done."

"She's always been different," Angela said. "You said so yourself—in fact, it's why you admire her so much. Or did. Because she's not like other ladies who only want to find husbands for themselves. And Mrs. Stowe says—"

"Oh, *do* tell me what the learned Mrs. Stowe says," Stephen said, aware of the petulance in his tone. But his sister was placing a mirror in front of him and he wasn't fond of the reflection he saw.

"Mrs. Stowe says that many women crave independence, and they should not be denied."

"But with independence comes responsibility—a woman making such a wish must take responsibility for her own actions and suffer the lack of security, having to fend for herself. And no woman wants that for herself."

"Perhaps, for some women, they do not have the privilege of choice, and instead must suffer the misfortune of circumstance."

What preposterous nonsense was Mrs. Stowe filling Angela's head with? But as Stephen opened his mouth to reply, he recalled the sight of the chaperone's misshapen hand, which not only gave her discomfort, but also shame, such that she strived to hide her pain.

Some women kept secrets to protect themselves, and others.

And some, no matter how misguided they may be, acted out of good intentions, and the wish to do better.

I've been a fucking fool.

"Brother!"

Bugger, he'd spoken aloud. "Forgive me, Angela."

"It's not my forgiveness that's in doubt, but Lady Portia's," Angela said. "Perhaps you ought to beg for it. I can come with you, if you like. After all, I'm the reason you shot her."

He shook his head. "She didn't seem at all angry that I'd shot her. Her brother was furious, as expected, but Portia…"

He recalled her expression not half an hour earlier when he'd stepped into the drawing room brandishing the bouquet of roses—the bouquet that he'd tossed aside with such contempt. Not a trace of anger or hatred, or even dislike, had he seen. Instead, though she'd seemed apprehensive, the delight in her eyes as he presented her with the bouquet had soothed his soul.

Whether or not Portia was the Farthing—whom he'd described as the most vile person alive—she had a good soul and a kind heart. And she was a better person than he could hope to be.

Oh, Portia—my Portia!

There was a knock, and Mrs. Stowe appeared together with a maid brandishing a tea tray.

"Set the tray over by the window, please, Millicent," Mrs. Stowe said. "Colonel, Angela, I'll leave you to your tea."

"No, please come in," Stephen said. "Angela considers you a friend, and your original plans were to have tea together without my getting under your feet. I have no wish for you to take your tea alone." He glanced at Angela and smiled. "I've a very particular errand to run."

"Shall I bring you a cup for when you return, sir?" the maid asked.

"No need, Millicent," Stephen said. "I have committed a grave transgression, you see—and the time a man needs to make amends should be in proportion to the gravity of his sin. In which case, I fear I may be some time."

Mrs. Stowe smiled. "A penitent man is always to be admired," she said. "The majority of the male sex lacks not only the propensity to recognize when he's sinned against another, but also the willingness to apologize and atone. I trust your quest will be successful."

He bowed, took his leave, then exited the building and retraced his steps toward the Foxton residence, darting behind a wall when he caught sight of Lady Thorpe and her son.

By the time he arrived, the sun had shifted toward the horizon, and shadows of the trees lining the road lengthened across the pavement. He knocked on the door, and it opened to reveal the butler, who arched a dark brow and glared at him.

"Yes?"

"Is Lady Portia at home?"

"You've just missed them, I'm sad to say," the butler said in a tone that expressed anything but.

Behind, Stephen could discern footmen bustling about the hallway. Two carried a trunk across the floor, while a third placed a dust sheet over a chair. Another opened the longcase clock at the foot of the staircase, stopped the pendulum, then closed it again.

A little shiver of apprehension rippled through Stephen.

"May I call on them after they have returned?"

"His Grace has left for the country."

"Somewhat unexpected," Stephen said. "Why—"

"It's not my place to ask," the butler interrupted. "One must never question whether the duke acts in a manner that those of lower ranks expect."

"And Lady Portia?"

The butler gave a cold smile. "She was *most* eager to leave. She particularly asked me to tell *you*, were you to darken our threshold again, that you were no longer welcome."

"How dare you speak to me with such incivility!" Stephen said.

"Both his Grace and Lady Portia gave me leave to speak to you as I saw fit," the butler said. "I cannot entertain the notion of one such as you crossing my master's threshold, tainting his name with your own family's disgrace—your sister's ruination, not to mention your taking part in an illegal duel. I'm sure the Society gossip columns would take a great interest in the former, and the authorities in the latter."

"Surely you wouldn't—"

The butler's lip curled in a sneer. "Lady Portia was most precise in her instructions before she left."

Portia…

Stephen caught his breath as nausea swelled in his gut. Then the butler gave a cold smile, inclined his head in the slightest of acknowledgments, and shut the door in his face.

Portia had gone. She was lost to him.

CHAPTER TWENTY-FIVE

Forthridge Park, Hampshire

OVER THE PAST weeks, the lush green of the Hampshire countryside had dulled, before brightening again into vibrant reds and oranges, then settling into warm browns and yellows. Soon, the leaves would disappear altogether, falling to form a soft brown carpet through which Portia could kick her way, breathing in that very particular aroma that heralded the demise of summer.

Not that she minded the end of the summer. The corsets Nerissa laced her into were uncomfortable at best, but under the intense heat of the sun, her undergarments restricted her breathing, and her skin grew irritable and itchy. The onset of autumn signaled a return to some comfort, even if she were unable to completely shed her corsets and stays—at least when visitors came to Forthridge Park.

Not that any visitors of note had arrived.

By visitors of note, you mean him.

She silenced the voice in her mind and rose from the love seat in the window, shifting position to the shade. She'd had to move several times already, being chased by the sun as it stretched across the floor. In less than an hour it would disappear altogether, sliding below the line of firs on the horizon, illuminating them with a pink and orange glow, after which the light would fade, followed by the coolness of night when she could, at last, breathe properly again.

Of late, her corsets seemed to have grown tighter, the gap

between the edges widening, no matter how tightly Nerissa pulled on the laces.

Why didn't men have to deal with stays and petticoats? True, her brother seemed to obsess over his collection of cravats, insisting that they were pressed daily, sprayed with cologne, and tied to perfection. Nerissa had once told her that Adam's valet had been asked to retie his cravat six times before it was declared fit to be seen.

Adam could be forgiven his little peculiarities. Nevertheless, a perfectly tied cravat did not pain him as much as this damned corset was paining her, squeezing at her ribs until she couldn't draw breath.

Was it any wonder she'd wanted to masquerade as a man? Even if it had cost her…

No. Do not *think of it.*

She pulled her mind back from the brink before it embarked upon the path to despair. But her hand involuntarily touched the scar on her arm, her fingertips running along the little bumps in the flesh where Euphramia had stitched it. The scar might be a mark of her flaws, but it served as a reminder that, though she may have regretted having loved and lost, the man who'd inflicted that scar would never have loved her as she wished to be loved. In the end, he couldn't accept her as she truly was—with all the flaws and imperfections that came with a flesh-and-blood woman.

Stephen had wanted a paragon. And no such woman existed—at least not among Portia's friends, all misfits in some way. And whatever he may have declared while he was courting her, he had proved the point that all men wanted a woman who did his bidding, not one who challenged him at every turn.

The door opened and her brother entered the parlor. He approached the window and sat beside her.

"Much as I find plenty to occupy myself with in London," he said, "I shall never tire of the view from this window."

"This part of the garden has a natural beauty, certainly," she replied. "You'd never think it had been landscaped only last year. Arabella's husband is to be commended—he has an eye for beauty."

"That he does, having bagged one of Society's premier beauties. Baxter's not only a competent businessman, he's a shrewd suitor."

"They never set out to wed," she said. "It was hatred at first sight, or so Bella says. But there's no denying how deeply they love each other. You only have to look at them to see that." She let out a sigh. "Why is it that people can only be truly happy in pairs? It's as if a single person is an incomplete soul, drifting—unfulfilled and unsatisfied—until they can find that one person who completes them. Like thousands of keys and locks, all of different shapes and sizes, submitting themselves to the hand of fate, which decides whether they're a perfect fit and can truly love each other."

"Love's overrated, puss," he said, giving her hand an affectionate pat. "It only leads to misery."

"How would you know, Adam? It's not an emotion you harbor for anyone, nor are ever likely to."

"I may not understand the concept, but I can see it in your eyes." He smiled. "But I didn't come here to speak of love—I came to see if you're any better. Your maid said you didn't touch your luncheon."

"Does Nerissa report my activities to you?" she said, wincing at the sharpness in her voice. Then she shook her head. "Forgive me. I've been somewhat irritable lately."

"Tell me something I haven't observed," he said good-naturedly. "She and I are merely concerned about your health. Had that wound festered…"

"But it didn't," she said, resisting the urge to scratch the scar, which still itched some two months after the duel.

"Then perhaps it's Miss Lucas's cordial that's making you unwell. After all, she's only the *daughter* of a doctor."

"And by virtue of her sex, she knows nothing about medicine?"

"You must admit, you've been taking it almost a month, and you're not any better. In fact, if anything, I'd say your sprits are lower than they were when we left London."

"I felt unwell before Euphramia sent the cordial," Portia said. "Besides, it's to prevent putrefaction, not lift the spirits."

"Then what the devil is wrong with you?" he said. "Perhaps I ought to send for Dr. McIver."

"I can't have him knowing what's happened."

"You trust him, surely?"

"Of course," she said, "but I can't bear the thought of his knowing that my donations were the result of…"

She made a random gesture in the air, and he nodded, understanding in his eyes. Then he rose and offered his arm.

"Care to permit me to escort you to supper?" he asked. "I've had the cook make her chicken broth—the one you used to love so much when we were children. She's been boiling the bones all day."

"Then I mustn't disappoint *her*, at least."

He squeezed her hand. "You're not a disappointment, puss. We can try again next Season, find you a husband worthy of you. I daresay Devereaux could be persuaded."

She shivered at the notion of the silent, brooding earl. Handsome he may be—savagely so—but he carried an air of menace.

"Perhaps not." Adam chuckled. "But you could at least consider the benefits of having a husband who doesn't answer back."

"A similar quality to that which you're looking for in a wife."

He laughed again, then escorted her to the dining room.

Though she was unable to finish her soup, Portia made, according to her brother, a "passable attempt." But the sight of the lemon syllabub, the creamy white cloud billowing in the glass before her, threatened to turn her stomach, and she excused herself and retired early, her brother's eyes focused on her beneath his frown as she exited the dining room to his promise to bring her a cup of tea.

Dear Adam! He might be arrogant and overbearing, but few brothers would have suffered such wild behavior in a younger sister without either subjecting her to a severe thrashing, or sending her away to the sort of schools where the mistresses were little more than gaolers. Or worse, he could have sent her to an asylum. He might declare that he had no intention of loving, but imagine what he might be capable of if he found the other part of his soul—the woman to make him complete?

Nerissa was already waiting in Portia's chamber.

"Have you taken your supper?" Portia asked.

"Mrs. Charlton's set some aside for me once I've got you settled."

"You make me sound like an invalid," Portia said, standing obediently, arms raised, while Nerissa removed her dress. The maid drew back the bedcover and pulled out Portia's nightgown, which she'd wrapped around the warming pan earlier. She held it up and studied it, her brow furrowed in concentration.

"Lady Portia," she said, her voice tight, "do you recall when I asked you about your monthly bleed, that morning at Rosecombe? And you said…"

"I recall what I said," Portia said, her face hot with shame.

Nerissa nodded. "Yes, that it wasn't your monthly bleed. "Well, I've not had to launder your nightgown for…" She gestured to the center of the garment.

No…

"I-I wondered, perhaps, seeing as you had…" Nerissa blushed scarlet and clutched the gown to her breast. "You've been feeling unwell."

Dear Lord, no…

She gestured to the discarded corset. "You've said it's been getting tighter. I've not been able to lace it completely closed."

The pit of Portia's stomach dipped and she pitched forward, her legs crumpling beneath her. Nerissa took her arm and steadied her as she drew in a deep breath, willing her trembling body to obey her will.

"Do you think, perhaps…" The distress in the maid's eyes, which brimmed with tears, was almost too much to bear. "F-forgive me. I cannot say it!"

"Then let me," Portia said, the need to comfort her maid overpowering her own selfish desires. "You're asking me whether I am carrying Colonel Reid's child."

Portia startled at the sound of shattering porcelain. She turned to see her brother in the doorway, a pool of dark brown liquid at his feet, together with the remnants of a teacup.

"Oh, Your Grace!" Nerissa cried. "What a mess. That'll need clearing up."

He tilted his head to one side, his eyes the color of midnight as he fixed his gaze on Portia.

"Yes," he said quietly, "the *mess* will need a great deal of clearing up."

CHAPTER TWENTY-SIX

THE BENEFIT OF the London Season having come to an end was the fact that almost all of the preening young bucks had left—either returned to their country seats to learn how to run their papas' estates or, in the case of the youngest ones, to Oxford or Cambridge to subject themselves to an education that few of them deserved or would make use of in their charmed lives.

Stephen himself, to his shame, had spent little time with his books while at Oxford, despite the dean of Balliol College expressing hopes that he might be a distinguished scholar. But the tradition in his family was that second sons joined the militia, for which they merely needed the ability to wield a sword, shoot straight, and order others about. He'd have been more suited to the life of a scholar, but not even the third sons in his family had been permitted to decide their fate, destined as they were for the church, whether they were fit to do the Almighty's work or not.

Another benefit of the Season having come to an end was that a man could find a quiet corner in the clubroom at Boodle's without having to jostle other members for a place. And there was little risk of encountering the worst members of the *ton*, who considered any club other than White's beneath their dignity.

He relaxed into the button-backed leather chair and closed his eyes, relishing the quiet murmur of voices and gentle chink of glasses as the footmen milled about, distributing brandy, newspapers, and cigars. While he often considered letting his membership of Boodle's lapse, he had to agree with the general maxim that a gentlemen's club was his haven from the rigors of the world outside brought about by female company.

Namely his sister and her chaperone. Angela had yet to forgive him for "chasing away Lady Portia," as she put it, and whenever he was in her presence, she turned her soulful, judgmental gaze on him. Mrs. Stowe, though she remained diplomatically neutral, refused to be drawn into their arguments, always seeming to display the sort of deadly dull good sense that reminded him of an overbearing parent.

He let out a sigh and admonished himself. Angela was not to be blamed for Lady Portia's disappearance, and Mrs. Stowe was far more pleasant company than almost every woman in London.

Every woman except…*her*.

"I say, Reid!" a familiar voice said. "I *thought* it was you. We've not seen you here for some time. How goes things?"

Stephen opened his eyes and recognized his old university friend—one of those rare fellows who had made use of an Oxford education and earned his degree on merit, as opposed to by virtue of a generous donation to the dean of Balliol.

"Wormleighton!" he said. "I thought you'd be in the country this time of year."

"I leave tomorrow." Wormleighton gestured to a footman at the far end of the clubroom, then lowered himself into the chair next to Stephen, the leather creaking as he settled into the seat. "How about you?"

"We leave for my brother's seat next week," Stephen said. "Frederick is spending the winter in Italy with his family."

"Is your sister going with them?"

Stephen shook his head. "Angela is staying with me, but she'll be accompanied by her chaperone, so she will at least have some female company."

The footman appeared with a glass of amber liquid, and Wormleighton plucked it from the tray and drained it.

"Excellent!" he said with a sigh. "The Armagnac at Boodle's is always superior to anything a fellow could find at White's."

"The company, also," Stephen said.

"Another, if you please," Wormleighton said to the footman, "and whatever my friend's having. Unless it's not too early to take a bottle of champagne? Is there one you recommend?"

"We ordered a case of the Veuve Clicquot 1810 for the Duke of Wellington, of which we have two bottles left," the footman said. "It's easy on the palate, though a little on the sweet side. If you're thinking of dining here, it would be an excellent accompaniment to the Dover sole."

"I'm not dining, but celebrating," Wormleighton said. "But I doubt His Grace would take kindly to just anyone taking one of his bottles."

"Any *civilian*, perhaps, sir," the footman said, gesturing to Stephen, "but a soldier, and fellow *veteranus* of Waterloo, could never be described as *just anyone*."

"Very well, then," Wormleighton said. "I'll take advantage of being in the company of a hero and take a bottle. But I insist it's put on my ledger."

The footman bowed, then disappeared, and returned shortly after with two glasses filled with a pale liquid, within which a stream of bubbles ascended in a straight line from the bottom to the surface, where they dissipated around the rim. Wormleighton plucked a glass eagerly from the tray and took a sip.

Stephen followed suit. "What are we celebrating, other than the fact that we're both escaping London?"

Wormleighton's eyes sparkled with pleasure. "Kitty is expecting our first child."

"Congratulations."

"It's long overdue," Wormleighton said. "We've been married almost three years, and we despaired of having a child of our own."

"And now you have an heir on the way."

"Whether we have a son or daughter matters not to me," Wormleighton said. "All I wish for is a healthy child."

"And Katherine?"

"Kitty wants a son—I think because she felt her father's resentment of her sex until her younger brother was born. Lord Tate's desperation for a male heir is not something I share." His eyes took on a faraway look, as if he could see, over the horizon, a state of ultimate bliss. "To think," he said, sighing, "I'll soon be holding my child in my arms. I cannot think of anything a man could wish for more than that. Save, of course, a loving wife— and I've already been blessed with my sweet Kitty."

"I envy you," Stephen said before taking another mouthful of champagne.

"It'll be your turn soon. Weren't you courting that Hawke girl—Lady Portia? I'll wager that before the year is out, you'll be holding *your* child in your arms."

The image swam before Stephen's mind—a tiny child in his arms, with a head of thick, dark hair and wide, brilliant blue eyes, curling a fat pink fist around his forefinger.

Then he shook his head. "I think it'll take a little longer than that."

"Rejected you, has she?" Wormleighton shook his head. "Foxton always was one who set too much store on rank, but I thought Lady Portia had more sense. At least she's sensible enough not to have been taken in by Sir Heath Moss's charms."

Stephen's breath caught as he tightened the grip on his glass. Had Sir Heath broken his promise to remain silent about Angela?

I swear, Sir Heath, if you say one word about my sister, I'll cut off your—

"Lady Cholmondeley-Walker is his latest conquest," Wormleighton continued. "Almost cost him his life."

"I beg pardon?"

Wormleighton's eyes widened, and he leaned forward. "You've not heard? It's all over White's." He glanced over his shoulder to the clubroom's other occupants, then lowered his voice. "Sir Heath's sporting an injured leg—he's been limping about Hyde Park to elicit sympathy from the fairer sex. Apparently a woman unable to apply reason finds an injured man damnably attractive."

"No matter his character or honor?" Stephen said. "Is he badly injured?" he added, tempering the little voice in his head that issued a cheer.

"Most likely it's just a scratch," Wormleighton said. "Of course, if you ask him, he'll say he was on the brink of death. But at least he fared better than his opponent. Cholmondeley-Walker is, by all accounts, preparing to meet his maker."

Dear God!

A series of tuts and the rustling of newspapers told Stephen that he'd spoken aloud.

"I daresay he'll survive—he's a resilient chap. But it wasn't a certainty yesterday, by all accounts." Wormleighton shook his head. "That's what happens when unskilled men engage in a duel. A stray bullet can cause irreparable damage. It's a pity the Farthing seems to have disappeared. Had he been present, I daresay the duel would have ended in one combatant sustaining a slight scratch and the other the loss of fifty pounds."

"Surely you're not condoning the *Farthing*?" Stphen said.

"Why not?" came the reply. "He's fought countless duels—at least ten, I'd reckon—all with the purpose of ensuring that nobody is hurt, at least no more than superficially."

"You speak nonsense," Stephen said, suppressing a shudder at the notion of Portia placing herself in danger on so many occasions.

Dear Lord—what if she'd been shot?

But she was shot—and left for dead.

"Haven't you noticed the number of gentlemen wandering about Town this Season sporting scratches to the ear, or the hand?" Wormleighton said. "Think on it—each and every one of them could have been maimed or killed. But instead of losing their lives, they chose to lose fifty pounds instead."

He sipped his drink and leaned back in his chair. "I'd say that's a fair bargain. A man as skilled as the Farthing could easily have sent his opponents to their graves, or employed his skills for more nefarious means. Instead, he chose to ensure that only a little blood was spilled. Don't you recall what happened to Lord Green last summer? Do you think he lost his leg in a riding accident? Or Mr. Frankland, who lost his life? Granted, they were both unpleasant sorts of fellows, lacking in honor—but no man deserves to suffer or die for the sake of honor."

Stephen set his glass aside as nausea swelled in the pit of his stomach. "Y-you think the Farthing acted out of honor?"

His companion nodded. "Of course. A lesser man wouldn't remain anonymous—he'd be unable to resist boasting of his prowess among his acquaintances. He might continue to wear his mask to preserve the dignity of others, but it'd be the worst-kept secret in London. However, nobody—*nobody at all*—knows the identity of the Farthing."

Except me.

"Though," Wormleighton continued, frowning, "I wouldn't consider it entirely honorable to pocket fifty pounds each time."

"Perhaps he was in need of funds," Stephen said quietly. "For his family, perhaps—or others."

"A masked crusader?" Wormleighton's eyes shone. "Mayhap he used the funds to help the poor, or the sick. That would make him a hero, would it not?"

A clock chimed in the distance, and Wormleighton set his glass aside.

"Best be off. Can't keep my Kitty waiting. Come and pay us a visit in the country, Reid—when you can stomach the sight of our marital bliss, that is. No, don't get up," he added, as Stephen rose. "Finish the bottle."

"I'm not thirsty," Stephen said.

...and I have nothing to celebrate.

The two men exited the club, parting at the front door, and Stephen set off toward home, where a judgmental, angry sister awaited him.

Angela had every right to be angry—but she couldn't be as

angry as he was with himself.

Or as disappointed.

As expected, Stephen's sister greeted him coolly as he entered the morning room. She then excused herself, leaving him alone with Mrs. Stowe.

"As least she spoke to me this time," he said. "I thought she'd forgiven me, but ever since…"

"Ever since Lady Portia left London, Angela has blamed you?" Mrs. Stowe suggested.

Did she possess the ability to read his mind?

"Your sister will see reason eventually—she just needs to reconcile what's happened with her conscience."

"Have you spoken to her of the folly of her actions?" he asked.

"Your sister's an astute young woman," Mrs. Stowe said. "I merely provide the understanding silence that gives her the space to work it out for herself—the blank canvas on which she paints the portrait of her folly to enable her to understand the consequences of her actions."

He stared at her, and she smiled.

"It sounds all rather grand, does it not?" she said. "But I fear you'd not appreciate any degree of frankness today."

"On the contrary, Mrs. Stowe, I *insist* you be frank."

"In which case, I would say that Angela will need time to reconcile with her conscience the fact that her folly resulted in the brother she loves shooting Lady Portia Hawke."

He drew in a sharp breath. "How the devil did you know?" He shook his head. "Has Angela been gossiping?"

"Of course not," she said. "But it's plain to see if you look closely enough. Just because I'm unnoticeable, doesn't mean I'm also blind. For what other purpose would you have taken a turn about the park at dawn? And I can think of no other reason why you'd abandon your courtship of Lady Portia. Even the meanest intelligence could discern that you…" She made a dismissive gesture. "It matters not. I ought to see to your sister."

He caught her hand, and she let out a low cry. He released it, but not before he'd felt the misshapen fingers—the lumps and bumps and sharp shards, almost as if…

…almost as if someone had smashed her hand to pieces.

"Forgive me, Mrs. Stowe," he said. "I meant no harm."

She cradled her hand, then tugged at her glove to hide the scars peeping out from beneath the hem.

"I rather suspect you're a great deal more intelligent than you'd have Society believe, Mrs. Stowe."

She gave a wistful smile. "Society will believe what it wants," she said. "There's nothing I—or any woman—could do, or say, to convince the world otherwise."

"Perhaps the world you've occupied has failed to appreciate you, Mrs. Stowe, but the little corner you occupy at present places great value on your qualities. In many ways, you remind me of…"

Lady Portia.

She approached the door and reached for the handle with her right hand, then hesitated and took it with the left. Then she turned to face him.

"Might I be so bold as to make a suggestion, Colonel Reid?"

"Please do."

"You could always pay her a visit."

There was no need to ask to whom she was referring.

"Lady Portia has left London, Mrs. Stowe."

"I'm aware of that," she replied, "but Forthridge Park is en route to your brother's seat. It's a short detour—barely five miles, on the outskirts of Saddleforth village."

"You know the place well?" he said. "Have you visited? Forgive me, I had not known you were acquainted with Lady Portia."

"I have not had the pleasure of an introduction with her."

"Then her brother, the duke?"

Her eyes widened, then she shook her head, her cheeks reddening. "My late husband was a little acquainted with His Grace, I believe, though he wouldn't recall it, for it was only a slight acquaintance."

"And Foxton isn't one to recall anyone he considered beneath him," Stephen said. "Not to impugn the late Mr. Stowe, of course, but Foxton's the most frightful—"

"I should go to Angela," she said. "I fear that if I do not encourage her hourly, her trunk will never be packed in time before we leave."

"Forgive me, I didn't mean to distress you," Stephen said, "or to pass judgment on your late husband." He lowered his gaze to her misshapen hand.

"It was nothing," she said, smiling, though her eyes retained a gleam of sadness as she shifted her hand behind her back. "And you must forgive *me* for speaking out of turn. I have no wish to disrupt our journey to Somerset, and have no right to tell you what you must do."

"But that doesn't mean I should not at least listen," he said. "When an insightful woman speaks, it is wise to take note."

She nodded, then slipped through the door, closing it softly behind her.

Mrs. Stowe was right. In fact, Stephen had fought the urge to follow Portia and beg her forgiveness. She was generous-minded enough to give him a chance. After all, in their discussions *he* was the one who'd displayed arrogant intransigence. His fear that she might reject him was born of a fear that she might be like him.

But she was a better person than he—a better person than the rest of the world. And, perhaps, if she forgave him, she might teach him to aspire to reach her level of goodness.

There was nothing to lose if he tried.

CHAPTER TWENTY-SEVEN

AFTER TRAVELING WHAT seemed like several miles through the trees, the carriage rounded a corner, and the trees thinned to reveal the landscape.

A lake dominated the foreground, and the drive wound around one side of it, following a slight incline leading toward the main house, a building of soft gray stone. The central section was topped by a dome with a flagpole, the flag fluttering in the breeze, and was flanked by the main body to the building—two halves that extended either side, with row upon row of windows that stared out across the landscape.

Angela leaned out of the carriage window.

"My heavens—it's *huge!*" she said. "I've never seen anything the like. It must be ten times the size of our home. And Lady Portia lives here with her brother? How can one building house only two people?"

"Not just two people, Angela," Mrs. Stowe said. "There will be a whole household living there. Not to mention the steward whose offices are likely to occupy some of the rooms."

"How would you even begin to take care of a house that size?"

"The housekeeper will see to that," Mrs. Stowe said.

"Overseen by the mistress of the house, I suppose," Angela said. "But it doesn't have a mistress at present."

"I daresay Lady Portia keeps house for her brother, at least while they're both unmarried."

"I wonder how she'll feel when the duke marries?"

"Relieved, I'll warrant," Stephen said, tempering his apprehension at the anticipation of seeing Portia again.

Assuming she's willing to receive me.

"You don't think she'll be disappointed to be supplanted by another?"

Stephen smiled. "I doubt that. Your sympathies are better directed toward the future duchess, whomever she may be. What do you think, Mrs. Stowe—would you relish being mistress of Forthridge Park?"

Mrs. Stowe shrank away from the window, as if she feared the building watched her. Then she drew her shawl around her shoulders.

"It's not something I'm likely to experience."

"You were mistress of your former home, were you not?" Angela said. "I overheard Lady Staines say—"

"Angela, I think perhaps you'd do well to remain in the carriage when we arrive," Stephen said, aware of the distress in Mrs. Stowe's eyes.

"You can't leave me in here!" Angela protested.

"Only until I've seen Lady Portia," he said. "I fear my conversation with her may at first be of a somewhat delicate nature."

"And whose fault's that?"

"Angela," Mrs. Stowe said, a tremor in her quiet voice, "I'm sure your brother knows best."

"Would *you* accompany me, Mrs. Stowe?" Stephen asked.

Her eyes flared with fear. "I-I hardly think that's appropriate."

"A respectable widow is the best advocate for a man begging forgiveness."

"I doubt anyone would wish to hear anything *I'd* have to say."

"Not Foxton, perhaps," Stephen said, and she flinched at the mention of the duke's name. "But Lady Portia's a sensible sort. She'll not dismiss anything you have to say merely because of your sex—or your rank."

The carriage drew to a halt. Stephen climbed out and helped Mrs. Stowe down. Angela folded her arms and slumped in her seat, sticking out her lower lip.

"Sit up straight, Angela," Mrs. Stowe said. "Remember what we said about posture."

"There's nobody to see me here, stuck in the carriage."

Mrs. Stowe gave a nod, her expression impassive, and, at length, Angela straightened her stance. Then Stephen offered his arm and escorted the chaperone to the main doors.

They opened even before they reached the threshold, to reveal a black-clad butler with the same cadaverous appearance as Foxton's butler in London.

"Yes?" he said sharply.

"Is the family at home?" Stephen asked.

"Are you expected?"

"I'm acquainted with the family."

"So that's a 'no,' then."

"Please say that Colonel Stephen Reid begs an audience."

"And…?" The butler turned his disapproving gaze to Stephen's companion.

"And Mrs. Stowe."

"Very well, Colonel Reid and…*Mrs. Stowe*. Wait here."

"Perhaps we should leave," Mrs. Stowe said as the butler shut the door. "Or at least let me wait in the carriage with Angela. I fear my presence will do no good."

She glanced about the building, fear growing in her eyes. Then footsteps approached and the door opened once more.

Mrs. Stowe let out a little gasp and tightened her hold on Stephen's arm as Foxton regarded them both with disdain.

"To what do I owe the…*pleasure* of this visit?" he said.

"We're come to see Lady Portia," Stephen replied.

Foxton curled his lip in a sneer. "Are you come to tell my sister that your tastes now run to dowdy widows?" He let out a cold laugh.

"Foxton, if you'd permit me to say—"

"No, I do *not* permit."

Foxton took a step forward. Stephen held his ground, but Mrs. Stowe moved back.

"How dare you?" Stephen said. "Of course, I'd *expect* a man of your rank to bully your fellow men—it is, after all, how dukes assert their superiority. But no man has the right to bully a woman."

"Perhaps you should have thought of that before you shot my sister and left her for dead," Foxton snarled. Then he turned his gaze to Mrs. Stowe. "Do I shock you, madam, with the revelation that your protector has a penchant for shooting the women he beds?"

Mrs. Stowe inhaled sharply, then glanced at Stephen.

"At least let me see her," Stephen said.

"I'm delighted to say that's impossible," came the reply. "She's not at home."

"You lie."

"For what purpose would I lie?" Foxton said. "To keep the knowledge of your presence from my sister? She wishes to see you even less than I do. You don't matter enough to lie to, Reid. Whereas I have nothing to hide." He stepped forward again. "My sister's not in the county. She's taking a vacation—a rest cure."

A pulse of fear swelled in Stephen's gut. "Is she unwell? Has her wound festered?"

"I don't think that's any of your business," Foxton said. "My sister is *my* concern."

"It's about time."

Foxton's eyes—the same shape and color as his sister's—darkened with dislike.

"I hardly think you're in a position to lecture me on my sister's welfare," he said. "Now go, and take your drab little woman with you."

"But—"

"Go!" Foxton roared, and Mrs. Stowe flinched. "I'll give you to the count of ten to get off my land—then I'll set the dogs on you."

Stephen remained still, and Foxton tilted his head and roared, "Moore! Let loose the dogs…and fetch my shotgun!"

Stephen's companion tugged at his sleeve. "Please…" she whispered.

"This isn't over, Foxton," Stephen said.

"It will be if you remain here."

Footsteps approached and the butler appeared, brandishing a shotgun with a polished wooden handle.

Stephen retreated, escorting Mrs. Stowe to the carriage. Angela's concerned face appeared at the window.

"Would she not see you?"

"She's not at home," Stephen said, helping Mrs. Stowe in and then following her. He rapped on the side of the carriage, and it lurched forward, turned in a wide circle, then set off down the drive.

CHAPTER TWENTY-EIGHT

Solthwaite Manor, Cumberland

S NOW HAD BEEN falling for days. Even the windows were white with frost, and the sounds of nature were muffled by the cold white shroud—almost as if the world outside no longer existed.

If only that were true.

Portia pressed her hand against the windowpane, fingers splayed out, until the cold seeped into her bones. Then she lowered her hand, leaving an imprint on the glass where the frost had melted, through which she could discern the Cumberland landscape. A line of fir trees stretched toward the horizon, thickening to a forest in the distance, before thinning out as the land stretched toward the foothills, undulating softly across the land. And beyond…

Beyond were the mountains. Her gaze followed the gentle slope, which grew steeper higher up, toward the snow-capped peaks that glowed a soft pink as the day drew to a close.

Soon, the winter sun would dip behind the mountain, and the world would slip into darkness.

Darkness to match that the depths of her heart.

Portia rose to her feet, wincing at the soreness in her body.

Stephen!

She blinked and shook her head to dissipate the memory of his name—a name she had cried as her body had been almost torn apart less than a fortnight ago, when the snow had closed in, as if Nature wanted to muffle her cries and hide her disgrace.

You're to go to Solthwaite to hide your disgrace from the world…

A rest cure, her brother said he'd tell the world—as if the fruits of her love were an ailment to be cured, a disease to be obliterated.

My love…

However much *he* might hate her now, her child was conceived out of love.

I cannot think of her as…

Almost as if Portia's thoughts had been read, a wail rose up from within the manor. Portia held her breath at the familiar tug in her heart. She placed a hand over her aching breasts and closed her eyes, willing the tears to subside. But they stung her eyes as she tempered the surge of envy. Soon the crying would subside as the wet nurse—a young girl from the village who had recently lost a child—would see to her needs.

And, in a matter of days, if her brother got his way, Portia would suffer the same loss. Her child might be alive, but Portia would have to live out her life knowing that her daughter would never know her. Strangers would witness her first steps, hear her first words. Strangers would comfort her at night to chase away the demons in her dreams, would sing her lullabies at night…

She curled her fingernails into her palm, focusing on the pain in her hands to drive away the pain in her heart. But the instinct of a mother, the urge to comfort her child, threatened to shatter her resolve.

"No…"

If she were to crumble now, she might never be able to part with her, and Adam would have to tear the child from her arms.

The wails increased, turning into a crescendo, until screams of distress cut through the air.

Portia's heart cracked, and she darted across the floor, threw open the door, and sprinted along the corridor.

She arrived in the nursery to see the nursemaid bending over the cot.

"Mrs. Leaney, what are you doing?"

The woman turned and fixed her with a grimace. "Aren't you

supposed to be resting, miss?"

"It's *Lady Portia*," Portia said, eyeing the woman with distaste. She might be the sister of the local vicar, with a proclivity for quoting scripture on a whim, but Mrs. Leaney was the least godly creature Portia had met—more pious than godly. "Why is the baby crying?" Portia said, eyeing the cot. "Is she hungry?"

The nursemaid wrinkled her nose in distaste. "Jilly has already been. The child's been fed."

"Then what's wrong?"

"Merely a little petulance."

"Petulance?" Portia said. "She's a baby, less than a month old."

She approached the cot, and the woman stood in her path.

"Let me pass, Mrs. Leaney," she said, tempering her anger.

"His Grace's instructions were that you were not to touch the child, Lady Portia—for your sake."

"But she's distressed."

Portia pushed the woman aside. Mrs. Leaney caught her wrist, and Portia shook it free.

"Do *not* touch me again," she said. "You may be in my brother's employ, but I'm the mistress of this house."

"The brat mustn't be allowed to—"

"How dare you!" Portia cried. "She's my child!"

Her resolve shattering, she scooped up the baby and held her to her breast. Her whole body shook with a visceral need to comfort and protect.

"Lady Portia, I—"

"Be quiet!" Portia said. "Leave us."

"His Grace needs to be told of this."

"Go, then," Portia said, dipping her head to place a soft kiss on the child's ear, breathing in her beautiful baby smell. "Go and tell your tales."

The nursemaid dipped into a curtsey, her eyes glittering with dislike, then she exited the nursery.

Portia closed her eyes. "I'm here, my darling," she said. "Mama's here."

The baby let out another cry, and Portia adjusted her blanket, tucking it in place around the baby's neck. Then she froze.

A red weal adorned the child's shoulder—the size and shape of a fingertip.

Portia pulled down the blanket and let out a low cry as she caught sight of two more marks, the same size and shape as the first, but darker in color—like bruises.

"Oh, my love!" she cried. "What has she done to you?"

Footsteps approached while she sobbed.

"I *knew* it!" her brother said, his voice dark with anger. "This cannot be borne."

"No, Adam," Portia said, "it cannot. I insist you dismiss Mrs. Leaney immediately."

"We've already discussed this," he said, "and I'll not discuss it further. You promised to let the child be after your confinement." He folded his arms. "I only agreed that we should remain here until you recovered from your confinement. I knew I should have sent the child on—I bloody *knew* it!"

"She's not *the child*, Adam," Portia said, her voice cracking. "She's your niece—my daughter."

He sighed. "I understand your distress, I really do, but this behavior is not in your, or the child's, interests."

"I'll tell you what's not in my child's interests, Adam," Portia said, pulling down the blanket. "Can you see what your pious Mrs. Leaney has been doing? My child is not some brat she can abuse. Do you want me to hand her over to those who would harm her?"

"The Bensons are good people," he said. "And loyal—they've farmed on Forthridge land for generations. And they have wanted a child for years. Would you deny them that?"

"As you are denying me?"

"I thought you'd agreed to this."

The child in her arms let out a satisfied grunt, and Portia caught her breath at the rush of love, the urge to protect the little creature who called to her soul.

"May I not change my mind, Adam?"

"Of course, provided you're fully aware of the consequences."

"Many women have children."

"Not in your circumstances," he said. "What will you do, Portia, if you keep the child?"

"She has a *name*."

He let out a sharp sigh. "She has no name in the eyes of the world in which we live."

"Then the world is wrong."

"Perhaps, but we cannot change the world," he said. "All we can do is change it for those we care about. And believe it or not, I care about you. And"—he gestured to the baby in her arms—"the child."

"*My* child," Portia said, "who needs her mother."

The baby stirred, and Portia cradled her head, rocking to and fro until she quietened once more.

"She knows her mother."

"Don't be a fool," he said. "Babies lack the wit to know one person from another. They rely on instinct rather than rational thought."

"Her instinct tells her that she's safe with me," she said. "Unlike with Mrs. Leaney."

"I can dismiss Mrs. Leaney, but does that not give credence to what I've said all along?"

He stepped closer, and she retreated, tightening her hold on her daughter.

"An unmarried woman with a child will be vilified wherever she goes," he said.

"Then I'll go where nobody knows who we are."

"To live in obscurity?" he said. "Among strangers, masquerading as a widow, arousing suspicion, living in fear of your secret coming out until one day it does, and you're forced to move on again?"

"I can weather the insults of others."

"But can *she?*" He gestured to her child, and she turned away as if to protect her from his gaze.

His expression softened, and he thrust his hands into his pockets.

"If the Bensons take her, she'll want for nothing—a home, a mother, and a father. And, most of all, respectability. Her birth will not be questioned. She'll not be subject to whispers and stares as she goes to school. Nobody will treat her differently because of her birth. And she'll make a respectable marriage with some young man on the estate, where she will be cared for by our family."

Portia closed her eyes, willing him to disappear, but the image filled her mind—of Olivia Whitcombe struggling to find her way after her come-out, the taunts and whispers she was subjected to on account of her birth, despite being the half-sister of a duke. Olivia had everything Whitcombe could give her—a champion in Whitcombe's duchess, a dowry—but even that had not been enough to protect her from the stain of her birth.

When Portia opened her eyes once more, the child in her arms stared straight at her out of dark, deep-set blue eyes, her round, pink face surrounded by a shock of blonde hair. Portia's heart stuttered at the expression of complete and utter trust in the baby's eyes—trust that she would be safe, and happy.

A sob swelled in Portia's throat, and her brother took her hand.

"Little puss," he said, "it's for the best. I know how painful it must be for you—"

"How would you know?" she said. "I daresay you've not given a second thought to the bastards you've littered the countryside with."

He flinched, and his eyes flared with anger. Then he placed a light hand on her arm.

"I cannot begin to understand how you feel," he said. "Men are different. Besides, I was always careful to make sure that the women I…" A slight color tinted his cheeks. "It matters not," he continued. "As far as I'm aware, I have no natural children."

"And the natural children of whom you are not aware?"

"I'm better off not knowing," he said. "As are they. I'm not like you, Portia—I am incapable of loving another."

She dipped her head to kiss the baby's cheek. "You don't know that until you hold your child in your arms."

"And that is where we differ, puss," he said, squeezing her arm affectionately. "But one thing I do know about love is that if you love another, you will do what is best for them, even if it might give you pain."

"I-I know, but…"

"You love her, don't you?"

Her heart shattered at the softness in his voice—a softness that her harsh, arrogant brother so rarely displayed—and she nodded, her eyes stinging with tears. Then he approached the mantelshelf and tugged at the bellpull. Shortly after, a footman appeared, and Portia heard a murmur of voices, then the footman glanced at her, bowed, and disappeared.

"What was that?" she asked.

"I think, perhaps, it's better if you say your goodbyes now," he said. "The pain of separation will only increase the more you prolong the inevitable."

"No!" She clung to the child and retreated while he held out his arms.

"I'll not force you," he said quietly. "It must be your choice."

Footsteps approached, and there was a knock at the door.

"Come in," Adam said, and Nerissa stepped into the room.

"Lady Portia! I thought you were resting."

"I've just given orders to have Mrs. Leaney dismissed," Adam said.

Nerissa wrinkled her nose. "Not before time, Your Grace, if you don't mind my saying."

"No, I don't mind, Nerissa," he said. "I've summoned you to take care of your mistress today—and for the next few days, until I return."

"But sir, I always—"

"Your mistress will be in need of a little more care over the next few days."

Nerissa glanced toward Portia, and her face creased in sorrow.

"Oh, Lady Portia!" She took a step toward Portia, and Adam caught her wrist.

"One moment, if you please." He held his arms out to Portia, then grew still and waited.

Biting her lip to stem the pain, she stepped forward. She caught her breath as, her body trembling, she handed the little bundle to her brother.

The child stirred and let out a cry, and Adam held her close to his chest.

"Hush, sweet one," he said. "Everything will be all right. You'll be loved and cherished by those with whom you will live, and"—he glanced at Portia, his gaze softening—"and by those with whom you cannot. Perhaps, when you are a little older, you may be fortunate enough to have a benefactress."

Portia stepped forward, then forced herself to remain still as she fisted her hands at her sides, clutching at the fabric of her skirts. Her brother approached the door, cradling the precious bundle in his arms.

"Adam!" she cried as he reached the threshold.

He turned toward her. "Portia, you know it's for the—"

"Her name," she said, her throat catching. "Please tell them..." She drew in a sharp breath as convulsions began to rack her body. "Her name is Stephania."

"Portia, I can't just..." He hesitated, then nodded. "Stephania."

He retreated to the doorway and closed it behind him. His footsteps began to fade while she remained, her body vibrating like a coiling spring.

Then the spring snapped. She flew toward the door, a primal cry of loss tearing from her throat. Nerissa caught her and held her firm while she struggled to break free, until her legs gave way and she collapsed, her maid holding her weight as she screamed, finally yielding to the pain.

Her voice grew hoarse as the cries swelled in her chest, thick, dark waves of sorrow that burst forth, tearing at her throat until she could cry no more, while her maid rocked her to and fro.

At length, she caught the distant sound of hoofbeats. Ignoring Nerissa's protests, Portia raced to the window to see the carriage moving along the drive, growing smaller with each turn of the wheel.

She lifted her hand and placed it on the pane of glass, where the imprint in the frost was still visible. By the time the frost had threaded through her body and reached her heart, the carriage had turned a corner and disappeared.

CHAPTER TWENTY-NINE

Hyde Park, London

THE EXTRAORDINARY THING about the color green was the variety of shades to be found in nature. While Stephen was not a true connoisseur of art, he knew enough to appreciate the subtle nuances of color in even the drabbest places—from the pale green of the lawns to the dark, glossy green of the bushes lining the path.

Most of his acquaintances considered Hyde Park to be exceptionally dull in February. Trees, devoid of their leaves, stood in a forlorn row along the Serpentine, like bones stretching toward the sky. The iron-hard ground glistened in the sunlight, dusted with frost, and the grass, brittle in the cold, crumpled underfoot, leaving imprints that formed winding patterns across the lawn.

Stephen smiled to himself as he caught sight of a pair of footprints disappearing into the rhododendrons, with no corresponding footprints coming back out again—clandestine lovers, perhaps.

He allowed himself a small smile.

"Colonel Reid!" a voice called.

A familiar figure approached, and he suppressed the little flutter of embarrassment as he recognized Lady Staines. But the sharp-featured frown she'd given him the day she broke their engagement was long gone, replaced by the serenity of a woman at peace.

"Lady Staines, a pleasure," he said. "Are you not spending the winter in the country?"

"We arrived in London last week," she said. "Besides, the winter is almost over."

"Tell that to Mother Nature," he said. "The ground underfoot is covered by frost."

"But if you look closely, you'll see the first signs of crocuses." She gestured toward a row of trees. "Just a few familiar shoots. I can't tell you how many times I've had to tell Gabriel not to pick them. He seems to think that if he picks the shoots and takes them home, they'll turn into flowers."

"Is your son here with you today?"

She nodded. "His father has taken him to see the swans while I have a few moments to myself." She gave a shy smile. "I love my son completely, but he's at that stage where he's filled with life and laughter, and I need a little respite. And, of course, I appreciate the time a boy needs to spend alone with his father to discuss"—she made a random gesture in the air—"oh, whatever it is that you gentlemen find the need to talk about when ladies are not present."

"His father?" Stephen said. "I thought…"

"My *husband* is Gabriel's father."

"Of course. I meant no disrespect."

"You've said nothing I've not heard elsewhere," she said. "Fatherhood is more than a blood tie, you know. But, of course, that's something you are yet to understand."

Now it was Stephen's turn to blush as he recalled his first declaration of love to her—when she was Miss Howard.

She placed a light hand on his arm. "Forgive me. I didn't mean to distress you, colonel. My life is complete now I have a family to love. Gabriel is my world, and it makes my heart sing to see how deeply Andrew cares for him."

"And quite right," Stephen said as he caught sight of a young boy further along the path, jumping by the water's edge, laughing animatedly, while the man next to him held his hand. "He's a charming boy." He held out his arm. "May I?"

She hesitated, and he tempered the shame at his former infatuation. Then she smiled and took his arm.

"Of course," she said. "We are acquaintances, are we not? And, if I may be so bold, I think we can call ourselves friends. We both wish each other happy, which is the mark of true friendship."

He steered her along the path toward Lord Staines and the little boy, who were too engrossed in the swans to notice anything else.

"My sister is in Town," she said.

"Is she well?"

She colored and gave a soft smile. "I'm sure she won't mind my telling a friend, but she's expecting her fourth child. Montague is, of course, terribly protective of her, but she insisted that he remain in the country while she came to Town. A doting husband is a joy to behold—but he can get a little *too* protective. He made Eleanor promise to send word if she felt unwell, and he made me promise to visit her daily. But I fear she'll soon tire of my company. I'm sure she'd appreciate a fellow admirer of art. After all, didn't you take her to see the Royal Academy exhibition the year before she…"

Her voice trailed away and her cheeks reddened. Stephen's heart have a little cry at the distress in her eyes as she evidently recalled the scandal that had driven her sister from London.

"I did not have the pleasure of escorting your sister to the exhibition," he said. "I believe she left London to spend a few days by the sea."

A strained silence fell as they continued along the path. Then they approached a clear patch of grass, and Stephen's stomach cramped in horror as he recognized the spot where the Farthing had fallen—where he had shot the woman he loved then walked away, not bothering to look back.

No wonder she hates me.

"I beg pardon?" Lady Staines said.

"Forgive me. I was beset by a memory."

"A painful memory?"

He nodded.

"You must embrace it, colonel, for it is unwise to bury it. Memories—and secrets—have a way of resurfacing when you least expect. And if you're unprepared, they can breach your defenses and lead to heartbreak."

"Surely it's better to look to the future."

"Perhaps," she said. "But one day, my Gabriel will discover the truth about his birth. I'd rather he heard it from me than the gossipmongers. Did you know that I"—she hesitated—"almost gave him up?"

She turned to him, and his heart ached at the pain in her eyes.

"I only considered it for a moment—and I was subject to the influence of others—but even so, that moment will haunt me. My mother—"

"Lady Staines, there's no need to tell me."

She drew in a deep breath, then let out a sigh.

"Society can be a cruel beast," she said. "Unforgiving, relentless in its capacity to judge others it considers unworthy, yet it directs envy and spite at those it seeks to praise. I myself am more guilty than most of harboring envy."

"Whom do you envy?"

She smiled. "I envy every woman who has yet to experience the judgment of the world—women who enjoy a successful Season, who avoid the attention of undesirables, who aren't driven to act out of desperation, and…"

She caught her breath as the little boy ahead turned and waved at her, the sunlight catching his hair to form a halo.

"My poor child," she whispered. "Before my confinement, Mother insisted I hide away in disgrace. I was required to utter falsehoods to explain my absence from London. A rest cure, Mother told her acquaintances." She let out a snort. "A *rest cure*, indeed! Little did I know that most women in Society are fully aware of what that actually means."

A rest cure…

Where had he heard that term before?

"Forgive me for burdening you with my sensibilities. I'm afraid..." Her blush deepened, then she dipped her head. "I believe I can trust you, colonel—despite how cruelly I treated you."

"Lady Staines, you were never cruel," he said. "In breaking off our engagement, you ensured your own happiness, and furthered the cause of mine. No matter the manner of the delivery, or the words you used, you committed an act of kindness."

"It is *you* who are kind." Then she lowered her voice to a whisper. "It's not only Eleanor who's with child," she said. "We came early to London to see Dr. McIver—I really couldn't bear to see anyone else, and I refused to make the poor man travel all the way to Radham Hall. He has instructed me to take plenty of fresh air, and occasional respite from my rambunctious son. I find that my spirits often rise and fall in a heartbeat, but Dr. McIver assures me that's perfectly healthy, and to be expected."

A rest cure...

Of course! It was what Foxton had said about Portia. Which meant...

"Dear God Almighty!"

Lady Staines recoiled. "Colonel!" she cried.

The man and boy at the water's surface turned and strode toward them.

Lord Staines reached them in a heartbeat, the little boy trotting at his heels.

"Is anything the matter, Juliette my love?" he said, eyeing Stephen with disapproval.

"Forgive me, Lady Staines, I meant no disrespect," Stephen said. "I-I was just thinking about..." He hesitated, but Staines stepped closer.

"Yes?" His voice may have a mild tone, but it carried an undertone of steel.

"I was thinking of Foxton," Stephen blurted out. "But it matters not."

"Have you seen him?" Lord Staines said.

"He's in the country, is he not?"

"He was at White's last night, though he's returning to Forthridge in a day or so for his shooting party. I daresay you'll see him there. You're not a member of White's, are you? I confess, I prefer Boodle's myself, but the chef at White's does an excellent roast beef. Not the least bit overdone—and I'm very particular about beef, am I not, my love? I know our cook at Radham Hall despairs of my fastidiousness."

Lady Staines looked at her husband with adoration in her eyes, while the little boy bowed toward Stephen.

"Colonel Reid," he said. "It's a pleasure to see you today. A fine morning for a walk in the park, is it not?"

Lady Staines looked at her son, love and pride shimmering in her eyes.

"What a polite and gentlemanly young man!" Stephen said. "Your mama and papa must be very proud of you."

Lord Staines scooped up the boy in his arms, and Gabriel squealed in delight.

"Yes," he said. "We are. Children are such a blessing."

A rest cure…

The whispered voice circled in Stephen's mind, taunting him while he shook his head to dissipate it.

"Colonel, are you well?" Lady Staines said.

"I-I think perhaps I might call on Foxton," Stephen said, trying to keep his voice even. "Do you happen to know if Lady Portia is in Town also?"

Lady Staines frowned and tilted her head to one side, fixing her clear blue gaze on him, her eyes a little paler than the rich sapphire eyes of another.

"I believe she's been on vacation in the Lakes."

"Are you sure, my love?" Lord Staines said. "I thought it was Derbyshire."

"She wrote to Mimi—forgive me, Duchess Sawbridge, I should say—before Michaelmas, though her note was a little brief. I daresay she's returned to Forthridge by now. I was disappointed not to hear from her myself. I wanted to ask her opinion on our holding an archery competition at Radham Hall this summer."

"You must write to her," Lord Staines said.

"I will, but you must remind me, my love. I find I'm somewhat forgetful of late."

"Well, that's to be expected, given that—" He broke off, a flush of pleasure on his cheeks.

"I'm afraid I've told Colonel Reid our news," she said. "But I can trust him to be discreet, can I not, colonel?"

"Of course you can," Stephen said, offering his hand to Lord Staines. "Permit me to be the first to congratulate you on your forthcoming arrival."

Lord Staines grinned and took the proffered hand. "Our third child," he said, his smile broadening. "I am the most fortunate of men. When your turn comes, I trust you'll realize your good fortune, and I'll take much pleasure in offering you my congratulations in turn."

He bowed and clicked his heels together, then he released Stephen's hand and caught his wife's arm.

"Now, my love, it's time to return so you can take your rest. With luck, Mrs. Bragg will have baked those ginger biscuits you love so much." He winked at Stephen. "My Juliette cannot get enough of them. When she was expecting our second child, she ate a whole batch."

"Andrew!" Lady Staines swatted her husband over the arm, and he grinned. Then he dipped his head and snatched a swift kiss, and Stephen's heart gave a little jolt at the expression of love they shared.

Laughing, they took their leave, and Stephen stood alone in the center of the path, watching them make their way to the park gates—a man and woman very much in love, with their beloved child walking by their side.

When your turn comes…

As soon as they were out of sight, Stephen turned and released the tide that had been swelling in his mind.

What if my turn has already come?

Could it be true?

Surely if it were, she'd have written, or Foxton would have come raging, pistol in hand, demanding honor be met?

Or perhaps they thought him of too little consequence to seek retribution or revenge.

Perhaps he did not matter enough.

CHAPTER THIRTY

S TEPHEN TURNED INTO St. James's Square, and his stomach fluttered as his gaze landed on the Foxton townhouse. Three stories of windows stared out over the street—huge eyes, dark in contrast to the white-fronted façade.

Was *she* inside?

As he approached the building, he caught a flash of light and his heart gave a flutter. Then he shook his head, cursing his folly. It was merely the reflection of the sunlight, caught in the windowpanes as he crossed the street.

Like much of the square, the building seemed empty, abandoned by all save a handful of staff to guard against marauders and air the rooms. But in a matter of weeks, the place would be bustling with life as the residents returned from wintering in the country to drink in their clubs, visit their modistes, and take tea with their acquaintances to gossip about who might secure the notice of the queen and become the premier debutante of the Season.

Then the world outside London would cease to exist, as would those individuals who resided outside Society, either due to their location, their lack of fortune or social status, or…

…or their ruination at the hands of another.

Stephen's sister had chosen to remain in the country with Mrs. Stowe, who was proving to be an adept teacher as well as chaperone. Angela's ruination seemed to have been avoided, with

Sir Heath Moss remaining tight-lipped, not once speaking of his seduction of her despite having boasted of numerous other conquests.

Angela's reputation seemed to have escaped unscathed from the events of last Season.

But as for another woman…

If what Stephen suspected were true, *her* reputation had been destroyed by an act of…

An act of love.

As he reached the main doors, Stephen closed his eyes at the memory—the way her eyes darkened with desire util they were almost black, as the final moment of surrender, when she offered her body to him, and…and how her body had welcomed him into her warmth, rippling and pulsing with pleasure until it had burst forth, drawing him in as he claimed her as his.

He blinked, and moisture stung his eyes as the burden of guilt pressed on his soul.

He raised his hand, but before he could knock, the door opened to reveal the black-clad butler.

"It's Reeve, isn't it?"

The butler arched an eyebrow, his face seeming to creak with the effort. "Are you expected?"

"Is Lady… I mean, the family, are they at home?"

Stephen stepped forward, moving his foot into the doorway. The butler lowered his gaze, then curled his lip in a sneer.

"Wait here."

He turned his back and disappeared into the house, where Stephen could discern the blurred shapes of items of furniture still covered in dust sheets.

At length, the butler returned, his slow, steady footsteps clicking over the floor.

"Follow me."

Without awaiting a response, the butler led Stephen to a small parlor near the back of the house. All the furniture within, like the items in the hall, was covered in white sheets.

"Is the duke intending to stay in Town?" Stephen asked.

The butler ignored him, instead giving the slightest of bows before disappearing, closing the door behind him.

Stephen crossed to floor to the window that overlooked the garden. A thin layer of dust covered the glass, and he ran his finger along the sill before inspecting the tip and wiping it on his jacket. The faint smell of damp and dust lay heavy in the air.

Then the door burst open.

"I thought I'd already said that you weren't welcome in my house."

Stephen turned to face the Duke of Foxton. "At Forthridge, yes," he replied. "You said nothing about your townhouse."

Foxton's eyes narrowed. "Whatever qualities my sister believed she saw in you are well hidden," he said. "If they exist at all."

"Is Portia at home?"

"*Lady* Portia is not your concern," Foxton said. "I thought I'd made that perfectly clear when you turned up uninvited at Forthridge"—he twisted his mouth in a sneer almost identical to the butler's—"with your brat of a sister and that dowdy mistress of yours."

"I have no mistress," Stephen said.

"Understandable," Foxton said. "After all, once you've had a taste of the choicest cut of meat in my sister, you're unlikely to want to take a bite out of a bit of scrag end, are you?"

Anger boiled in Stephen's gut and he curled his hands into fists. "How *dare* you insult her!"

Foxton let out a chuckle and thrust his hands into his pockets. "You must have set your cap at that old woman if you're so vehement in your defense of her."

"I meant your sister!" Stephen said. "She deserves better than to be spoken of in such a manner."

"Oh, *really*? She deserves better than the brother who has her best interests at heart, who is devoting his life to ensuring that she's never placed in danger again?" Foxton let out a sour bark of laughter. "I suppose you think *you* deserve her? Reid, you never came close."

"In that, if nothing else, I agree with you," Stephen said, tempering the urge to obliterate the arrogant expression on Foxton's face. "At least permit me to see her, speak to her."

"She's not at home."

"You lie," Stephen said. "If you're as protective as you say, you'd be by her side at all times."

"I'm not in Town for long," Foxton said. "Not that it's your concern. I return to Forthridge this evening."

"Then permit me to—"

"You're not welcome," Foxton said. "Step onto my estate and you'll regret it. My gamekeeper has orders to shoot you on sight."

Stephen flinched and dug his fingernails into his palms, focusing on the sharp stab of pain to drive away the memory of gunfire. "You wouldn't dare."

"Wouldn't I? You and your wretched family have cost me more than you deserve. I—" Foxton broke off, then shook his head. "Just go, before I do something I regret."

"What do you mean, my *family* has cost you?"

Foxton made a dismissive gesture. "I'm referring to my sister's virtue. You ruined her."

"I love her!" Stephen cried.

"You took her virtue, then shot her and left her for dead," Foxton said. "Are those the actions of a man in love?"

"How many times must I tell you, I didn't know it was—"

"I care not!" Foxton roared, advancing on Stephen, his powerful frame filling the room. "If it were up to me, I'd have your throat slit in the night while you sleep, preferably while that damned sister of yours watches. Had she kept her legs closed, none of—"

"My sister did nothing!" Stephen said. "She was seduced by a rogue, a man who deserves to be cut down."

"As my sister was similarly seduced—and the man who ruined *her* deserves to be cut down," Foxton said quietly. Rage still simmered in his eyes, but the cold, measured calm in his tone sent a shiver of fear through Stephen's heart.

Foxton was a man without a heart—and such a man was a dangerous enemy, for he would carry out his threats unhampered by conscience or remorse.

Nevertheless, the question that had been burning in Stephen's mind needed to be asked, even if it cost him his life.

"Did she have a child?" he said.

For a moment, Foxton's composure seemed to falter. His lips thinned, then he tilted his head to one side and smoothed his expression, the momentary flash of fury disappearing.

It was enough to confirm Stephen's fears.

A child…

My child.

"Sweet Lord Almighty," he whispered as the world shifted out of focus. The walls of the tiny parlor seemed to pulse and throb, moving in and out, pressing on his chest until he fought for breath.

"The Almighty has nothing to do with it," Foxton said. *"I'm my sister's only salvation now, and I'll do everything in my power to protect her, like any man would a fragile female, from the dogs that come sniffing around her."*

The anger swelling in Stephen's heart shattered and burst forth.

"You fucking bastard!" He lunged forward, and pain exploded in his hand as his fist connected with Foxton's face.

The bigger man teetered backward, his eyes widening in surprise, then crashed to the floor.

"What about the child?" Stephen cried.

Foxton winced, then wrinkled his nose. "There is no child," he said. "The only family my sister has is the brother who'd kill to protect her."

"You lie."

Foxton laughed. "I've no need to lie to a man such as you." He lifted his hand to his cheek, which was covered in an angry red mark.

Stephen shook his hand to dispel the pain, then approached Foxton, extending his other hand, but it was slapped away. "Foxton, I—"

"Don't touch me, you dog!" the duke snarled, struggling to his feet. Then he slipped and fell back. "Bugger!"

He reached inside his jacket and drew out a pistol, and Stephen froze, tightening in fear as his gaze was drawn to the muzzle of the weapon—a perfect circle at the end of the barrel, pointed at his heart.

Foxton moved his thumb and cocked the pistol with a crisp click.

"Make no sound, Reid," he said, lowering his voice to a whisper so quiet, it was almost as if he had crawled into Stephen's mind. "Go," he continued, his voice cold and even. "You have until the count of ten to leave my house, or I'll shoot you dead. That's how long you gave my sister, was it not?" He tilted his head up. "Reeve!"

Footsteps approached, and the butler appeared, his eyes only widening a little, as if his master prone on the floor aiming his pistol at a guest was a regular occurrence.

"Yes, Your Grace?"

"Show this…*person* out. Make sure he never returns."

"Very good, Your Grace." The butler turned to Stephen and raised his eyebrows. "If you please, sir."

"But—" Stephen began.

"One," Foxton said.

"I—"

"*Two!*"

Raising his hands, Stephen retreated while Foxton rose to his feet, counting steadily. On the count of five, Stephen reached the doors. Foxton uncocked the pistol then retreated deeper into the house, leaving Stephen with the butler.

"Reeve, I think—"

"You heard the master, sir. You're to leave immediately."

"But the child…"

The butler raised an eyebrow again, then tilted his head to one side. "I can assure you that there is no child." He reached for Stephen's collar, and Stephen slapped his hand away.

"Don't touch me!"

"Then please go, as my master directed," Reeve said. "He's given me leave to toss you out on the street like the ruffian you are."

Stephen retreated, and as soon as he'd stepped over the threshold, the door slammed. His foot caught in the door as it closed, and he fell back, tumbling onto the pavement.

Footsteps approached, followed by a familiar laugh. Stephen's stomach churned as he turned to face the man he loathed above all others sauntering toward him, cane in hand, tap-tapping on the pavement.

The man tipped his hat, then regarded Stephen with his pale-blue eyes, the sun catching his hair to form a soft halo around his handsome face. To those who cared only for outward appearances, he was the epitome of an angel.

"Well, well, what's this? A soldier grubbing in the dirt?"

"What do you want, Sir Heath?" Stephen said.

"Very little, thanks to Foxton," Sir Heath replied, glancing toward the doors through which Stephen had just been evicted. Then he lowered his gaze to Stephen's hand and laughed. "I see your tendency to assault your betters has not abated, even though you've taken to using your fists rather than a pistol."

Stephen glanced at his hand and caught sight of the broken skin around the knuckles.

"You should get that seen to," Sir Heath said. "Dr. Lucas would oblige—or at least, he *would* have had he not been struck down by the pox. But, of course, you're partial to that charlatan McIver, are you not?"

"Leave me be," Stephen growled.

"Or what?" Sir Heath laughed. "You'll give me a facer? From where I'm standing, you've come off worse than Foxton, seeing as you're sprawled on the street. You took quite a tumble just now—most entertaining."

"Go to hell."

"With pleasure." Sir Heath chuckled. "But let me give you some advice. I'd stay on the right side of Foxton if I were you."

"Foxon cares for nobody but himself," Stephen said. "Find another duke to ingratiate yourself with."

"No need, old boy," Sir Heath said. "All you need do with Foxton is seduce an innocent and he'll buy your silence." He chuckled again. "Is that why he tossed you out on the street? Tired of paying for your sister's indiscretion?"

"What?"

"Didn't you know?" Sir Heath gestured toward Foxton's house with his cane. "Our very generous duke paid me a *substantial* sum for my silence in the matter regarding your sister. He didn't look too pleased about it, and threatened to shoot me if I reneged. But five hundred's a respectable enough sum, enough to cover the expenses I incurred in paying the Farthing."

"Why you…" Stephen began to rise, but Sir Heath side-stepped him.

"Aren't you going to thank me for maintaining my silence?"

"I'd rather shoot you dead."

"Yes, I gathered that," Sir Heath said, grinning. "Though you managed to dispatch my proxy well enough. Well, I must be off." He tipped his hat once more. "Ladies to see, you know how it is." He winked, then twirled his cane before continuing along the path.

"Bastard," Stephen spat as he struggled to his feet. He caught his foot on paving slab and fell back. "Shit!"

"Sir! Are you hurt?"

Swallowing his embarrassment, Stephen looked up to see a young woman—barely out of girlhood—in a maid's uniform standing before him.

"Oh, Colonel Reid!" she exclaimed. "I didn't recognize you at first." She limped toward him, hand outstretched. "Let me help you up."

Ignoring the proffered hand—for surely a girl that slight couldn't support his weight—Stephen struggled to his feet and brushed the dust from his breeches.

"F-forgive me, colonel," the girl said. "I didn't mean to be so forward in offering my hand. Mrs. Platt's always saying to mind how I act toward folk that's better than I. I mean…"

"You acted out of kindness," Stephen said. "It's not every day you find a colonel sprawled at your feet on the street." He let his gaze wander about her form. "Do I know you, Miss…?"

"Not really," she said. "I mean, we've not been introduced. But I saw you once at St. Agnes's, when you visited the captain just before he went home."

"Captain…?"

"Captain Broom," she said, her face flushing. "Ever so kind he was—that is, when I spoke to him. We weren't supposed to talk to the gentleman patients, of course, but he brought me some wildflowers and grasses after I"—she frowned, and a flicker of pain shone in her eyes—"after Dr. McIver treated me. He said that he and I were the same. Imagine that! A captain in the army saying that I was the same as him! So kind."

"In what way were you and he the same?"

She blushed. "Forgive me, colonel, I must get back. Mr. Reeve is ever so particular about promptness."

"Reeve?" Stephen asked, glancing at the door from which he'd just been evicted. "You're a maid at the Foxton residence?"

"I'm employed at Forthridge Park—that's their country es-tate, you know. Mrs. Platt's the housekeeper there, but I was sent here to help tend to the house while His Grace visits London."

"And your name is…?"

"Tilly, sir," she said, dipping into a curtsey. She lost her bal-ance and pitched sideways, but Stephen caught her in his arms and set her back on her feet. "Forgive me, sir, I'm still not used to…" She looked away.

"Of course!" Stephen said. "You're the young woman Dr.

McIver spoke of, are you not, who hurt your foot in an accident, and he had to…"

She nodded, lowering her gaze to her right foot.

"And the duke took you in?" *Perhaps Foxton isn't as much of a bastard as I've always thought.*

"It was Lady Portia that took me in," Tilly said. "She insisted." She gave a soft smile. "The kindest lady that ever lived, is Lady Portia. I just wish she wasn't so—" She broke off, blushing. "Oh dear. Mrs. Platt's always telling me not to rattle on about my betters. I've no right to speak of her."

"You have every right if you care about her, Tilly," Stephen said. "What do you wish for her?"

"That she wasn't so unhappy. I know gentlefolk's not the same as us—they don't have feelings like the rest of us—but Lady Portia always seems so *sad*."

Stephen hesitated, his stomach fluttering in anticipation. "Why do you think Lady Portia is sad?"

"Mrs. Platt says it's not for me to ask. When I arrived at Forthridge, Lady Portia had just returned from a period of convalescence. A long illness, Mrs. Platt said, but I must not speak of it."

"Do you see much of Lady Portia?" Stephen asked.

"She spends most of her time in her chamber—even last week, when the weather was so fine, she remained inside." The maid smiled. "Except when she visits the children. She sometime takes me with her, to help with fetching and carrying and the like. Ever so patient, she is, seeing as I can't walk fast."

"The children…of the estate?" Stephen asked, willing his voice to remain calm, yet aware of his heart hammering against his chest. "Is she fond of the children?"

"Oh *yes!*" Tilly said. "The young girl, Jenny, at Willow farm is a bit of a handful—she likes to climb trees and such, and her pa caught her pretending to play at sword fighting with her brother, but Lady Portia tells her that girls are as good as boys at sword fighting and marksmanship."

"Often they're *better* than boys," Stephen said, smiling.

"That's just what Lady Portia said!" the maid said, delight in her voice.

"And"—Stephen hesitated, praying that the eagerness in his voice was not audible—"are there any other children Lady Portia is fond of?"

He held his breath for what felt like a lifetime, though it was likely only a heartbeat or two.

"There's the Bensons' little one," Tilly said. "Ever so sweet, she is. Sarah told me—"

"Who's Sarah?"

"The head housemaid at Forthridge. She said that the Bensons had been wanting a child for years, and nobody thought they'd be able to have any, seeing as Mrs. Benson had been ill after they married. And—" She broke off, blushing. "Forgive me. Mrs. Platt's told me I shouldn't gossip."

Stephen lowered his voice. "I'll not tell Mrs. Platt," he said. "And it's not gossip if you, or Lady Portia, have good intentions."

"Lady Portia dotes on the child," Tilly said. "Such a tiny baby, she is!"

Stephen's heart gave a flutter.

A baby...

Surely it was merely a coincidence?

"She?" he whispered.

Tilly nodded. "A baby girl. Gentlefolk don't tend to take to the little ones, but Lady Portia has taken such an interest in the child. And no wonder. She's the sweetest little angel, and is so good for her ladyship, never fussing when she holds her. Lady Portia gets so sad when it's time to leave her, but she talks to Miss Price about her next visit. That's her lady's maid, you know— Miss Price. She's promised to show me how to dress Lady Portia and fix her hair, so I might take up a position as a lady's maid myself. Though, of course, no lady would want me, what with my foot."

"I think you'd make an excellent lady's maid."

Tilly gave a shy smile. Then she glanced toward the house and sighed. "I ought to be getting along," she said. "Will you be all right now, sir?"

"Tilly…" Stephen hesitated, the question on his lips—but in asking it, would he reveal too much?

"Yes, sir?"

"The child," he said, his mouth dry. "I mean, the baby…"

"Baby Stephania? What of her?"

Stephania…

A cold fist punched through his gut and curled steel fingers about his heart. The breath left his lungs and he bent forward.

It was no coincidence.

"Stephania…"

"Sir?" Tilly's concerned face swam into view as Stephen wiped the moisture from his eyes.

"No matter," he said. "I was merely wondering… if Lady Portia is still recovering from her illness, whether she ought to be out visiting. But I'm sure she'll be well if she has you to take care of her."

"Thank you, sir."

Tilly bobbed a curtsey, listed sideways, then regained her balance and descended the steps leading toward the basement.

Stephen stared after her, then shifted his gaze to the heavy wooden doors.

By rights he ought to break those doors down and confront Foxton. But what he wanted—no, *yearned for*, with every fiber of his soul—was not in London.

The key to his heart was at Forthridge Park—where he was at risk of being shot on sight.

But it was a risk worth taking. If he couldn't be with the woman he loved, and the daughter she'd borne, then his life mattered no more.

CHAPTER THIRTY-ONE

PORTIA LAY ON her back, eyes closed, while the hushed voices of her companions whispered in the air, set against the backdrop of the gentle shush of the breeze through the trees.

In the far distance she could discern the murmur of male voices. By now, Adam's shooting party would be gathering in the field at the north edge of the woods, and soon the sound of gunfire would fill the air. But at least she would be spared their company, tucked away in her favorite part of the estate—a neglected meadow at the edge of a copse, where the ground shimmered with color, as the bluebells had begun to bloom.

With luck, by the time she returned to the house, Adam's friends would be long gone. Company was no longer something she craved. Instead, she preferred the silence of solitude, free from judgmental eyes and the sight of the happiness of others—of all her friends who had found fulfilment and bliss in their lives. Whereas she…

Whereas I have lost everything that made me whole.

Sometimes, particularly when she was asleep, or occupied in some embroidery or other that Nerissa had tasked her with, she could forget. Or, if not completely forget, she could at least push the pain deep enough into the recesses of her mind that it dulled to a constant, throbbing ache. It was a welcome respite from the sharp agony that had taken hold of her heart that day at Solthwaite Manor—from the moment the carriage had disappeared out of sight.

No matter how many times she visited the Bensons' farm, on some pretense or other of benevolence, or a wish for the lady of Forthridge Park to be neighborly toward the tenants, the pain never lessened. It might abate for a moment when she held her child in her arms, but each time she handed Stephania back to Mrs. Benson it returned, cutting that little bit deeper.

But pain was to be celebrated. Pain meant that she was still a living soul capable of feeling. The day the pain left would be the day she no longer existed.

She drew in a lungful of air and caught the faint, sweet scent of the bluebells. The soft pink glow of the sun penetrated her eyelids and she turned her face toward the sun, letting its warmth caress her skin.

"Lady Portia, are you well?"

She opened her eyes to see the concerned expression on her maid's face. Then she reached up and Nerissa took her hand, her work-roughened fingers interlocking with Portia's.

The compassion in Nerissa's eyes almost breached Portia's defenses, and she bit her lip to stem the swell of sorrow.

"The fresh air will help," Nerissa said. "It's better than any medicine."

Portia sighed. "Does it heal the soul as well as the body?"

"It will—in time."

"Shall I pour you a glass of lemonade, Lady Portia?" a light voice asked, and Portia tilted her head up and smiled at the young woman sitting beside Nerissa.

"No, thank you, Tilly," she said. "But take some yourself. Mrs. Charlton made plenty for our picnic."

"I don't think it's my place to—"

"I insist," Portia said. "It wouldn't be right if I ate everything myself."

"You've hardly eaten anything," Tilly said. "You must—"

"Tilly, hush," Nerissa said. "Lady Portia has been unwell."

"But you said His Grace wanted—"

"Tilly!" Nerissa admonished the girl.

Portia sat up, shading her eyes from the sunlight, to see her maid frowning at Tilly. "Perhaps I *will* take something," she said. "I wouldn't want everyone's efforts on my behalf to go to waste. What did Mrs. Charlton pack for us?"

"Apple pie," Nerissa said, lifting the cloth from the picnic basket. "Still warm to the touch. Perhaps you could take a slice of that?"

"Mmm, it smells delicious," Tilly said, sniffing, "but not like any apple pie *I've* had."

"Mrs. Charlton puts cinnamon in her apple pie," Nerissa said. "It's Lady Portia's favorite."

"Cinnamon? What's that?"

"It's a spice," Portia said. "Why don't you try some?"

"I don't think I—"

"Nonsense!" Portia said, forcing brightness into her voice to drive away the young maid's apprehension. Poor Tilly had known nothing but hardship in her previous household. Adam had objected to taking the girl in at first, but relented. In fact, he'd agreed to many of Portia's requests of late.

Save one.

Nerissa reached into the basket and pulled out the pie and three plates, together with a knife.

"Let me cut it," Tilly said. "Neither of you should be serving *me.*"

"Why not?" Portia said. "I'm capable of doing what you do. After all, I have arms and legs just as you..." She broke off, cursing herself as her gaze drifted to the maid's leg.

But Tilly merely smiled and nodded. "Then let me pick some bluebells for your bedchamber," she said, rising to her feet. She teetered sideways, and Portia reached for her.

"Tilly, do take care. Perhaps you shouldn't..."

"It's no trouble, Lady Portia, beggin' your pardon," Tilly said. "Dr. McIver said I was to walk on it as much as possible, so I could get used to it."

"Ah yes, my brother said he'd sent for him when you were in Town."

"It was ever so kind of His Grace," Tilly said. "To think—a doctor taking the trouble to visit, just to see *me*. And then there was…" She shook her head. "It doesn't matter. Mrs. Platt tells me I oughtn't gossip, especially about folk above stairs."

"Quite right," Nerissa said.

"I daresay my brother had plenty of visitors while in London," Portia said.

Including one who'd given him a rather impressive bruise just below the left eye. Adam had insisted—a little too vehemently—that he'd stumbled against a door. But Mrs. Scarlet was known for her fiery temper. And, at least according to William Congreve, the fury of a woman scorned was not to be taken lightly. Perhaps he'd insulted his mistress somehow, or perhaps Mrs. Scarlet had suffered the misfortune of falling in love with him, resulting in his inevitable rejection of her.

"I saw only one visitor for His Grace," Tilly said, "but Mr. Reeve told me not to speak of him. He's so strict, I think…" She hesitated, blushing. "Beg pardon for saying."

Portia smiled. "Shall I tell you a secret, Tilly? Reeve has been strict with me ever since I was a child. I often wonder if he believes I'm a child, still."

"I'd best fetch them bluebells," Tilly said. "They won't pick themselves."

"Pick enough for your room also, so you may benefit from your efforts as much as I."

"Ma'am," Tilly said, bobbing a curtsey. She listed sideways, then regained her balance and limped toward the copse.

Portia caught her breath as the sadness swelled within her, and Nerissa squeezed her hand.

"You'll recover in time, Lady Portia," she said.

Portia shook her head. "Every waking moment, I question whether I did the right thing. But…" She caught her breath, but a soft sob escaped her lips. "H-how can I care for her when I can barely care for myself?"

"You're stronger than you think," Nerissa said. "Think how you've cared for young Tilly there. She's thriving here, and it's thanks to you. There's no other ladies I know would be willing to take her in, and you stood up to your brother when he objected, and—" She broke off. "Forgive me for speaking ill of His Grace."

"You've said nothing I've not said myself," Portia said. "I cannot forgive him for…"

She shook her head and drew in a shuddering breath.

"No, *I'm* the one who did wrong," she said. "I let her down, abandoned her for my own selfish reasons. One day I might forgive my brother—but how will I ever begin to forgive myself?"

"She is well," Nerissa said, "and she has two loving parents. The Bensons…"

She trailed off as Portia shook with sorrow.

"Oh, Lady Portia!" Nerissa drew her into an embrace. "Forgive me. I know they're not her real parents. I know you're…"

"I-I'm her m-mother," Portia said quietly. "Steph—" She broke off, the urge to speak her daughter's name conquered by the rising blackness of loss.

She curled her hand around Nerissa's arm while her maid rocked her to and fro, as she had done most nights since their return to Forthridge Park.

"My brother says it's for the best, a-and he does love me. B-but every day I see her…" She caught her breath again, as her maid's soft caress breached her defenses. "Every day, it breaks my heart a little more to leave her."

"Then perhaps His Grace could—"

"No," Portia said, shaking her head, her eyes stinging with moisture. "He mustn't know how unhappy I am. If he knew, he'd insist I don't see her again."

"He can't stop you, Lady Portia."

"He was so insistent at Solthwaite that I found myself handing her over to him before I could think of a reason not to." She drew in a shuddering breath. "I-I know he thinks it's for the best—for me, for her…" A sob swelled in her throat, and she caught her breath. "It's like a part of me has been ripped from my soul… Like…"

She gestured toward Tilly, who was limping back, clutching a posy of deep-blue blooms.

"Tilly will carry the scars of what happened to her for the rest of her life. My scars may not be visible, but they exist all the same—even if I may not speak of them."

Portia wiped her eyes as Tilly approached, her brow furrowed in concern. "Oh, Lady Portia, you don't look well."

"A slight headache, that's all," Portia said. "The sun's so bright today, one could be mistaken for thinking it was summer already, even though last week there was frost on the ground." She picked up the pie plate. "Now, how about a slice of—"

A volley of gunshots echoed in the distance, and, with a cacophony of squawks and caws, a multitude of black shapes exploded from the treetops, forming a cloud that seemed to fill the sky, circling like smoke particles until they settled into a formation and began spiraling down to settle once more in the trees.

"Sweet bleedin' arseholes!" Tilly exclaimed. "What…" Her voice trailed off and she paled as she turned to Portia. "Oh, beggin' yer pardon for cursin', Lady Portia."

"Sweet bleeding arseholes, eh?" Portia said, smiling. "I'll have to try that one on my brother."

"Oh no, please!" Tilly cried. "He'd be ever so cross."

"With me, not you," Portia said. "My brother has always despaired of my propensity to curse."

"Oh, lawks!" Tilly said. "Hear he comes. Do you think he heard me?"

Portia glanced about, wincing at the sunlight in her eyes, and caught sight of a lone figure approaching from the far end of the meadow, striding through the grasses.

"That can't be my brother," she said. "He's coming from the wrong direction."

"It could be the duke," Nerissa said, shielding her eyes. "The shooting's stopped."

Portia paused, straining to hear the gunshots, but other than the wind through the trees, she could only discern shouting in the distance. Most likely the beaters calling to each other to flush out the unfortunate birds destined to grace the dining table.

Then another gunshot rang out, and the figure paused, seeming to cringe, before resuming.

Tilly held up her hand to her eyes. "Oh my!"

"Can you see who it is from where you're standing, Tilly?" Nerissa asked.

"It's *him!*" came the reply. "What's he doing here? Mr. Reeve said—" Tilly broke off.

"What did Mr. Reeve say?" Nerissa asked.

"It's not my place to say. Mr. Reeve said I wasn't to—"

"Tell me what he said, Tilly," Portia said, looking up at the maid.

"He's the one who visited His Grace in London. He spoke to me."

"My brother spoke to you?"

"No, the gentleman. He seemed kind enough, but when I next saw the duke, his face…"

"Help me up, Nerissa," Portia said, struggling to her feet, drawing in a sharp breath at the rush of lightheadedness. Her maid took her arm and steadied her while the figure continued toward them, the blurred silhouette morphing into the shape of a man—a man carrying something in his arms.

Then a high-pitched wail came from the figure, resonating through Portia's bones. She caught her breath and her legs gave way. Two arms caught her and Nerissa whispered in her ear, "I've got you, Lady Portia."

"B-but it's…" Portia began to shake. "It's…"

"Who is it?"

The cry came again, and there was no mistaking it. The bond that had formed between them, though weakened by their separation, could never be fully broken.

Stephania…

Clinging to her maid, Portia took a step forward.

"Stephania!"

She took another step, and her maid pulled her back.

"Have a care, Lady Portia. You're not well."

"What are you doing with her?" Portia cried. "Who are you to torment me so?"

The figure paused, then resumed his approach. Portia blinked, and tears splashed onto her cheeks. She wiped her eyes, and her vision cleared as the shape morphed into a familiar form: the solid, steady gait she'd have known anywhere—the broad shoulders she had clung to as he'd declared his love, and…

…and the golden head of hair that caught the sunlight like a halo—hair she'd buried her hands in as he'd buried himself inside her to claim her as his.

"Dear Lord…Stephen!"

His features swam into view, and she winced in anticipation of the face that haunted her dreams, its features twisted with anger, dark eyes filled with accusation.

But instead, she saw penitence, regret, and a sorrow to match hers. His eyes glistened with moisture as he lowered his gaze to the precious little bundle in his arms—the soft blanket that contained a piece of her soul.

Then another gunshot sounded in the distance. He stiffened and closed his eyes. When he opened them again, she saw a flicker of fear that turned into determination—a determination to protect the child in his arms.

"Wh-what are you…" She gestured toward him, blinking in the sunlight lest he were a mirage sent to torment her.

"I'm here for you," he said softly. "And for *her*."

He dipped his head and placed a kiss on the blanket. Then a small pink hand appeared, reaching up, fingers extended, until it grasped a tendril of his hair, tiny fingers curling around the ends. He let out a soft laugh.

"My sweet one," he breathed, kissing the little hand. Then he glanced up at Portia, his eyes red-rimmed and shining.

"Stephen, I..." Portia's voice caught as her throat tightened and she took a step toward him.

"No loving mother should be parted from her child," he said, his voice wavering. "Not for propriety—not for *anything*."

"But she's..." Portia said. "I've already..."

"Was it your choice to give her up?" he said, his voice tightening.

Ignoring the chasm of loss in her heart, she nodded.

"Say it, Portia," he said. "If that's what you truly believe, then *say* it."

"Stephen, I cannot..."

"Listen to your heart, Portia," Stephen said, "your soul. If it weren't for Society, propriety, or your brother's wishes, would you have willingly given her up?"

He moved closer, and a whimper escaped Portia's lips as she caught sight of the child's face—rounded and pink, with deep-set eyes that mirrored her own, gazing at her from beneath a furrowed brow.

The ache in her soul shattered her denial.

"No!" she cried. "Of course I wouldn't have given her up! She's everything—my soul, my whole world... I'm nothing without her!"

She shuddered with sobs as she stumbled forward, and her soul slid into place as Stephen lifted the little bundle into her arms.

"Oh, my darling!" she cried. "My sweet baby—can you ever forgive me?"

"Lady Portia, please don't distress yourself," Nerissa said. "You're not strong."

But as Portia held her child in her arms, the strength that had eluded her for so many weeks seemed to flow through her veins, and she stood, erect and firm—a mother tigress willing to defend her cub from those who would take her away.

"Lady Por—"

"*Leave* her, Nerissa," Stephen said. "She's strong for her child. Can you not see that?"

"But my lady's been ill."

"Aye—and she now holds in her arms the one thing that will make her well again."

The voices in the distance seemed to grow louder, while Portia closed her eyes and breathed in the beautiful aroma of her child, then a single voice roared in anger.

"What the bloody hell do you think you're *doing*?"

Portia glanced up to see her brother, red-faced, eyes dark with fury, striding toward them, a shotgun over his arm. Behind him, two figures followed: Earl Thorpe and Lord Devereaux, the taciturn gentleman who'd been in hiding in Whitcombe's study the night of the house party—the man who carried an air of brooding menace about him.

"Adam, I—"

"Be quiet, sister!" her brother roared. "I'm talking to *you*."

He waved his gun at Stephen, who stepped back, raising his hands.

"Foxton, I—"

"You address me as *Your Grace*," Adam said, his strides lengthening. Then he grasped the shotgun and snapped the barrel in place.

"No!" Portia stepped toward her brother, but Stephen leaped in front of her, shielding her with his body.

"Shoot me if you like, *Your Grace*," he snarled, "but you'll not harm a hair on Portia's head—or our daughter's."

Adam drew in a sharp breath, and his companions exchanged glances.

"Reid, you've lost your wits. That child is not—"

"Yes, she is!" Stephen cried. "Portia's a mother, and you separated her from her child! What sort of man does that to his sister?"

"What about *you*?" Adam said. "You ruined her, abandoned

her, then shot her, leaving her for dead, while she carried your child! What sort of a brother would I be if I let that pass?"

"Adam, please!" Portia said. "Put the gun down—you know how Stephen fears…" She hesitated. "F-forgive me, Stephen. I didn't mean to—"

"No, say it," Stephen said. "I care not if your brother knows that I have relived the war every night, such that the sound of gunfire returns me to the nightmare of the battlefield, the cries of pain, the stench of bodies of the men I failed to save. But I would willingly endure a thousand gunshots to protect the woman I love—and the child she bore me."

"Well, stap me," Earl Thorpe said, thrusting his hands into his pockets. "When you insisted we accompany you after you received your message, Foxton, you didn't say it would lead us to such an interesting experience."

"Speak one word about this and I'll shoot you down," Adam said, swiveling round and aiming the shotgun at Thorpe. "I asked you to come with me to rid my land of vermin. At least there are those among my staff are loyal to their master." He glared at Nerissa. "Unlike some. I suppose you've been encouraging my sister to fraternize with the child after I expressly forbade you."

"You never forbade me outright," Portia said.

"But I did tell you that if you continued to visit the child, it would end in heartbreak."

"She's not *the child*, Adam. She's your niece—my daughter!"

Adam turned to Stephen. "Did you come to expose my sister? Not content with shooting her, are you here to spread gossip about her ruination?"

"No, Your Grace," Stephen said. "I come to claim the woman I love—and the daughter she bore me."

Adam gritted his teeth, his eyes darkening until they were almost black. "You'll have to tear me down first."

"With pleasure."

Stephen strode toward Adam, into the line of fire.

"No!" Portia cried. "Stephen, don't! *Please!*"

He curled his hand around the barrel and wrenched the gun from Adam's grip. He uncocked it and expelled the cartridge, then dropped the gun on the ground.

"How's your eye, Foxton?" he said. "Care for a matching pair?" He gestured toward Thorpe and Devereaux. "Or have you brought your friends to throw me off your land as you threatened to do in London? Well, I'll not be thrown off your estate so easily this time—not now I've found your sister."

"Y-you came her before, looking for me?" Portia said.

"Aye, I did."

"And again, in London?"

"Aye." Stephen turned toward her. "I would walk to the far ends of the earth to find you, Portia. I cannot live without you." He wiped his eyes and shook his head. "I cannot begin to describe how much I hate myself for hurting you—and for placing judgment on you when it is I who ought to be judged. I was angry, aye, when I discovered that you were the Farthing—angry because I believe you'd deceived me. But I never stopped loving you, Portia. And though you've every right to hate me for bringing you to harm and for abandoning you, I know, in here"— he placed his hand over his heart—"that our child was conceived from an act of love between us."

"Ahem," Thorpe said, and Portia glanced up to see him shuffling from one foot to another. Undeterred, Stephen stepped toward her, arms outstretched, palms upward in supplication.

Then he lowered himself to his knees.

Thorpe drew in a sharp breath and shook his head. Adam's lip curled in a sneer, while Devereaux's eyebrows lifted a fraction— the only sign of reaction in his otherwise emotionless expression.

Undeterred, Stephen reached toward her and caught her skirts. Then he dipped his head and kissed the fabric.

"As undeserving a creature as I am, Portia, I offer myself to you now—my body, heart, and soul, which are, and have always been, yours. I offer everything I have, and everything I ever will be, and though you may rightfully deem me unworthy even to kiss your skirts, I ask, with hope and no expectation, that you consent to be my wife."

Her heart have a little pulse of hope, then she tightened her grip on her child.

"And Stephania?"

"She is my child, and I would recognize her and love her as such. Do you think I care whether she was born in wedlock or not?"

"I say…" Thorpe muttered. "Time and a place, Reid."

"That there is, Thorpe," Stephen said. "The time is now—and the place is here—for me to declare my love for Lady Portia and our daughter."

"And if my sister refuses you?" Adam said. "What if there's no dowry, if I cut her off and leave her penniless?"

Stephen let out a laugh. "Are you so foolish as to think I care for wealth and titles as much as you, Foxton? If your sister had no fortune, still I would love her. If you abandoned her and refused to consent to our marriage, still I would love her." He tilted his head toward the sky, as if addressing the Almighty. "If Lady Portia Hawke had nothing but the clothes she stood in and the child in her arms, *still I would love her!*"

"And if she refused you?" Adam continued.

Stephen's eyes narrowed, and Portia caught a glimmer of pain there. But he turned toward her brother, still clinging to her skirts.

"Still I would love her," he said. "And I would be the champion of her happiness until the day I drew my last breath. I would fight you at every turn to ensure that she is not parted from our child, even if she denied me the chance to love our child—even if she denied me herself."

His chest rose and fell as he drew in a shuddering breath, then he lifted his head and met Portia's gaze, his eyes shining with emotion.

"That is what love is," he said. "That is the joy of love, but the pain also. But the pain, even though it may be enough to tear a man's heart to shreds—every ounce of that pain is worth it for even one second of the joy that love can bring. And I want nothing more than to give you that joy, Portia, my love—to love and protect you."

"To protect me?"

The corner of his mouth lifted into a smile, though his eyes shone with moisture.

"You are brave and strong, my love," he said, "more courageous than I could ever be. Perhaps it is I who should ask you to protect us—me, and our beloved daughter."

Our beloved daughter…

Her heart opened toward him. "Stephen…"

He rose to his feet, then placed his hands on her arms and drew her close, and she inhaled the familiar, woody scent of him.

"Oh, Stephen!"

She leaned into his embrace, placing her head on his shoulder, drawing strength from his athletic form, the firm muscles of his arms that claimed her as his.

"What about the Bensons?" Adam said. "What have you told them?"

"What about Portia?" Stephen said. "It's Portia I love. Her happiness is all I care about. It's you who must make amends to those who have suffered harm—not only your sister and your niece, but those to whom you made a promise that was not yours to give. You stripped your sister of her soul, forced her to make a choice that you believed to be easy. I now beg you, Foxton, to do that which is not easy…but what is *right*."

"And if I don't?"

"Then you must reap the consequences," Stephen said. He placed a soft kiss on Portia's forehead. "I have made my decision."

Portia lifted her head to see him looking at her, his eyes wide with entreaty, filled with love and desire and asking—as the soul asks in its moment of vulnerability—not to be hurt.

"And so have I," she said. She tilted her head, offering her lips for a kiss, and he lowered his mouth to hers, flicking his tongue along the seam, begging entrance, which she granted, gladly. His tongue caressed her gently, curling round her own in a gentle dance, before he withdrew, his eyes shining, then whispered in her ear, his warm breath dancing on her neck.

"And there, my love, I taste the moment of joy."

"Oh, bloody hell."

Portia looked up to see her brother, hands on hips, resignation in his eyes.

"I suppose you really do love her," he said, and she braced herself, anticipating his usual jibes about a man being a milksop if he admitted to having a heart.

Instead, the corners of his eyes creased into a smile.

"And do you love him, puss?"

She nodded against Stephen's broad chest.

"Then I suppose I've no choice but to give my consent," Adam said. "But mark my words, Reid—you harm a single hair on my sister's head, aversion to gunfire or not, I'll shoot you down."

Stephen placed his hand on the back of Portia's head and caressed her hair. "I would not have it any other way."

"Then come shake my hand."

Stephen released Portia from his embrace and approached Adam's outstretched hand. Then he took it, and the two men stared at each other for several heartbeats before they released their grips.

"I'll make the arrangements," Adam said. "It will be my gift. The archbishop can have no objection to your being married at St George's. We can have the banns read on Sunday."

"No!" Portia said. "Please, Adam."

"Don't you want a Society wedding?" he said. "I thought every young woman—"

"I thought you'd already admitted that I'm *not* every young woman," she said. "I'd prefer a quiet ceremony, with the people I love—with Eleanor and Juliette, and Angela of course, if she wishes it."

"My sister would never forgive me if we didn't invite her," Stephen said. "And she most certainly would never have forgiven me had I not reconciled with you."

"And…" Portia hesitated. "I want Stephania to be there, at the ceremony. I'll not have her hidden away."

Her brother raised his eyebrows, then, at length, he nodded.

"Of course," he said. "I can arrange a special license and you can be married privately here, if you like." He turned to Portia's maid. "Nerissa, could you speak to Mrs. Platt about making up a chamber for Colonel Reid?" He met Portia's gaze and smiled. "And for the chamber next to my sister's to be prepared for my niece, now she has come home."

Portia smiled at her brother.

Thank you…

"And now, I think it's time we rejoined the other gentlemen," he said. "Thorpe, Devereaux, I thank you for your service, but it seems you're not needed after all. Nerissa, perhaps you could take my niece back to the house—young Tilly can help, and I'll speak to the Bensons."

"But my mistress…"

"Is, I think, eager to be reunited with the colonel," Adam said, a glint of mischief in his eyes. "Is that not right, Portia?"

A low growl reverberated from the broad-chested man next to her, and Portia nodded, her cheeks warming.

Nerissa approached, arms outstretched. "Let me take you, precious one," she cooed, and the baby gave a satisfied little grunt as the maid took her in her arms. "I'll take care of her for you, Lady Portia—for as long as you need."

"Shouldn't we stay for—" Tilly began, but Stephen interrupted.

"Your mistress will be quite well with me."

A ripple of desire threaded through Portia as he took her hand, linking his fingers through hers, and lifted it to his lips. Then she blushed as her brother's knowing gaze settled on her, a glint of wickedness in his eyes.

Tilly bobbed a curtsey, then linked her arm through Nerissa's as the two maids set off toward the house. Adam turned and retreated toward the woods, his companions in his wake.

As she watched them disappear, Stephen's warm, solid arms drew her close. Then he steered her toward the picnic blanket and sat, pulling her down beside him.

"Now, my love," he said, his voice low and hungry. "What shall we do?"

"There's apple pie," she said. "I was about to cut a slice when…"

She paused, biting back tears.

He touched her chin, then tilted her face up with his fingertip. "When…?"

"When you appeared out of nowhere, like an angel come to deliver me from sorrow into joy."

He dipped his head and claimed a kiss.

"W-would you like a slice of pie?" she said.

"I can think of something far more delicious to satisfy my hunger," he said, his voice a low growl. "Your brother tasked me with taking care of you. I would not wish to disappoint him."

Oh heavens!

Desire swelled and throbbed inside her body, and she lay back, relishing the sharpening scent of her own need. He lifted her skirts, and she caught her breath as the cool air caressed her skin.

"May I take care of the woman I love?" he whispered.

"Yes, Stephen," she breathed, "you most certainly may."

He entered her swiftly, and she gave a soft moan as pleasure flared at the feel of him inside her—pleasure that grew as he began to move in and out of her, slowly at first.

"Is it not most terribly wicked of us?" she whispered. "Out in the country?"

He grew still. "Perhaps we should wait until we're married."

"Would you torment me?" she said, arching her back to chase the pleasure.

"No, my love, I would worship you. I intend to spend the rest of my days worshipping you, if you would permit me."

"You have my permission," she said, and he moved once more, letting the pleasure build, slowly, "as you have everything of me, including my heart. Stephen, I—"

He silenced her with a kiss and quickened the pace, until she could speak no more. Their twin cries of pleasure filled the air as they sealed their forgiveness, their reunion, and their love.

EPILOGUE

STEPHEN LED HIS wife out of the chapel amid the cheers of the guests. Portia had never looked more beautiful, her glossy, dark locks in contrast to the bone-white gown trimmed with lace. In her arms, she carried their daughter, wearing a christening gown of matching silk. As they reached the carriage, bedecked with white roses courtesy of the children from the Forthridge estate, Angela approached, Mrs. Stowe at her side, and held out her arms.

Portia handed the baby over.

"Take care of her for me, Angela."

"Of course," Angela said. "She's my favorite niece."

"She's your *only* niece," Stephen said.

"Perhaps not for long," Angela replied, a smile dancing in her eyes. "I want at least six nieces and nephews."

Stephen steered his wife toward the carriage, but she paused and turned to Angela.

"She likes her toy cat," she said. "Make sure she has him with her at night."

Angela nodded. "Yes, Portia—you told me everything she likes. I'll not let you down."

"And—"

"My love," Stephen said, "our daughter's in good hands with so many to care for her and love her. Angela will be here during our vacation, and you have Nerissa and young Tilly. She'll not want for care—or love."

"But I hate to leave her."

"I know, my love, but it's not for long. And are you not looking forward to visiting the Lakes?"

She curled her fingers around his, and for a moment he caught a flare of sorrow in her eyes—the memory of her last visit to Cumberland, perhaps.

Then she smiled.

"Of course," she said. "The hills thereabouts are very beautiful, and I'm looking forward to exploring them with you."

"And taking a picnic or two," he said, tempering the desire swelling in his groin. "I took care to ask your maid to pack the picnic blanket."

A delicate bloom colored her cheeks. "Stephen!"

He leaned toward her, brushed his mouth against her neck, then nipped her earlobe.

"Oh yes, my love," he said, "I look forward to hearing your name on my lips—many, many times."

Foxton approached and offered his hand. Out of the corner of his eye, Stephen saw Mrs. Stowe retreat and join the rest of the party—Lord and Lady Staines, Earl and Countess Thorpe, and Whitcombe and his duchess. Of Whitcombe's sister Olivia, there was no sign, despite her having been invited as Angela's particular friend, but the dark scowl on Whitcombe's face prevented Stephen from asking.

He took the proffered hand, recognizing the warning in his brother-in-law's eyes and the firmness of his grip, as if he'd spoken the words aloud.

Remember your oath to love and cherish her, Reid.

Then Foxton released him, and Stephen helped Portia into the carriage before climbing in after her.

Amid cheers, the carriage set off and rolled down the drive. Portia leaned out of the window, her gaze fixed on the chapel building until the carriage turned a corner and it was out of sight. Then she sat back in her seat and smiled.

"Well, Mrs. Reid," Stephen said, "a very successful day so far, I think. I have gained a wife, and our daughter has been christened—and now, I have the prospect of your delicious company for three weeks. I think I shall advocate for hasty marriages."

Her smile slipped. "Not all hasty marriages are to be celebrated," she said. "Did you not notice Olivia's absence?"

"Whitcombe's sister is *married?*"

She nodded. "Eleanor's most distressed. Of course, being Eleanor, she insisted on coming today to celebrate our union. I have promised we'll call on her as soon as we're able. I hope you don't mind."

"Of course not," he said. "What my wife wishes is also what I wish."

"And what do you wish at this moment?"

"That we can find something to occupy ourselves to pass the time. It's a long ride to the inn."

He shifted closer, his thigh touching hers, and she suppressed a gasp at the small surge of pleasure. How could she be so eager for him, even though they'd indulged in a little illicit premarital bedsport only last night?

"Perhaps," he said, placing his hand on her shoulder, "we might count the number of carriages we pass."

"That seems like a sensible suggestion," she said. He leaned close, his breath hot and urgent against her neck, and her skin tightened with want as he shifted his hand lower, to caress her throat.

"Or mayhap we could count the number of inns we pass before we reach our destination for the night?"

"I must congratulate you, sir, on your propensity for excellent ideas. I—Oh!" she caught her breath as his hand slipped below her neckline and cupped a breast. Her nipple beaded against his palm, and a fizz of need sparkled in her center as he flicked the little bud with his thumb.

"And I must congratulate your modiste, madam," he said, his voice thick and low. "An excellent gown—though I have been in agony of want in my desire to remove it from your person."

He dipped his head and placed a kiss on the top of her breast, and she squeezed her thighs together at the wicked heat between them that surged as he flicked his tongue over her skin. He gave a soft chuckle as she arched her back, offering her breast.

"Ah," he said. "I have it!"

"Stephen?"

"Exactly," he said, his lips curving in a smile against her breast. "How about we count the number of times you scream my name while I'm buried inside you?"

Oh my...

The ripple of desire throbbed in her center, and she drew in a deep breath, willing her body to calm, lest she come to pleasure too soon.

"I think my wife approves of my suggestion," he whispered.

"Oh yes," she said, before his lips claimed hers. "She most certainly does."

About the Author

Emily Royal grew up in Sussex, England, and has devoured romantic novels for as long as she can remember. A mathematician at heart, Emily has worked in financial services for over twenty years. She indulged in her love of writing after she moved to Scotland, where she lives with her husband, teenage daughters, and menagerie of rescue pets—including Twinkle, an attention-seeking boa constrictor.

She has a passion for both reading and writing romance with a weakness for Regency rakes, Highland heroes, and Medieval knights. *Persuasion* is one of her all-time favorite novels, which she reads several times each year, and she is fortunate enough to live within sight of a Medieval palace.

When not writing, Emily enjoys playing the piano, baking, and painting landscapes, particularly of the Highlands. One of her ambitions is to paint, as well as climb, every mountain in Scotland.